ALSO BY MIKE BROOKS:

Dark Run

MIKE BROOKS

DARK SKY

DEL REY

1 3 5 7 9 10 8 6 4 2

Del Rey, an imprint of Ebury Publishing
20 Vauxhall Bridge Road,
London SW1V 2SA

Penguin
Random House
UK

Del Rey is part of the Penguin Random House group of companies
whose addresses can be found at global.penguinrandomhouse.com

First published in the UK in 2016 by Del Rey

www.eburypublishing.co.uk

A CIP catalogue record for this book is available from the British Library

ISBN 9780091956653

Typeset in India by Thomson Digital Pvt Ltd, Noida, Delhi

Printed and bound in Great Britain by Clays Ltd, St Ives PLC

Penguin Random House is committed to a sustainable future for our
business, our readers and our planet. This book is made from Forest
Stewardship Council® certified paper.

MIX
Paper from
responsible sources
FSC
www.fsc.org   FSC® C018179

To Janine.
For everything, pretty much.

The Grand House on New Samara was exactly what its name suggested. Luxurious without being ostentatious, it eschewed the garish, dancing holos or blinking neon used as advertisements by those gaming establishments that lacked its pedigree. The outer walls were plated a rich, deep green so dark as to be near-black, with only the most delicate touches of decoration here and there: a few tiny, winking lights which served merely to outline and define its bulk, tasteful uplighting on the two small balconies open to the sky and, most important of all, no visible name. The Grand House was an imposing, dark green iceberg taking up a sizeable plot of hugely valuable land in the middle of the richest district on all New Samara: if you didn't know what it was, you didn't belong inside.

The tower at one end, not so tall as the surrounding skyscrapers but sharing their curved aesthetics, was a hotel affordable only to the rich. There was no requirement to visit the gaming floors while staying in the hotel, of course, but few would pass up the opportunity given that 10 per cent of their bill was refunded in the form of credit chips. It did, however, explain why patrons were always charged in advance. The Grand House would not wish to see a guest suffering any complications with regard to their accommodation following an unwise flutter. After all, there were standards to be maintained.

Ichabod Drift couldn't help but feel he was automatically lowering them simply by being present.

He more or less looked the part, of that there was no doubt. His suit, the first such item he had ever owned, was a midnight blue, his shirt was silky smooth and starched at the collar and cuffs, and he'd abandoned his long-serving military-surplus boots for a fancier, shinier pair of shoes (which nevertheless had enough grip to run and enough weight to kick, as Ichabod Drift was in many ways a cautious man). He'd even re-dyed his hair to match the suit, abandoning the violet colour he'd sported for the previous eighteen months or so, and had persuaded Jenna to polish the small amount of visible metal on his augmented eye.

It was the darnedest sensation. Here he was, in New Samara's Grand House, a casino so posh you weren't even allowed to call it a casino, dressed like a toff and gambling huge amounts of money . . . and not one bit of it was a lie. There was no angle, no scheme in the works, and they weren't scoping the place to rob the vault. He and his business partner Tamara Rourke had actually done that once, but in far less opulent surroundings. Even then they'd needed to assemble a one-off team of nine specialists, which meant the payout hadn't been that great after being split so many ways. Such a venture would be suicide in the Grand House, however, so it was just as well that he was, for once, completely honest and above board.

At least, if you ignored the fact that the money he was gambling with had come from one of the private accounts of a man named Nicolas Kelsier, former corrupt government minister turned terrorist, and now thankfully and quite definitely dead.

'So,' he asked, sighing with pleasure as he surveyed the scene of well-moneyed gambling laid out in front of him, 'what do you feel like hitting tonight?'

'You.'

Tamara Rourke was short where Drift was tall, her skin was the colour of black tea instead of the golden almond tone his Mexican heritage had bestowed upon him, and her hair was an unbroken black cropped close to her skull rather than a rich, shoulder-length blue. Nevertheless, they both had a wiry build and shared a general attitude that money was better in their pockets than in other people's. She seemed far less comfortable in this place than he did, though, because while Drift had always possessed the manner of a born showman, Rourke was happiest in the shadows, and for all its low-level lighting and relaxed atmosphere, the gaming halls of the Grand House hardly counted in that respect.

'I'd have thought you'd enjoy a chance to relax for once,' Drift said mildly, casting a sidelong glance at his business partner as a robot waiter purred past carrying a silver tray of expertly mixed cocktails.

'Watching the rest of you dress up like idiots and lose money doesn't qualify,' Rourke snapped, shifting her shoulders slightly.

'It was your idea we come here,' Drift reminded her.

'*Come* here, yes; show up, get the funds, maybe find an easy job or two while we stayed out of Europan space until all the fuss died down,' Rourke replied testily. 'I said nothing about gambling it away.'

'A. and Kuai could do with some recovery time.'

'I'm not arguing that,' Rourke sighed. Apirana, their hulking Maori bruiser, and Kuai, the *Keiko*'s Chinese mechanic, had both taken recent gunshot wounds and were recuperating with stoicism and self-pity, respectively. 'It's just that . . . this isn't our place, Ichabod. We might have the money, at the moment, but we're out of our depth in this sort of society. Something's going to blow up in our face, and I don't like the feeling of being exposed.'

'Maybe you should try to fit in more, then?' Drift suggested. New Samara's fashions favoured ostentatious outfits that sometimes bordered on the scandalous but Rourke had, typically, ignored them. She couldn't get away with wearing one of her favoured utilitarian, skin-tight bodysuits but had got as close as she could: knee-high black boots encased tight, dark green leggings which were nevertheless stretchy enough to allow her to run, crouch or kick someone in the head as needed, and her black shirt was free of frills and other extraneous frippery that might get in the way. She'd also refused to abandon either her wide-brimmed, flat-topped black hat or her long, enveloping coat, and she'd been mistaken for a particularly short and rather delicately built man on more than one occasion so far.

'You are *not* getting me into a dress, if you can even call what they wear here "dresses".' Rourke's voice had taken on a dangerous edge which Drift had last heard when she'd been considering shooting him, so he decided not to push his teasing any further.

'Fine, fine.' His comm beeped the message he'd been waiting for, so he checked his cuffs and nodded towards the poker tables. 'Back to seeing if I can relieve any heirs and heiresses of the family fortune. Enjoy whatever you decide to do.'

'I might go and join Apirana,' Rourke muttered, 'at least his choices are interesting to watch.' The big Maori was usually found on the first subterranean level at the Grand House's combat sports arena, where you could see anything from ground-based grappling contests to full-contact cage fights, along with weaponised contests such as kendo and even low-powered laser shoot-outs.

'Poker is a game of tactics and subtlety!' Drift protested.

'Not the way you play it,' Rourke sighed. 'Just try not to bleed the account dry, okay?' She turned and walked away towards the elevators, scudding across the floor like a small but determined thundercloud. Drift watched her go for a couple of seconds, then shook his head and ambled towards the poker tables with an expression of affable good nature, and a slight alteration in the tone of his facial muscles to suggest the onset of drunkenness.

Drift would never have considered himself to be a professional gambler, unless trying to make a living as a freelance captain in this uncertain galaxy counted. Even so, he was well aware that the process of reading your poker opponents should start before you even got to the table. The Grand House attracted its fair share of prestige players, the men and women who would sit down, calmly bet enough money to buy a starship and make a comfortable living from it; these people would wipe the floor with him. Instead, he'd registered for one of the tables where the bored cousins of oligarchs, nephews of sheikhs and third-in-line to the family business were playing for what was, to them, pocket money.

He rejoined his likely, finely dressed group around a table near the edge of the poker area. There were eight other players, each of whom had already laid down the buy-in of 5,000 stars (the currency of the Red Star Confederate, who took a simple if unimaginative approach to naming it when they combined the yuan and the rouble). He shook some chips idly in his hand as he wandered back to them, the better to give an impression of slightly inebriated overconfidence.

'*Hola*,' he hailed them merrily, and slightly too loudly, 'are we ready to go again?'

One of the women, a really rather good-looking brunette with a porcelain complexion, turned to regard him with sparkling eyes surgically altered to shine like diamonds. Her dress of a glistening burgundy fabric wasn't strapless so much as mainly composed of straps, cunningly anchored to prevent 'very suggestive' becoming 'blatant'. She gave him a predatory smile, probably because he'd made a point to be careless in their first session and she now had him pegged as an easy mark. 'Are you, sir?'

Drift smiled ruefully and raised his glass to her. 'As ready as I'll ever be, I expect.'

The sentence was technically correct. It wasn't his fault if this group of peacocks misread it as an admission of weakness.

They sat down and got back to their play. The big blind was posted by one of the other male players, a blond-haired fop barely into his twenties judging by appearances, and using a thin mesh vest to flaunt a physique surely created at the point where narcissism met art, or possibly surgery. The small blind fell to a stunningly beautiful woman in a cream dress which Drift recognised as a fabric that became more and more transparent as the owner's heartbeat and body temperature rose. It was designed for the hedonistic club or party scene: wearing it to a poker table was an unsubtle statement of confidence in one's own self-control.

Drift had lost some chips in their first session, but only one of their table had been in real trouble at the break. He was an athletically built man with a narrow moustache whom Drift guessed had Chinese ancestry, and who was the only other player at the table with clothes of similar quality to Drift's own. His suit might have got him in past the door staff but it hadn't garnered him any respect at this table, and nor had his playing style. He was overly conservative, bleeding chips and reluctant to take any form of risk. When he did go all-in, with a desperate bid to salvage his game, he ran a pair of tens into pocket jacks from the girl in the cream dress, who wiped him out and took his chips without her dress losing a shred of opacity. Drift wasn't sorry to see him go: the man had a dangerous air which the rich kids around them seemed to have completely missed, and if he wasn't something like a gangland enforcer blowing his pay then Ichabod Drift was a left-handed ham sandwich.

The next player to fall by the wayside was the girl in the straps, who watched Drift bluff his way to a couple of fairly small hands in quick succession with nothing cards and then went head-to-head with him as the others folded again, perhaps sensing a trap. This time Drift didn't need to bluff, but made sure to chew the inside of his cheek in the exact same way as he had previously. She fell for it and saw her pair of fours from the table with an ace high get utterly trounced by the three fours Drift made using one of his hand cards. He didn't get her completely, but her attempt to save herself in the next hand saw her lose her few remaining chips to a bald man with a narrow goatee who was wearing some modern-fashion inter-pretation of a twenty-first or twenty-second century military uniform, chewing some form of dried meat and smoking a genuine, hideous-smelling cigar.

The well-muscled young fop bled himself slowly dry with poorly thought-out risks, and left muttering dire imprecations at somebody. The third woman in the group, a plump blonde with a dazzling smile and pleasing cleavage, or possibly the other way around, coolly eliminated a genial old man shortly afterwards. He'd been paying too much attention to her low-cut dress of midnight purple, and the tiny lights like distant fireflies that crawled all over it but seemed to pool most often over her breasts. Drift had no doubts at all as to how coincidental that particular detail was.

'Will you at least let me buy you a drink for a game well played?' the man she'd eliminated huffed jovially, heaving himself to his feet. He spoke Russian, as had most of them during the game, but Drift heard him in English thanks to the commpiece in his left ear, which provided an almost instant translation in its pleasant, neutral tone via the translation function on his pad.

'You already have,' his conqueror replied, gesturing to her pile of chips, and that was that.

They took another short break at that point, which Drift used to visit the nearest bathroom. He was making his way back when the last of their group of players, an androgynous youth of few words, fell in beside him before he'd even realised they were there. Their hair was an artfully asymmetrical mess of lengths and colours ranging from pure white to the darkest violet imaginable, and they wore a forest green sarong with what looked to be a deliberately shapeless sleeveless black top. It was probably in fashion.

'So,' they began, too casually, 'whose feathers have you ruffled?'

Drift frowned sideways at them. 'I beg your pardon?'

'Someone's taken an interest in you,' his opponent said mildly. 'Don't tell me you haven't noticed?'

'This is a pretty poor psychological game,' Drift snorted. 'Worried about your chances?'

'I've seen at least two security watching you,' they told him, carelessly flicking a strand of hair back from their face, 'and someone else who I'm sure is one of the House's plain-clothes people. You've attracted someone's attention.'

'The only thing I attract is the ladies,' Drift replied with mock politeness, 'but thanks for your concern.'

'Don't sell yourself short,' the other player said with a faint smile, before leaving his side to resume their seat at the table. Drift returned to his own place, but despite his best efforts he couldn't completely shake what they'd said. He made a pretence of looking around to see where the bald man in the pseudo-military uniform had got to, but in reality he was checking out the location and numbers of the nearest of the Grand House's floor staff. He saw nothing untoward, but when he turned back to the table the youth was smiling at him.

Damn it.

Play restarted and Drift made an effort to resume his tipsy act, but his heart wasn't in it. He told himself that it would be less believable now anyway given that he'd played astutely enough to avoid elimination so far, but he still would have preferred some sort of additional bluff between him and his opponents. The fact was that he was undeniably distracted by what he'd just been told, even though there was no reason for him to be. He hadn't broken any laws here, he wasn't trying to game the casino and he wasn't wanted in Red Star space, so far as he was aware. Unfortunately you couldn't skate as close to the edge of legality as he habitually did without getting a bit paranoid about the authorities, and someone had found a way to play on that.

Well, at least the game wouldn't be boring.

He got back into the swing of things by eliminating the blonde woman with the lights on her
dress, who was aiming for two pairs with her pocket
queens and the two eights on the table, but fell foul
of Drift's pocket threes that allowed him to snatch
a full house. The youth in the sarong followed not
long after, when their queen-high clubs flush lost
out by the narrowest of margins to the cigar-smoker's
king-high. That left Drift, the bald man with the
cigar (now on at least his third) and the woman in
the cream dress.

It was, on the face of it, a fairly even match-up:
each of them had around fifteen grand in their stack,
although the automated reading on the table showed
that Drift was slightly ahead of both his competitors.
However, the cigar-smoker seemed as implacable as
a concrete wall, and the woman in the cream dress
hadn't allowed her apparel to grow the faintest bit
translucent throughout the game's duration. This was
purely a hobby for each of them, he suspected, and
the stakes weren't enough to make them blink. For
Drift, on the other hand, a potential win of over
40,000 stars was enough to make him start sweating.

He was abruptly tired of the game. Cheap trick by
the youth in the sarong or not, he had become
convinced that the bald security guard standing
against the wall opposite *was* watching him, and he
didn't like it. Nothing good ever came of having
security interested in you. He was dealt his next cards,
checked them – the ace of spades and the queen of
clubs – and came to a decision.

The cigar-smoker checked his cards, as unreadable
as ever, and pushed in his bet: 5,000 stars. It was a

hefty opening gambit, and one probably designed to intimidate, but it didn't work.

'All in.' The woman in cream shunted her entire stack forwards, close on 15,000 stars. The cigar-smoker's eyebrows climbed a little, but he said nothing.

Drift scratched the skin around his right eye for a moment, then shrugged. 'Go big or go home, I guess.' He pushed his stack in too, and looked enquiringly over at the bald man. 'Are you game?'

The cigar-smoker just grunted. He did, however, push his remaining chips in to match Drift as closely as he could. Everyone was in and the winner would essentially take all.

They all turned their cards over, since betting was now at an end. The woman in cream had queens in hearts and diamonds and the cigar-smoker had . . . kings in diamonds and clubs. A faint smirk crossed his face: they all knew he had the best chance of taking this hand. The woman in cream swallowed slightly, and Drift thought he caught the faintest beginnings of translucency in her clothes. A pair of queens was a strong starting point, but it looked like she'd played aggressively at the wrong time.

The dealer flopped the next three cards.

The seven of clubs, the queen of spades and the three of spades.

The woman in cream puffed her cheeks out and gave a small, semi-nervous laugh, while the cigar-smoker's already stony expression fell a fraction. Three queens on the table suddenly made *her* the huge favourite, and Drift's paltry two queens meant he could almost see his pile of chips sliding across the table in her direction.

The turn card revealed the four of spades, and suddenly Drift breathed again. Any spade for the final card would see him sweep the table with a flush, which meant the cigar-smoker had only one hope left: the king of hearts, to give him three kings without Drift getting the spade he needed. However, the woman in cream was still winning as it stood.

The dealer, with a disappointing lack of drama, turned over the river card.

The two of spades.

'Mother*fucker*! Seriously? On *kings*?' The cigar-smoker shot to his feet and stormed off without a backwards glance, his implacability finally crumbling away. The woman in cream simply smiled ruefully as the dealer pushed the pile of chips towards Drift's waiting arms.

'Well played, sir.' She quirked an eyebrow at him. 'Although I think you have luck to thank for it.'

'A win's a win,' Drift grinned at her, sliding a couple of thousand-star chips back the dealer's way as a tip. 'I admire your confidence in your wardrobe, by the way.'

'Oh, it would take more than this table can offer to get me excited,' she replied, not without a hint of mischief.

'Well, I seem to have an abundance of cash,' Drift said, getting to his feet. 'How about I use some of it to buy you a drink and test that theory?' She might have quietly sneered at his clothes when they'd first met, but Drift wasn't the sort to hold grudges. Well, not when the other person had the kind of features you'd expect to see in a fifty-foot hologram advertising make-up, anyway.

She opened her mouth as if to respond, but then something in her face changed. She composed her features and took a step backwards. 'Perhaps another time.'

Drift blinked in surprise. He'd been almost sure she was going to . . .

A hand landed on his shoulder. Startled, and not a little annoyed, he looked around to see which of his crew had spotted him and come over to interrupt his flirting.

'Excuse me, sir,' said the bald Grand House security guard, two of his colleagues standing at his shoulder. 'I must ask you to come with us.'

'**E**xcuse *me*?!' Drift found his voice rising more than he'd have liked, and not one part of it was a result of play-acting the drunk. 'I think there must be some mistake.' He turned back towards the beauty in the cream dress but she'd already disappeared, presumably not wanting to risk being caught up in whatever this was.

'No mistake, sir,' the guard said, his expression not shifting by a jot. 'Please come this way.'

With three guards in close proximity, Drift didn't really have an option. He pocketed his chips, ruining the line of his suit in doing so. 'Can you at least tell me what this is about? I can assure you, I won that game fair and square.' Their little group garnered several curious glances from players at tables as he was shepherded across the floor, and he briefly wondered how many games they'd mildly disrupted before his mind went back to windmilling through the possibilities. Was this some sort of trick played by the person in the sarong? But what purpose could it serve now the game was over?'

'I apologise, sir,' the first guard said quietly from his left, 'but Mr Orlov has told me to ask if you will accept an invitation to meet with him.'

Drift didn't exactly stop dead, but he certainly stumbled a little as his train of thought was thoroughly derailed. 'Wait . . . Mr Orlov? Mr *Sergei* Orlov? The owner?'

'Yes sir,' the guard replied neutrally.

Drift chewed the inside of his cheek for a second, the mild pain helping him to focus his thoughts slightly. Sergei Orlov, owner of the Grand House, was what you got when a gangster was so respectable he barely counted as a gangster anymore. He was a businessman with enterprises that stretched far beyond the establishment where his family had first made their name, and was probably immune from ever being arrested, even without the fact that he had the slickest lawyers around. If Sergei Orlov's businesses started to struggle, then a third of the system's population might find themselves economically disadvantaged in one way or another.

Sergei Orlov was very much the big fish in the New Samaran pond, and by comparison Ichabod Drift was . . . some sort of water beetle, perhaps? Maybe a fly larvae. Old Earth biology had never been his strongpoint.

'Just so I'm clear on this point,' he said slowly, looking sidelong at his escort and with a sinking feeling that he already knew the answer, 'is this invitation an "invitation" or an *invitation*?'

'I assure you sir,' the guard replied, 'you are free to choose whether to see Mr Orlov or not. If you do, we will take you to him. If not, you are free to go. However, he suggests that seeing him would be more profitable.'

Drift digested that and thought furiously. His first instinct was to cut and run, to bring his crew's stay on New Samara to an abrupt end and get the hell away from whatever had brought him to the attention of Sergei Orlov. Was it simply a velvet-lined trap, enticing him with soft words and financial rewards instead of disrupting the House's atmosphere by having him dragged away? Playing on his ego by claiming that Sergei Orlov wished to see him personally when that was about as likely as the planet's twin moons dancing a hornpipe if he played the flute?

He sighed. If someone in authority, be that Orlov or no, wanted him removed from the House floor then he would be removed. He might as well play along on the off chance that this was actually as benign as it sounded. Besides, if it genuinely *was* Orlov who wanted to see him then he was intrigued despite himself.

He gave the bald guard his best smile. 'Lead on, then.'

The guard nodded to the others, who melted unobtrusively away. Drift blinked his one natural eye in surprise, a motion his remaining escort apparently picked up on.

'Mr Orlov wished to give the impression of you being removed from our establishment when you left the table,' he explained, extending a hand in front of him to direct Drift towards an elevator situated in a curve in the wall, 'but there is no need for my colleagues now.'

'Curiouser and curiouser,' Drift muttered, falling into step alongside him, then adding, 'said Alice.'

'I beg your pardon?'

'Mmm? Oh, nothing.' Drift waved a hand dismissively. *No one appreciates the classics anymore.*

The elevator shaft was as curved as the rest of New Samara's architecture, with a mainly oval footprint that was flattened at the narrow ends. The guard entered a security code on a pad, shifting his body to block Drift's view, before pressing the floor button. Drift supposed that this was to prevent just anyone from dropping in to see Sergei Orlov, then bit his cheek again at the realisation that yes, perhaps he *was* about to see the Grand House's owner. What were the odds?

Well, he was in a casino. Whatever the odds were, they were almost certainly against him.

The elevator rose, passing through two other floors judging by the display above the doors, before slowing to a halt with a *ping*.

'Don't be alarmed,' Drift's companion muttered, seconds before the doors slid aside and he was confronted by a short, narrow corridor and two more guards, each pointing a pistol at him.

'Well, this is depressingly familiar,' Drift sighed. His own guns were back in his hotel room, since the Grand House took a very dim view of patrons going armed onto the gaming floors. However, to his shock the two guards holstered their weapons after a second's scrutiny and stood back, one against each wall.

'Sir?' The guard beside him stepped forwards, quirking the fingers of one hand to motion Drift to follow him. After a moment of checking that he was certain this wasn't some elaborate trick, Drift did so.

'Roman? Did he come?'

The voice was rich, with a faint burring of the initial 'r' but not an extravagant roll. The Russian accent was strong, but it was a statement of identity rather than an inability to adapt to a different language's vowels and consonants.

'Yes, sir,' the man called Roman replied, stopping at the point that the corridor opened into a room and extending one hand to invite Drift forwards.

'I suspect you already knew that I came,' Drift said, stepping out, 'or you'd have probably said that in Russian . . .'

He tailed off, impressed despite himself. He wasn't quite sure what he'd been expecting, but being shown into Orlov's personal penthouse suite certainly wasn't one of them. This was the top floor of the main casino, narrower than the rest of the building below but still considerably larger than the entirety of the *Jonah*, Drift's *Carcharodon*-class shuttle currently sitting in New Samara's spaceport. He experienced a burning moment of envy at the opulence and size, and briefly wondered exactly why he'd spent most of his adult life in the relatively cramped conditions on board spacecraft instead of settling on a planet where your home didn't need to also contain engines and cargo holds.

Oh yeah. 'Freedom.'

'Captain Drift!'

Sergei Orlov was rising to his feet from a recliner and approaching him, a glass tumbler in one hand and the other empty, his arms spread wide in greeting. Drift sized him up in a second: late forties from his looks, with a peppering of dark stubble across cheeks that were starting to sag into jowls, and thickening slightly at the waist while still being physically fit. Orlov's hair was cut short at the sides and slightly longer on top. He was wearing loose, pale trousers, gathered at the ankle in the Arabian style, paired with a dark green roll-neck top, and his bare feet sank into the plush carpet on the floor.

All in all, he hardly looked like a man seeking to make an intimidating impression; not that he needed to, of course. Regardless, Drift's spirits rose a little further and he accepted the warm handshake which was proffered.

'Thank you for accepting my invitation,' Orlov told him sincerely, looking him in the eyes while they traded grips for a second or so, 'I hope you do not object too much to the manner of it?'

'I've experienced considerably ruder ones,' Drift replied with a smile. 'So, um . . . what can I do for you?'

'Captain Drift, I hope you may be able to help me with a small problem I have,' Orlov said simply, standing back. 'Roman, you may go.'

Drift caught a very slight tightening in the guard's features, but this was clearly a man who knew better than to question his boss's orders, certainly in front of strangers. Roman simply nodded and turned to leave. However, this brief distraction did little to take Drift's mind off what Orlov had just said.

'I see,' he replied, trying to keep his voice level despite his surprise. 'Well, I'd be happy to help, of course.'

Orlov chuckled. 'You seem a little confused, Captain, and without wishing to be arrogant, I can understand why. After all, I am Sergei Orlov, yes? I have dozens of starships at my disposal. But, if you will, walk with me outside and I will explain why I have taken an interest in you.' He pulled aside a sliding door and stepped out onto the flat, white-tiled roof of the main casino, under the stars.

Drift followed, for lack of any other real options, and felt the cool kiss of the night air against his skin. It was this air, the naturally occurring oxygen-rich atmosphere, that made New Samara such a haven for the Red Star's moneyed classes. Set comfortably inside the habitable zone of the Rassvet System's star, New Samara had needed the barest touches to be able to support plant life. Virtually the entire planet was an agriworld, devoted to producing food crops in bulk and, with the exception of the thinly spread farming crews, the majority of the human population lived at the cold poles or on the edges of the baking deserts where plants struggled to grow. The Confederate had allowed for one temperate city on the entire planet, the capital which shared its name, and with land at such a premium outside its borders it was no surprise that only the rich could live here.

'Firstly,' Orlov said as he trailed his fingers through the fronds of a line of soft, ornamental conifers, 'let me address who you are. Ichabod Drift, captain of the *Keiko*, who arrived here in my city some two weeks ago and *immediately* went to the main bank to withdraw funds which did not, by any reasonable standard, belong to him.'

Drift froze in place, but when Orlov looked around his expression was not mocking but mildly amused. 'Please, Captain. You are aware of who I am. It should not come as a surprise to you that I have contacts in many places, no? And as a result of who I am, I have no great concern about who takes money from whom, so long as it is not taken from *me*. On this occasion the money was taken from an account belonging to a man named Nicolas Kelsier.'

Drift bit the inside of his cheek and didn't trust himself to answer.

'Word travels across this galaxy, Captain,' Orlov said, turning and walking back towards Drift, 'especially to someone like me. I hear of unusual events on a small Europan backwater world involving a shoot-out in a market between two groups of off-worlders. Not particularly noteworthy in and of itself perhaps, but when eyewitnesses suggest that the Laughing Man was there . . . well, then anyone notable enough to perhaps one day fall under that *der'mo*'s crosshairs is far more likely to pay attention.'

Drift swallowed. He'd lost a crewman to Marcus Hall, the cold-hearted bastard of an assassin better known to the galaxy at large as the Laughing Man. Micah van Schaken had been . . . well, he'd been an abrasive, easily dislikeable mercenary, but he'd been reliable, and he hadn't deserved to die with Hall's razor-edged stardiscs puncturing his throat.

'And then,' Orlov continued, 'the Europans announce that they've taken action against the man who was behind that explosion in the North Sea on Old Earth, that botched bombing attempt? That man was Nicolas Kelsier, would you believe? One of their former ministers. And here you are, spending his money, with your bright hair and your metal eye, your colleague Miss

Rourke with her hat and coat, and your big Maori friend with those distinctive tattoos of his; all people mentioned in that shoot-out in the marketplace. Captain, this leads me to one, simple conclusion.

'You are quite clearly not a man to piss off.'

Drift blinked. 'Er . . . what?'

Orlov chuckled again. 'I'm sorry, that lead-up probably sounded a little menacing, didn't it? I assure you, I was simply proud of my own deduction.' He raised his glass to Drift and took a small sip in salute. 'I don't believe you are Europan agents, Captain Drift, but you must have been involved in some way with the downfall of Kelsier, or how would you have got his account details? I strongly suspect that he angered or provoked you in some manner and you brought down retribution on his head. Suffice to say, I have no intention of making the same mistake. I do not like to underestimate people. I believe you and your crew can be fearsomely capable when the need arises. This makes me simultaneously want to hire you, and to ensure that you do not see any need to make my life difficult in ways I could probably not even imagine.'

'That's . . . very good of you,' Drift managed, still stunned at what he was hearing. Here was the most powerful man on New Samara, arguably the most powerful man in the entire *system*, basically saying that he was going to tread carefully around the crew of a battered freighter. It was welcome, but he wasn't sure he believed a word of it.

Then again . . . he and his crew *had* ruined Nicolas Kelsier, based on nothing but an epically ambitious web of bullshit and the fact that they'd had no other

option. It had been him or them, and by the time
Kelsier had worked out what game they were playing
he'd pretty much already lost. If Orlov had heard the
right parts of it he might not have realised how tenu-
ously desperate the whole mess had been.

'So that, Captain Drift, is why *you*,' Orlov said,
pausing for a moment to look up at the few stars
above them that could be seen through the capital's
light pollution. To one side of them a muffled booming
grew in volume before fading again: the sound system
of someone in an open-topped hovercar. 'I must say
that I was also impressed with your play in the casino
tonight. You showed an admirable mix of caution
and risk-taking.'

Drift decided that this was not the time to admit
that he'd gone all in on the final hand simply because
he'd been getting spooked by Roman and his companions and wanted out of there.

'As to what you can help me with,' Orlov continued,
'are you familiar with the planet Uragan?'

Drift frowned. 'That's in this system, isn't it?
Further out, some sort of mining planet? About the
only thing I know about it is that I have no plans to
go there.'

'An understandable position,' Orlov nodded. 'It is
not a world for sightseers, certainly. My government
plunders the crust for metals and the populace shelters
underground from the toxic atmosphere. It is . . .'
He paused for a second, selecting the correct word.
'. . . *grim*. However, I need a piece of information
from a man who works in Uragan City, whom I will
not name unless and until you accept this job. He
cannot transmit it to me, and I certainly cannot go

there myself. I need someone to retrieve this information and bring it back to me, in person. They will need to get in and out again before the next of Uragan's regular hurricanes hits the mining complex in two days standard, at which point no shuttle travel will be possible through the atmosphere for roughly seventy-two hours.'

'And you don't have anyone in your own employ who could do this?' Drift said dubiously. 'Forgive me, Mr Orlov, but this sounds like something far too simple to need an outside contractor.'

Orlov's face pulled into a grimace, his lips twisting as though he'd bitten down on something sour. 'Captain, when you sit as high as I do, there are always people trying to take the chair out from under you. I have rivals who are trying to infiltrate my organisation; I say "trying", but I have no doubt they have succeeded in some part. How large a part, I am not sure. Of one thing, however, I *am* sure: none of these rivals have had any reason to try to bring *you* into their service, as you yourself were not aware that I was offering you employment until just now. Also, you will need to leave more or less immediately, so they will have no chance. You have some small reputation as a reliable contractor, the job itself is not taxing, and I will pay you the sum of 100,000 stars if the information I require reaches me before the next storm on Uragan has begun to lift.'

Drift nodded thoughtfully. One hundred thousand stars was a thoroughly respectable sum for a few days of courier work, for all that the currency was worth less, unit for unit, than the USNA or Europan dollars. Sure, he'd just made forty-odd, but he had no illusions that poker was a future career for him. Orlov's proposal, on the other hand, sounded like his bread and butter. He did have one concern though, given the source.

'Is this job illegal?'

Orlov's face twitched into a small smile again. 'There are certain parties who might not wish me to have the information you would be retrieving, it's true. They concern shipping schedules, cargo destinations and the like.'

Drift frowned. He'd heard no stories of pirates operating in the Rassvet System, and surely that was the only reason to know a cargo and destination? Then he remembered who he was dealing with, and comprehension dawned. 'And the reason you want them before the storm lifts is so you can know how much of what has been mined recently, to get a head start on buying and selling shares before the next shipment can actually take off?'

'You are a perceptive man, Captain,' Orlov nodded, 'but the information would be valuable only to someone with enough financial capacity to take advantage of it, and so time-sensitive that you would struggle to find another interested party with that capacity before it was useless. Hence I am confident that you would find it simpler to come straight back to me for your payment as opposed to, ah, "shopping around". Whereas should I choose the wrong employee from *my* organisation to retrieve this piece of information for me . . .'

'. . . they might know *exactly* who to go to with it, and buy their way into someone else's good graces,' Drift finished, nodding in his turn. He turned the offer over in his head and failed to find any obvious flaws. The logic for his selection was sound enough, the payment was generous but not so high that he was concerned Orlov was trying to blind him with greed, and the job sounded feasible and only mildly illegal, if that. Most importantly, Orlov had no history with him and therefore presumably no reason to set him up.

'As a small additional matter,' Orlov murmured, sipping his drink, 'while you are of course being financially compensated for your time and effort, you would also have my gratitude for your assistance. It is not limitless, of course, but may be of some small use should you ever find yourself inconvenienced somewhere my name carries weight.'

Drift scratched at the skin around his right eye. Perhaps this was actually a good idea, given that his crew's loyalty was still somewhat up in the air. Nicolas Kelsier had employed him in years gone by, then had resurfaced suddenly to blackmail him into transporting a mystery package to Amsterdam by threatening to reveal his darkest secret to his crew. The package had turned out to be an armed nuclear bomb, and in the aftermath of *that* spectacular shitstorm his big secret had come out anyway: Ichabod Drift, freelance merchant captain, had once upon a time been known as Gabriel Drake, ruthless pirate. What was more, he'd had to admit that instead of dying with his crew, as the galaxy thought, he'd actually opened all the airlocks on the *Thirty-Six Degrees* and let them suffocate, making it look like an accident, then jettisoned in an escape pod.

It was a betrayal of trust, which had been haunting him for over a decade, and it wouldn't be inaccurate to say that it hadn't gone down well with his current crew.

Apirana had nearly strangled him, and Rourke had threatened to shoot him. Kuai had declared his intention to leave, and his sister Jia had been teetering. They'd stayed for long enough to take Kelsier down before the old bastard could eliminate the only people who knew he'd tried to nuke Amsterdam, and Drift had promised them a share of the funds they'd gleaned, but the simple truth was that once this money was gone he didn't know if they'd stick around.

He liked his crew and didn't want to lose them, let alone find new ones. They'd have little reason to refuse a nice simple job with a decent payday, and it might be exactly the sort of thing needed to ease everyone back in to being a team again. If this went well then maybe anyone still harbouring ideas of leaving the *Keiko* could be persuaded that it wasn't such a bad way to make a living after all.

Besides, if Drift had been afraid to take a gamble he'd have never set foot in the Grand House. He stuck his hand out with a smile.

'Mr Orlov, I do believe we have ourselves a deal.'

URAGAN

'That,' Jia Chang said thoughtfully as she brought the *Keiko* into geostationary orbit and activated the chime that called all crew to the cargo bay, 'is one ugly-ass piece of rock.'

'Congratulations, Ichabod,' Rourke said, clapping the Captain on the shoulder, 'you've found us a planet that looks like a giant bruise.'

Jenna McIlroy, the youngest member of the *Keiko*'s crew, made her way over to the viewshield and peered out at Uragan. The light of the Rassvet System's star was behind them, and Uragan City, their destination, was in the middle of one of its fourteen-hour days (not that the solar cycle mattered much to the inhab-itants, who almost never saw natural light anyway). Sure enough, the planet's atmosphere was an ugly yellowish-brown – large amounts of sulphur dioxide, according to the records – and reminded her of nothing so much as pus.

'It might not look like much,' Drift admitted, 'but we're not here for the aesthetics. We're here for business, and business waits for no one. And nor will *that*,' he added, pointing to a menacing swirl in the clouds visible even from this far up: the next ravaging storm due to strike. 'That's our timescale, ladies, and it's closing in. Let's go and find Mr Orlov's contact.' He glanced over at Jenna. 'Do we have a landing window?'

'Seventy-two minutes until we can start final approach,' Jenna replied, checking her self-built wrist console. 'I could always bump us up the list a bit, if you want?'

'No,' Drift said firmly, shaking his head. 'I appreciate the thought, but we *should* be able to get this done without breaking any laws, so let's not jeopardise it with any unnecessary jiggery-pokery.'

Jenna raised her eyebrows. '"Jiggery-pokery"?'

'What?' Drift protested, looking mildly hurt. 'I like that word!'

Jia rotated around on her chair. 'Is that just one word, or actually two—'

'*Move.*' Rourke clapped her hands twice. 'C'mon, we've got over a standard hour to wait before we can break atmo, you can all discuss language once we're on the *Jonah*.'

They trailed through the corridors of the *Keiko*, down towards the main cargo bay where their shuttle sat. Jenna had often thought it was in some way a waste of the cavernous space to have most of it taken up by a shuttle with a far smaller capacity, but that was simply how it was. Humanity had developed an Alcubierre drive that could compress space–time and allow travel far faster than the speed of light, but the doughnut-shaped structure had to encircle the ship's midriff and no one had yet succeeded in constructing one that wouldn't disintegrate upon entering even a moderately thick atmosphere. As a result, if you ever wanted to be able to land on a planet without relying on someone else's transport, you needed a separate shuttle of your own . . . and that meant you needed to store it somewhere while you travelled between stars.

Drift palmed open the airlock and they stepped out into the cargo bay. Jenna looked up at the grey and somewhat battered shape of the *Jonah* with almost equal parts fondness and loathing. The two ships felt far more like home than they had done but she'd been brought up on Franklin Minor, a planet which, like New Samara, had needed very little terraforming before it was suitable for human habitation. As a result, she'd spent the first twenty or so years of her life used to open skies and wind on her cheeks. The *Keiko* was just spacious enough that she could feel a little like she was in one of her old university buildings, even if most of the room was given over to functionality. The *Jonah*, on the other hand, was unmistakably a small, enclosed tin can in space.

'Back into the rat trap, eh?' a voice rumbled, and Apirana 'Big A' Wahawaha appeared from around the other side of the shuttle. The big Maori was an imposing, not to mention intimidating, sight. Possibly a shade closer to seven feet tall than six, and at least three times Jenna's weight, his hands could form fists nearly as big as her head with battered, scarred knuckles attesting to their historical use. Then there was the *tā moko*, the dark whorls of tattoos spiralling across his face, which lent his features an exotic look to Jenna's eyes when in repose, and a truly terrifying one to anyone's when angered. That was the point, to a certain extent: for all that they were a mark of his heritage, Apirana had them done when he was an angry teenager being used as muscle for a local gang back on Old Earth. His hold on his temper was better these days, although not perfect, but his sheer presence had caused many a potential fight to stop before it even started.

He was also, to Jenna's mind, the best company on board. She liked Drift, and was grateful for his willingness to give her a berth and a job when she'd been desperate to find passage away from the Franklin system, but his mind was like quicksilver. It was forever flitting from scheme to scheme, hard to follow and impossible to truly keep up with. There was a knot of secrets in there too, and she didn't think for a moment that his previous identity as Gabriel Drake was the end of them. There was also the fact that he was entirely capable of shooting people dead without an apparent second thought, should the need arise. No, the Captain was not just all smiles and camaraderie.

Rourke was as unreadable as a blank steel wall and about as friendly: a former Galactic Intelligence agent who'd abandoned working for the USNA government for reasons she chose not to share, she was ferociously competent but hardly warm. As for the Chang siblings, Jia was pleasant enough most of the time but a raging egomaniac when it came to her flying skills, and Kuai had apparently healed well enough from his gunshot wound to ease out of the mild depression he seemed to have fallen into and start being passive-aggressively pessimistic about everything again.

'It's not that bad,' Jenna laughed, honestly enough, 'at least it's just a surface trip this time.'

'A surface trip down to a subterranean warren where everyone speaks Russian,' Apirana replied, pulling a face. As a New Zealander by birth, he too had grown up under the open sky, although he'd had longer to get used to being enclosed than she had – including over a decade in prison on Farport for various crimes which he'd declined to list, but was open enough to admit had included violence and drug-running offences.

'Everyone on, c'mon,' Drift urged from behind them, making shooing motions with his hands and looking around as though to check he hadn't forgotten anything. 'Everyone got what they need?'

'What *do* we need?' Jia shouted from the top of the ramp. 'Thought this was going to be a cakewalk?'

'That's the theory,' Drift replied, 'but when was the last time something went exactly as planned? You got your pilot hat?'

'Yeah.'

'Well then,' the Captain beamed up at her, 'we'll be fine, won't we?' He looked down at Jenna and his gaze slid to her bare right wrist. It was normally taken up by a chunky metal bracelet she usually pretended was a health monitor, but was in fact a device she'd designed and built herself to knock out electronics. 'Not taking the EMP?'

'I don't much fancy locking us into an underground prison,' Jenna smiled at him.

'I'm glad,' Drift said, flashing a grin. 'I'm not certain if I'd trust the backup power relays in a Red Star mining complex.' He turned away and headed up the ramp, leaving Jenna to follow.

'It's in your bag, ain't it?' Apirana said softly at her shoulder.

Jenna nearly stopped in her tracks and deliberately didn't look down at her satchel. 'Was it that obvious?'

Apirana shrugged. 'I might not be smart like you, but I can spot an evasion when I hear one. Kinda surprised the Captain didn't, to be honest, but I guess he's got other things on his mind.'

'I just feel better with it around,' Jenna said, trying not to feel guilty. She walked the last few steps into the cargo hold and hit the control that raised the ramp behind them. 'It's not like I'm going to set it off for no reason.'

'Nah, I know that,' Apirana assured her. He smiled. 'An' I won't tell, either.'

A distinct, muffled rumbling started up, and the deck vibrated ever so slightly beneath their feet. Kuai had started up the main engines, which meant they were about to leave the *Keiko*. Above them, an intercom speaker crackled before exuding Drift's exasperated voice.

+*Jenna? Get your narrow little butt up here, will you? These inconsiderate bastards have got all their systems in Russian.*+

Jenna frowned and picked up the cargo bay handset. 'What about the translation protocol? We were using it for New Samara!'

+*Yeah, well*, someone's *pressed* something *and it looks like it's reset to Swahili.*+

She sighed, and rolled her eyes for Apirana's benefit. 'Time to go babysit. Strap in; I hear Uragan's windy even when it's not blowing a full storm, and you know what Jia's flying is like.'

'I've been on this boat the best part o' six years, and she ain't killed me yet,' Apirana snorted, then grimaced as the *Jonah* lurched forwards out of the *Keiko*'s forward doors. 'On second thoughts . . .'

They were still on time for their re-entry window, even with the small delay while Jenna adjusted their systems so everyone could once more read what they needed to, and Uragan began growing beneath them as Jia angled them down into its thick, hostile atmosphere. Jenna had found herself clutching at her terminal with whitened knuckles during her first couple of descents on the *Jonah*, but had soon worked out that for all her arrogance and bluster, Jia was, pretty much, every bit as good a pilot as she boasted.

Even so, it seemed that Uragan was testing Jia, judging by the fact that roughly halfway through their entry she snatched her 'pilot hat' up and jammed it on her head. It had a thick, furry lining, with a peak at the front and a fold-down piece on each side, presumably to keep one's ears warm. Jia would never admit to it, but it was clear that she regarded it as some form of lucky charm in much the same way as her brother would absent-mindedly play with his dragon pendant.

'That bad, huh?' Drift asked brightly as the cockpit tilted sideways thanks to another gust.

'Shut up, *bái chī*.' Jia adjusted thrusters or flaps or . . . something – Jenna had about as much idea about piloting as Jia did about slicing into high-security information systems – and they started to level out a little. 'O-*kay*, should be below the worst now. You wanna make yourself useful and check what berth we're getting?'

'Me?' Drift looked hurt. 'Your Russian's better than mine!'

'Yeah, but I'm flying,' Jia replied shortly. 'Don't bother asking Kuai, either; I need him concentrating. Don't wet your pants, they'll have a translation program. Probably.'

Drift muttered something uncomplimentary in Spanish under his breath and opened a comm channel. 'Uragan City Port Authority, this is the shuttle *Jonah* requesting permission to land, over.'

There was a short pause, then the speakers crackled into life with the stilted, pre-recorded voice of the *Jonah*'s own translation program.

+*Shuttle* Jonah, *this is Hurricane City spaceport. Please state your language of choice so we may calibrate translation software.*+

Drift directed a glare at the back of Jia's head. 'English.'

+*Acknowledged. Please repeat your initial transmission.*+

Drift sighed, and did so. The resulting conversation made no sense to Jenna as she looked down at the barren plain beneath them, but Jia clearly received some sort of coordinates as she began to bank their shuttle to the left. She'd just levelled out again when the cockpit door slid open to admit a somewhat vexed-looking Tamara Rourke.

'Have you finished trying to kill us yet?' the older woman asked bluntly.

'Excuse me?!' Jia's head whipped around. 'You see the sort of crosswinds I was dealing with there? I know you din't, because *I'm* the one with the readouts and—'

'The spaceport,' Rourke interrupted her, pointing out of the viewshield, 'it's that way. Not over here.'

'One day,' Jia replied, pointedly waiting a couple of seconds before turning back to her controls, 'you will have to fly this crate without me and then, god help you all, that's all I say.'

'If only that *was* all you said,' Drift grinned, unstrapping himself and standing up before leaning on the back of her chair.

'Don't need you lookin' over my—'

'*Cristo*, I'm just looking outside!' Drift pointed downwards and made a thoughtful noise. 'Huh. See that? Never seen a spaceport like that before.'

Jenna released her own webbing and peered out as best she could. There, laid out below her, was the surface of Uragan City.

The city was in the partial lee of a ridge, but she couldn't imagine that shelter would make a great deal of difference when the near-thousand mile per hour hurricanes swept down across this dusty, rocky wasteland. That would explain the barely visible nature of the city: nothing protruded more than a few feet above the surface and what could be seen was curved and rounded, designed to let the wind flow over it with the least resistance. Some things were clearly meant to be skylights, although how often they remained clear of obstructing detritus was doubtful, but the most common features were low, hooded structures all facing west. These were dotted everywhere, and it was a few seconds before Jenna realised they must be wind turbines. With the Rassvet star distant, weak and often obscured by clouds or airborne dust, harnessing the readily available wind power was the logical way to keep everything running here.

She couldn't see the spaceport at first, looking as she was for a large open area crowded with shuttles and other atmosphere-capable craft, but then she realised her mistake. Big and heavy though such ships were, they would still be vulnerable in the teeth of a Uragan storm. The only place that could provide any meaningful shelter would be the same as for the human population: underground. Sure enough, she now saw that at one point the other features gave way to regular, oblong shapes of retractable roofs set into the ground, a little like the covers for swimming pools in her parents' neighbourhood back on Franklin Minor, albeit somewhat larger. Some of them were drawn back for craft to enter or exit, and it was towards one of these that Jia was steering them.

'Throttling back . . .' Jia murmured as she reduced their speed, 'engaging mags . . . okay, takin' us down.'

The *Jonah* described a lazy half-circle in the air as Jia killed their momentum and began to lower them carefully down into what had seemed from afar to be barely big enough to accommodate their ship, but which now proved itself to have already admitted three others. Jenna realised that without any familiar structures to give her a sense of scale, her estimates of size had been rather out: each 'cover' was about the size of a sports field.

'So which one's this?' she asked, on the basis that if she waited until she'd become separated from the rest of the crew somehow, it would be too late.

'Grazhdansky Dok 2,' Jia replied as they sank down below the rim of the bay.

Jenna frowned, turning the syllables over in her head. 'Civilian Dock?'

'Pretty much,' Jia confirmed with a snort. 'Guess they don't have many non-government ships here.'

'I . . . guess that makes sense,' Jenna nodded slowly. 'Well, maybe we'll have friendly neighbours.'

'Don't bet on it,' Rourke said suddenly, her voice flat and grim. Drift turned to her, immediately picking up on her mood.

'Trouble?'

Rourke's breath hissed out and she shook her head slightly in what looked like a mixture of frustration and anger. 'Take a look over there at that *Corvid*-class and tell me what you see.'

'*Corvid*-class?' Drift frowned and peered out of the windshield. Jenna followed his gaze, trying to make out whatever it was that had perturbed Tamara Rourke. She wasn't an expert on ship makes but there was only one choice where Rourke had been looking – a long, sleek shuttle with a design that had clearly been inspired by military vehicles, despite being a commercial craft. It was painted a dark green and its rounded rectangular snout appeared to have had additional decoration applied at some point: the heat of re-entries had blackened, faded and obscured the work, but it was still just about recognisable as . . .

'Teeth?' Jenna asked the cockpit in general.

'Oh, shit,' Drift sighed, with the air of a man who's just found out about an unannounced visit by his mother-in-law the tax inspector. 'Of all the fucking . . . that's the *Pouco Jacare*.'

'Shit,' Jia added with finality, although she didn't stop their descent.

'The what now?' Jenna asked, struggling to recall what Portuguese she'd learned. *Pouco* meant 'little', didn't it . . .?

'The *Pouco Jacare*,' Drift repeated as their hull set down on the metal deck beneath them. 'The *Little Alligator*. A shuttle belonging to one Ricardo *fucking* Moutinho.'

'Who exactly,' Jenna asked as she trailed the others back towards the cargo bay, 'is Ricardo Moutinho?'

'Ricardo *fucking* Moutinho,' Drift corrected her, without turning around. The Captain's mood had taken a definite nosedive since spotting the shuttle that was sharing a bay with them. 'He's absolute scum: he's a thief, a smuggler, a trickster, a looter, occasional bounty hunter—'

'So basically, everything we are?'

'Exactly!' Drift turned round and wagged a finger at her. 'He's a *rival*! Weren't you listening?' He spun away again, hands checking the position of his pistols in their holsters.

'Also,' Jia whispered hoarsely to Jenna, 'he has a massive cock.'

'He *is* a massive cock!' Drift barked from ahead of them.

Jenna looked at Jia in shock. It had only been a couple of weeks ago that she'd found out their pilot had secretly been sleeping with Micah van Schaken, their now-deceased gun hand. The notion that she'd also had a liaison with some sort of old rival, presumably also behind Drift's back, suggested a near-superhuman ability at conducting affairs.

Jia shook her head slightly and, with her fist tucked in close to her stomach, pointed ahead of them.

Jenna frowned in confusion. The Captain had a healthy – perhaps more than healthy – appetite for the female form, but she'd never seen any indication that he was interested in men. She mouthed his name as a silent question.

Jia rolled her eyes for an answer and pointed again, this time with expressive raised eyebrows and a head tilt for good measure.

Comprehension still refused to dawn for Jenna. The only other person ahead of them in the corridor was . . .

Wait.

As though her attention had been summoned by some unearthly rite, Tamara Rourke stopped dead and turned back to look at them, eyes dark and dangerous beneath the brim of her hat. They halted in their tracks simultaneously, each unwilling to get any closer to that countenance.

'Are you expecting to live through this job, Jia?' Rourke asked coolly, while Drift's footsteps *clanged* off towards the cargo bay.

'Uh, yeah?'

'Then I suggest you stop spreading rumours.'

'How'd you know——?'

'The only time I can't hear your voice is when you're saying something you don't want me to hear,' Rourke told her firmly. She walked towards them and jerked a thumb over her shoulder. 'Go find your brother.'

For once, Jia didn't argue or mouth back and hurried away towards the engine room. Rourke turned her gaze to Jenna, who was still trying to prevent herself from looking shell-shocked and not feeling that she was succeeding very well.

'So surprised?' Rourke said, and her voice was softer than Jenna had expected; almost thoughtful, in fact. 'Is it so very hard to believe that I might have had sex a few times in my life?'

'Uh, I . . .' Jenna wondered briefly how the hell she was supposed to get out of this one. 'You've never . . . I mean, that is, not that I . . .'

'Nor have you,' Rourke pointed out. 'When was the last time *you* found the opportunity to get intimate with someone, Jenna? Unless you were also sleeping with Micah, which quite frankly I doubt.'

'Um,' Jenna swallowed. So far in her career on the *Keiko* she'd either been keeping a low profile or they'd all been in mortal peril, and an inability to small talk in Russian had somewhat limited her chances on New Samara. 'Does "too damn long" count as an answer?'

'It does,' Rourke nodded, with possibly the vaguest hint of a smile. Then she sighed. 'Since it's out now – and you're the only one not to know, especially since Ichabod does like to remind me of the fact – I did sleep with Ricardo *fucking* Moutinho. Once. Many years ago now, and incidentally before we realised what a royal pain in the ass he was capable of being.

All it really did was confirm to me that I hadn't been missing a great deal by never finding time for it, in all honesty. Unfortunately, the fact that I didn't fall at his feet afterwards and worship his overlarge manhood seemed to piss him off, as did the fact that *we* ended up smuggling out what he viewed to be *his* contraband. As a result, things haven't exactly been rosy between our crew and his whenever we've encountered him since then.'

'And you've encountered him a lot?' Jenna asked in surprise.

'The galaxy's huge, but humanity's still only settled pinpricks of it,' Rourke replied, turning and leading the way towards the cargo bay once more, 'and people who've made a career of doing the sort of things we do . . . well, we tend to cluster around the same pinpricks. It's the nature of the business.'

Rourke slapped the airlock and they came out above the cargo bay. Drift was already by the control to lower the ramp, talking with Apirana in a low voice while the big Maori nodded soberly. The airlock on the other side hissed aside and the Changs appeared, Kuai still limping slightly.

'Right!' Drift said loudly, turning to look up at them. 'Given that we've got that little shit-stain Moutinho wandering around here somewhere, I think some of us should stay behind and watch the ship; besides which, too large a crowd might scare our contact, or draw attention. So I'm going to go with Jenna, since she can encode and store the data in a way that will mean anyone who checks our stuff won't know what we've got, and Kuai, since although this guy Shirokov apparently speaks good English,

I might need someone with a better grasp of Russian than I have to make myself understood.'

Out of the corner of her eye, Jenna saw Jia nudge Kuai. The little mechanic coughed.

'Ah, my leg's aching today. Can Jia go instead?'

Drift sighed and turned his attention to Jia, waiting for the inevitable sibling argument to ensue as she accused her brother of laziness or foisting work off onto her.

'Good idea,' Jia said, clapping Kuai on the shoulder and hurrying down the steps to the bay floor, 'I want to see this place anyway.'

Drift looked from one to the other suspiciously, but when there were no immediate signs of the apocalypse he nodded cautious agreement.

'Am I seriously that scary?' Rourke murmured into Jenna's ear. Jenna decided that the question was rhetorical.

'There's no guns allowed down there, unfortunately,' Drift continued, unbuckling his gun belt and placing it in a locker, 'and their laws say all firearms should be stowed securely. Still, laws or no laws, we have to be able to defend our property if Moutinho decides he wants to make trouble, so make sure you've got the keys to hand. With any luck, though, we should be in and out before he even knows we've been assigned the same goddamn berth as him.'

'Maybe you should take A. with you,' Rourke spoke up. 'No disrespect to Jia or Jenna, but if something kicks off you might want a bit of muscle.'

Drift frowned and looked around at the Maori. 'What do you say, big man? That hole in your belly healed enough?'

'Don't worry 'bout my *puku*, bro,' Apirana told him, slapping his side. 'You need me, I'm ready.'

'Good to know.' Drift beckoned to Jenna, who began to make her way down the steps. 'Let's get moving, then; our man's going to have finished his shift any minute.'

'Is the bay ready?' Jenna asked, not anxious to step outside into choking fumes of sulphur dioxide.

'Roof shut and oxygen restored,' Drift confirmed, checking the readouts and punching the release. The ramp started to whine downwards, and he looked back at the rest of them. 'Remember, this isn't New Samara, where everyone shits platinum and pisses fine wines; this is a government-run mining planet. Outsiders like us are welcome enough because we bring in money, but *only* if we stick to where we're meant to be and what we're supposed to be doing.'

'Good job we never break any rules, hey?' Apirana grunted.

Gaining access to Uragan City as a pedestrian consisted of stepping onto a long moving walkway which took them to the immigration suite, since the spaceport berths were large enough to make walking there something of a chore. Then they passed through a scanner, which confirmed that none of them were carrying any firearms, and had their identification checked by a group of black-uniformed *politsiya*, the local law enforcers, who most definitely were. That done, they skirted the escalators leading to the tram station and exited on foot down steps that led them into a world of grey.

'This place,' Jenna commented, looking around them, 'is grim.'

'That's the exact same word Orlov used,' Drift remarked, scratching at the skin around his right eye. 'I'm not inclined to argue with either of you.'

Uragan City was mainly lit by sunbulbs, designed to emit a frequency of light as close as possible to that of the sun from the First System, but even that concession did little to make it feel any warmer or more welcoming. It was a thoroughly utilitarian place, a network of square tunnels of varying sizes shod in grey and silver with slightly raised sidewalks for pedestrians flanking streets of humming vehicles, many of them official-looking. Red Cyrillic script on the walls or floor gave directions but there were no translations such as were provided on more cosmopolitan planets. Jia could read them anyway and the Captain's mechanical eye was equipped with a visual translation program, but Jenna and Apirana would have been reduced to scanning things with their pads to work out where they were. Even the occasional mural or piece of artwork looked tired and uninspired. The people were not dissimilar, although for a mining planet Jenna could see precious few dressed in mining gear.

'They'll be much deeper, actually working at the face,' Drift pointed out when she mentioned this. 'This is the commercial district, since it doesn't make sense to transport all the off-world goods any further from the surface than you have to.'

'It's a bit like walking around a giant hospital,' Jenna commented.

Apirana snorted. 'I swear, I've been in *prisons* cheerier than this.'

'We'll make interior designers of the pair of you yet,' Drift said as a maglev tram hissed around the corner ahead, its buzzer hooting at a pair of women who'd begun to venture across the street. 'Jia, can you see the nearest public comm?'

The pilot scanned their surroundings, then pointed at a junction ahead of them. 'Looks like we got one a block that way.'

'I could always slice into the system?' Jenna offered, but Drift just clucked his tongue.

'Again, let's keep this simple. I've got no idea how close an eye Uragan security keeps on their comms network, so let's stick to what's provided. We're only asking a guy to meet us so I can pass on a present from his dear old granddad, after all.' They dodged across the street, avoiding the traffic, and soon found what they were after around the next corner: an old-style comm unit, the handset attached to the main body by a strong metal-wrapped cord.

'Not taking any chances on it being damaged, are they?' Apirana noted.

'That would cost public money to replace, my friend,' Drift replied, pulling out his pad and bringing up a line of digits. 'Okay, here we go.' He flipped the comm to its loudspeaker setting and dialled. The call tone buzzed once . . . twice . . . three times . . .

+Privetstviye?+

The voice sounded . . . weary, was Jenna's best description. Male, middle-aged and weary.

'Mr Aleksandr Shirokov?' Drift asked.

+Da?+

'My name is Ichabod Drift,' the expression on the Captain's face clearly indicating his hope that Shirokov's English was as good as Orlov had claimed it would be, 'I ran into your grandfather on New Samara and he asked me to deliver something to you.'

+*I see.*+ Shirokov's voice had taken on a slightly livelier edge, but had Jenna been of a gambling persuasion she'd have put money on it being an act. +*How is he?*+

'He was well when I left him,' Drift recited, completing the planned exchange. 'Is there somewhere you'd like to meet?'

+*There is bar called Cherdak on Level Five. You should find map when you exit transit elevators, which can direct you to it. I will sit as close to rear window as I can so you find me.*+

'We'll be there as soon as possible,' Drift assured him.

+*We?*+

'Yeah, a couple of my crew are with me, they wanted to look around,' Drift assured him. 'Will that be a problem?'

+*No, no problem. No problem. I will see you soon, Mr Drift.*+

The connection cut off. Drift looked at the comm unit thoughtfully. 'Did he sound entirely happy, to you?'

'Probably just tired,' Apirana offered.

'*Si*,' Drift sighed, 'I just wonder . . . oh, never mind.'

'Like he might not like all the demands his grandfather's putting on him?' Jenna offered, careful to stick to the language they'd been using so far.

'Hmm,' Drift nodded thoughtfully, then snorted. 'Well, we're not here to fix anyone's family issues. Let's go and give Mr Shirokov his present, see if he's got a message he wants us to take back, and get off this rock.'

evel Five was hardly an improvement on Level One, where they'd begun, but at least it wasn't noticeably worse. What Drift was less impressed by was the fact that after paying a fare for a shuttle tram to the transit elevators, he'd then found that they needed to pay a further fare to use the elevators, and then yet another to get a shuttle tram to the district where Cherdak was. He'd gritted his teeth and tried to tell himself that they were small expenses in the scheme of making 100,000 stars from Sergei Orlov, but he couldn't help counting up the costs.

They'd ended up in an area Jia identified as lodging for off-worlders, which might have been why there seemed a high percentage of bars, gambling houses and the like. The higher-budget ones advertised themselves with flashing holo displays while the cheap settled for glowing neon, some with signs in the windows saying 'ENGLISH SPOKEN', or the equivalent in

Spanish, Swahili, Arabic and so on, which Drift viewed would be unlikely to be necessary elsewhere in Uragan City. This was not, after all, a highly cosmopolitan metropolis like New Samara; this was a Red Star mining town, and an almost exclusively Russian-rooted one at that.

Cherdak was at least easy to find, as its name was written over the door in Cyrillic, Western and Mandarin alphabets. Drift gave it a quick once-over from the outside and decided he approved of it as a meeting place; not too flashy, insofar as that was possible down here, but also not completely down at heel. It was an unremarkable bar, which meant they wouldn't be that remarkable going into it.

Well, except Apirana. He looked back at the huge Maori, who had raised the hood on his top as per usual. While he liked Apirana and valued his presence immensely, Drift couldn't help wishing that he didn't stick out *quite* so much.

Might as well wish for an entire engine refit while I'm at it, that'll probably happen sooner.

He pushed the swing door open and stepped inside, holding it for the other three and engaged in a quiet but meaningless conversation with Jia while doing so, the better to take a look around while trying to look natural. One or two people glanced up at them, but no one seemed overly watchful or suspicious. There were four groups in, probably ship crews judging by their clothes and general demeanour, with a few other individuals scattered around. The well-dressed Arab gentleman scowling at his pad might be a trader or broker, a middle-aged woman with a Japanese cast to her features could have been anything from a dealer in mining equipment to a diplomat on what had to be one of the most boring assignments available, the two Chinese men . . .

'Triax,' Jia whispered as they approached the bar.

'Really?'

'Tattoos.'

Drift frowned. He didn't want to look again, but although he'd seen tattoos on both of them he hadn't recognised anything which he knew to be a Triax gang sign. He sighed, and wondered again how much it would cost to get one of those recording chips with a playback function for his artificial eye. He had heard that sometimes caused the implant to run quite hot, however, and that just didn't sound like a good trade-off.

The landlady smiled at them as they approached, with more genuine warmth than Drift would have expected in this place. Still, four new customers were four new customers, and he supposed you probably got used to the dreariness of Uragan City after a while, especially if you'd never been anywhere else. He smiled back – she was actually rather pretty, and fairly young, with large blue eyes and hair so blonde it was almost white – and pulled out a credit chip, scanning the bottles lined up behind her.

He ordered the drinks – two bottles of Cerveza del Diablo, his favourite beer, for Jenna and him, a vodka and Star for Jia and a plain Star Cola for Apirana – and glanced over towards the rear of the bar. Sure enough, sitting in the far corner by a window that let in very little light, there was a solitary man who hadn't seemed to pay much attention when they'd walked in but was now studying them. Drift touched Jia lightly on the arm and began to wend his way between stools and other customers, while Jenna and Apirana chose a table at the opposite end, out of the way but able to watch the door.

'Aleksandr Shirokov?' Drift asked quietly when they'd approached to within a few feet. 'My name is Ichabod Drift, captain of the *Keiko*, and this is my pilot, Jia Chang.'

'Then please, sit,' Shirokov replied, gesturing to empty chairs. Drift complied, studying the other man as he did so.

Aleksandr Shirokov was probably in his mid-forties if you looked closely, but the lines on his face and the grey in his dark, thinning hair gave him the appearance of a man a decade older. He wore tired office clothes: black shoes with frayed laces, a dark blue suit from which the years had stripped whatever true lustre the material may have originally possessed and replaced it with a well-worn shine, and a mostly white shirt pulled open at the collar. The jacket was the cut favoured by the Red Star government, with an almost breastplate-like front panel buttoned at the right side of the chest. Drift had been expecting a miner, but this made far more sense: no miner would be likely to have access to the sorts of production quotas and shipping arrangements Orlov wanted.

Drift produced a small box from one of the pouches on his belt and set it on the table. 'Your grandfather asked me to pass this on to you. Did you have a message for me to take back?'

Shirokov didn't reply. Instead he stared at the box with an unreadable expression.

'Mr Shirokov?' Drift prompted, after a few seconds had elapsed with no reply forthcoming.

'I have no message for my "grandfather",' Shirokov said, looking up and meeting Drift's eyes, 'but I have message for you, Captain.

'Get me out of here.'

Drift blinked, not welcoming the sensation of the metaphorical ground shifting beneath his feet. 'Excuse me?'

Shirokov reached out and flipped the box open to reveal a small silver oblong. 'Do you know what this is?'

Drift had already looked at Shirokov's payment to make sure that he wasn't going to be smuggling anything illegal into Uragan City, but made a show of inspecting it for the sake of politeness. 'It appears to be a power cell.'

'It is,' Shirokov nodded. He tapped his knuckles on his left leg, which was unyielding. 'I lost this leg at mine face when I was thirty-two. Industrial accidents not uncommon here, although mine was worse than many. I could not afford prosthetic, even from Universal Access Movement; they can provide good basic items, but my nerve damage too bad. I could only work in office and had to move by wheeled chair. My reading and writing not good, but I seemed to have knack to learn when I needed to. Also learned English; half well, I feel.'

'Your English is certainly better than my Russian,' Drift acknowledged, wondering when Shirokov was going to get to the point.

'I got lucky,' the Russian continued, although his lips twisted. 'Or so I thought. Wealthy businessman visit our office, shocked how government does not help its injured workers. Organise for me new leg: proper, powered, matched with nerve endings, perfect balance. I can walk again! He tell me: any problems, I can reach him.'

'I think I can guess his name,' Drift muttered.

'I think you can too,' Shirokov sighed. 'After eight months, power supply fails. I cannot find manufacturer to replace, brand too specialist for Universal Access Movement to supply. I contact businessman; he say, of course I can get you new one! I send someone to bring you replacement. This man come just before big storm. He tell me—'

'I can guess what he told you, too,' Drift sighed, pinching the bridge of his nose. Goddamn it, was it too much to ask for Orlov to have found someone willing to talk for money instead of this little entrapment scheme? But of course, if you wanted regular information you needed your mole to have a regular need for whatever you were paying him. He thought for a moment about what he'd do to ensure his mechanical eye kept functioning.

Yeah, quite a lot.

'So you want out?' he asked, gloomily.

'*Da*,' Shirokov said firmly, a tone of urgency entering his voice for the first time as he dropped it lower. 'Here is *my* deal to you: you get me and my Pavel off-world and I give you information you need. This planet took my leg and I am sick of living in this *svalka*, sick of waiting for someone to realise I pass information for last ten years! Maybe I can find how to get new power supplies myself, maybe I just learn to do without one leg again. But I want to leave. I want to *live*.'

'And if I don't get you off-world?' Drift asked wearily. Shirokov sat back, arms folded.

'Then you fly back to New Samara and tell Mr Orlov you could not do his job.'

For a moment, just a moment, Drift was tempted to do just that. Or, hell, just leave the system entirely; pack up and head off, forget about Uragan and New Samara and Sergei Orlov. Kelsier had left other stashes of money around the galaxy, after all.

But . . . the hundred grand from Orlov was a payoff not to be sniffed at, and one of his reasons for taking this job was to prove to his crew that they still wanted to be a crew at all. Cutting and running from something as easy as this would not reflect well on his leadership credentials, or their chances of making a living from following him.

Besides, Orlov might not bother coming after them, since it wasn't like they'd taken anything belonging to him yet apart from the power supply sitting on the table in front of them, but what if he decided they'd found a higher bidder elsewhere and sold Shirokov's information on? That would be a slight he could not overlook, regardless of whether he had any genuine concerns about their ability to cause chaos when provoked. And there was also their reputation with the rest of the galaxy to consider. Ichabod Drift, abandoning a simple fetch-and-carry information run because it got too hard? All Orlov would have to do would be to circulate that rumour and their employability would take a terminal nosedive.

'And Pavel,' he said, trying to buy some time to think, 'he would be . . . your son?'

'My husband,' Shirokov replied. Drift nodded; at least a second adult would be easier to move than a child . . . *Why in God's name am I even considering this?*

'You understand that this is a slightly different situation to the one we were anticipating?' he asked, amazing even himself with his understatement.

'Of course,' Shirokov nodded. 'You may wish to get used to this, if you keep dealing with Mr Orlov.'

'Right, thanks for that,' Drift muttered. 'Can you just up and leave when you like?'

'*Nyet*,' the other man sighed, shaking his head. 'We will need emigration papers, and these the governor does not often grant. Who would stay, otherwise?'

'Who indeed?' Drift paused, then realised to his horror that Shirokov expected him to be able to do something about this. 'Wait . . . what sort of clout do you think we have, exactly?!'

Shirokov shrugged. 'I do not know. A lot, I hope.'

'Great.' Drift looked at Jia, then back at Shirokov. 'I'm gonna need to discuss this with my crew, so if you'll excuse us . . .'

'Please.' Shirokov gestured to indicate they should leave the table if they wished. 'We have until next storm arrives.'

'Thanks for the reminder,' Drift said, trying not to grit his teeth too hard, and pushed his stool back. He drained the rest of his beer with one long swig and turned to head for the bar, Jia at his elbow.

'What we gonna do?' the pilot hissed.

'The way I see it, we don't have many options,' Drift muttered. 'I mean, do you think Apirana would beat the information out of him?'

'Nope.'

'No, me neither,' Drift agreed, 'and I wouldn't want to do that, anyway. That leaves us with—'

'Rourke might.'

Drift frowned. 'You might be right. Maybe. Even so, I still wouldn't like it. I think we're going to have to do this the hard way and get both Shirokovs out of here.' He smiled at the landlady and held up his now-empty bottle as she wandered over to them. 'The same again please, *krasotka*.'

'Why do you know how to say "pretty lady" in *every* language?' Jia hissed as another beer found its way into Drift's hand, courtesy of a slightly blushing landlady. Good to know he hadn't lost his touch.

'Because there are pretty ladies everywhere,' he replied, taking a sip. 'Okay. We obviously can't get them proper emigration papers, so—' He stopped, taking in Jia's suddenly widening eyes. 'What?' He glanced around as much as he could without moving his head, trying to see if there were any mirrors or other reflective surfaces nearby, and lowered his voice to a whisper. 'Did someone just come in?'

A hand landed on his shoulder and he was spun around before he could even move of his own accord. He found himself staring up, which didn't happen often, into the face of a man he didn't know. The newcomer was pale, with a slightly overlarge nose and hair an unremarkable shade of brown that fell shaggily to his jawline, and an artificial eye much like Drift's own.

He wasn't alone. Drift registered three others, all shorter, two men and a woman. Then someone else sidled into view, hair as black as a New Samaran night

and his face weathered and tanned by actual atmospheric exposure. He was wearing a red-and-white
neckerchief, a matt black armavest and heavy-duty
trousers, the sort Kuai favoured with hundreds of
pockets and reinforced knees. His mouth, under that
stupid damn moustache, was twisting into a smug
grin.

'*Olá*, Ichabod,' Ricardo Moutinho sneered. 'Long
time, no see.'

'Could you imagine actually *living* in a place like this?' Jenna asked in a low voice, looking around the bar. Apirana took a swig of his drink and followed her lead, trying to let his preconceptions go.

The buildings down here had clearly been built to specification; this was going to be A Bar, in the same way as the block across the street had been constructed (or should that be excavated?) as A Hotel or similar accommodation. It was a strange contrast to other mining planets or moons he'd been to, where old tunnels had been sold on by the mining companies to development agencies, and then on further to whoever could pay. On Uragan, the Red Star Confederate had come in and planned this entire subterranean city from scratch, then built it. It was ordered, functional and . . . well, more than a little soulless. Then again, if he was given a choice between living in the lower tunnels on somewhere like

Carmella II or living in the lower levels of Uragan City, Apirana would take the pre-planned version every time.

'I don't think it's that bad,' he said honestly. 'It's clean, you got good air provision,' he gestured at the large, functioning fans in the ceiling, 'you got running water an' sewage an' that. Good lighting. Probably got grow galleries with sunbulbs in too, so you can at least get some fresh fruit an' veg local.'

'I'd miss the sky,' Jenna said sadly, her face turned towards the darkened window which overlooked the street outside.

'I would, too,' Apirana nodded, 'an' I'm not saying it'd be ideal. But you can get used to it. Main thing is the people you share a place with. If you've got good people with you, you can put up with just about anything an' keep going. If you're surrounded by assholes, you won't be happy anywhere.'

'You think that?' Jenna asked, turning to look at him. Apirana shrugged.

'I know it. If that weren't true, I'd still be in New Zealand.'

Jenna winced, clearly uncomfortable with the reminder of his history: to be fair, it wasn't a pleasant story. However, something else occurred to Apirana as he looked at her.

'An' I'm thinking that you might still be on Franklin Minor.'

Jenna's face didn't move, but that in itself was an indication that he'd hit close to the mark; it wasn't a lack of reaction so much as her expression freezing in place.

'What do you mean?'

Apirana sighed. 'Look, I ain't meaning to pry, but you talking about how you'd miss the sky, an' given how shook up you got with that business in the asteroid – an' don't get me wrong, you had every right to be shook up, that was some nasty shit an' I don't just say that cos I got shot – I'm just thinking, it sounds like you *should've* been happier on Franklin Minor. Got a breathable atmosphere, plants, animals, your family must've had some money, you went to university . . .' He tailed off and swirled his drink around in his glass, looking down at it to avoid pressurising her with his gaze. 'It sounds like a good place to be. But I know it don't always work out that way. Just seems to me more likely that it's people what meant you ended up with us, not that you had some sorta wanderlust.'

Now he did look up. Jenna was staring at her own drink, lips pressed tightly together.

'We don't have to talk about our pasts.'

'Not trying to make you,' Apirana said gently. 'I'm just speculating. Could be wrong, could be right. But sometimes having a secret can be draining. Sometimes people wanna talk about something an' don't know where to start. Sometimes it's easier if someone else's done some of the groundwork for you, if you know what I mean. Told you before, I ain't in no position to judge anyone for what they've done or didn't do, because odds are I did worse.'

'Okay, just to get this straight, *I* didn't do anything wrong,' Jenna snapped, 'so you can stop that line of speculation.'

'You didn't do *anything* wrong?'

'No!'

Apirana couldn't prevent a slight smile touching his lips. 'So you just turned up on our ship with all that slicing knowledge which had been *purely theoretical* beforehand, then?'

'Uh . . . that's . . .'

'An' it's not like you told me an' the Captain about how you'd got the stuff to make your EMP,' he continued, winking at her. 'Y'know, when you talked about how you'd been to a well-equipped university an' you were good at getting around security systems?'

Jenna glared at him, but she had the decency to look slightly ashamed. 'There was a context.'

Apirana couldn't help but laugh. 'Like I said, I ain't judging. You're *whānau* o'mine, an' I trust you. You say there was a good reason, I ain't gonna call you a liar. Probably a hell of a lot more sensible decision than I was making when I was your age.'

'Maybe,' Jenna replied, and he was relieved to see that she was smiling slightly, too. 'A. . . . does it bother you that you're *still* employed just as . . .' She trailed off, as though looking for the right word.

'A thug?' Apirana suggested. She winced again, and he placed his hand briefly over hers to show he wasn't offended. 'Hey, don't worry. It is what it is. An' no, it don't bother me, for two reasons. One, cos that's not the case; the Captain don't just view me as muscle with no brains, he'll listen if I talk to him an' he won't ignore something I say just cos it's me what said it. Second, he *asked* me. Didn't trick me, didn't pretend to be my friend an' manipulate me, then tell me I owed him for favours. Came up to me in that bar on Farport an' asked me if I wanted in on his crew, made no secret that I'd be expected to look threatening when needed and throw down if it came to it.' He shrugged. 'I'm good at both, but it ain't no different to you an' slicing. It's something we *do*, not something we *are*. I can bring the thug out when he's needed, an' the rest of the time I'm just Apirana.'

'Well, good,' Jenna smiled. 'I prefer Apirana.'

To his astonishment, Apirana felt his stomach flutter. He coughed to cover his momentary confusion. 'Well, yeah. Most people do.' What the hell? Where had that come from all of a sudden? Okay, Jenna was a pretty girl, and intelligent, and he enjoyed talking to her, and it was true enough that his life hadn't exactly been full of pretty, intelligent, companionable girls telling him that they liked him, but . . .

Ah, shit.

'A.?' Jenna was frowning, and now she placed *her* hand onto *his*. 'Are you okay?'

'I . . . yeah, I . . .' Apirana looked around for a distraction and saw an all-too-unwelcome one filing in through the bar's main door. 'Oh, no.'

'What's up?' Jenna asked, apprehension colouring her voice as she presumably followed his gaze. 'Who're they?'

'Ricardo *fuckin'* Moutinho an' whatever *uku* he has working for him right now,' Apirana growled. 'Ain't seen him since that mess on New Shinjuku, where one of his goons stabbed me up.' He could feel his pulse quickening as the memory of hot, silver pain flashed across his right shoulder. Drift was at the bar talking urgently to Jia, and Moutinho's crew had clearly spotted him. They made a beeline for the Captain, Moutinho already smirking smugly. Apirana stood up, hands clenching into fists.

'A. . . .'

'Don't worry,' he told Jenna without looking at her. 'Just hold that thought, yeah? Looks like we might need the thug.'

When he'd been growing up as a young teen in Rotorua, Apirana had been a massive fan of the holo-show *Boomer Izaak* about a rough, tough sheriff on a planet he could no longer recall the name of. The actor who'd portrayed Boomer had given him a specific walk when it was time in the episode for heads to be cracked and fists to fly; it wasn't fast but it had an unstoppable aura, with a rolling of the shoulders to emphasise his size and build. Apirana had practised it back and forth across his parents' living room, at least when his father hadn't been around to shout at him. In the years that followed he'd adopted it for real, when he'd been trying to exude intimidation to keep the Mongrel Mob's enemies in line. These days, he fell into it as automatically as holding his breath before going underwater.

Apirana spent a lot of time trying to minimise his size by hanging back or stooping a little, partly to avoid making people uncomfortable where possible and partly because he got enough stares as it was. Now, however, he threw his head up and his chest out, sucking in air through his nose and setting his face into a hard stare. It was a physiological change as much as anything else; he only moved like this when he was ready to throw punches, and wanted to advertise that fact.

And as much as he liked to pretend otherwise, every once in a while it felt good not to be tiptoeing.

The biggest man in Moutinho's crew had grabbed Drift and spun him around. Moutinho himself was just sneering something when one of the others – a pasty-faced male youth with 'tribal' tattoos on his skinny arms which were, in Apirana's opinion, shit – caught sight of Apirana bearing down on them. The youth panicked and turned, pulling a knife and drew back his arm to strike.

That was his first mistake. Apirana didn't give him a chance to make a second.

He lurched out of the Boomer walk into a quick two-step run-up which terminated in a lunging kick that drove the sole of his right boot into the kid's breastbone. Apirana had well over 300 pounds of momentum to play with and nearly three decades of fighting behind him, on streets, in bars and in prisons. He knew how to kick.

The kid might have weighed half what he did, and all of that weight went flying back into the bar with the sort of sickening, dull thud that only comes when a skull meets an unyielding surface. He slumped down and Apirana instantly dismissed him. Even if he got back up, he wouldn't be in a position to menace so much as a kitten for a couple of hours.

Of course, he hadn't *meant* to start a fight, but the kid's colleagues were unlikely to stand off now. A blur of motion to his immediate left was the only warning that the guy in a turban had swung a punch. Fortunately Apirana had been expecting it, and his greater height allowed him to easily trap the swing beneath his right arm. From there it was a moment's work to grab the back of the other man's skull and pull him into a headbutt – technically against *tapu*, but Apirana had never really bought into that spiritual shit – then pull him down face first into a rising knee. *Two down*.

A smashing sound dragged Apirana's attention sideways, but it was only Drift. The Captain had taken advantage of the distraction to knock the end off his beer bottle and now held the jagged remnants to the throat of the big man who'd grabbed him, his other hand tangled in the crewman's hair and pulling his head back. Apirana looked between Moutinho, whose face was a picture of shock, and the wiry *pākehā* woman with a scar down her cheek who'd just picked up a stool by one leg.

'Now,' Apirana said to her levelly, holding up one fist for emphasis, 'you don't look that dumb. How about you three,' here he nodded towards Moutinho and the big man, whose eyes were somewhat wild as the broken glass pricked his throat, 'take your friends outta here before this gets *really* unpleasant, *mārama*?'

The woman looked to Moutinho for guidance. To Apirana's relief, the captain of the *Jacare* nodded at her before bending down to scoop up the kid with the tattoos; none too gently, but that was none of Apirana's concern. For her part, the woman dropped the stool she'd picked up and moved forwards warily to help support her crewmate in the turban back to his feet, on which he was rather unsteady.

Moutinho looked at Drift, the swagger completely absent from his manner now, although there was more than a little resentment burning away in his eyes. 'What about Dugan?'

'Your friend here?' Drift replied, nodding towards the man he was holding prisoner. 'How about the rest of you walk out that door, and then I'll let him go.'

'And if we don't?' the woman spat. Apirana winced internally and readied himself to step in. *Shit, do* not *try to call his bluff . . .*

'Just get out the fucking door, Lena!' the man called Dugan wailed, clearly reluctant to be the subject of this confrontation.

'I'll remember this,' Moutinho snarled at Drift, but he was backing away.

'See that you do.' Drift's face was thunderous. 'Maybe you'll think twice about trying to throw your weight around when other people are just trying to have a quiet drink.'

Moutinho scowled, but chose to drag his groaning burden towards the door instead of answer. Lena and the man in the turban followed, the latter still moving like someone who'd overindulged in the bar's wares. The door banged shut behind them, although Apirana could see them waiting on the other side of the darkened glass.

'So, your name's Dugan, right?' Drift said to the man he had at bottle-point.

'Fuck you!'

'Listen, there's nothing personal here,' Drift said seriously. 'I'm just going to give you some advice. First of all, stop flying with that man. Second, if you don't take that advice, find out who it is he wants you to intimidate before you start doing it. You'll live longer.' He pulled the broken bottle away and shoved Dugan hard in the back in one motion, sending the larger man a few lurching steps across the floor. Apirana stood back to give him room, but Dugan didn't seem inclined to linger. He was through the bar's door a second later, and Apirana breathed a sigh of relief as the shapes of Moutinho and his crew turned away instead of coming back for another go.

'*Cristo!*' Drift threw his hands up as soon as the door had banged shut for a second time. 'Why'd you have to start a fight, A.?'

Apirana fought down a brief impulse to slap Drift, but he knew where that would end: Drift had made very clear before that if Apirana ever laid a hand on him again then he would find himself out of a job. Still, he didn't keep the bass out of his voice. 'He pulled a fuckin' knife on me, bro! What was I supposed t'do?!'

'He did?' Drift's eyebrows rose. 'Ah. Didn't see that.'

'*Da!*' To Apirana's surprise, the landlady was now holding a length of metal which might have been a decapitated broom handle. 'I saw it!'

Drift turned to her with an apologetic expression on his face. 'Madam, I am so, so sorry—'

'Hssht!' She held her hand up. 'They been in here too many times, last few months. I don't like them. Bad people, rude. Not polite like you.' She lowered her voice, leaning forwards a little. 'Sometimes come in here with others, too: local people, but trouble-makers. Won't be sorry if they stay away now.' She picked up a comm handset. 'You want I call *politsiya?*'

'Ah, no. No, thank you,' Drift assured her hastily, 'we're kind of pushed for time here, and we need to leave before the next storm. We'd rather avoid having to give statements, all that sort of thing. Uh, have you got anything I can clear this glass up with? I seem to have made a bit of a mess . . .' He smiled and, as it usually seemed to, it did the trick. The landlady smiled back and waved him away.

'See? Polite. Don't bother yourself, I do it.' Then, to Apirana's surprise, she turned to him. 'You.'

He frowned. 'Me?'

'You ever need job, you come see me about security work, *da*?'

Apirana smiled at her, on the basis that it seemed to be a good plan. 'Sure thing, ma'am.' He registered a presence at his elbow and turned to find Jenna standing there, and was suddenly acutely aware that he'd ended their previous conversation by beating down two men. *Smooth, A.*

'You okay?' she asked him, brushing one of her disobedient strands of hair back from her face as she looked up at him.

He smiled. 'Yeah, I—'

'Good.' She switched her attention to Drift. 'We need to leave, now.'

'How come no one ever asks if *I'm* okay?' Drift asked, hurt.

'Because no one cares,' Jia said bluntly. The pilot had stayed well back from the fighting, which Apirana was thoroughly grateful for given what usually happened if her or her brother tried to get involved. 'Shut up and listen to Jenna, she's got her serious face on.'

Jenna gave a brief nod of thanks to the other woman, then looked back at Drift. 'We need to get out of here; I think someone's called the cops already.'

Drift frowned. 'How do you . . .' He tailed off as Jenna tapped her left forearm meaningfully, where her wrist console was hidden by the sleeve of her jumpsuit, then glared and lowered his voice to a hiss. 'What did I say about not slicing into *anything*? Let alone security communications!'

'That was before we got involved in a fight half an hour after we touched down,' Jenna pointed out. 'You want to tell me off, fine, but can we at least do it somewhere else?'

Drift scowled at her. 'Just for *that*, you've volunteered to solve our latest little problem.' He threw a look over at the corner where he'd been speaking to the person Apirana assumed to have been Aleksandr Shirokov, but the table was empty. In fairness, several of the other drinkers had made a quick exit through the rear door during or in the immediate aftermath of their brief scuffle, but the sight seemed to infuriate Drift further. He waved his hands at them. 'C'mon, back to the ship, *now*.'

Apirana threw his hood up before they even stepped outside: it wouldn't help much when it came to avoiding detection, but it was better than nothing. Thankfully there was no sign of Moutinho and his crew anywhere, and at least the inability of civilians to carry firearms meant they wouldn't walk into some sort of ambush like the one that had claimed Micah's life.

'You get what we need?' he asked Drift as they walked towards the shuttle tram stop as fast as they could without drawing attention.

'No.'

'Ah.' Apirana had heard that tone of voice before, and it never boded well. It usually meant that something completely unexpected had gone wrong, which the Captain always seemed to take as more of a personal affront than expected complications like breakdowns, law enforcement officials and Jia's piloting. 'That'd be the "latest little problem" you mentioned, then?'

'One of 'em.' Drift pulled out the contact number they had for Shirokov and keyed it into his comm.

'Shouldn't you use a public—' Jenna began.

'Don't care right now,' Drift snapped. Clearly he was answered, because his next words made no sense otherwise. Not that they made much sense to Apirana anyway. 'Pack your bags and wait for my call.'

'Uh, why is he meant to be packing his bags?' Jenna asked as Drift jabbed his comm earpiece off again. The Captain snorted humourlessly.

'*That* is our latest little problem.'

UNWANTED ENTANGLEMENTS

'That's the best we can do?' Drift asked with what Jenna felt was a wholly inappropriate dubiousness. She sighed, exasperated, and shoved the documents under his nose.

'I *told* you: I'm a slicer, not a forger! The electronic component was no trouble, but the *plasticwork* . . .' She shook her head in disgust. What sort of planet still relied on physical media? 'It looks more or less okay, I think, but it's probably the wrong thickness and maybe the wrong texture, probably the wrong weight, and the holographic watermark's not going to stand up to any sort of real scrutiny.'

She watched Drift pore over the thin plaspaper sheets she'd just managed to coax out of the *Jonah*'s on-board printer. You were never going to get everything handled digitally, of course, which was why they still even bothered to carry such an archaic piece of equipment. Some people simply wouldn't take anything but a person's signature on a physical contract, or at least expected it as part of a transaction; a sort of ceremonial accompaniment to a genescan, fingerprint or what-have-you. However, to find an entire planet where the government actually used it as standard . . .

Well, in a way she supposed it was fiendishly clever. It was so outdated that no one would even consider needing to be prepared to forge something like this unless they already knew about it.

'Well, we've got no real option,' Drift concluded. He ran his finger down one of the pages, then rubbed it gently between thumb and forefinger and held it up to the light. The flag of the governing conglomerate rippled in the top-right corner, a holo fluttering in a non-existent breeze.

'Except turning around and heading back to Orlov,' Rourke suggested from the cockpit doorway. 'We could tell him his mole refused to cooperate, explain Shirokov's demands.'

'I don't think that will help anyone,' Drift replied pensively, 'least of all us. Orlov won't pay us, at the very least, and we'd be lucky if he didn't spread it around that we couldn't handle a simple information transfer. He doesn't get to make his killing in the stocks, and Shirokov is still stuck here. No, if we get the mole off-world and he gives us the data then he gets what he wants, Orlov gets what he wants and by extension, we get what *we* want.'

'Orlov gets what he wants until he next wants a jump on the ore market, you mean,' Rourke pointed out, folding her arms. 'How do you suppose he'll react when he finds out we've taken his meal ticket away from him?'

'Nothing to do with us if Shirokov somehow bought his way off-world,' Drift shrugged. 'We'll be long gone from New Samara by that time anyway, even if we linger for a few days so our disappearance isn't suspiciously quick.'

'Except that Orlov is bound to have enough influence to access the shipping records here,' Rourke said, her tone taking on a slight edge of exasperation, 'and they'll record his emigration on the *Jonah*.'

Jenna raised a finger, feeling for an incongruous moment as though she were back on Franklin Minor watching her parents bickering over some small grievance. They'd never really fallen out, but the other person's idiosyncrasies had clearly started to grate over time. 'Uh, I can sort that. The Shirokovs might be *recorded* as leaving on the *Jonah*, but I can alter that as soon as we're clear from the docking bay.'

'Which, incidentally, cannot come quickly enough,' Rourke muttered, casting a dark glare over at the shape of the *Pouço Jacaré*. She shook her head, a disapproving twist to her lips. 'I suppose it's too much to hope that Apirana actually knocked some sense into anyone's heads?'

'A couple of them might think twice about trying something again,' Drift conceded, 'but I won't believe Moutinho's out of our hair until I see him take off or we leave him in our trails. They haven't been up to anything, I take it?'

'Saw him and that big guy you mentioned unloading some cargo,' Rourke replied, 'but they didn't so much as look this way. I don't like it, the bastard's up to something. He'd be pissing up against the side of our ship, normally.'

'He's welcome to,' Drift laughed, showing the first sign of genuine good humour Jenna had seen in him since they'd set foot in Uragan City, 'petty malice doesn't worry me. We'll just have to stay sharp in case he tries anything more meaningful.' He started to fold the plaspaper and nudged the comm on with his elbow. 'A., get your boots; we're going back in.'

Ten minutes later Jenna was watching Apirana carefully slide her forgeries into the secret compartment in the sole of one boot. The Maori was so tall that the extra half-inch of height given by the slightly thicker soles of this pair didn't look at all incongruous, and since he had the biggest feet on the crew it provided slightly more space in which to smuggle sensitive items. Nothing big, of course . . . but things didn't have to be large to be valuable.

'Right,' Drift was saying, checking his wrist chrono, 'same set-up as before. A., Jenna, Jia and I are going in to find the Shirokovs, Tamara and Kuai will watch the ship and be ready to leave as soon as we get back. We have—'

'Three standard hours,' Rourke put in.

'—at the *most* until the next storm hits and this place closes for three days or so,' Drift continued, 'so we can't afford any delays. This has already taken longer than it should have done.'

'Let's go, then,' Apirana grunted, and hit the door release. Was it Jenna's imagination, or was he avoiding eye contact with her? She was sure she'd already caught him looking at her oddly once, when he'd seemed to think that *she* was looking somewhere else.

Maybe he thought she should have done a better job with the forgeries, too. She was getting a little tired of feeling like everyone expected her to work miracles, for all that it was sort of flattering.

Uragan City didn't get any more inviting on the second visit. She tried to look at it differently, seeing the positives Apirana had listed, but she still couldn't get past her initial impression of the entire place as a giant, underground morgue with a populace that just happened to be walking about at the moment. Glass City on Hroza Major had been far more to her liking, with its views of the skies and its natural light, or New Samara and its fresh air.

So, the wealthy places we've been to recently. Yeah, not like you're showing your background at all, rich kid.

Drift wasn't wasting any time; he made his way to the same public comm that he'd called Shirokov from before and punched in the Uragan's contact code, then switched the unit to its speaker setting again. Jenna leaned against the wall, a faintly coarse artificial surface of some sort rendered in a mild cream, and cast a deliberately casual glance up the street in the direction they'd just come from. Seeing no immediate signs of *Jacare* crew or roving law enforcers, she turned her head to check the other way and found Apirana looking back at her, apparently having had the same idea. To her surprise, the Maori dropped his gaze and seemed to find an immediate interest in the comm riveted to the wall. Yes, this was definitely getting weird now.

The comm stopped ringing. +Privetstviye?+

'Mr Shirokov, we're ready for you,' Drift said briskly, managing to keep most of the annoyance out of his voice. 'We'll meet you at the same place as before to go over final arrangements. When can you be there?'

+*I . . . One moment, please.*+ There was a quick buzz of muffled conversation in fast Russian; Shirokov had presumably placed a hand over his comm's mouthpiece, but it probably wouldn't have made much difference to the crew's ability to understand. +*Thirty minutes.*+

Drift winced. 'Don't be late. We're working to a tight schedule here.'

+*I understand, Captain. I assure you, I do not wish delay.*+

'Best get moving, then,' Drift said, and killed the connection. He exhaled, and grimaced in obvious frustration as he checked his chrono.

'Easy, Cap,' Apirana rumbled, 'we got plenty of time.'

'Only if nothing goes wrong,' Drift countered, 'and given our luck so far, I'm not holding my breath on that front.'

'Why you wanna meet him there again, anyway?' Jia asked as they began to move towards the nearest tram stop. 'Ain't this just gonna cost us more money?'

'Yeah, but we need somewhere to hand over the documents out of sight,' Drift muttered, nodding slightly in the direction of Apirana's feet, 'and I don't trust that *someone* isn't listening in. I don't want to name locations or mention us taking them off-world, so that leaves us with precisely one option of where to meet.' He sighed. 'Well, at least the landlady's pretty.'

Cherdak was still open, and busier. The slightly dimmed lighting in the streets was an indication that

Uragan's artificially imposed day cycle was moving towards its arbitrary 'night', and while Jenna suspected that shift work would be continuing down at the mine faces it seemed that a lot of the population were taking the chance to sink a few before turning in. The bar was thick with the sound of chatter, almost all of it in Russian, and the locals now outnumbered the off-worlders.

Despite the crowd, it only took a moment to spot the Shirokovs. Jenna nudged Drift in the ribs and pointed to where two men were sitting, each with a wheeled suitcase beside them. 'That them?' She hadn't got a close look at Shirokov before – or Aleksandr, as she supposed she should think of him, given that there were now two – but these were the only people in the bar who looked ready to travel anywhere.

'That's them,' Drift nodded, and began to make his way through the bar. Jenna followed, slipping easily past crowded tables and rowdy punters, and found herself looking at the two men for whom she had recently spent so much time forging documents.

Aleksandr was the older man, that much was clear immediately. Dark-haired and with grey showing both on his head and in his stubble, his face carried deep-scored lines of fatigue or stress, or possibly both. He was wearing a turtle-necked, long-sleeved top in a very dark blue, worn black trousers with smart black boots, and the face he turned to them carried a warring, badly concealed mix of eagerness and apprehension.

His partner, Pavel, was a contrast; at least ten years younger, if Jenna was any judge, and with a shaggy mop of light blond hair framing smooth-cheeked, clean-cut features that were decidedly easy on the eye. He wore a sleeveless, collarless white shirt that displayed well-developed arms, and dark green dungarees with one strap left carelessly unfastened. However, he too looked tired. If he was a miner, as Jenna suspected, then while the work might have benefitted his physique it didn't seem to have done much for his general well-being.

'*Señores.*' Drift sat down without preamble and nodded for Apirana to do the same on the other unoccupied stool. The big Maori did so and crossed his right leg over his left, leaning forwards as if to massage his ankle. Jenna and Jia were left standing, although they were far from the only ones in the room to be on their feet, and the pilot sidled around until she was blocking all lines of sight to Apirana and his boot.

'Captain,' Aleksandr nodded. Nervousness was currently winning out on his face. 'Do you have what we need?'

Drift nodded. 'We do.' Apirana's huge hand appeared from beneath the table, two folded sheets of plaspaper gripped in his fingers. He opened them up enough for the Shirokovs to see the holographic watermark, but drew his hand back as Aleksandr reached for them.

'Captain?' Aleksandr's voice was level but his eyes were on Apirana, and not happy. Still, he wasn't foolish enough to make a grab. People rarely tried to take things from Apirana by force.

'You got what *we* need?' Drift asked, his voice cold. Aleksandr's jaw moved for a second, but then he pulled out a small datachip.

'Here. All schedules for next shipments after storm clears.'

Drift held out his hand.

'Captain, you must think me a fool,' Aleksandr said, his eyes narrowing.

'You're the fool, Mr Shirokov, if you think I'm letting you on my boat with nothing but your say-so that you have what I need,' Drift replied, leaning forwards slightly. 'Give me the chip, and we will verify its contents. Then, and only then, will we go to the spaceport and you'll get off this rock.'

Jenna watched Aleksandr while he chewed that over for a few seconds. She couldn't exactly blame him for his reticence, since the information was literally the only leverage he had. For a moment she thought he was going to hold out and deny the Captain, but then the older man's face folded and he pushed the small piece of plastic and silicon grudgingly across the table's surface.

Jenna snatched it up before he could change his mind and pulled back the sleeve of her jumpsuit to expose the dataport of her wrist-mounted console. The chip slotted in neatly and the console immediately began scanning it. Cyrillic characters scrolled across the screen for a moment, but then her translation program kicked in and it resolved into lines of familiar letters and numbers. She searched them for meaning, feeling her forehead crease into a frown as she did so.

'Jenna?' Drift asked.

She nodded. 'Looks like we've got amounts, product codes, dates and destinations . . .' She pulled the chip back out and handed it to him. 'I'd say it's good.'

'I hope so.' Drift took the chip between thumbs and forefingers and snapped it.

Aleksandr spat something in Russian which Jenna didn't need a translator to catch the general gist of. Pavel even started to rise to his feet, but Apirana landed one massive hand on his shoulder and pushed him gently but firmly back into his seat. The blond lifted his arm as though to swat the obstacle aside, but whatever he saw in the Maori's tattooed face clearly made him think better of it.

'We don't know what sort of searches you'd be subjected to, going through security as emigrants,' Drift explained calmly, letting the halves of the chip drop. 'I certainly can't risk this being found on you. So now it's with us.'

Jenna was only half listening as Drift continued talking. Instead, her fingers were dancing over the keys on her console to activate encryption and disguise programs. Simply encrypting data might protect it but it was suspicious as all hell, so she'd developed a further tactic: hide it as something innocuous. Her three go-to options were the schematics of the *Keiko*, a series of pictures of attractive men wearing very little clothing, and the beginnings of a hilariously bad amateur screen-play cobbled together for this exact purpose by her and Jia when they'd both been rather drunk.

She went for the men. It was that sort of day.

'A.,' Drift was saying, 'I think they can have their documents now.'

Apirana passed the emigration plastics over to the Shirokovs, who took them with badly concealed haste. Pavel frowned at his as he opened it, then spoke in a light tenor which Jenna found slightly surprising given his frame, his words heavily accented. 'This . . . will work?'

'They don't come with any damn guarantees,' Drift replied testily. 'You wanted the impossible on very short notice, you've got the best we have. Jenna?'

'Data's coded,' she replied, watching the last set of impressive pectorals resolve. 'I can transmit it to the shuttle now, or . . .'

'Not yet,' Drift told her, 'I don't want to throw anything into the Uragan system if we don't have to.' He looked back at the Shirokovs. 'Well, *señores*, time to get moving.'

Jenna let out a small breath she'd not really been aware she'd been holding. She hadn't been sure if Drift would follow through on his end of the deal once they had the data, given how angry he'd been about being seemingly manoeuvred into a corner. It was probably the wiser course of action rather than risk a scene here which might delay them, of course, but every now and then the Captain did something a little irrational in a fit of pique.

The Shirokovs didn't need telling twice: they rose to their feet and took hold of their suitcases, and were heading for the door almost before Drift and Apirana had joined them. Jenna fell into their wake, then frowned to herself as her wrist console vibrated. But she'd turned all notifications off except . . .

Shit.

Her throat was suddenly dry as she clawed back the fabric of her sleeve again, then swiped the display.

Shitshitshit.

'Captain!' Several heads turned towards her in addition to her crew, but she didn't care. Drift's expression was already grim; he must have known automatically that she wouldn't risk drawing attention to them if the need weren't dire.

'What?'

'We . . .' Jenna trailed off hopelessly as both doors to Cherdak burst inwards, disgorging black-clad *polit-siya* in body armour and riot masks with guns trained on them. She hit the key that would send Shirokov's information winging through the Uragan Spine and – hopefully – to the databanks of the *Jonah*. 'Never mind.'

Angry Russian filled the air, none of it coming from the other punters who were all busily throwing themselves to the floor to get out of any possible line of fire. The Shirokovs tried that as well, but were clearly viewed to be guilty by association judging by the way they were hauled back up again. Jenna found herself staring down at least three gun barrels belonging to men shouting words she didn't understand, and made an assumption that raising her hands with her palms outwards was a universal gesture for 'please don't shoot me'.

'Drift!'

That shout was clear enough, although Jenna couldn't work out which mask it had come from. The Captain, who had already raised his own hands, coughed slightly.

'Uh . . . yeah?'

Two men approached Jenna while the third kept her covered. Her arms were wrenched down and cuffed behind her back with some sort of auto-constricting, segmented metal manacle. The same thing was happening to the others, including the Shirokovs.

She noticed Apirana resisting for a moment, just to show that it would take more than one man on each arm to budge *him*, before he relented and allowed himself to be secured.

One of their captors stepped forwards and shouted in Russian again, leaving Drift looking uncomfortable and blank all at the same time. 'Uh, I'm sorry, I don't—'

'He says we're under arrest,' Jia provided miserably.

'I kinda got that,' Drift snapped, clearly exasperated, 'but my translator's not working properly with all this noise. What the hell *for*?'

'Uh . . .' Jia raised her voice. '*Za chto?*'

'*Kontrabanda oruzhiem!*'

Jenna knew the expression that flooded Jia's face then. It was one of complete and total bafflement.

'Guys, you ain't gonna believe this . . .'

'*Gun-running?!*' Drift spluttered. 'That's ridiculous!'

Security Chief Alim Muradov looked at him levelly across the desk in the small, grey-walled interview room. He was probably somewhere in his forties, with his black hair slicked back and his moustache neatly trimmed. His skin held a richer tone than most of the other Uragan natives Drift had seen, and if the crescent moon pendant at his throat was anything to go by, he was a Muslim: at a guess, Drift would have put his ancestry somewhere in the historically Russian-influenced Middle East. Given that bigotry was far from absent in the galaxy, especially on more insular worlds like Uragan with largely homogenous populations – ethnic Russian Orthodox Christian, in this case – the odds were that to reach the rank of security chief Muradov would either have to be a corrupt toady or formidable at his job.

Drift didn't get the feeling it would be the former. He relaxed a little, despite the cold metal around his wrists. For once, his crew were completely innocent of all charges being brought against them, and any halfway-competent investigation would show that. His nerves were jangling at the time they were wasting, though. It had been two hours since they'd been arrested in Cherdak, and the storm would be closing in fast.

'Ridiculous or not, Captain, these are not allegations my force can ignore,' Muradov replied calmly. His English was good, although his accent seemed to remove a lot of the emotion from the words. Or maybe there just wasn't that much there to begin with. 'This is your crew's first visit to Uragan, yes?'

'Mine, certainly,' Drift nodded, 'as for my crew, no one said they'd been here before. It's not the sort of place you'd forget about, I think it's fair to say.'

'Nor one you would visit twice without good reason,' Muradov replied. Drift started to nod again, then caught himself; was that dry humour, or a camouflaged accusation? The Chief seemed to notice his momentary confusion, and snorted. 'Come, Captain, we are hardly a tourist destination. Still, utilitarian though my planet is, it is my job to keep it secure and its people safe.'

'Of course,' Drift agreed, 'but if you've searched my shuttle you'll know the only weapons we have are for personal use, and while in your spaceport they're locked away securely, in compliance with your laws.'

Muradov's teeth showed for a moment beneath his moustache, a flash of a grin that didn't reach his eyes.

'And there speaks a man who has had to talk his way out of trouble with the law before, I feel.'

'Not your law and not your planet,' Drift countered, 'I've done nothing wrong here.' *Well, apart from furnishing two citizens with fraudulent documents, but we'll say nothing of that.* 'If you have any evidence to the contrary, please . . .' He spread his hands invitingly in front of him.

Muradov looked at him for a second, and Drift fought the urge to smile. *You've got nothing. If you had, you'd have brought it out by now.*

'So, Captain,' Muradov said instead, 'why would we get these allegations?' He quirked an eyebrow inquisitively.

'Probably because you listened to Ricardo *fucking* Moutinho of the *Pouco Jacare*,' Drift replied promptly. He'd had suspicions about the source of this latest inconvenience from the moment the police had burst into Cherdak.

'Captain Moutinho?' Muradov actually seemed surprised. 'The tip was, in fact, anonymous. Captain Moutinho is well known to us, however; he has been a regular visitor over the last few months. What makes you think he would do such a thing?'

'Moutinho and I are both freelancers,' Drift told him flatly. 'We own our own ships and take whatever jobs we can. You do that for a living, you tend to run into other captains who try to undercut you, steal your work or sabotage you. Moutinho and I had a falling out a few years ago and he's tried to make my life difficult every time we've run into each other since.' He shrugged. 'It would be his style, probably just to annoy us. I'm surprised he made up something as far-fetched as gunrunning, though.'

'Far-fetched?' Muradov snorted. 'Perhaps not so much as you think, Captain. Still, I cannot deny that we found no weapons, and our security feeds show that you have offloaded nothing since you landed.'

'So I'm free to go?' Drift asked. He didn't want to seem so eager he drew suspicion, but he also didn't want to be trapped by the storm. In any case, who would want to remain in custody longer than they had to?

'Not just yet,' Muradov told him, raising one hand. Drift forced himself to appear calm.

'Well?'

'You landed here something like eight hours ago,' the other man said, fixing Drift with a steady, dark-eyed gaze. 'You have offloaded nothing, and you have loaded nothing. You describe yourself as a freelance captain, so I have to wonder: what brought you to my world?' He drummed his fingers on the desk, as if genuinely contemplating the problem.

'Signal transmission across our system is not instant-aneous, Captain, but we are not out of range. Your ship was recently docked in orbit over New Samara. *New Samara!* With its clean air, its plants, its . . .' Another half-smile appeared briefly. '. . . its *rich people*. Why, after spending time there, would you choose to fly to my storm-lashed little rock? For the views?' He snorted. 'I think not.'

'Looking for work,' Drift replied immediately. 'We'd taken some shore leave on New Samara, yes; my crew had been cooped up for too long. Since we were in the area, I thought I'd see if we could make a bit of cash.' *Technically true*. He let his face take on a rueful expression. 'But of course, all the haulage out of here is handled on governmental contracts.' *Also true. I just knew that before I came.*

'And your two passengers?' Muradov queried. 'This was not arranged before you got here?'

'Can't say it was,' Drift replied easily. 'I met the older one in Cherdak earlier today when I went there with a couple of my crew; I guess he was hanging around an off-worlders' bar trying to find a transport. I don't normally take on passengers, but I figured it would cut our losses a little.'

Muradov nodded, as though this was all reasonable. 'And the fare?'

Drift hesitated for a split-second, sensing a trap. Should he make a figure up? But they'd probably already asked the Shirokovs the same question, so he went for as close to the truth as he dared. 'We hadn't agreed a price, I was taking them to see the ship.' He essayed a mercenary grin. 'If you wait until the passenger can almost taste their destination, they're generally a little more willing to part with their cash.'

Muradov watched him for a couple more seconds without saying anything, then finally chuckled and shook his head. 'Captain, I do not trust a single word you are saying to me, but I have no reason to hold you further. Everything you have said hangs together . . . *just*.' He pressed a button on the wall next to him, and the door buzzed open to admit a junior officer. 'Please escort Captain Drift to his crew. They are to be released without charge.'

Muradov fixed Drift with a steady gaze while his subordinate activated his collar comm and passed on the instructions. 'I am sure you are intelligent enough to work this out on your own, Captain, but I think it might be best for your sake if you gave us no further cause to investigate you during your stay here.'

'No fear of that,' Drift replied, getting to his feet and holding out his hands towards the other officer. 'I'm going straight to my shuttle and leaving. No offence, but I've had enough of Uragan.'

'None taken,' Muradov nodded, 'but I am afraid you will have to wait a while. The storm rolled in faster than we were expecting. I hear the spaceport was closed about twenty minutes ago.'

Drift stared at him in horror, barely registering the cuffs being removed from his wrists. 'What?'

'Meteorology is not an exact science, especially on a planet as volatile as this,' Muradov explained. He raised his eyebrows. 'Why, was there somewhere you needed to be?'

So that was it. The quick-and-easy hundred grand from Orlov and the associated benefits of having the goodwill of the area's major crime lord, gone just like that thanks to Aleksandr Shirokov's wanderlust and Moutinho's pettiness. In fact, forget about good-will: they'd be lucky if Orlov didn't decide to make an example of them.

Drift controlled his expression with an effort, trying to ignore images of some New Samaran thug taking a vibrohammer to his knees. The shit icing on a cake of crap would be if Muradov decided that his eager-ness to leave before the storm was suspicious.

'It just means I'm going to have a crew kicking about my ship for three days with nothing to do and no way to earn any money,' he grumbled.

Muradov stood. He was not a tall man, and lean with it, but he had a certain air to him that suggested he was not to be trifled with. The security chief didn't present himself as the sort of man who would take massive issue with you accidentally spilling his drink, for example, but woe betide the person who squared up to him should he accidentally spill theirs.

'Unfortunately, Captain, that assessment is not entirely accurate.' He sounded genuine, but Drift could feel that cool gaze watching him. 'It is Uragan City policy that no crew may remain in their ships while the spaceport is shut for a hurricane.'

'I . . . *what*?' Drift tried to fight down the sensation of increasing frustration. 'Why not, for the love of God? Where are we supposed to go?'

'We have had too many people trying to get out,' Muradov shrugged. 'Some idiot decides they can fly through a hurricane and finds some way to open the bay doors, then you get half a ton of sand and three rocks the size of apartments dropping in before anyone can shut it again. As for where you go, Uragan City is well-equipped with accommodation for visitors.'

'Which will cost more money,' Drift replied through clenched teeth as he stepped out of the interview room, 'and probably goes up in price drastically when there's a storm, am I right?'

'Is capitalism not wonderful?' Muradov followed him out and clapped him on the shoulder. 'Chin up, Captain; I am sure a resourceful fellow like you will be able to survive the loss. I will arrange for your crew to be escorted to your shuttle to collect essentials for the next couple of days, but no dallying.' He turned and walked away, leaving Drift to trail in the footsteps of the officer who'd released him from his cuffs.

He found his crew in the main reception area, signing for the possessions they'd had confiscated upon arrest. He'd clearly been the last to be interviewed, but from what Muradov had said it sounded like they could have all been held had he slipped up and uttered a provable falsehood. He exchanged a glance with Jenna as she fastened her wrist-mounted console back onto her arm and booted it up again, but she didn't seem concerned at what she saw so Drift assumed that there was no sign her files had been compromised. A quick scan of the area found the Shirokovs standing to one side, looking very uncomfortable. He didn't feel in the slightest bit sympathetic.

'Can we leave before the storm hits?' Rourke asked him urgently as he scrawled and thumbprinted to recover his comm, personal pad and credit chips.

'Too late,' he replied bitterly, 'we're stuck here until it blows over now.' He turned back to face them, saw the mixture of disappointment and anger on their faces and decided to usher everyone out before any comments about not getting paid landed them in further trouble. 'C'mon, let's get out of here.'

'So what now?' Kuai asked once they were safely out of the front doors of the *politsiya* building.

'I vote we go find Moutinho an' kick his ass,' Jia said forcefully. 'Bet you anything he was behind that pile of *hùnzhàng*!' Drift couldn't deny the appeal of the idea but he gritted his teeth and shook his head.

'I asked the captain interviewing me if it was Moutinho – he said the tip was anonymous. They know Moutinho though, apparently he's been here a lot recently, and now *they* know *I* think it was him.' He sighed bitterly. 'I'd love to take that bastard down a peg or two but we can't afford to do anything that might bring these guys back down on us, and I'd bet good money we'll be under surveillance for a little while.'

'Brings me back to my question,' Kuai pointed out. 'What now?'

'We need to find somewhere to stay until the storm blows over,' Drift said as calmly as he could, although the frustration inside him was clamouring for at least a minor release by, for example, kicking his infuriating mechanic in his bad leg. 'We can get an escort to collect clothes and so on from the *Jonah*, but let's make sure we have somewhere to put them first. All the outsider accommodation is likely to be priced exorbitantly right now but, *luckily*, we have a couple of guides who know the city.'

As one, the entire crew of the *Keiko* swivelled until they were staring at the Shirokovs, who had tailed them out and then stood at a distance like a pair of anxious puppies. Drift wasn't looking at his companions, but he was well aware that his own expression probably did not consist of sweetness and light. Aleksandr's gaze skittered across them, and he licked his lips nervously.

'Um,' he said.

A NIGHT ON THE TOWN

It was two standard hours later, the storm on the surface was in full swing and the turmoil in Ichabod Drift's head was nearly matching it. According to his chrono it was slightly past 23.00 hours on Uragan City's twenty-four-hour clock, but the bars didn't appear to be quietening down much. In fact, there seemed to be a certain nervous energy about many of the patrons of Labirint, where they were currently drinking. Perhaps this was what happened when Uragan was on shutdown during a storm? Drift certainly felt cut off and isolated, unable to get back to the comforting freedom of space. Still, you'd have thought the locals would be used to it by now.

He took a sip of whisky, and pulled a face at the taste. There clearly wasn't much market for the stuff here, and if it tasted like this he could see why, but he'd never really got on with vodka either. On the other hand, he'd bought it so he was damn well going to drink it. On either side of him the Chang siblings were sipping at *báijiŭ*, which seemed to have hit closer to their expectations, and across the table the Shirokovs were mainly looking uncomfortable.

It had quickly become clear that the two men had handed in the key cards for their apparently tiny apartment in the expectation of getting off-world on the *Jonah*, and that now they'd done that there was no going back. As a result they were essentially tied to Drift, unless they wanted to approach another captain and try to find passage off-world with them. For his part, Drift had toyed with the notion of just leaving them here since the information Aleksandr had provided was useless now in any case. The contract had been to bring it back to Orlov in person since it was too sensitive to transmit, and there was no way they could even get to the *Jonah*, let alone take off into the teeth of a raging hurricane. However, in the end he'd decided to stick to his side of the deal with Aleksandr, on the condition that the Shirokovs find them accommodation while they were marooned here.

As he'd expected, there were places to stay that weren't in the districts set out for off-worlders; these were hotels normally used by other Uragans travelling from one of the other, smaller mining centres scattered across the planet, and they were far cheaper. The staff also didn't speak much except Russian, but with the Shirokovs along as translators and Rourke and the Changs having a decent grounding in the language, they'd got along well enough.

Drift hadn't been in the mood to stay in their somewhat cramped accommodation, however, and had come out to find a drink. Jia and Kuai had been eager to accompany him and he'd dragged the Shirokovs along more out of contrariness and the desire for a local guide than because he really wished to spend time with them. Rourke, Apirana and Jenna hadn't been interested, and were presumably playing cards or something equally tame at this very moment.

'What's the matter?' he asked Aleksandr, trying to ignore his whisky's unpleasant aftertaste. 'I'd have thought you'd be eager to say goodbye to this place properly, given how you were just about to up and leave with no notice.'

Aleksandr glowered at him between furtive glances around the bar. 'Will you please keep voice down?'

'What's the matter?' Drift demanded. He was being needlessly abrasive, he knew, but he'd had a bad day and just enough alcohol to not really care. '*You* are still getting what you want. The best *I* can do right now is try to lose as little money as possible.'

'And maybe you not take us when you go!' Pavel spoke up angrily, his English considerably more broken than his husband's. 'Maybe this all trick!'

Drift sighed, eyeing the angry young miner. 'You know, once upon a time you might have been right. But I'm a man of my word now.' He assessed the blankness of Pavel's expression and sighed. 'I mean, I don't break deals.'

'And you would tell us if you did, of course,' Aleksandr snorted.

Drift bristled. 'If you think—'

'Please.' Aleksandr raised both his hands, palms outwards. 'I understand you are angry, Captain, but we did not cause delay. We trusted that . . .'

He looked around them again, then leaned closer and spoke more quietly. 'We trusted that documents you give us would work. I give you information you needed. We were coming with you. We did not summon *politsiya*.'

'No, of course you didn't,' Drift muttered. He sank the last of the whisky from his tumbler. 'Still, I'm surprised you're not seeking out friends. Or have you already said your goodbyes?'

'Saying goodbye would need explanation,' Aleksandr muttered. 'I have none. Not just "why?", you understand, but also "how?". This I cannot say to them.'

'Huh.' Drift nodded slowly. 'Guess that makes sense. So, why did you want to get out of here anyway?'

'Aside from the obvious,' Jia put in loudly. 'I mean, you've been living in an anthill all this time, why's it bothering you now?'

Aleksandr frowned. 'Anthill?'

'Oh, for . . .' Jia waved her hands derisively. '*Ants*. You know?' She launched into a slightly inebriated explanation in Russian, trying to get across a concept that simply didn't have much inherent meaning for natives of a planet that had never seen colonial insects. Drift left her to it and looked around the bar again, trying to put his finger on what was bothering him about the place, and for a sudden, surprising moment found himself missing Micah. The mercenary had always been more than just a gun hand; he'd shown an unexpected ability to read tactical situations on several occasions, spotting inconsistencies and drawing conclusions that Drift simply hadn't seen, or at least would have taken longer to put together.

He went back to his roots: reading people. Many of Labirint's patrons appeared normal, so far as the definition could ever be used of someone, whether that be sitting and drinking quietly or laughing raucously with friends, but not everyone seemed so relaxed. He let his eyes wander, trying to single them out without being too obvious about it.

There. A man with dark, thinning hair, heavy-set insofar as could be told beneath his jacket, a thin sheen of sweat showing on his forehead and what could be seen of his pate. He sat alone, but unlike the other solitary drinkers visible here and there he wasn't staring into his drink, lost in his thoughts. He was looking expectant, almost nervous, and kept checking the pad on the table in front of him with only the tiniest movements of his hand.

Someone waiting for a friend, or for a date? Possible, but now Drift thought about it the guy had been there on his own since they'd come in half an hour previously. It was always possible that the person he was meeting was tardy . . . but it was kind of late to be meeting someone now, wasn't it? Still, perhaps he was a Uragan night-shifter on a day off.

Drift cast his eyes around casually, looking for anyone else who didn't seem quite right. He caught a couple of people looking back at him, but he'd expected that and none of it seemed malicious; a blue-haired Mexican on Uragan would just stick out like a sore thumb in a way that simply wouldn't have happened on a more cosmopolitan planet like New Samara.

There. A man and a woman, her as pale and blonde as Pavel Shirokov and he with a thick brown beard which was longer than the buzz cut atop his head. They were nominally part of a group standing and chatting at the bar, but both seemed slightly reserved, as though a little preoccupied. The woman casually checked her pad – simply keeping an eye on the time, or waiting for an important message or call? – and tucked it back into the pocket of her . . .

Jacket.

Drift felt his gut tense. It wasn't like coats and jackets were only worn on planets with atmospheres, because climate control didn't always work, or one person might still be cold where another person would be fine, or you wanted more pockets, or you simply liked that jacket and how it looked – Rourke was practically inseparable from hers. But that woman was sweating a little, judging by the slight lankness of her hair, and it was far from chilly in this enclosed bar packed with people. So why wear it?

And the guy she was with was wearing a jacket too. And so was the lone drinker in the corner.

And, looking around, every one of the half-dozen people he could see in a jacket all looked a bit too warm and just slightly on edge.

There was one other reason to wear a coat or jacket: to conceal something. Drift concentrated again on the man and woman at the bar, since they were both standing and, if he was right, would be most likely to give themselves away. Another round had just been bought, but the man hadn't yet finished his current drink, held in his right hand. He started to remove his left hand from his jacket pocket to accept the new glass, hesitated, then did so awkwardly and reluctantly.

Beneath where his left arm had been resting until a moment ago was a bulge. Judging by the way the fabric of the jacket was pulled downwards, it was a fairly heavy bulge.

The uncomfortable feeling in Drift's gut crystallised into the sort of apprehension that simultaneously dried his throat and reminded him exactly how long it had been since he'd last emptied his bladder. It wasn't that he was scared . . . exactly. Not yet. But he had the sudden notion of how Micah had actually felt in that story he used to tell about when his patrol had once walked into a minefield without realising it.

He leaned forwards, interrupting whatever the conversation had morphed into while he'd been distracted. 'Everyone finish your drinks. We're leaving.'

'What?' Jia waved her glass in objection. 'This ain't bad!'

'Why?' Aleksandr asked him at the same moment. 'What is it?'

'There are half a dozen people in this room with guns,' Drift said, keeping his voice as low as he could. 'I don't want to find out why. *Don't look round!*'

Aleksandr froze, then returned his gaze to Drift's face and nodded slowly. 'You're right. We should leave.'

'I thought Uragan law said no guns?' Kuai asked, frowning.

'It does,' Drift replied quietly, staring hard at Aleksandr, 'which is why I'm a little surprised you're not more shocked, my friend.'

Aleksandr got to his feet, the legs of his stool scraping over the floor as he pushed it back while he muttered something in Russian to Pavel, who blanched and hurriedly downed his drink. His husband looked back at Drift. 'Do you want to leave, or do you want to talk?'

Drift ground his teeth. He'd encountered security doors easier to read than the older Shirokov. 'Oh, I'm fine with leaving, so long as we're not going to run into anything worse out there.'

Aleksandr shrugged, eyes flickering from side to side. 'Who can say?'

'Fine.' Drift really, *really* missed the reassuring weight of his pistols on his hips right now. 'Let's get out of here, and then you can tell us what the hell's going on.'

They were halfway to the door when they heard a swell of chanting from outside.

'That can't be good,' Jia said, looking around anxiously at him. Drift pushed forwards and opened the bar door to take a look out into the boulevard, now relatively dimly lit in imitation of a city at night. It wasn't that he thought it was going to be anything but trouble heading for them, but it was usually better to know exactly what manner of trouble you were facing.

The chanting was coming from his right, borne from the throats of a mass of Uragan citizens moving slowly up the street and effectively filling it widthways from shop front to shop front. His Russian wasn't good enough to make out much of what that many voices were raggedly shouting, but they were carrying placards and banners strewn with slogans in Cyrillic script and a whirling, yellow-on-black pattern that was repeated over and over: a simplified depiction of a spiral galaxy.

The symbol of the Free Systems.

'*Shit*.' Drift ducked back in, brain whirling. A few faces had turned towards the doorway as the noise had leaked in, but the bar in general didn't seem to be aware of the approaching mass of humanity yet. However, one or two of the patrons he'd pegged as carrying guns seemed to be taking an interest. 'We've got a full-blown Free Systems protest going on out there.' He cast a look at Aleksandr, whose face had taken on an even more hangdog expression than usual. 'This anything you want to talk to us about?'

'Discontent has been brewing,' Aleksandr replied, speaking urgently but quietly, 'there have been some small protests, always put down quick by authorities.' He grimaced. 'This also why we want to leave. This planet not safe now.'

'Uh, did I just hear "put down by authorities"?' Kuai asked. 'Should we still be here?'

'No,' Drift admitted, 'but I don't fancy going out front. Maybe there's a back—'

The bar suddenly exploded into noise; not the chatter of assembled drinkers or the chants of the protesters outside, but the full-blown wail of a *polit-siya* siren. It took Drift a second to realise that the sound was coming from the speakers, which until a second previously had been emanating nothing but quiet, upbeat background music. Clearly, when the Red Star Confederate had built this city they'd ensured that no one would be left unaware of any civic emergencies.

Words cut through the noise, a female voice speaking in firm, strident tones over the sirens.

Drift grabbed Aleksandr's shoulder and raised his voice to be heard over the din. 'What's it saying?!'

'Is standard emergency broadcast!' the Uragan shouted back. 'All citizens remain calm, stay indoors until told!' All around them, the bar's customers were milling in various different levels of panic; several pushed past to the doorway, then retreated much like Drift had when they saw what was outside. Others crowded to the windows, trying to find out what was going on.

'Yeah, fuck that,' Drift said decisively. There was a crush of anti-government protesters coming up the street one way and the local law would likely be coming down it the other way very shortly, which meant the last place he wanted to be was stuck anywhere nearby, especially when there were people with guns in the immediate vicinity. Suddenly the reason for Muradov's comment about the likelihood of gunrunning was becoming uncomfortably clear. He pointed towards the rear of the bar and gave Jia a shove to get her moving. 'That way, before it all kicks off!'

Labirint was crowded and most people were moving towards the front of it, so it took a combination of agility and strength to fight against the tide, but suddenly they were through. The bartender, a bear of a man with a thick black beard long enough to brush his chest and touched with grey near the roots, took half a step away from his bar and held up one hand to stop them. His eyes flicked from one face to the other and he clearly settled on English as some form of *lingua franca*. 'You stay!'

Drift debated pushing past him, but only for half a second; there wasn't enough space and he didn't fancy being grabbed by an angry Uragan ogre, so he settled for looking as urgently sincere as he could and waving his hands to indicate how very serious everything was. 'Big problem! Riot outside! People with guns in here! Guns!'

'*Da.*' The bartender's left hand reached under the counter and came up holding a genuine pump-action shotgun; not exactly the cutting edge of firearms technology but more than enough to greatly inconvenience them all, especially at such close range. He worked the action to rack a shell and aimed the barrel straight at Drift's face. 'I know. You stay!'

Drift's brain started pin-wheeling away, but his body took over admirably in its absence, raising his hands and even stuttering out a shaky '*D-da,*' of appeasement. He glanced over his left shoulder and saw that his companions had followed his example, which was reassuring. He didn't have either of the Changs down as the type to suddenly launch themselves at an armed giant, but you could never be entirely sure.

He looked back questioningly at the bartender, who gestured with the barrel of his weapon for them to return to the front of his premises. Drift turned smartly and ushered the others away with outstretched arms, taking the opportunity to check on the other patrons he'd pegged as being armed while he did so. At least two of them were looking at him and his companions, which was precisely the sort of attention he'd hoped to avoid, but it was too late for that now.

Suddenly the callbeep of his comm went off in his ear. He instinctively moved one hand towards it to answer, but a shout from his right arrested him; one of the patrons had pulled a handgun and was pointing it in their direction. Drift froze, then carefully lowered his hand again, but while everyone seemed to have been facing the wrong way to have noticed the bartender's firearm, this new development had attracted attention. Someone screamed, heads turned and there was an abrupt scramble for the doorway.

Beside him, Drift heard Jia's callbeep going off, but the man covering them – the slightly balding one Drift had noticed earlier – still had his weapon trained on them and the little pilot showed no signs of moving to answer it. Probably for the best; the bar had exploded into near-panic now, and that was a bad situation to be in when people had guns. Especially when Drift was not one of those people.

Shouts from the street outside dragged his attention towards the front of the bar again. About half a dozen patrons had fled into the street, but the mass of chanting Free Systems protesters – and why had they come this far only to stop in place? – didn't appear to be an attractive proposition for them. Instead they turned to the left and began to flee the other way . . . directly towards the dark line of riot police which had materialised since Drift had tried to leave via the back door.

There were about twenty officers, fully kitted out in body armour with full-face helmets and small but undoubtedly powerful loudhailers on the shoulders, armed with shockguns, shocksticks and large, rect-angular flashshields. Still, the mob outnumbered them by at least ten to one, if Drift was any judge, and that wasn't counting anyone in the buildings on either side of the street. Some of whom had guns . . .

'*Me cago en la puta*,' he breathed, then raised his voice a little so the Changs could hear him. 'This isn't a protest, it's a goddamn *trap*!'

As a rule, riot police were rarely likely to respond well to people running towards them. The small group of ex-patrons suddenly spasmed and fell as dark, snub-nosed guns spat what Drift could only assume were shockbolts: small, short-range devices that pierced the skin shallowly and delivered a single, powerful electric pulse sufficient to cause brief loss of muscle control. They were theoretically non-lethal but were capable of causing heart failure, especially if someone was hit by more than one, but that didn't seem to be of great concern to the advancing *politsiya*.

The mob roared and resumed chanting whatever slogan it was they had – probably something about freedom and justice, it usually was – but they didn't press forwards. Apparently emboldened by this, one of the *politsiya* activated his loudhailer and his stern voice filled the air, tinged with metallic distortion. Drift couldn't make out much more than 'go', but he didn't need to; the protest was undoubtedly being instructed to disperse and return to their homes, probably with threats of arrest for anyone who didn't comply. However, while this message was being delivered the *politsiya* continued their steady advance . . . and now they were level with the main windows of Labirint.

Whereupon, everyone inside the bar who was armed hauled out their guns and started firing.

Glass shattered and fell outwards and the screaming started in earnest, as patrons switched from apprehensively watching one gunman to seeking cover from multiple ones. Drift dived to the floor, dragging the Changs down with him. So far as he was concerned the Shirokovs could look after themselves, and indeed they hit the deck a moment later, cowering face down and covering their heads with their arms. Labirint's windows were full-length, and even from his poor vantage point Drift could see the riot squad staggering and falling under the fire. Four were already down and another fell backwards, blood erupting from his thigh. Two or three others had pulled themselves together and turned their flashshields towards the bar; the electrified surfaces were meant for corralling rioters, but they would provide at least some protection from small-arms fire. Another one had dropped his shield and was fumbling behind him, then wrenched around a bulky, wide-barrelled weapon which had apparently been slung in the small of his back.

Drift just had time to yell, 'Gas!' before the launcher thudded with a violent release of previously compressed air and a small, dark shape trailing yellow fumes arced through the broken windows and skittered across the floor. A moment later the trickle became a flood, and breathing inside Labirint suddenly became impossible.

he small games room of the Otpusk Gostinitsa was filled with sound.

'Hah!'

'*Hah!*'

'Urgnnk!'

'Yes!'

'*HAH!*'

'Oh, you *bastard* . . .'

'Booyah!' Apirana punched the air as the holographic air puck he'd propelled towards Jenna's goal with a mighty sweep of his right arm fizzed through her shambolic defence and sounded a buzzer. '7–4! Game *over*!'

Jenna scowled at him while synthesised trumpets officially announced his victory, her quick breathing sending strands of red-gold hair quivering where they'd fallen in front of her face. Holo-hockey was not an exertion-free pastime. 'Don't do it.'

Apirana grinned at her. 'Don't do what?'

'You know what.'

He raised an eyebrow. 'You mean . . . this?' He cleared his throat, stood straighter and lifted his voice in song: '*E Ihowā Atua, O ngā iwi mātou rā . . .*' He'd never been the best at carrying a tune and he was a little short of breath after his exertions, but he managed the first couple of lines of the Maori version of 'God Save New Zealand' before he was interrupted.

'Shut up, shut up, shut up!' Jenna peeled off one of her holo-gloves and threw it at him. 'God, you are *insufferable* when you win at something!'

'Just enjoying the moment,' he protested, although he couldn't keep a straight face.

'I'm amazed you don't do the haka beforehand, too,' Jenna muttered, crossing her arms.

Apirana let a wide grin spread across his features. 'Now *there's* an idea!'

'If you even—'

'Nah, it's probably overkill for something like this,' he agreed, unfastening his own gloves.

'"Probably"?'

'Fine, fine.' He held up his hands. 'I'm sorry if I get a bit competitive. Not my most endearing feature, I guess.'

'I can assure you that it isn't,' Jenna smiled crookedly.

'Which means there's at least something endearing about me,' Apirana informed her soberly, reaching for his soda, 'so I'll class that as a compliment.' He was taking a sip before Jenna spoke again.

'You're cuddly.'

He swallowed, carefully, and looked around at her. '*What?*'

'Cuddly,' Jenna repeated, looking thoughtful. 'At least when, you know, you're not kicking people into next week.'

'He had a kni—'

'I know, I know, I'm just sayi—'

'If someone pulls a knife on you then—'

'Jesus, A., I was trying to be nice!' Jenna shouted, frustration suddenly clouding her face. 'What is *wrong* with you? You've been weird with me ever since we left the *Keiko*!'

Apirana blinked, suddenly wrong-footed. He had?

Jenna sighed. 'Forget it. I'm going back to my room. Thanks for the game.' She turned to leave and Apirana felt something twist inside him. It wasn't that he'd ruled out saying something to her, exactly, but he'd been trying to work out exactly what he *was* feeling before he attempted to fit words around it. Suddenly he got the impression that, no matter how clumsy the attempt might end up, he should probably say *something* right now.

'Uh, hey, wait a second.' He'd half expected Jenna to ignore him and keep walking, which would have been disappointing in one respect but a relief in another. Instead she stopped and turned to look back at him, her expression neutral. He swallowed again, nervously this time, and attempted to force his thoughts into some kind of coherent and hopefully eloquent order. 'I . . . look, um . . . I didn't mean to be—'

He was cut off by an ear-splitting siren. 'What the bloody hell . . . ?'

Jenna had visibly jumped when it went off, and was now looking around with her hands over her ears. 'Jesus, that's loud!'

Sirens rarely boded well in any case, but Apirana had landed hard on the wrong side of the law when he was fifteen and hadn't properly crossed back since; for him, the sound had long since been hard-wired into his fight-or-flight reflex. He had a light-pool cue in his hands almost without thinking, feeling the weight and heft of it.

'What's that for?' Jenna asked, cautiously removing her hands from her ears but still wincing at the volume.

'Dunno yet,' Apirana admitted. A female voice started to speak over the siren; in Russian, predictably. 'Check the local Spine, see if it says what's going on.'

'On it.' Jenna retrieved her wrist console from where she'd taken it off to play holo-hockey and fired it up with a few quick taps, then shook her head in frustration. 'It's some sort of universal alert, but all it says is to stay calm and stay indoors.' She looked up at him and shrugged helplessly. 'That could be anything from a ventilation malfunction to a planetary invasion, for crying out loud!'

'Won't be an invasion with the storm going, at least not here,' Apirana replied absently, trying to run through the other options in his head. Unfortunately, there were too many; he didn't know what level of problem would cause the Uragan authorities to react on this scale, and the damned siren wasn't helping him think. The only certain conclusion he could come to was that the Captain and the Changs were out in whatever it was. 'You're a slicing wizard, you can get more info than that, surely?'

Jenna gave him a level look. 'Do you have any idea—' The alarms suddenly ceased, the recorded message apparently having been delivered the requisite number of times. 'Christ, that's better. Do you have any idea how hard it is to slice government-level encryption on the fly, through a translation program and a goddamn *character proxy* so you're using the right frigging alphabet?!'

'Nope,' Apirana admitted, 'but that's why I'm asking *you* to do it.' He was no stranger to the Spine, but his technological skills were more focused towards spanners than terminals. 'I'm gonna go find Rourke.'

'No need.'

Apirana's ears were still ringing in the aftermath of the siren, which was probably why he hadn't heard footsteps behind him. He turned to see Rourke standing in the doorway to the games room, her face grim and looking past him at Jenna. 'You got anything?'

'Working on it,' Jenna muttered. 'It has to be something either big or local to us though, right? I mean, the levels can be sealed off from each other, so if there was a fire one level down or something, that wouldn't be anything to worry about here.'

'I'm gonna call the Captain,' Apirana said, keying his comm, 'see if they're okay.' The call tone buzzed in his ear, and kept buzzing.

There was no answer.

Rourke was already frowning, and trying her own comm. She waited for a few seconds, then looked up. 'Jia's not answering either.'

'Shit.' Apirana looked from one woman to the other. 'So do we stay here an' hope they come back, or head out an' try to find 'em?'

Rourke looked indecisive, one of only a handful of times Apirana could remember the former GIA agent being uncertain. 'I don't know . . . I'm not sure it's a good idea to go out there without knowing what's going on, but the worse it is the more likely the others will need our help.'

'And what happens if *we* go out and *they* come back?' Jenna put in without looking up from her console.

Rourke pursed her lips and seemed to come to a decision. 'I'll go and check a couple of the nearest bars; I've got the best Russian of the three of us anyway. You two stay here and call me if the others show up.'

Apirana grimaced. 'Okay, but keep in touch, yeah? Last thing we want is for you to get arrested for breaking curfew, or whatever this is, and we didn't—'

He was cut off by an angry explosion of Russian from the hallway behind Rourke, at a pitch and pace that ruled out any chance of him being able to decipher it: a male voice, and clearly unhappy. Rourke whirled around and took two quick but unhurried steps backwards. Moments later the doorway she had been standing in was filled by the shouting shape of Mr Vershinin, the hotel's proprietor.

Apirana supposed that most people would consider Vershinin to be a big man; he certainly towered over Rourke and was comfortably taller than Jenna, who was far from the shortest girl Apirana had ever seen. He was also obviously agitated. Apirana surreptitiously adjusted his grip on the light-pool cue, just in case.

Vershinin shouted something again, and Rourke raised her hands to try to placate him a little. 'Please, sir! Slowly, or in English!'

Apirana hadn't thought that the hotel owner's face could get any more thunderous, but he'd been wrong. The burly Uragan's mouth twisted, and he spat out some heavily accented words.

'You leave! Now! Foreign *otmorozki*, get out! *Out!* Go join your friends!'

'Sir,' Rourke said, keeping her voice calm with what was clearly some effort, 'we don't know exactly where our friends are—'

'They're outside!' Vershinin roared, gesturing back the way he'd come while advancing into the room, circling around as though to herd them towards the door. 'Get out! Police come! I have no foreigners here!'

Apirana caught Rourke's eye and inclined his head, very slightly, in the direction of the apoplectic proprietor. Rourke gave an infinitesimal shake of her head in response, and a splay of the fingers of her left hand. *Wait.*

'Sir,' Rourke tried again, addressing Vershinin, 'if you'll allow us to return to our rooms and get our things—'

'*Nyet!*' Vershinin lunged for Jenna, grabbing her by the shoulder and shoving her in the direction of the door. Jenna slapped his hand away, but Apirana had abruptly had enough. He whipped the cue up, holding it across the Uragan's chest crosswise and pushing him firmly backwards.

'Listen bro, we—'

He didn't get any further with the sentence because Vershinin yelled in rage and slammed both hands into Apirana's chest in what was half a shove and half a double palm strike. It didn't take Apirana off his feet or even knock him back much, and the sensible thing to do would be to back away from the incandescent proprietor and get all three of them out of the room before things escalated further . . . all of which he realised about half a second after he'd dropped the cue and slammed his fist into Vershinin's enraged face.

The Uragan dropped like he was a puppet whose strings had abruptly been cut. Apirana backed away from the fallen man, his knuckles stinging and bitter recriminations already rising in the back of his mind. 'Guys, I'm sorry, I—'

'Don't be,' Rourke cut him off clinically, 'we don't have time.'

'Let me at least check he's okay,' Apirana asked, hearing the pleading in his own voice. A small hand took his arm in a firm grip, and he looked back to see Rourke's dark eyes regarding him steadily from beneath the shadow of her hat.

'A., you just hit him as hard as you could. Either you've simply knocked him out, in which case he's going to wake up in a few seconds and we need to get out of here, or he's not going to wake up any time soon, in which case we still need to get out of here.' Her jaw tightened slightly. 'If it makes you feel better, I was about to do the same thing anyway. No one touches my crew.'

Apirana looked back down at Vershinin and thought he caught a faint flutter of eyelids. Something seemed to loosen a grip on his heart; not completely, but enough. 'Okay,' he found himself saying, 'let's go.'

'What about our things?' Jenna asked, looking from him to Rourke. They'd only been allowed to take a bare minimum of items from the *Jonah*, chivvied as they had been by impatient *politsiya* officers.

Rourke grimaced. 'Thirty seconds, then we're out the front door. Essentials only!' she yelled after them as Apirana and Jenna sprinted out of the games room and towards the main stairs, located in the foyer. Jenna swung herself around the bannister pole at the bottom and onto the second riser, an action Apirana would have normally expected to draw the disapproving attention of the sour-faced check-in clerk standing behind the reception desk, but she wasn't even looking at them. His gaze followed hers, out through the glass panes in the double doors and onto the plaza outside, and suddenly he forgot all about getting anything from their rooms.

The plaza was a mass of people, with more streaming in even as he watched. There seemed a roughly even split of men and women of varying ages, with even a few children present, but what they pretty much all had in common was their appearance: cheap, plain clothing, many still in dust-caked mining gear after however many hours at the face.

Well, and the Free Systems banners and placards.

Apirana winced as the reasons for Vershinin's attitude suddenly became a little clearer. Governments liked to blame each other for stirring up discontent in their own populations, since that was easier than admitting a planet's people had spontaneously decided to rebel. Off-worlders might well be detained on suspicion of being involved in rabble-rousing, and their choice of accommodation would likely be scrutinised closely. With this sort of gathering outside his business's front door, it was little wonder Vershinin had got edgy about his foreign guests.

'Tamara!' He raised his voice and looked back over his shoulder, ignoring the start of surprise the sudden noise elicited from the clerk. 'I think we gotta problem!'

Rourke was already approaching, having shut the door of the games room to hide Vershinin's prone body for at least a few more seconds, but she quickened her stride at his shout and came alongside him with her coat billowing behind her. He saw her lips purse as she assessed the situation.

'Shit.'

'Yeah, that was pretty much what I was thinking,' Apirana agreed. 'You still wanna go out there?'

'I don't really see that we have much choice,' Rourke admitted. 'We won't have long, though; the *politsiya* will be here soon, and they'll be armed to the teeth. Standard Red Star protocol for a protest gathering of more than thirty people is full riot gear and a maximum ten-minute response time.'

Apirana frowned at the matter-of-fact way Rourke had delivered that piece of information. 'How'd you know that?'

Rourke looked at him sideways, with perhaps the faintest flicker of amusement in her eyes. 'Once upon a time, it was my job to *organise* things like this.'

Apirana wasn't certain if he'd missed something. 'Organise what? The response?'

'The riots.' Rourke turned away from him towards the stairs. 'Jenna! We need to go *now*!'

'Okay, okay!' Jenna appeared at the top of the stairs, clutching a couple of overstuffed bags she must have hastily rescued from their suites. She stopped when she saw Apirana and glowered at him. 'Weren't you going to help me?'

'Yeah, uh . . .' He jerked his thumb over his shoulder. 'Something came up.'

'*Now*, Jenna,' Rourke snapped, making an impatient beckoning motion, but the young slicer was already taking the stairs two at a time.

'Fine, fine, what—?' She stopped when she reached the bottom and looked out at the gathering crowd. 'Oh.'

'Yes.' Rourke snatched a bag from her. She passed it to Apirana without looking, who slung the strap across his chest so it rested on his left hip. Rourke also took one and so, relatively equally loaded, they looked out at the mass of people.

'Want me to clear a path?' Apirana asked, pointing at the mouth of a street directly opposite them. That was the way Drift and the Changs had gone earlier, although whether they were still in that direction was anyone's guess.

Rourke shook her head. 'It's too thick, and the crowd looks tightly wound. We don't want them turning on you for giving them a shove. We'll have to go around . . .' she paused for a moment, apparently thinking, '. . . the right-hand edge. Circle about and get down that street in the corner if we can so we're at least going sort of the right way, but I don't want to stick around any longer than we have to.'

'Works for me,' Apirana nodded. He took a deep breath, cast a fervent wish for good fortune towards any form of deity that might be listening, and pushed open the big glass door.

There were four steps down from the frontage of the Otpusk Gostinitsa, and as soon as he'd stepped off the last one Apirana was in among the crowd. They were busy chanting in Russian and waving home-made banners and placards – simple cloth or plascard ones, nothing fancy like the 3D holos he'd seen used outside the G2000 summit on the news as a kid – but they still stood aside when they saw him bearing down on them with the two women at his heels. He quickly saw that Rourke was right to suggest taking the outside route, as he could almost taste the powder-keg atmosphere around them. Had a large, strange-looking foreigner tried to barge through the middle of the protesters . . . well, he didn't like to think what the reaction of this mob might have been.

'Do you want me to try the Captain again?' he heard Jenna ask behind him.

'Don't bother,' Rourke replied, 'he'll see A. called him. If he can make contact, he will. Besides, I doubt the comm network is even still functioning right now.'

'What?' Apirana turned his head to look at her, jogging along in his wake with a grim expression on what he could see of her face beneath her hat. 'Why not?'

'The Red Stars almost always cut public communication channels during civil unrest to prevent dissenters from being able to coordinate their movements,' Rourke explained, swerving around two youths with bright dyed hair and everything below the bridge of their noses obscured by makeshift cloth masks.

'Great,' Apirana snorted, 'so how are we going to find the others now?'

'I ask people if they've seen a tall, blue-haired Mexican who was with Chinese siblings!' Rourke called back. Apirana had to concede that might have some merit to it. It wasn't like their crew weren't distinctive in this largely homogenous city.

'Or we could just head for the *Jonah*,' Jenna suggested, 'if there was trouble kicking off, the Captain would probably go there to make sure our ship's okay.'

Rourke growled something in a language Apirana didn't speak, but it sounded like a curse of some sort. 'You're right. Hold up!'

Apirana slowed – there was entirely too much of him to arrest his momentum with any alacrity – and turned back to find the other two standing in place. 'What?'

'Jenna's right,' Rourke said uncomfortably, her eyes scanning the crowd, although Apirana guessed that was probably more out of habit than because she expected to see Drift making his way towards them. 'He'll try the hotel first, but after that his first instinct will be to make sure we keep a way off this rock.'

'Plus he loves that ship,' Apirana put in, trying not to sound too breathless. It wasn't that he was out of shape, as such, more that he was only in shape for certain things.

'That too,' Rourke acknowledged. 'Okay; we'll try to find them quickly, but if we get no luck we'll head for the *Jonah* and hope they do the—'

Her last word was drowned out by a loud crack from the other end of the square, and her head whipped around so fast Apirana thought her hat was going to fly off, but frustration clouded her features as she stood futilely on tiptoe. 'Damn it! A.?'

The shouting of the crowd had taken on an uglier, angrier edge, at least in that direction. Apirana drew himself up to his full height, but although he could see over most of the gathering his vision was still obstructed by the furiously waving signs many protesters had brought with them. 'I'm not sure, I . . .'

There. Between two banners he caught sight of a black-helmeted head, then another and another. The crowd was roiling, some pushing forwards and others trying to retreat. 'Cops,' he summarised.

'That sounded like a gunshot,' Rourke said uneasily. 'Never mind trying to reach the others for now, let's just—'

More cracking noises cut through the air, and their repetition brought certainty into Apirana's mind: definitely gunfire. Shouts were replaced by screams and then cries of warning as dark shapes trailing greenish-white fumes arced into the air above the plaza.

The mood of the protest shifted direction quicker than Jia trying to outmanoeuvre a missile. Ten seconds ago the plaza had been filled with righteous anger, the sort that could spiral out of control into full-blown aggression if handled incorrectly. Whoever was in charge of the *politsiya* had clearly decided that the softly-softly approach was not for them, and that the only course of action was to hammer the protest so hard that it cracked before it evolved into a riot under its own steam. The security officers opened up with live ammunition and gas grenades, and the cauldron of simmering resentment abruptly swirled into a frenzy of fear and self-preservation that responded by stampeding directly away from the threat.

Which meant that, all of a sudden, a few hundred panicking people were heading directly for the three crew.

'Run!' Rourke yelled, and Apirana obeyed. There was no standing against a tide like this, big though he was. He didn't even set out for a destination, just went with the flow towards the nearest street which led off the plaza, but he was being outpaced. Desperate men and women clawed past him, many of them cursing him in Russian, towards the inevitable bottle-neck forming ahead of them as half a plaza of people tried to fit down one street. His shoulder blades were itching, expecting a *politsiya* bullet to strike between them at any moment. He looked back to see if there was anyone left between him and the guns, caught a brief glimpse of the sea of faces still behind him . . .

. . . and tripped over something unseen. He hit the ground hard, palms stinging and forearms jarring as they took the brunt of the impact, but that was the least of his worries now. He hadn't even landed prop-erly before someone tripped over his leg; then someone stood on his arm, causing a spike of pain so bad he wondered momentarily if they'd broken it, *then* someone landed on his back and drove the breath from his lungs.

The anger flared up inside him and he tried to roar, tried to surge up to his feet flailing at anyone within reach in revenge for the pain he was suffering, but he simply couldn't. Every second brought a new impact on a leg, an arm, his head, his back, knocking him back down again. Someone landed across his shoulders and smashed his face into the ground, bringing a new flare of agony married to a sudden sick wooziness, but for the first time he could remember there was no corresponding surge of rage-filled adrenaline.

His left side had taken a blow somewhere and he felt like he'd been shot again; had his wound ripped open? He tried to brace his arms beneath him and push up, no longer in a fury but now simply mechanically attempting to rise, but a body landed on top of him and crushed him back down, then another before the first had even managed to scramble away.

His ribs were burning from the weight. His lungs were burning from lack of air. His head was swimming. Every limb felt like it had been beaten by a team of men with sledgehammers.

Somewhere on the hard rock floor of Level Five of Uragan City, for the first time since he was fifteen, Apirana Wahawaha stopped fighting.

Therehad been one chance for a good, deep gulp of air before the gas had flooded everywhere, and Ichabod Drift had taken it with both lungs. The fumes weren't just unbreathable, they stung the eyes and made it impossible to see clearly as well: that was, unless you happened to have at least one mechanical one. As a result Drift found himself to be in considerably better shape than pretty much anyone else inside Labirint, which was why he was able to get to his feet, hoist up a bar stool and crack it over the head of the balding man who'd been holding a gun on them scant seconds before.

Now bent double and coughing, the man dropped his handgun to the floor. Drift snatched it up and checked his options. His mechanical eye couldn't see through gas as such but it was hardly an opaque wall, it was just that once inside it most people couldn't see because their eyes were burning and filled with tears. The front of the bar seemed like a bad option; sounds of fighting suggested that the rioters had surged forward to engage the *politsiya*, despite the gas and the shockbolts. On the other hand, the back way was possibly locked and, if it was, he didn't have the breath to spend finding another option.

The huge bartender stumbled into view, obliviously hacking his lungs up but with his shotgun still clasped in one meaty hand. Drift aimed for the man's head, agonised with himself for half a second over what the right course of action was, then shot him in the knee instead. The bartender cried out, an agonised roar which died in a strangled gurgle a second later as the gas continued its ugly work, and fell on his face. He still clutched the shotgun, but Drift stepped up and kicked him smartly in the head before he could get ideas about pulling the trigger.

So, if the back way wasn't viable, it would have to be the front after all. Drift tugged the shotgun free, put the safety on the handgun and tucked it into the waistband of his pants, then turned back to where he'd left the Changs and the Shirokovs. His chest was now starting to feel uncomfortably tight thanks to the frantic pace at which his heart was running, but he spared some of his tightly hoarded breath to shout instructions into the foul-tasting gas as he hauled Jia up from the coughing crouch he found her in and shoved her in the direction of the shattered front windows. 'Go! Get clear!'

Under any normal circumstances Jia would have been likely to argue the call about stepping through shattered glass into a full-blown fight, but Drift was counting on the fact that when running low on air, people would tend to obey any instructions coming from someone who sounded like they knew what they were doing. Sure enough, his usually quarrelsome pilot scrambled forwards as well as she could, with her brother tailing her near-blindly. Drift wasted one more second debating about the Shirokovs, but there was still a chance to squeeze some manner of profit from them so he pulled Aleksandr up, with Pavel clinging to his husband like a choking drunkard to an unopened spirits bottle, and sent them the same way.

He followed after them, eager to get out into what passed for fresher air despite the fact that it seemed at least one gas grenade had gone off in the mass of protesters, but paused for a second with glass crunching underfoot as he was about to follow his crew members and whatever manner of nuisance the Shirokovs now counted as up the street. Not ten feet away, nine black-armoured *politsiya* cowered behind flashshields and occasionally lashed out desperately with shocksticks against a mass of protesters who had only failed to overwhelm them so far due to some relatively minor breathing difficulties and the electric charges of the shields. However, even such purpose-built riot technology couldn't maintain a constant output, and the frail defensive line was going to crack at any second. In most cases Drift would have shrugged and walked away, but something about the way the officers appeared to be not just desperately defending themselves but also their fallen colleagues tugged at him.

This had been a trap, an ambush. This wasn't a protest that had got out of hand; whoever was in charge of organising it had fully intended for these men and women to walk down this street to a point where they could get shot at. Whatever trouble the law enforcers here had caused him, Drift wasn't quite certain that its officers deserved to be lured in to be slaughtered in the name of a better world.

Secondly, and more compellingly, until he heard otherwise he had to assume that the spaceport – and therefore the *Jonah* – was under the control of Uragan authorities. That meant he wanted to keep on the good side of those authorities, and given Chief Muradov's thinly veiled hints of what would happen if Drift drew his attention again, that was probably going to be hard to achieve at the best of times.

Let alone when walking hurriedly away from the likely deaths of nearly two dozen of Muradov's officers while in possession of illegal firearms.

Sometimes, as an entrepreneurial independent businessman, there was no clear choice of how best to proceed. There was simply the task of playing the odds and selecting the least shit-spattered course of action from a series of unappealing options. Usually that was to keep your head down and avoid notice, but when that wasn't possible . . .

Drift grimaced, took a couple of lungfuls of air that was bitter-tasting but at least breathable, and discharged the shotgun into the air just over the heads of the rioters.

The kick was powerful; whatever the weapon lacked in sophistication it made up for in grunt, and its roar was loud enough to attract attention even above the noise of the melee. Drift worked the action to pump another shell into the chamber, sending the spent one clattering off to the side, and fired again forty-five degrees to his left, then once more to the right. Even though he hadn't hit anyone, the rioters were stumbling backwards; it was one thing to charge a line of *politsiya* with their non-lethal riot control gear, and quite another to have a blue-haired Mexican opening fire on them. A few seconds later and discretion had become the better part of valour for the mob, who turned to flee through the wisps of gas remaining in the street and those still leaking out of Labirint, leaving several of their number stunned or incapacitated by shocksticks or flashshields.

Expressionless riot masks turned to look at Drift, their wearers either sagging with released tension or already on the ground having hunkered down behind their shields to protect themselves. He spent a useless half-second wishing he could see their faces, then gave up on that idea and just trusted that he'd got at least some credit with them after potentially saving their lives.

'Come on!' he said, not needing to try hard to inject urgency into his voice as he pointed at the gas-filled Labirint, 'there's still people with guns in there! We need to get out of here!'

Two of the masks turned to look at a third, whom Drift now noticed had three yellow stripes on each shoulder. The sergeant hesitated for a moment, then nodded and said something that Drift couldn't hear clearly through the mask but which was communicated to the rest of the squad via comm, judging by the way the ones still on their feet all turned and moved towards their fallen comrades. Drift judged that a further gesture of assistance was in order and made furious beckoning motions back down the street towards the Changs and the Shirokovs, who had paused some distance away and were watching curiously. They seemed to get the gist and returned cautiously to begin offering assistance to the injured *politsiya*, and the party began to retreat up the street with Drift acting as rearguard, hefting the shotgun and trying to look menacing.

He became aware that the sergeant had fallen in beside him and was removing the riot mask, then found himself looking at the slightly blocky features of a woman probably about his own age, her auburn hair cut short and her face pale with the aftershock of adrenaline. She cast him a quick glance, but didn't take her eyes off the street for long.

'Those guns are illegal, you know,' she said simply.

'They're not mine,' Drift replied, 'and you're welcome to them when we get somewhere safe. I didn't want to leave them with the previous owners, though.'

She snorted a somewhat tense laugh. 'You have my thanks. Who are you, Mr Blue Hair?'

'Ichabod Drift, starship captain.' He looked over his shoulder, just to check there was no new mass of protesters cutting off their retreat. 'And you are?'

'Sergeant Ingrid Lukyanenko.' She still had her flashshield strapped in place on her left arm and was keeping it between her and the rest of the street. 'I think you have picked a bad time to be visiting Uragan, Captain Drift.'

'The thought had occurred to me,' Drift agreed grimly. 'I don't suppose any of your colleagues are on their way to lend a hand, are they?'

'I hear they are two blocks away,' Lukyanenko replied. She started speaking rapidly in Russian, which caught Drift off-guard for a moment until he realised she was talking into her commpiece and that she had probably just heard an update in her ear. That triggered another thought and he hastily activated his own comm to call Rourke, but got nothing except static. He frowned and looked over his shoulder.

'Kuai! Is your comm working?'

'No!' the little mechanic shouted back, he and Jia each under one arm of a *politsiya* officer who appeared barely able to walk. 'Could it be the gas?'

'All civilian communications have been shut down,' Lukyanenko said from beside Drift, her conversation apparently having been concluded. 'It is to prevent activists from coordinating their activities.'

'Wonderful,' Drift muttered, feeling his stomach start to sink. 'How am I meant to get in touch with the rest of my crew?'

'You are not meant to,' the sergeant replied, and Drift sighed in frustration.

'I meant, how *can* I get in touch with the rest of my crew?'

'You cannot.' Lukanyenko turned as howling sirens began to assert themselves over the background noise of the city, and a little of the tension seemed to leave her features. 'The Chief is here. Perhaps he can help you; I will tell him what you did.'

'The Chief?' Drift followed her gaze and saw that they'd nearly come to a confluence of streets, a plaza where five roadways all converged into a pentagonal open space. The sirens were almost shockingly loud now, and reverberating off the walls and ceiling three storeys above so that it was hard to tell which direction they were coming from. That mystery was quickly solved, however, when the first armoured transport barrelled in from the second exit and slewed to a halt directly ahead of them.

It was not only armoured but armed as well, Drift noted. The black-clad, six-wheeled vehicle had a turret on the roof that rotated, pivoting to face over their heads and down towards Labirint. The central barrel looked to be a water cannon, but mounted directly on either side were two narrower apertures which were almost certainly ballistic weapons for use if the natives got too restless to be constrained by conventional riot control techniques. He instinctively ducked, which caused the barrel of the pistol tucked into his pants to dig into his lower belly and remind him that he was in front of a *politsiya* vehicle while carrying two illegal firearms.

He was still debating with himself about whether to throw them both away and risk looking guilty or hold onto them and risk getting shot when Security Chief Alim Muradov strode around the vehicle's cab, flanked by a pair of white-clad medics and a team of riot-armoured officers carrying guns.

'*Drift?*' Muradov's voice was tinged with incredulity. 'What in the Prophet's name . . .?'

Someone in the new riot team had noticed the shotgun, and for the third time in the last twenty-four hours Ichabod Drift found himself on the wrong end of multiple gun barrels.

'*Stoi!*' Sergeant Lukyanenko interspersed herself between Drift and the squad, to his great relief and their apparent confusion. He took the opportunity to set both the shotgun and the pistol down with exaggerated care while she spoke in rapid Russian to Muradov, and was pleased to see the Chief's expression changing from shocked anger to only mild residual suspicion. When the sergeant finished her explanation, Muradov nodded and said a few words, and suddenly the squad had lowered their firearms and were filing past Drift, taking up station across the street.

Drift allowed himself to breathe out, and felt a sudden burning urge to take a shower; he was feeling rather fragrant, what with all the risk of being shot. Muradov beckoned him over and Drift approached cautiously, exchanging a slightly uncertain look with Jia while stepping around the medics who were now attending to the worst-injured members of Lukyanenko's squad.

'Captain,' Muradov greeted him with a slight nod.

'Chief,' Drift responded in kind, awaiting some sort of cue. Muradov spent a couple more seconds studying his face, then pursed his lips.

'I currently have what appears to be a full-blown uprising going on in my city,' he said quietly, and Drift was suddenly struck by the realisation that the man's anger had not been removed; instead it was merely suppressed, and bubbled just beneath the surface. 'My officers have been fired upon and wounded; possibly fatally, in some cases. And here are you in the middle of it, Captain Drift, with your too-easy smile and your too-ready answers, holding a shotgun and with only the word of one of my senior sergeants saving you from being a victim of . . . what is the phrase you North Americans use?' His gaze drifted sideways for a second, then refocused on Drift's face with an almost palpable heat. 'Ah yes, "Shoot first, ask questions later."'

'I'm very grateful to your sergeant,' Drift replied fervently.

'I am going to ask you this question *once*,' Muradov said. 'Why. Are. You. Here?'

Drift swallowed. 'The hotels for off-worlders were extortionate so we got the Shirokovs to find us one in this district—'

'Which one?' Muradov cut in.

'The Otpusk Gostinitsa,' Drift replied immediately, glad he'd bothered to memorise the name before he went drinking but unable to prevent himself from pronouncing it with his best stab at a Uragan accent. 'Anyway, I fancied a—'

'The Otpusk Gostinitsa on Tsink Ploschadi?' Muradov demanded, his eyes narrowing.

'I . . .' Drift was wrong-footed momentarily. 'Yes, I think so.' Something in Muradov's expression was worrying him. 'Why?'

'We have another riot taking place on Tsink Ploschadi,' Muradov said grimly. 'My officers have just opened fire with live ammunition.'

'*What?!*' Drift nearly grabbed the other man by the webbing on his flak jacket, but restrained himself at the last moment.

'Calm down, Captain,' Muradov said, turning away from Drift and raking the streets around them with his eyes. 'So long as your crew obeyed the emergency broadcasts and stayed inside the hotel, they should be perfectly safe.'

THE WRONG COMPANY

Tamara Rourke liked crowds. They were good cover if you knew half a thing about blending in, and she'd always had the ability to read the movement of people within them. Ichabod or Apirana seemed to view a crowd as a separate thing and used their height or breadth to try to force a way through; Rourke had always thought of herself as part of any large group of people she was in, and could find the gaps to slip through in any direction.

That was, of course, providing the crowd in question wasn't in a headlong stampede away from gunfire.

The banners and placards had been abandoned, dropped and trampled underfoot like the incriminating evidence they were. Here and there Rourke could see some item of clothing with a slogan on it discarded as well, and wondered briefly how many topless Uragans would be trying desperately to get

back into their homes before the *politsiya* tracked
them down. A highly visible protest was all very well,
but it could backfire spectacularly if the authorities
decided to play hardball.

One thing that *wasn't* highly visible was the rest
of her crew. She'd lost sight of Jenna almost immediately, and she hadn't even caught a glimpse of
Apirana in the few quick backwards glances she'd
managed to snatch as the press of bodies drove her
inexorably forwards. Still, she didn't fancy trying
to navigate against the tide and towards live
weapons fire, crowd negotiation skills or not, and
she was sure the other two would be able to cope
without her.

Something caught her eye: a flash of darker skin
through the crowd of desperate, pale faces that
surrounded her. She frowned, wondering how Apirana
could have got ahead of her, then reassessed when
she saw that instead of the massive Maori it was a
smaller man with a thick beard and scarlet turban.
A moment later she caught a second glimpse of him
and noticed his jacket, a style most common in the
planets of the South Asian Treaty.

More interestingly, there was a young man in
typical Uragan clothing tugging at his arm and
gesturing urgently, as though trying to shepherd him
in a direction slightly at an angle to the main crush.

Rourke had pegged the man in the turban as a
fellow off-worlder immediately. Right now, separated
from her crew and in a city that was rapidly becoming
increasingly hostile, trying to tag onto another
outsider who appeared to have some sort of local
connection seemed like an excellent plan. She cut

diagonally through the crowd as best she could, employing her elbows viciously when she needed to and taking a couple of knocks herself in the process. For a galling moment she thought she'd lost them, but then the man's turban flashed into view again and she got another fix. They seemed to be heading for an alcove set back slightly from the street, just visible above the heads of the people around her. There was a brown-painted door there, plain and unadorned, possibly the rear entrance to a shop that fronted onto the plaza?

She shouldered aside a determined-looking Uragan woman who had her head down and her skirts bunched in her hands as she ran, ricocheted off a teenager of indeterminate gender, collided with a large incineration bin and used its weighty bulk as a mustering point to fight her way into the alcove, all the while feeling somewhat like one of those big fish that swam up waterfalls back on Old Earth. She found herself face-to-face with the Indian man, who looked startled, and *just under six feet tall, early thirties, a shade over 200 pounds, more fat than muscle,* and the Uragan youth, *no older than twenty, five feet eight and 150 to 155, something long and straight in his left leg pocket which could well be a knife with a roughly six-inch blade,* who looked at her suspiciously and quickly stopped tapping an entry code into the keypad next to the door.

'Please,' Rourke gasped, doing her best to look desperate and pitching her voice slightly higher than usual, 'English? You speak English?'

'Yes,' the Indian man nodded, which was entirely the point: get someone to agree to something you said, no matter how trivial it was, and they'd uncon-sciously be more likely to agree again.

'Can I . . .' Rourke continued, not needing much acting to appear a little breathless. 'Can you get in here?' She pointed at the door, but didn't wait for an answer. 'Can I come in with you, *please*? I just want to get out of the way, they're using real bullets, I'm sure of—'

'No,' the Uragan man broke in sternly. He was little more than a youth, really, but was trying to look older by cultivating the side-whiskers-and-moustache combination that seemed to be some sort of fashion here. 'No, you must go.'

Rourke ignored him and returned her attention to the Indian man. 'Please? I won't be any trouble, I just want to get off the street but I can't get back to my hotel.' She paused a second, anxious not to come across as histrionic and therefore a potential liability. How did Drift manipulate people so easily? She had to think about her body language, pace her delivery, time things carefully . . . he just breezed ahead and *did* it. She tried an appeal to a shared concern. 'I think the cops might blame this on us off-worlders!'

The man's face twitched behind his beard. She'd struck a nerve there, although she couldn't say what or why exactly. He looked at his companion uncertainly.

A gunshot sounded, and suddenly the shouts of the tide of people crammed into the street turned into screams again. Rourke poked her head out for half a second, then ducked back in again. She hadn't seen anything, but the other two didn't need to know that. 'They're coming!'

'Open it,' the man in the turban said, gesturing to the door. The Uragan hesitated, but his companion looked none too relaxed himself and slammed his fist against the metal. 'For fuck's sake, man, open it!'

Rourke turned her face a little, as though she was peering anxiously for signs of approaching *politsiya*, but her sideways glance was enough to see and memorise the combination punched in by the scowling Uragan. The lock buzzed open, the noise barely audible over the crowd still piling past in their rush to get further away from the plaza, and the two men slipped inside. Rourke darted after them before either of them could change their mind, pressing up close behind her new friend in the turban.

She found herself in a white-walled stairwell. Steep and narrow concrete steps, marked with yellow safety strips at the edge and flanked by metal handrails with flaking blue paint, rose up about a storey's height to another door, which was slightly ajar. The Uragan youth cast a dark glance at her and went up first, followed by the Indian man. Rourke brought up the rear, surreptitiously double-checking the hidden wire sewn into the sleeve of her bodysuit. It wasn't that she distrusted these two any more than she would any other pair of strangers, but it was always best to keep your options open and close at hand.

The upper door opened into a room which continued the white theme, but rather than paint over rough concrete the walls here were polished panels interspersed with mirrors. The tiled floor was also white and one side of it was occupied by swivelling, padded chairs upholstered in what had to be fake leather, given how expensive the genuine stuff would be down here. Here and there on the walls were prints of good-looking men and women sporting a selection of unlikely hairstyles, with a couple showing off the same style of whiskers sported by the young man who'd led her up here.

They were going to be taking shelter in a hair-dressing salon, apparently.

More surprising than the location was the fact that they weren't alone. There were already three other Uragans, judging by their appearance and clothing, none looking much older than the one she'd entered with. Still more curious was the presence of another two off-worlders: a pale, skinny kid with tribal tattoos down one arm, *standing slightly hunched, either poor posture or in some sort of pain,* and a middle-aged man whom Rourke would have pegged as having Native American ancestry if she'd had to hazard a guess, *left-handed and not happy to see me, given the way he started to reach for a gun at his left hip that isn't there.*

'Skanda?' the older man said, jerking his chin at Rourke with a suspicious look on his face. 'Who's this?'

The man in the turban, apparently named Skanda, looked suddenly rather less certain than he had when thumping the door downstairs. 'Ah . . . she was outside with us, and the cops were coming . . . I guess she must have followed us in . . .'

Rourke didn't like the sound of that at all, and it took no acting effort to protest indignantly. 'Hey, wait a second, you let me in!' The whiskery Uragan was scowling and she appealed to him. 'He let me come in, right? You didn't want me to come in, but he told you to open the door anyway.'

The young man's eyes flickered between her and Skanda, apparently uncertain which of them he currently disliked more. He settled for biting out a sullen, 'Yes,' and folding his arms.

'Okay, but look, I didn't know you guys were gonna be here *too*,' Skanda protested, waving his arms to encompass the salon. 'I thought me and Ruslan were just gonna duck in here and then leave after.'

'That's all I want!' Rourke spoke up, raising her hand. 'I don't know if you're having some sort of gathering or . . . or what, really, but I don't want to get in anyone's way. I just want to stay off the streets until the shooting stops and then I'll be out of your hair.' She was getting a nasty feeling about this group; she'd clearly stumbled into something less innocent than a simple group of salon employees and their off-world friends. She edged towards the salon's window which overlooked the plaza, hoping to catch a glimpse of Jenna and Apirana from a higher vantage point, but was interrupted by a door banging open. It was the salon's main entrance this time, rather than the back way she'd come in by.

'—the hell you think you're playing at?' a male voice was shouting angrily in English.

A Uragan woman stormed in first, her dirty blonde hair cut into a bob with a fringe. There was nothing to visually set her apart from her compatriots in the room apart from a few additional years, but Rourke noted how everyone, including the off-worlders, moved aside for her. The new arrival threw one arm up in a motion clearly intended to dismiss the ranting of whoever was following her, then slightly spoiled the effect by turning in place to address them.

'This is the start,' she retorted at the closing door, 'this is what we have been building towards for *years*! This is what you have been working for!'

The door ricocheted open again before it had fully shut, admitting a black-haired, well-tanned man with a thick moustache and a red-and-white spotted neckerchief. '*I* have been working to get *you* some damn guns and get *me* some damn money,' he retorted, jabbing a finger at her and his own chest alternately to furiously underscore his words. 'I don't give a flying fuck what you *do* with them, but getting us caught up in a fucking *war* when we're stuck down here with you doesn't seem like—'

He broke off in mid-rant, staring at Rourke with an expression of stunned fury.

'*Ta tudo fodido* . . .' He looked around the room. 'What the fuck is *she* doing here?! Huh?'

Rourke centred her weight, dropped her bag and folded her hands in front of her stomach, so she could easily draw her garrotting wire from her sleeve. She relaxed her face and let her voice come out naturally, free from the artificial strain and pitch she'd injected to make herself seem more vulnerable, and allowed the man's name to slide from her lips with an appropriate amount of scorn laced into it. There was no point acting now.

'Ricardo *fucking* Moutinho.' She sighed. 'I should have known this would be your fault somehow.'

When Jenna saw Apirana fall, her first thought was that he'd somehow been shot through the crowd.

Rourke was nowhere in sight and she had no idea if the other woman had even seen their crewmate go down. She tried to fight down the sudden sucking dread in her chest and angled herself ever so slightly across the flow of the crowd, nearly tripping over someone's legs and only staying on her feet through good natural balance and sheer bloody-mindedness. Someone's elbow caught her in the side of the head and she staggered, but the flash of pain kick-started a violent response. She lashed out in anger and frustration, hitting someone to her left and gaining a half-second of space as the nearby Uragans veered away from this sudden minor disturbance, which gave her an opening to head for where she'd seen Apirana fall.

She was on him almost before she expected, the only warning being the people directly in front of her stumbling slightly and suddenly shifting direction. Then she caught sight of one of his boots and the familiar navy blue of his jumpsuit on the ground, and shouldered a dark-haired woman aside to scramble down into a crouch by his side.

'A.!' The big man's arms were covering his head and he was breathing, but he was face down and otherwise motionless. She couldn't see any obvious wounds on his body, but—

Someone fleeing headlong tripped on Apirana's foot and nearly went over, only saving themselves by dint of planting a foot into his back. Jenna heard a quiet moan of pain as air was expelled from the Maori's lungs: she nearly got a knee in the head before she could react, then the man was gone into the throng.

She came up to her feet snarling, unslung the bag of hastily grabbed possessions from their hotel room and starting swinging it in a figure-eight, straddling Apirana's prone body and yelling wordlessly at the onrushing Uragans. The sight of a screaming, red-blonde girl using a backpack as a weapon seemed to do what a fallen Maori couldn't, and within a couple of seconds the crowd was parting around her.

Of course, they were still fleeing from *politsiya* using live rounds, and the mass of onrushing bodies was already starting to thin out into stragglers; the older, the younger or the infirm. When even they were gone, Jenna would be left to face the authorities down with nothing but bad language and a bag that was already making her arms ache. She caught her first glimpse of black body armour through the thinning press in front of her. She had to get away, and get A. away too, but to where? And how?

Two more pale-faced Uragans split apart to pass on either side of her, revealing a dark-skinned man behind them. He was wearing a red bodysuit decorated with a lattice of gold lines that formed geometric shapes, and the sight of him made Jenna falter where she stood. There were three metal studs along one side of his shaven head, his eyes were covered by a thin visor and the outline of his torso was strangely angular as though it wasn't flesh and blood beneath the fabric he wore.

A Circuit Cult logicator.

He slowed from what had been little more than a jog and Jenna saw the brief downwards tilt of his head as he took in Apirana's body beneath her. Then he stepped forward and spoke a sentence in rapid Russian.

Jenna shook her head, shrinking back instinctively. 'I . . . I don't . . .'

'Ah, North American, yes?' the man replied, switching to English with what sounded like an accent from the Federation of African States. He gestured down at Apirana. 'Your friend is hurt.'

Jenna wriggled her fingers, checking her grip on her bag in case she needed to swing for him and aware of how fast her heart had suddenly started beating. *God*, but she hated circuitheads. 'I think so, I haven't been able—'

'His ankle is broken,' the logicator said, pointing. Jenna followed his gaze, realising almost absently that the circuithead's mere presence seemed to be enough to divert the remains of the fleeing crowd away from them. Sure enough, one of Apirana's feet was twisted at what looked to be slightly the wrong angle. She hadn't had time to notice it before, being too busy trying to ensure that he didn't get trodden on.

Well, that was it. She'd been watching via co-opted security cameras when they'd assaulted Kelsier's asteroid base with the Europans, and she'd seen the Captain trying to support Apirana's weight when the big man had been shot. He'd barely managed to help Apirana move thirty feet, and Drift was certainly bigger and stronger than she was. Apirana probably weighed well over twice what she did, there was no way she could—

'We will help,' the man said, pressing a button on one of his wrist cuffs. 'I am Kunley Ngiri, of the Universal Access Movement.'

'You'll help?' Jenna was taken aback, and becoming even less comfortable with the situation.

Kunley appeared to take her reaction as a comment on his modest size and build. 'I have friends,' he said with a smile, and suddenly there they were at his shoulder: two Uragans, a man and a woman, in white jackets with the Circuit Cult's gold lattice on the sleeves, although the fabric did little to disguise the unnatural shape of their limbs. Jenna swallowed, uncomfortably aware of exactly how strong augmentations could make a person. These two could certainly pick Apirana up and move him even if he wasn't able to do anything for himself.

They could also likely break pretty much any bone in her body if they got hold of her.

Now Kunley seemed to get an inkling of why she was hesitating. His face, so far as she could read it with his natural eyes obscured, fell into an earnest expression. 'Please, we only wish to help. We can take him to our workshop and fix his leg.'

Workshop. Damn circuitheads don't even call it a surgery. 'What about them?' Jenna asked, pointing at the *politsiya*. They weren't firing anymore, but were now roughly apprehending and cuffing anyone who had fallen in the crush or had been overcome by the gas, the remnants of which were starting to drift around them, making her throat feel like she'd swallowed powdered glass.

Kunley's smile returned. 'In a mining town, the Universal Access Movement is well thought of. Everyone has family or a friend who we have helped after an accident, even the police. You will be safe so long as you are with us.'

Translation: you're not safe unless *you're with us.* But then, Jenna had pretty much known that anyway.

She stood back from Apirana's body and knelt down by his head again. 'A.? Listen to me, there's some . . . people . . . who're going to help you up, okay? *Don't* try to use your left leg. If they hurt you, let me know.'

He still didn't respond and she sat back, biting her lip with worry, then looked up at Kunley. 'What if it's not just his ankle that's broken? Should we even move him? There were people *standing* on him, what if his neck's—'

'His ankle is the only break,' Kunley replied calmly. He raised a finger to his visor. 'I scanned him.'

X-ray visor. Right. Jenna was dubious for a moment, but the Circuit Cult were all about replacing or enhancing people's limbs with mechanical augmentations so she guessed it kind of made sense for their leader to be able to scan for broken bones. She stood back, admitting defeat. She still couldn't bring herself to trust a circuithead, but it wasn't like she had many options. 'Fine. Uh . . . go ahead, then.'

Kunley nodded to his two companions who stepped forwards and squatted down next to Apirana and, murmuring things which were doubtless meant to be soothing but which probably did nothing as Apirana didn't speak much Russian, started to roll him carefully onto his back. Jenna caught her breath: the big man's face was visibly scraped and battered even under his tattoos, and although he appeared conscious he showed no sign of being aware of where he was. She started to reach out to him, but pulled her hand back – she certainly wouldn't want to be touched on her face if it looked like that – and settled for quickly unhooking the satchel he'd had slung across his shoulders.

The man took Apirana under the shoulders and the woman got his legs by the knees, then they lifted him up and set off at a steady pace towards the edge of the plaza without any real sign of effort. Jenna found herself staring open-mouthed at this casual display of strength.

'Come,' Kunley said, placing one hand briefly on her shoulder and gesturing with the other, 'we should go.'

'Yeah.' Jenna started walking with him, but unzipped her bag as she did so and pulled out her EMP generator bracelet which she secured around her forearm. It would knock out the circuitry in their augmentations if she activated it, which was why she'd built the damn thing in the first place. It was far from the best option this far underground, but she desperately felt the need for some sort of equaliser.

'What is that?' Kunley asked, his tone no more than mildly curious.

'This?' Jenna tried to look casual. 'Health monitor. It's . . . been a rough day.'

'I see,' Kunley nodded. 'Forgive me for asking, but are you already augmented at all?'

'Me?' Jenna shook her head, trying to suppress a grimace. 'No.'

'Have you considered it? Even for those who appear to be in good natural health, the benefits can be—'

'Best discussed elsewhere,' Jenna cut in, pointing towards the far end of the plaza where movement had caught her eye behind the *politsiya* she'd been watching distrustfully. 'Run!'

She was ten feet into her sprint and rapidly gaining on the two circuitheads carrying Apirana when the firefight started in earnest.

Everyone was staring at Rourke. This was when she felt the absence of Drift most keenly: he always knew when to make a big show and attract the attention of an audience, thereby allowing her to make preparations for their exit.

At least, she'd always supposed he did that consciously. It was always possible that he was simply an egomaniac.

'She came in with Skanda,' the First Nations man said to Moutinho, who looked about ready to haul off and hit someone.

'Oh, thanks, Jack,' Skanda retorted with heavy sarcasm. 'Seriously, that's really—'

'*Shut up!*' Moutinho thundered, rounding on him and pushing him up against the wall. '*You* brought her in here? Why?!'

'Why *not?*' Skanda demanded, although his face didn't look half as confident as his voice. 'Who the hell *is* she, anyway?'

'I was about to ask the same thing,' the older Uragan woman put in, eyeing Rourke warily.

'My name's Tamara Rourke,' Rourke said simply, before Moutinho could respond. The skinny kid gave a small start of surprise, while Jack nodded sourly as though she'd simply confirmed a suspicion he'd started to hold. Skanda just closed his eyes and looked like he wanted the ground to swallow him.

'I'm from a ship called the *Keiko*,' Rourke continued, 'where I'm a business partner with its owner, Captain Ichabod Drift. This man has crossed paths with us a few times before over the years, and we aren't friends.' She nodded at Moutinho, then addressed him directly. 'It was you who left that anonymous tip about us being gunrunners, am I right?'

'Is all that true?' the Uragans' leader asked Moutinho.

'As near as makes no difference,' Moutinho growled, clearly angry at having his thunder stolen, which had been Rourke's intention: when the truth was going to come out anyway it was best to reveal it voluntarily yourself. That way you could avoid others putting less complimentary spins on it.

'Including the part about the tip-off?' the Uragan asked, and suddenly there was an edge in her voice. Moutinho was sharp enough to catch it. He released his hold on Skanda's shirt and turned to face her, his brow furrowing.

'Drift and his crew are troublemakers, Tanja, always have been. If they'd caught wind of what we were up to they'd have run to the law the first chance they got and sold us out. Then where would *you* have been? No,' he shook his head emphatically, 'we tarred them with the only brush they could have used on us, cos that way they'd have been ignored if they'd tried it.'

'You *told* the *politsiya* that there was gunrunning going on?!' Tanja shouted in response. Rourke saw Jack shift his stance slightly. The First Nations man suddenly seemed to be counting heads and realising that his crew were one short compared to the Uragans present, none of whom were looking particularly relaxed now. Two short, if Rourke was classed as an enemy.

'They're not as dumb as you want 'em to be,' Moutinho snorted. 'I've heard about that Muradov, he's a sharp card. This was gonna be our last drop here, anyway; I didn't fancy running the risk again. No customs official can be bribed to look the wrong way for ever.'

'You told me you wanted to help!' Tanja snapped.

Moutinho shrugged. 'I *did* help. You got any other contacts who'd be willing to risk their asses hauling illegal firearms into this place? I'm not a revolutionary, I'm a businessman, and business is looking better elsewhere.'

'What about her?' the Uragan youth Rourke had followed in asked, pointing in her direction. Tanja looked at Rourke thoughtfully, pursing her lips, then sighed with every appearance of genuine regret.

'She knows too much, now.'

Well. That doesn't leave me with many options, does it?

'Actually,' Rourke spoke up, 'I don't know anywhere near enough if I'm going to help you.'

Tanja's brow furrowed. 'Excuse me?'

'You're clearly heavily involved in planning and executing a Free Systems revolution and we are' – Rourke made a show of checking her wrist chrono, – 'approximately seven minutes after the general alert sounded. The security forces have already deployed live rounds. That means they've escalated response by two levels, so civilian communications through the public hub will have been cut off, correct?'

'You mean your comm doesn't work?' Moutinho snorted. 'That's not hard to spot.'

Rourke gave him a thin and completely false smile, then turned her attention back to Tanja. 'So given we're in a multi-levelled underground city and you therefore can't use independent short-range comms, I imagine you're getting around that by deploying hard-wired communication points that use the power lines, right?'

Tanja's eyes narrowed. 'How do you—?'

'But what you probably *don't* know,' Rourke ploughed on, 'is that standard Red Star anti-insurgent protocol in areas where hard-wired comm points are considered likely to be in use is to induce a power surge in order to knock as many of those units out as possible. That's meant to happen five minutes after the first officer reports that live rounds have been deployed, in order to give time for government devices to be switched off or otherwise protected, so . . .' She looked at her chrono again, then back up at Tanja. 'You're on the clock.'

Tanja stared back at her, then turned to one of the younger Uragans who was lurking near a cupboard and spoke in Russian. Rourke missed some of the words, but caught the gist: *Unplug the transmitter and tell the others.*

Ricardo Moutinho's expression was getting more and more incredulous as the youth opened the cupboard door and started speaking urgently into the transmission equipment concealed there. 'You're actually *buying* this?'

'A power surge will knock out a lot of things,' Tanja said, ignoring him to focus on Rourke once more with a weighing stare, 'we'll soon see if she's telling the truth. Where did you learn this information?'

Rourke raised her eyebrows slightly. She was aiming for authoritative without coming across as superior or condescending, but that was always a fine balancing act. 'Let's not rush into anything here. It sounded like you were planning on killing me a minute ago. That doesn't exactly engender trust.'

Tanja nodded. 'A fair point. If your information about the power surge is good—'

There was a bang as the salon's lights brightened momentarily, then went out with an air of finality. The only light left was from the muted communal lamps outside in the plaza, still mimicking the night-time level of illumination in an open-air city like New Samara.

Rourke sighed. 'I could have done with them waiting a few more seconds, really.' She allowed herself a small smile, which was at least partly due to the look of outraged consternation on Moutinho's face. 'How were you planning on ending that sentence?'

Tanja had the look of someone who wanted to believe something but was being assailed by the fear that it was too good to be true.

'I take it you've done this before?'

'Three times,' Rourke nodded. 'Don't bother asking me when or where.'

'I think I can take that on trust,' Tanja said slowly.

'How do we know she's not a spy?' one of the Uragan girls demanded.

'Because Captain Moutinho has already told us that he's known Ms Rourke for years,' Tanja smiled. 'A case of "right place, right time", perhaps?'

'More like "wrong place, wrong time" from where I'm standing,' Rourke admitted. 'I hadn't intended to do this again, but given the circumstances . . .' She gave a slight shrug. 'If I'm going to be mixed up in this, I might as well give myself the best chance of coming out alive.' She crossed to the salon's window and looked out, still half hoping to see some sign of Jenna and Apirana and half worrying that if she did, it would be because one of them would have caught a bullet.

The plaza was largely empty, but the drifting remnants of gas made the air hazy and it was hard to see many details. Rourke could make out the black-clad forms of *politsiya* moving here and there, securing and arresting the luckless ones who'd fallen, but she couldn't see any sign of her crewmates. Hopefully they'd managed to flee the plaza unharmed and had fallen in with better – or at least less potentially troublesome – company than she had.

A cluster of movement at the far end of the plaza caught her eye, visible even through the haze. At first she thought it was yet more law enforcement officers, perhaps ones who hadn't yet heard quite how thoroughly the protest had been dispersed. Then, however, she saw the unmistakeable shards of light which constituted muzzle flash. A fraction of a second later the reports reached their ears, muffled by the salon's window but still identifiable to anyone who'd been in a gunfight or two.

Wait until the riot squad think the threat's been dispersed, then attack from behind. Rourke nodded slowly, even as her stomach sank. *Goad them into inflicting a few civilian casualties to sway the populace to the justice of the cause. Callous, but effective: I might have planned this myself, other than the timing.* She was already slipping back into the insurrectionist thinking model. The Galactic Intelligence Agency had never particularly wanted any planet to genuinely defect to the Free Systems – any one of them could be the pebble that would cause a landslide across into USNA space – but a single bad apple could throw an entire system into disarray, or even more. That could be very useful in the right circumstances, and so the United States of North America had carefully planted GIA agents on planets belonging to rival governmental conglomerates. Then Rourke, and others like her, would harness pre-existing public unrest and turn unsettled mutterings into a chaotic, destabilising roar. The important difference this time was that she wasn't in control of the timetable, and she didn't have an extraction protocol.

Well, and she had a crew these days, the location of which she had no idea.

She looked sideways and met Tanja's eyes. 'You know what happens now, I hope?'

'Now,' the other woman said, a tight excitement visible in her features, 'we start to throw off this government that works our people to the bone to ship *our* natural resources elsewhere.'

Rourke sighed. 'I was thinking more that an incident of live ammunition fire on government personnel during an alert status calls for the imposition of martial law.' *I never liked dealing with amateurs, but at least I used to have a chance to coach them a bit before we unleashed hell on a population.*

Tanja was looking at her, her expression guarded once more. 'Martial law?'

'Shoot on sight, and shoot to kill,' Rourke said grimly. 'That applies to anyone seen on the streets, so I hope you've already done your rallying work.' On the plaza outside, even the body armour of the *politsiya* wasn't helping them. Some had thrown themselves to the ground to narrow the angles of fire available to their ambushers, but even so they were exposed in the middle of a flat, open space. There wasn't going to be a happy ending for them.

'Don't worry about that,' Tanja replied confidently, and not without some steel in her tone, 'the people will rise. This was just a taster for the dogs in charge.'

'Glad to hear it,' Rourke said. She checked her chrono again. 'Because the imposition of martial law means the planetary governor sending a signal to the system capital – so New Samara in this case – requesting immediate military aid. And that means that by the time the storm up top clears you're going to have half the Rassvet System's defence force sitting overhead in troop transports ready to land, so you'd better have finished the job by then.'

There was a stunned silence.

'Seriously?' Rourke couldn't keep a tone of incredulity out of her voice. 'You thought the Red Stars would just let one of their primary ore planets secede? There's no government in the galaxy that would give up resources like this without a fight.' She swallowed back further words. There was no need to tell them that even if they took the entire city, even if they held the planet, the Red Stars would simply blockade them in. At some point, someone here had had a dream of a life not ruled by a bureaucracy of interminable layers leading all the way back to Moscow on Old Earth, and that dream had spread far enough that people were willing to try to seize it even though it was impossible, simply because they couldn't bear not to any longer.

Focus, Tamara. You're not trying to set them up to destabilise the entire system. All you need to do is find your crew and get out of this hole as soon as possible.

Tanja seemed to have only got more determined. 'Then we *will* finish the job.' The other woman paused, then continued slightly more hesitantly. 'Will you . . . help us?'

It was a bigger question than it sounded, Rourke knew. Whether or not Tanja was in overall control of the revolution – if anyone was ever in overall control of a revolution, which in Rourke's experience was not the case – the Uragan woman was certainly the one doling out the orders around here. Taking advantage of the information Rourke had provided for free was one thing; asking for help was a concession that she didn't know everything and was, potentially, something that might damage the belief of her followers. And a revolution was nothing without belief.

But that really wasn't Rourke's problem.

She turned to Tanja. 'You understand that this isn't my world and it isn't my fight, and I'm not going to pretend that it is. You help me find my crew and keep them safe, and get us to the spaceport. You'll need to take that anyway, if you want to have a hope of stopping any invasion. You do that, and I will give you any and all advice and information I can.'

'You won't be able to leave until the storm subsides anyway,' one of the younger Uragans spoke up, 'and you said the troops will be overhead by then. How will you get off-world?'

Rourke fixed her with a steady gaze. 'I trust my pilot.' She looked back at Tanja and extended her hand. 'Do we have a deal?'

Tanja clasped her hand firmly. 'Ms Rourke, we have a deal.'

TO THE RESCUE

'They'll have guns too, you know,' Drift said.

Chief Muradov turned away from the officer he'd been speaking to, and glowered. 'Who will?'

'The protesters your people have just opened fire on,' Drift explained, as patiently as he could. 'It wasn't rioters who shot up the squad here, it wasn't people who'd found some guns from somewhere and decided to join a rally, they were in a bar! The protest was just bait to draw your squad in, and then they opened fire from the side!' He spread his hands, trying to look as convincing as possible. 'I'd say you've got a full-blown insurrection on your hands, planned out in advance.'

'The possibility *had* crossed my mind,' Muradov snapped, then frowned. 'Why do you care, anyway?'

'Because my business partner, tech officer and . . .' he searched for a term for Apirana and plumped for '. . . translator are in a hotel next to that protest, and the longer stray bullets go flying around the more likely one of them is to get hurt.'

'Translator?' Muradov's eyes flickered over to the Changs, apparently eliminating possibilities, then cocked an eyebrow quizzically. 'The big man?'

Well, he is very good at making himself understood. Sometimes he doesn't even need to use language. 'He's West Pacific,' Drift said instead, 'speaks Japanese like a native, and has pretty good Indonesian, too.'

'I do not doubt it,' Muradov said dryly, 'but please do not take me for a fool. I am fairly sure that is not his only role on your crew, Captain.' He frowned again, his eyes wandering slightly to the left, and Drift realised he must be listening to a comm report in his ear. Then he looked up again, fixing Drift with a stare. 'However, that is not my concern at present. We are needed elsewhere.' He turned and barked instructions in Russian, pointing at the armoured transports which the mass of *politsiya* with him had arrived in. Three of them quickly started filling up again, while it seemed two units would be left to chase down and disperse any remaining rioters in the local streets.

Drift turned to look over at the Changs, who were standing a little way away with the Shirokovs and generally trying to escape notice. Jia made a gesture that combined hands and eyebrows and somehow managed to eloquently ask what they were going to do now. Drift shrugged. Jia rolled her eyes and used a hand gesture that required no translation.

'Captain,' Muradov said from behind him, 'I need to ask you and your companions to come with me, please. Maximum of two to a vehicle.'

Drift turned, an uncomfortable sensation prickling in his stomach. 'I beg your pardon?'

'Uragan City will shortly be placed under martial law,' Muradov said grimly, rechecking the magazine of his rifle, 'and procedure in martial law is to shoot to kill anyone seen violating curfew.' He looked up and met Drift's eyes. 'You and your companions have no home to go to here, so it would be a dereliction of my duty to leave you in the street.'

Drift pursed his lips. 'And you don't trust me.'

'And, as you say, I do not trust you.' Muradov flashed a thin smile, fast as summer lighting over New Shinjuku. 'You also discharged a firearm at Uragan citizens—'

'Oh come on!' Drift protested. 'I aimed over their heads and I was trying to save some of your people's lives!'

'—and you are fairly distinctive,' Muradov continued firmly. 'Quite frankly, Captain, even if my officers did not shoot you I would half expect one of the rioters to find you and do it anyway. Consider it protective custody if you like, but *get in the damned vehicles.*'

'Well, when you put it like that,' Drift muttered. He turned and gestured to the Changs and the Shirokovs, who made their way over doing a collective impression of a study in variations of reluctance.

'We'll be riding with them,' he informed the others, jerking a thumb over his shoulder at the APC behind him, 'maximum of two in each, so I guess you folks pair off and I'll take this one. It's not negotiable and it's not my idea, so no yelling at me.' He aimed that last at Jia, who narrowed her eyes at him but kept her mouth shut.

'Are we in trouble?' Kuai asked gloomily.

'When aren't we?' Drift grinned at him, but the mechanic didn't seem to take it well. Even Drift had to admit that it was a fairly poor attempt at lightening the mood, so he covered the awkwardness by turning and climbing into the APC by the rear doors.

It wasn't his first experience of being inside a vehicle belonging to law enforcement, unfortunately, but it was certainly the first time he'd been in one of this size or bulk, some unholy cross as it was of bus, truck and tank. There were benches down each side for the riot officers to sit on, a gun rack halfway along each and a ladder in the centre up to the turret. At the far end was a hatchway through to the cab and what looked like a tactical comms station, and seated next to that was Alim Muradov.

'Captain!' he called, beckoning. Drift made his way uneasily over to him, trying to avoid getting in the way of the various officers currently taking up position and strapping themselves into their seats. One or two gave him a strange look as he passed, but he also got a couple of smiles.

'They have heard how you intervened for Sergeant Lukyanenko's squad,' Muradov said quietly, apparently picking up on Drift's confusion at the mixed messages as he sat down next to the security chief. 'It is rare enough that anyone will step in to help us, let alone an off-worlder.'

'Not everyone's heard, apparently,' Drift remarked. One of the larger officers, a middle-aged male with close-cropped ginger hair edging towards grey and a blunt moustache, was still eyeing him uncertainly.

'Oh, they all have,' Muradov smiled, 'but that does not mean all of them trust you. They are *my* officers, after all.' The last member of the team jumped on board and pulled the doors shut behind her, and the man sitting opposite Drift hammered his fist twice on the hatch leading through to the cab. Moments later the engine roared into life and the sirens began to wail, and the big vehicle started rolling forwards.

'Where are we heading, anyway?' Drift asked, fastening the restraints around him and feeling for a moment like he was in his chair back in the *Jonah*'s shuttle, waiting for Jia to perform a spectacularly stupid atmospheric manoeuvre.

'Tsink Ploschadi,' Muradov replied absently, watching a readout on the tactical station. Drift watched coloured dots and icons move slowly over green-on-black grids and presumed it was some sort of display of contacts between *politsiya* units and protesters or rioters, but he didn't know the key and lacked enough knowledge of Uragan City's geography to make head or tail of it. What he did realise as Muradov cycled between screens was that there was one for each level of the city. Some appeared clear of conflict, so far as he could work out, but even so he was impressed at the Uragan's ability to not only apparently make sense of what he was seeing but presumably remember it all.

'Has there been more trouble there?' he asked uneasily, a nasty image jumping into his mind of Jenna crumpled on the floor next to a window with a shattered hole through which a stray bullet had passed. 'I mean, I doubt you're making the trip just to get me back to my hotel.'

'Captain,' Muradov replied with strained patience while he frowned at the display in front of him, 'I am trying to coordinate an operation to return peace and safety to a city of slightly over two million people spread over a dozen levels. I'd appreciate it if you could—'

He broke off suddenly and Drift saw his eyes widen, then he jabbed at a switch on the console and shouted something in Russian. Drift didn't catch all of it, but judging by their sudden increase in speed, something had gone wrong somewhere.

'Was that—?'

'I do not believe that fate can be tempted, and I trust in Allah, not superstition,' Muradov said grimly, casting him a dark look from beneath his brows, 'but that said, Captain, I would appreciate it if you would keep your mouth shut until this issue is resolved.' He turned to the officers riding with them and spoke again. Drift caught the words for *gunfire* and *rebels* and didn't need to ask any further questions. It sounded like someone had employed the same ambush tactic he'd got mixed up in earlier. More and more, he was getting the uncomfortable feeling that he was getting caught in a burgeoning civil war.

Better just hope the other side doesn't have anyone too competent in charge, then.

They cornered sharply – it felt sharp, at least, although with no windows Drift couldn't say for sure – then accelerated again, and he was suddenly grateful for the restraints that prevented him from sprawling across the vehicle and into the lap of the officer sitting opposite. Still, it was nothing compared to flying into a storm system in a shuttle with no power like he'd done on his last visit to Old Earth. On the other hand, he did at least trust Jia's piloting skills and he had no idea about the competence of whoever was driving now.

Of course, whoever it was would have been selected by a system devised by Alim Muradov, who did not strike Drift as a man likely to tolerate the advancement of the unsuitable.

A voice came over speakers, presumably the driver. +Komandir! Barrikada!+

Drift saw Muradov grimace. '*Taran' eto!*' The Uragan security chief turned to him as the other officers held on grimly to their own straps. 'They have constructed a barricade, we are going—'

'—to ram it,' Drift muttered. 'I gathered.' He'd seen the massive dozer blades on the front of Muradov's APCs, and since he very much doubted the Uragans got any snow down here there was only one conceivable use for them.

The speakers crackled into life again, counting down. +Tri, dva, odin . . .+

There was a crunching sound audible even inside the vehicle and it lurched alarmingly, throwing everyone against their straps, but the driver gunned the engine and despite their rapid deceleration, the APC powered through with nothing but an audible scraping sound for a second as some part of whatever had been rigged up was dragged a short distance beneath them. Muradov shouted a command and he and the squad with him slapped their harness releases, snatched up their weapons and got ready to disembark.

'Well,' Drift said to no one in particular, 'that wasn't so ba—'

Something hit the underside of the vehicle like the hammer of a god, and suddenly gravity was at right angles to where it had been a moment ago. Drift fell forwards and downwards but was caught by his crash restraints as the opposite wall suddenly became the floor and the vehicle slid forward on its side, its considerable momentum carrying it onwards with an ear-splitting shriek of tortured metal on stone.

The *politsiya* squad, on their feet and unstrapped, were mashed together to become a pile of bodies beneath him and pelted by items flying off the overhead equipment rack. Alim Muradov was thrown into the tactical comms unit and rebounded off, landing on his back with a bloody gash above his right eye and displaying no obvious signs of consciousness. As they came to a halt, the squeal of their progress was replaced by the muffled but distinctive sound of cheering voices from outside.

And then, as Drift became aware that his neck hadn't liked that whole adventure very much, the cheering was replaced in turn by a hammering on the vehicle's rear doors.

EXPLOSIVES AND THE WILL TO USE THEM

Rourke looked up as an explosion loud enough to rattle the salon's glass in its frames reverberated around the plaza. Some way up the street on the far side of the open space, she could see a crowd of rebels – and they surely were rebels now, not just rioters or protesters – advancing on a large black shape. Her brain took a moment to process it until she realised it was on its side, at which point she recognised it as a standard-issue Red Star urban riot control vehicle.

'What the hell was that?' she asked, perhaps slightly more calmly than she felt. Did Tanja's people have access to a tank they'd failed to mention?

The other woman smiled grimly.

'Mining charge with a magnetic clamp, hidden in a barricade.'

HOW APIRANA GOT HIS ANKLE BACK

He felt like he'd swallowed a fork.

He coughed and the air ripped at his abused throat as it was forced outwards, making him cough again. The motion caused his body to spasm, and *that* produced its own problems because his body felt like it had been attacked with hammers all over, although in an oddly muted way. He reacted in the way he always did to pain.

He lashed out.

He was on his back on something hard and the lights above him were so bright he was nearly blind. He couldn't see much to hit at and he couldn't get much power into his arms, partly because he was lying down and partly because everything seemed to be made of cotton wool, especially his brain. A shadow moved, skittering away from him, and he made a grab for it, which overbalanced him as the edge of whatever he was lying on snuck up on him without warning. He nearly fell, but something grabbed him and pulled him back onto a level. He struggled against that, too, but whatever it was that had hold of him was terrifically, almost immovably strong. Then the shadow he'd grabbed for came back, cautiously, and warbled something. There were words there, but his brain couldn't make sense of them at the moment.

The light dimmed a little, and the shadow's face came into view as his eyes adjusted to the contrast. It had blue eyes, a slightly snub nose and a dusting of freckles on pale skin, framed with slightly reddish-blonde hair. It was a pretty face. He said some words, although he wasn't sure what.

Jenna. It's Jenna.

She pushed something towards his face, her arm seeming to extend crazily as she did so. It was a glass. With water in. He flinched back at first, then reached out a hand for it and became suddenly aware that the pressure that had been holding him back a moment ago had disappeared. He grabbed the glass on the second attempt, but getting the water into his mouth was a little more of a challenge and a fair bit of it leaked out down his chin. However, he managed to swallow enough that his throat felt a little better.

Something tugged at the glass in his hand. It was Jenna. She was saying words again, but he couldn't make them mean anything. He found himself answering in spite of that, but wasn't sure what he'd said and watched her face to see what effect it had had.

Then he fell asleep.

When Apirana came around for the second time his brain still felt slightly fuzzy, but thinking was a lot easier. He seemed to be in some sort of medical unit, not massively dissimilar to the one he'd been stitched up in on the Europan frigate after he'd taken a bullet while storming Kelsier's asteroid base. He raised his head, not without some effort, and looked around.

Jenna was standing several feet away by the wall, watching him with an expression of guarded caution on her face, even though there was a chair next to the . . . bed? Table? Whatever it was he was lying on, anyway – and there was the memory of pressure on his left hand which suggested someone had been holding it.

'What're you doing over there?' he asked, or tried to. The words seemed to come out a bit slurred. However, Jenna's face lit up with a smile and she stepped over to him.

'Last time you woke up you got a bit violent,' she told him matter-of-factly. Her voice buzzed in his head a bit, but at least the words made sense this time. 'General anaesthetic can make people react oddly, so I thought I was better safe than sorry. How're you feeling?'

'Sorry,' he muttered. He remembered now, that sensation of confusion and pain. As if responding to her question the pain suddenly returned, as though his body had been waiting until it was certain his brain would process it properly before offering it up for consideration. 'Ah, bloody hell. I feel like hammered shit.'

'You got sort of . . .' Jenna's face screwed up uncomfortably and she brushed some loose hair absent-mindedly back behind her ear, '. . . trampled.

In the crowd, when you fell over. I tried to get to you, but by the time I . . .'

The movement of her hair had revealed the beginnings of a livid bruise near her right eye. He winced in sympathy, despite his own pain. 'Ow. Your face alright?'

'Hmm?' She suddenly seemed to become aware of it and let her hair fall forwards again. 'Oh. Yeah, it's nothing, don't worry about it.'

Nice going, A. Draw attention to the big bruise, you dumb galoot. 'Sorry, I didn't mean—'

'No, it's fine, I—'

'I'm just still a bit . . .' He waved a hand near his face to try to indicate that everything was all a bit fuzzy. 'Probably don't quite know what I'm sayin', eh?' He smiled, but if anything Jenna looked a little more uncomfortable.

'So,' he said after a couple of seconds of deafening silence, 'I, uh, assume there's a reason I'm . . .?'

'Here?' Jenna finished for him, then shifted uncomfortably. 'Yes, I . . .You mean, you . . . Well, I suppose . . .'

He blinked at her. 'What?'

Her jaw moved for a second, then she pointed towards his feet and mumbled something incomprehensibly quickly.

'Pardon?'

'You broke your ankle! Or, well, someone else broke it, I guess they trod on it when you were on the ground . . .'

He lifted his head again and looked down, or possibly along since he was already on his back. Sure enough, his left boot had been removed and there was a lattice of plastic and metal around the lower part of his leg. The moment his eyes rested on it he became aware of a dull throb of pain from the interior of that limb, something bone-deep and noticeably separate from the other aches that seemed universally external in nature.

'Oh,' he said. He did remember a stabbing sensation of agony in his leg, but by that point he'd taken so many knocks to the head that everything had been somewhat blurred. Which, given the muddled memory he had of helpless pain, he was somewhat grateful for. 'But someone's fixed it up?'

'Yeah.' Jenna looked uncomfortable, then leaned close to him suddenly. For one startled moment he thought she was going to kiss him, which was a prospect he found simultaneously terrifying and exhilarating, but instead she just put her mouth next to his ear. 'Circuit Cult.'

'Oh.' That seemed relevant somehow, but it took his brain a couple of seconds to make the connection. '*Oh*. Uh. Thank you.'

She frowned as she pulled back a little. 'Well, I didn't find them, they found me in the crowd, I—'

'No, I just meant thanks for . . .' He lowered his voice a little and looked around to check there was no one else in the infirmary with them. 'I know how you feel about 'em. Means a lot that you'd stick around.'

'There was no way I was going to leave you alone with them,' Jenna hissed, her eyes flickering towards the door. 'Seriously, A., I know you think I'm paranoid but—'

He reached out and took her hand. 'I get it. I do. I wouldn't wanna be left alone somewhere being operated on by people I didn't know, anyway.' He suddenly registered something cold pressing against the edge of his palm and looked over at Jenna's forearm. Sure enough, her EMP generator was sat in plain view. 'Ah. Not takin' any chances, then?'

'Better safe than sorry,' she muttered again. 'That seems to be my motto, these days?'

'I've heard worse,' Apirana grinned. 'Hell, I wish that'd been *my* motto when I was . . .' *When I was your age*, he'd been going to say, but he abruptly didn't feel like reminding her of their age difference. 'Y'know. Stupider.' He coughed, and winced. 'Man, my throat feels rough.'

'They had air tubes down it, or something,' Jenna told him. She passed him the same glass she had before, now apparently refilled. He made a much better effort of getting the water into his mouth without spilling it or dribbling this time around.

'So,' he said after he'd swallowed a couple of times, 'what's been goin' on outside? You heard from the others?'

'Comms are still down,' Jenna grimaced, 'and there was apparently some sort of power surge on the grid, but the cult's got enough safeguards here that it didn't seem to affect them too much. We don't know what's happening other than apparently there's still a high alert in force and anyone who goes outside is liable to be shot on sight.'

'Say what?!' He broke off into a coughing fit again and took another swallow of water. 'What the hell kind of place is this?'

'It is a mining complex under the control of the Red Star Confederate which supplies resources directly to that government,' a male voice said smoothly to his right, 'and they do not take the security of such places lightly.'

Apirana looked around to see a man standing in the doorway to the infirmary. He was wearing loose red trousers with no shoes despite the cold metal floor and, more strikingly, no shirt. What was visible of his skin was several shades darker than Apirana's own, but much of his upper body was sculpted from metal in a form that mimicked the human thorax were it slightly more angular. As he spoke his chest gently flexed in and out, exposing small areas – also metal – between the pectoral plates in what seemed to be a perfectly natural breathing rhythm. He also had a visor across his eyes, which Apirana assumed was a permanent replacement rather than a fashion statement.

'A.,' Jenna said in a relatively level tone, although he could tell she was still somewhat uneasy, 'this is Kunley. He's the logicator, and the man who arranged for you to be brought here and . . . helped.'

Apirana nodded. He wasn't going to deny that Kunley's mechanical chest gave him the willies a little, but a man had to breathe and he'd had no bad experiences with the Circuit Cult himself, unlike Jenna. 'Well, thanks, mate. I owe you.'

'Actually, you don't,' Kunley said, taking a few steps into the infirmary, 'your friend here saw to that.'

Apirana looked sideways at Jenna. 'Eh?'

'Well, the Cir—' She stopped herself and continued as though she'd said nothing out of turn. 'The Universal Access Movement don't tend to provide things for *free*, just cheap. So I had to—'

'How much?' He asked, narrowing his eyes and looking towards Kunley.

'Five hundred stars,' the logicator replied promptly, 'which covers anaesthetic, the surgery and the materials. Your ankle has been braced with an advanced polymer which should fuse naturally with your bone, and you've been given a healing booster.' He raised his eyebrows slightly. 'I expect you will be unusually hungry over the next few days.'

Apirana grunted. Even with the after-effects of the anaesthetic, doing the mental calculation was easy for someone who'd spent most of his life outside prison moving goods, services and sometimes people between currency zones. 'That's very reasonable. Cheers, bro.' He looked back at Jenna. 'And thank you, as well.'

Jenna shrugged, and possibly blushed a little. 'Well, I didn't spend much of my share on New Samara and I had enough on me . . .' She smiled. 'Besides, I certainly can't carry you.'

'Ain't that the truth,' he muttered. 'Right, then. Healing booster, you said?' He sat up with a groan more theatrical than genuine and waited for the world to start swimming. Which it did, but neither as much nor for as long as he'd feared. He leaned forwards a little and knocked gently on the casing enclosing his ankle and heel. 'Okay, so how long before I can walk on this bad boy?'

'I would advise waiting at least ten days before you stop using crutches,' Kunley replied, nodding towards a pair leaning against the wall, before the blank stare of his visor returned to Apirana again. 'Come to think of it, given your height and build—'

'Don't diss the *puku*, bro.'

'—I would perhaps suggest two weeks,' Kunley finished, unperturbed. 'Unless, of course, you wished for a complete replacement? In that case you could be walking normally again after a day.' The logicator glanced briefly at Jenna, with perhaps the faintest hint of reproach in the set of his mouth. 'You were injured and distressed and we wished to stabilise your condition fast, so we did not wait to ascertain your wishes and Jenna here was very adamant that you should keep your existing foot.'

'Yeah, an' she was right to do so,' Apirana grunted.

'If it's a concern about the cost then we would of course count the fee already paid against any further work—'

'Mate.' Apirana held up his hand. 'I appreciate what you've done, seriously, an' I thank you for it. An' I know that maybe a fancy new robot foot would see me right, but I'm sorta attached to the bits of me what are already here, know what I mean? If it can be fixed up I'm happy for it to be fixed, an' I'll carry on my way.'

Kunley smiled. 'I understand. I once thought as you did. My first augmentation' – he momentarily placed one hand on his metal chest – 'was not a choice, but a necessity. It was only afterwards that I realised the boons further work could give me.'

Apirana smiled a little in return. Circuit Cult equivalent of a priest or not, Kunley had the manner of a born salesman and a voice which was pleasant on the eardrums. Which now he came to think of it, was probably a good set of skills for a priest too. 'What happened? If you don't mind me askin', that is.'

The logicator's face took on a more sombre aspect. 'I was working as a freighter crewman. It was not well paid, but I made enough. However, on one shipping trip we were attacked by pirates who announced themselves with a shot that took out our Alcubierre ring, rendering us unable to flee. Our captain was either in thrall to the prospect of the earnings from his cargo or in fear of his employers should he lose it, as he refused the pirates' demands to launch it in a shuttle for them to collect. So they came aboard and, fearful for our lives, I led the crew in trying to turn them back.'

Apirana winced. A civilian merchantman crew taking on pirates confident enough in their numbers and equipment to risk boarding another vessel was only ever likely to end one way.

'Three of my crewmates died,' Kunley said simply. 'I was shot in the chest three times. When we had surrendered they did not mistreat us further; they simply wanted the cargo as quickly as possible, and before our distress signal brought the authorities down on them. My vessel limped back to the port we had so recently departed from, barely in time for me since our medical facilities were relatively rudimentary.

'The damage to my lungs was too great; I would never breathe properly again unaided. But the Universal Access Movement were able to offer another option for a merchant crewman with little money put aside.'

'So you got a new set of lungs?' Apirana asked. 'Bloody nice of 'em.'

'The experience was enough to change me,' Kunley nodded solemnly. 'I wished to help the Movement help others as it had helped me, so I devoted myself to it. Fifteen years later, and I have become logicator on this planet far from the African systems where I was born.'

'Now, I'm not gettin' at you at all,' Apirana said, 'but I'd have thought that New Samara would've been the obvious place for a logicator, given that's the capital planet.'

Kunley smiled. 'The capital for money and politics, perhaps, but it is on mining and industrial planets where our work is required most urgently. New Samara's farm workers suffer their accidents, it is true, but there is nothing quite so unforgiving as a mine face . . . save open warfare, of course. Uragan City was originally only five levels, and it was here on the deepest level at that time that the Movement chose to establish our headquarters, so we could be the nearest to those who needed us. No, this is where I belong.' He frowned as a chime rang through the air, and looked towards the door. 'Excuse me; I shall return moment-arily. One of my colleagues wishes my attention.'

They watched him go. Then Jenna leaned in close to Apirana again. 'I'm not sure if I just heard a sales pitch or a sermon.'

'Bit of both, maybe,' he grunted, then paused as a nasty thought struck him. 'You don't suppose . . .'

'Hmm?'

'You know?' he said, casting a wary glance at the empty doorway. 'African freighter crew hit by pirates? You don't think it could have been the Captain?'

He saw Jenna's expression change as the possibility dawned on her, but she quickly schooled her features again and lowered her voice. 'I think there's been a hell of a lot of FAS shipping, and a whole lot of pirates going after it. Doesn't mean it was the Captain. More to the point,' she added, padding to the door and looking through it, 'we need to work out what we're going to do now.'

Apirana grimaced. 'Don't see how we've got a lot of choice. We can't call anyone, and I'm too big and slow to play dodge-the-bullet with a bunch of trigger-happy cops, even without a buggered ankle.'

Jenna sighed in frustration, drumming her fingers on the door jamb, then turned around and pulled the sleeve of her top back to reveal the wrist console on her left arm. 'To hell with this. The Spine might still be down, but there's got to be *some* way to find out what's going on.'

Apirana felt a twinge of unease in his sizeable gut. 'I dunno if that's such a good idea, Jenna; won't they be specially on guard against slicers if there's some sort of revolution taking place?'

She fired him a look from under lowered brows. 'Well, what do you suggest then?'

He swung his legs off the table and eyed the crutches resting against the wall. 'I reckon we're best off waiting.'

'*Waiting?* But we don't know what's going on!'

'Seems like a good time not to go walking out into it, then,' Apirana said. His right foot was on the floor now, but he wasn't going to chance standing on the left one and the crutches were out of reach. A quick hop, though . . .

'Oh, for goodness' sake.' Jenna reappeared in his line of sight, crossing the room from the doorway and passing the crutches to him. 'What about the others?'

'If they've got any sense, they'll be lying low,' Apirana told her firmly, 'an' if there's one thing the Captain and Tamara are good at, it's staying alive.' He pushed himself up onto his feet – or foot – and took a couple of practice strides up and down the infirmary. It wasn't the most graceful he'd ever been, but at least he had enough upper body strength that he shouldn't get too tired moving around. 'I just wonder how long—'

Only the faintest of scuffing noises announced Kunley's bare feet on the floor a moment before the man himself reappeared in the doorway, his face creased in concern. 'The situation is grave. The resistance we witnessed in the plaza has escalated, and it appears that a general uprising of the populace is taking place. People are in the streets and there are no *politsiya* to enforce the curfew; the rebels are claiming this area as theirs and say they have destroyed armoured vehicles sent in to put the riot down.'

Apirana looked at Jenna uncertainly. On the one hand, freedom to move around the streets was welcome. On the other, when the authorities came back with more force – and he was damn sure they would – he didn't want to be anywhere on the receiving end of it. He looked back at Kunley, and grimaced when he saw the other man's expression. 'You got a twist to your lip I don't like the look of, bro. That's the bad news, so what's the worse?'

'The rebel group appears to have started door-to-door searches,' Kunley replied, looking straight at him. 'We don't know who or what they're looking for . . . but they're moving in this direction.'

Drift wasn't too worried by the hammering on the doors, unwelcome though it was: it would be a poor riot vehicle that could be easily opened from outside, after all. However, his assessment of the situation changed a moment later when a loud hissing became audible and a spark of white light appeared around the central lock.

Laser torch.

It was depressing, really, the amount of industrial items that could be turned to malicious use by a determined mob.

He hammered at the chest-mounted release button on his straps, but his bodyweight was holding them at their full extent and there wasn't the fraction of give they needed to release. He momentarily considered pleading innocence in the faces of the rioters – or more accurately, guilt – but there was little chance of passing himself off as a prisoner without at least sporting a pair of handcuffs. Besides which, Free Systems rebels were unlikely to be emptying penitentiaries or freeing suspects unless those individuals were affiliated to them. They weren't trying to overturn society, just change government.

Also, he *had* opened fire on some of their allies not half an hour previously.

He couldn't remain strapped helplessly to what was now essentially the ceiling, especially as the centre of the vehicle's door was turning an alarming cherry red. Gritting his teeth, he reached up as high as he could and just managed to hook the fingers of his right hand into the wire of the equipment rack, then got some sort of leverage on what had previously been the floor with the heel of his boots and tried to ease his weight up off the strap buckle. He strained, pressed with his left hand . . .

Click.

Of course, this suddenly presented a new problem. 'Shit!' he bellowed in alarm as his momentary traction fled and gravity reasserted itself. His arms were still hooked into the straps, which he stupidly hadn't been prepared for, and instead of a clean, free-fall drop or hanging athletically for a second before smoothly disengaging, he instead only managed a descent combining the worst parts of both, and landed in a crumpled heap. On the other hand, that still put him considerably better off than Muradov and his riot squad: not one member had managed to regain their feet in the handful of seconds since the crash, nor were they looking likely to in the next few. In fact, several were giving voice to moans or fast, spittle-flecked breathing which Drift would usually associate with the stabbing pains that might accompany broken bones.

Sometimes a noise could be ominous, at other times it was the cessation of one which was most concerning. Such was the case now, when the hissing, spitting song of the laser torch abruptly died away. Either it had run out of charge, which seemed far too fortuitous to be possible, or . . .

One of the rear doors, now running horizontally, was levered outwards and crashed down to form what was effectively a shallow ramp, revealing a worryingly large crowd of legs and feet and letting in a triumphant roar from their accompanying lungs and throats. There was no time to think: Drift grabbed a rifle from the weapon rack that now formed part of the floor, slapped in a magazine and flicked off the safety with his thumb, then dropped into a crouch to get a better angle of fire, braced it against his shoulder and pulled the trigger.

It had been some time since he'd fired an assault rifle. It felt a bit like being punched repeatedly in the shoulder by a Wing Chun expert, and in the enclosed vehicle the roar of the action bordered on painful.

By some miracle he managed to keep the barrel more or less level and avoided hitting the other door that was still hanging down across half of the opening, which would have resulted in potentially lethal ricochets inside. Instead, the hail of fire tore across the legs of the rioters, with dramatic consequences. He probably didn't actually hit that many – even close together there was still a lot of space between legs for the bullets to fly into – but three Uragans fell screaming and the ones he hadn't hit fled abruptly rather than risk their knees. One of his three victims had caught another bullet somewhere more fatal as they fell, judging by her lack of movement, and a second had rolled desperately away out of his line of fire. That left him staring down the barrel of the assault rifle at a dark-haired young man, possibly in his early twenties, howling in pain and clutching at his blood-spattered trouser leg.

And with the pistol he'd been holding lying on the Uragan rock floor, still in easy reach.

What did he do? The kid had already dropped his weapon, albeit involuntarily. An instruction not to move was unlikely to be obeyed by someone who'd just taken a bullet in the leg, and Drift couldn't put the correct Russian phrasing together off the top of his head anyway. He was left with the option of shooting the youth dead, or waiting for him to become a threat again and *then* shooting him dead. He hesitated for a second in agonised indecision. *Damn it, this was easier when I was younger and less moral.*

The *politsiya* had wisely been keeping their heads down when he'd been firing, but now a couple of seconds had passed with no further shots, one or two of them had started to stir. The large man who'd been looking at him oddly before raised himself painfully up onto his elbows, looked at Drift, looked out of the door at the writhing rioter, looked back at Drift, then drew his own pistol and shot the kid twice.

Drift blinked. *Well, I guess he* was *involved in crashing this thing. Probably.* 'Ah, to hell with it,' he grunted aloud, and turned around to look at Chief Muradov who was sitting up and holding his bleeding head. 'You alright?'

Muradov responded with an emotion-laden burst of Russian, then gritted his teeth. 'No, I am *not* "alright"! We have just been ambushed! A *politsiya* armoured vehicle has been attacked! This is not a riot, these people have started a war! Do you understand me? They have started a *war*!' He pulled himself to his feet, using the tactical console which had knocked him out as a handhold. Drift realised with surprise that Muradov didn't look angry. Instead, the security chief looked to be on the verge of tears, and his next words contained only bitter sorrow.

'It is a war they cannot win.'

'You don't seem as happy about that as I'd have expected,' Drift offered.

'Captain, I have *seen* war,' Muradov bit out, 'and I have no wish to bring it down on the people I've sworn to protect. But this' – he gestured at the riot vehicle and his team, some of whom were now getting to their feet – 'this cannot be smoothed over and explained away to the governor.' He pushed past and shouted something Russian at his team in a manner that had more than a little military bearing to it, now Drift came to think about it.

Seven of the officers were now upright but three had remained on the floor, one of them unmoving and with his head at an angle that looked very unhealthy. Drift averted his gaze, feeling slightly sick, which meant he was looking directly at the hatch through to the cab when it fell open with a bang and the somewhat shell-shocked driver clambered through to find herself confronted with a blue-haired Mexican holding an assault rifle.

'Whoa!' Drift nearly dropped the gun as the woman wrenched her pistol out, stopped himself just in time when he remembered the safety was off and settled for raising one hand and using the other to hold his weapon at arm's length, pointing downwards. 'Chief?!'

'*Nyet, Vazirov!*' Muradov barked, and the driver – clearly rather surprised – stopped bringing her gun to bear.

'Thanks,' Drift muttered, then gestured at the rifle with his free hand. 'Uh, about this . . .'

'Captain, you have saved the lives of members of my force twice now,' Muradov said, picking up and loading an identical weapon without looking at him. 'So far as I am concerned, you can keep it until we are out of danger.' He barked more orders in Russian, ones which saw two of the able-bodied officers move to assist both of the downed wounded, then beckoned to Drift. 'In fact, come up here.'

'I'm not going to like this, am I?' Drift asked rhetorically, making his way to the Uragan's side.

'None of us will, I imagine,' Muradov admitted, tapping the comm in his ear, 'but the driver of the vehicle following says that there was no shot fired to knock us over. It must have been a trap planted in the barricade, and since the rebels could not know exactly where we would ram through it, there are likely to be more in the wreckage. The other teams dare not follow to get to us in case their transports are similarly damaged, so *we* must get to *them.*'

Drift swallowed nervously. 'So we're meant to run through a potentially booby-trapped barricade in an area of town where it seems everyone's out to get us?'

'That appears an accurate summary, yes,' Muradov nodded, 'although if we head for where this vehicle drove through, then any trap in that immediate area may at least have already detonated.' He frowned and looked back at Drift. 'I have to wonder, Captain, how an off-worlder caught up in all this remains so calm.'

Drift shrugged. 'I've made a career out of never quite being killed by everything around me going wrong.'

Muradov nodded. 'Admirable. You take 90 to 180 degrees.'

'I . . . what?' Drift blinked, then realised what Muradov had meant. 'Three o'clock to six o'clock. Right?'

The *politsiya* captain turned to look at the rest of his squad, settled a riot helmet in place over his head and pointed at the door in front of them. '*Vidvigaisya!*'

It was a strange sensation, trying to burst quickly and aggressively through what was now essentially a giant, half-length pet door. Drift wheeled to his right as soon as he was through and brought his borrowed rifle up to sweep the dimly lit street, letting the corner of the door rest on his right shoulder to try to make it easier for the officers supporting their injured colleagues. Not that he had any particular attachment to the wounded, but if he was going to get into even the dubious safety of another vehicle he needed to be with this group, and that meant he needed to ensure they all moved as fast as possible.

'Clear!' he shouted, trying to look everywhere at once but fairly certain he hadn't missed anything.

There were no other barricades or improvised fire screens set up, and the various windows that passed under the roving barrel of his gun stayed reassuringly empty. He could see movement on the plaza at the end of the street, but that was some distance away and none of it appeared to be focused on them. However, that caused an ugly question to bubble to the surface in his mind. 'Muradov! Are you still planning on heading to help out your boys on the plaza over there?'

'Keep your mind on the job!' Muradov shouted back, his voice rendered slightly metallic by the speakers on his helmet.

'Just checking whether I want to get into another of your cars, is all!' Drift replied, taking a few cautious steps backwards as the party began an agonisingly slow 'dash' away from their wrecked vehicle. He was terrified he was going to trip and fall during his backtracking, but he was damned if he'd turn around to see where he was going and let some Uragan rebel pop up to shoot him in the back.

'I have ordered anyone there who can still hear me to stand down,' Muradov replied heavily. 'We are pulling back to Level Four.'

Drift cursed under his breath. For all the risks involved, an armour-plated ride to his hotel's front door had seemed like his best chance of getting back in touch with Rourke and the others, but now that option was being taken from him. With no comms and no *politsiya* escort, he had no clue how he'd find them again. For a moment he considered grabbing the Changs and heading off in search of the other half of his crew anyway, but—

There was a flash from around the corner of what looked like some sort of shop and the air was torn by the report of a gunshot. Drift ducked instinctively and then, belatedly, fired back. His volley of shots tore holes in the wall near where the attack had come from, but a second after he released his trigger again a dark shape edged out just enough to aim a gun once more.

And promptly collapsed backwards as a single shot rang out.

Drift turned, despite himself, to see Muradov lowering his rifle. The *politsiya* captain barked another order and the group stumbled into movement again; Drift followed a second later, more certain than ever that when Chief Alim Muradov said he'd seen war, he hadn't been employing a metaphor.

They'd nearly reached the barricade now, a ramshackle collection of furniture and miscellaneous metal items, plus at least one door. It had stretched across most of the street at a crossroads, but there was a hole in it where their vehicle had punched through and the detritus from that impact was now making their footing troublesome. On the other side, with rear doors facing their group and turrets rotated so the water cannons and linked guns were covering them, were the other two armoured transports.

Drift, casting nervous glances over his shoulder, had half expected Muradov to send someone else through first in case another trap was detonated. Instead, still covering the twelve-to-three angles of their retreat, the *politsiya* captain made a dash for it and fetched up against the rear of the right-hand vehicle before anyone inside could even get the door open. The driver of their transport, who'd ended up taking the nine-to-twelve quarter, made it through next, followed by the two injured officers and their minders.

Drift had had enough. He turned and ran for the beckoning safety of the transports' opening doors, eager to put as much metal between himself and any incoming bullets as he could. Hell, he didn't even have a problem with these people! He was just trying to make a living and they had to go and have a damn revolution while he and his crew were—

Something hit him in the back like a thunderbolt, and he fell.

DECONSTRUCTING THE STATE

Tanja hadn't been exaggerating about the populace rising for the rebellion, Rourke noted. The protest in the plaza had melted away in the face of gunfire, it was true, but that wasn't necessarily surprising. However, there was almost a party atmosphere now that the security forces had been 'subdued' (most of them not fatally, she was pleased to see) and their reinforcements driven away, and the amount of people out in the streets with pro-independence placards and banners or just generally rejoicing was quite telling. Tanja was instructing everyone to announce that Level Five was now free of Red Star rule, which seemed slightly premature but was probably good for general morale, and reports trickling in from the lower levels suggested that similar things were occurring further underground.

'What we need to do now,' Rourke said, puzzling over a diagram of Uragan City's various levels, 'is to spread the word.'

'We have people on the streets,' Tanja replied, gesturing outside. They were on the first floor of a *politsiya* station which had turned out to be not far from Tsink Ploschadi, and which had apparently decided that opening its doors and playing nice was preferable to undergoing a siege. Rourke had immediately suggested it should be requisitioned as the new state's headquarters. This had been opposed by some, who'd argued that they wanted to distance themselves from the Red Star regime, but Rourke had pointed out that people tended to react to a change better if they had at least some familiar reference points. Besides, she'd added, the cells were a handy place to put the *politsiya* officers who'd surrendered until it could be decided what to do with them, and it would be good to have the armoury under their direct control.

That last point in particular had seemed to swing it.

'People on the streets is fine, up to a point,' Rourke said carefully, 'it shows that we're not scared of reprisals. Still, this isn't the twentieth century; we need to be broadcasting to everyone. Civilian comms are down, so unless people see us from their windows they won't know what's happening, and the government are probably playing this down as much as they can on the official channels.'

Tanja nodded, tapping one finger on her lips. 'We can probably get to the official broadcast wires and disable them. Once people are not hearing the government anymore they will know that something is happening.'

'It would be better if you could use them yourself,' Rourke pointed out. 'Everyone will know that the government imposes a communication blackout when there's any sort of disruption taking place. Imagine the impact it would have if you started broadcasting through that and announce your new state. They wouldn't be able to pretend it was all under control then.'

'That would be lovely,' Tanja said dryly, 'but you have to understand who we are. Most of us are miners. I've been a shift supervisor for twelve years. If we ask for people to build a barricade, or make a bomb from a mining charge, or fight for us, they will do it. But if your holoset or your comm goes wrong, you take it back to the shop. I doubt there are many people in the revolution who would know about broadcasting equipment.'

'There's a transmission hub on this level,' Rourke said, spinning the plans around with a sweep of her finger along the holoboard. 'It'll be standardised gear; there must be *someone* who can work it.'

'Probably Uptowners,' Tanja replied, jabbing a finger towards the ceiling. 'It is mainly us workers down here, and you do not get time to learn fancy skills when you work fourteen-hour shifts. I only speak English because my parents saved for lessons and insisted I learn as a child.'

Us workers. Rourke managed not to snort in derision. This sounded like it was a class uprising as much as anything else, but while maintaining the city's communications network didn't exactly match up to working at a mine face in terms of hard graft, she also doubted that the techs were swimming in money. Still, Tanja had played into her hands and Rourke didn't care whether this revolution took once she and the rest of the *Keiko*'s crew were clear.

'So we pull specs off the Spine and do it ourselves,' she shrugged, as though it were nothing. To be sure, even on a relative backwater like Uragan the Spine would contain an enormous amount of data, including innumerable manuals and user guides. However, there was one problem.

'The Spine is blocked off by the security protocols,' Tanja told her, sounding quite surprised that Rourke hadn't worked this out for herself.

'Well then,' Rourke replied, looking up with a smile, 'we need a slicer, don't we?'

Which was how Rourke, holding a Crusader 920 donated to her by the revolution since her own was still locked up on board the *Jonah*, was able to begin leading an organised search party for her crew. It wasn't that she didn't trust Tanja not to go back on her word, but each of them were smart enough to know that theirs was a marriage of convenience and Rourke wanted to bump her partner's side of the deal up the priority chain somewhat. Besides, having an expert slicer with a somewhat cavalier attitude to things like governmental authority was practically essential for a revolution. It wouldn't solve every problem, but it would reduce the pile considerably.

It was as she was leaving the *politsiya* station at the head of half a dozen of the revolution's best English-speakers that she caught sight of Ricardo Moutinho and his cronies. They were standing in the street and were clearly doing their best to smile and look cheerful as groups of Uragans bustled past in knots of nervous, excited energy, but every time they thought no one was watching they returned to a sullen huddle. Rourke weighed them up for a second then beckoned to her escort's leader, a grey-haired, retired spaceport worker named Nikita, and mustered her best Russian. '*Can you please start making enquiries around here? I need to speak to these people.*'

Nikita looked startled. '*I didn't know you spoke Russian. Tanja asked for English-speakers.*'

Rourke shrugged. '*Not all my crew do, and you may need to explain to them who you are. We are looking for a tall Mexican man with blue hair, a dark-haired Chinese brother and sister, a white American girl with blonde hair and a very big Maori man with facial tattoos and a shaved head.*'

Nikita nodded. '*We'll start asking.*'

'*Thank you.*' Rourke watched them drift off up and down the street, accosting people as they went, then strode over to her fellow off-worlders with her new rifle rested casually across her shoulders.

'What the fuck do you want?' Moutinho snarled as she approached.

'Best mind your language,' Rourke advised him mildly, 'you're talking to the revolution's chief advisor now.'

'I still want to know how the hell you span that bullshit,' Moutinho snorted. 'You're going to regret it when they figure out you're a fraud.'

'Why don't you let me worry about that?' Rourke asked. She frowned at the four of them: Moutinho, Jack, Skanda and the kid whose name she still hadn't picked up. 'You're running a smaller crew than you used to, Ric.'

'The others'll be along,' Moutinho replied, but the suddenly expressionless cast to his face told her everything she needed to know.

'With no comms, and fighting on the streets? I doubt it.' She glanced over her shoulder to check her escort had cleared the area, then leaned in a little closer to Moutinho. 'Truth is, I don't know where a damned one of mine are and I'm thinking you might be in the same predicament.'

'And you're telling me this because . . .?'

Rourke sighed. 'Neither of us planned to be caught up in this, you numbskull. I'm playing nice with the big bad revolutionaries because I don't give a shit who owns this planet, but I *do* need their help to find my crew so I can leave it as fast as possible.'

'You really think that all this is gonna help?' Jack threw in, arms folded and face stern.

'I was just being an innocent bystander until your captain here decided to blow my cover,' Rourke bit out, nodding at Moutinho. 'Then the head of the revolution that *you've* been supplying said I needed to die, and when someone decides to kill me I try to find a way to persuade them not to. So, I'm taking it you didn't realise that they were going to kick off their party here and now, when some of yours were elsewhere?'

'Hell, if I'd known this is what they were planning I wouldn't have even come back to this shithole,' Moutinho growled. 'I thought we were supplying a gang or something, not getting mixed up in *politics*.'

'Here's what I'm suggesting, then,' Rourke said, lowering her voice further and speaking fast. 'Help me look for my crew; they shouldn't be *that* hard to find. You help me with that and I'll talk to Tanja about helping you find your lost lambs. While we're at it, we all keep an eye out on what's going on and which way the wind is blowing, and we all try to get off here as soon as we can.' She looked from one to another, trying to meet their eyes. 'We're all off-worlders, we've got no loyalty to anyone here, and this is a bad thing to be mixed up in. I think we need to stick together.'

'You're saying you'd sell out this "revolution" if it came to it?' Jack asked, so quietly Rourke could barely hear him.

'I'm saying,' she replied with a meaningful look at Moutinho, 'that I'm a businesswoman, and business is looking better elsewhere.'

'Ain't that the truth,' Moutinho muttered. 'How do we know you can hold up your side of the bargain, though?'

'Out of the five of us,' Rourke retorted dryly, 'who has the revolution trusted enough to give a gun to?'

'C'mon, boss,' Skanda piped up, 'I think she's got a point.'

'You can shut up,' Moutinho snapped, rounding on his crewman and causing him to flinch back. 'It's your damn fault we're in this mess!'

'Actually,' Rourke offered, 'if he hadn't brought me in there then this revolution would already be faltering and you'd still be standing around wondering where your crewmates were, only you'd also be more likely to get arrested very soon.' She shrugged. 'I'm not saying I can give them success, but I might be able to swing it long enough for us all to get away while we're still flavour of the month.'

'Oh, fine,' Moutinho growled, and stuck out a hand with visible reluctance. 'But if you double-cross us, I swear I'll take your head off.'

'Noted.' Rourke shook his hand and fought the instinctive urge to wipe her palm on her bodysuit afterwards. It still perplexed her that she'd ever been to bed with this man, although admittedly it had more been out of curiosity than desire, and the experience had squashed her curiosity fairly comprehensively. It wasn't that he was physically unattractive as such, but his personality was so abhorrent that it almost polluted everything else about him. 'The only member of my crew you haven't seen is Kuai, the brother of the Chinese girl in that bar. They'll probably be together anyway, and with Ichabod; around here I'm *hoping* to find Jenna and Apirana.'

'I think we know what that big *babaca* looks like,' Moutinho grunted, a sentiment that seemed to be shared by his crew judging by the uncomfortable shuffling from Skanda and the kid. 'Okay, Skanda goes with Jack. Achilles, you're with me.'

Achilles? Rourke shrugged mentally as the skinny pale youth sloped over to Moutinho's side. There was simply no accounting for parents. 'So that I know, who are *you* looking for?'

'My first mate Lena and a guy called Dugan,' Moutinho said. His tone was all business now; the man might hold grudges, but he was able to keep his feelings in check when he wanted to. Rourke had worked enough deals with people she hadn't cared for personally to know that was a valuable skill when you were a freelance crew taking work where you could find it. 'They're both white American,' Moutinho continued. 'Lena's kind of wiry, dark hair, got a scar down on cheek. Dugan's a big guy, with quite long, brown curly hair.'

'Got it.' Rourke mentally filed the information away, then pointed back towards Tsink Ploschadi. 'I last saw Jenna and Apirana on the square, before we got separated, so I'm going to start there and try to find someone who saw them.'

'You wouldn't think it'd be hard,' Moutinho snorted, looking at his wrist chrono. 'Okay, Achilles and I are going this way,' he pointed into the narrow streets just off the main promenade they were currently on, then jerked his thumb in the opposite direction. 'Skanda and Jack go that way. We'll meet back here in half an hour, or as soon as you find anyone.'

Rourke watched them go. It wasn't exactly the help she'd have wished for, but beggars couldn't be choosers and she'd meant what she'd said to Moutinho: so far as she was concerned, any off-worlders on Uragan right now would do well to stick together. The Brazilian's crew might have been rivals and enemies of the *Keiko*'s, but the very same initiative and ability which made them so annoying as rivals would make them useful allies if needed. She just had to hope that A. or Jenna would stop to listen if they were hailed instead of punching someone in the face or running for it.

And where the hell is Ichabod? She shunted the thought away, slung the Crusader across her shoulders by the strap and started to trudge back towards Tsink Ploschadi. One thing at a time. Drift was a born survivor and she wouldn't be surprised to find him sheltering in a bar somewhere, having commandeered a bottle of the most tolerable whisky he could find. Probably seducing a barmaid while he was at it, if she knew him. Meanwhile, the Changs weren't the type to take unnecessary risks so long as Jia wasn't in a pilot's chair. They'd keep their heads down and ride it out.

She hoped.

CAT AND MAORI

Jenna felt her mouth go dry, but forced herself to remain calm. 'There's no reason for them to be looking for us. They're probably searching for hidden *politsiya* officers, or something.'

'As you say,' Kunley replied, although neither his voice nor his face held much certainty. 'You have no connection with either the rebels or with the government here?'

'Hell no,' Apirana rumbled, sitting down again. 'Sure, we all got picked up by the cops on some gun-runnin' charge, but it got dropped when they realised it weren't us.'

'Unless . . .' Jenna thought furiously, but the logic appeared to be alarmingly sound. 'What if Moutinho's crew were the real gunrunners?'

'Sounds feasible,' Apirana grunted, his tattooed face frowning, 'what're you thinkin'?'

'If they're the real gunrunners, then that means they're in with the rebellion,' Jenna said, growing more alarmed even as she explained it. 'If they are, then what if they've decided to paint us as some sort of . . . government spies, or something? Yeah, we got arrested earlier, but then we all got released without charge.'

Apirana grimaced. 'I wish I could say you're wrong, but you might just be right. I can imagine that *kai kurakura* spinnin' it to say that we got let out because we cut a deal to report back, or something. It's not like there ain't bad blood between us.'

'You think you may be in danger?' Kunley asked. He sounded concerned, but Jenna was willing to bet that the concern wasn't solely for them. The Circuit Cult here had treated them kindly and fairly, so far as she could tell, but there was a difference between taking someone in to attend to an injury for a reasonable payment and denying entry to armed rebels.

She looked at Apirana. 'Can you move if you have to?'

'Hell, I got three legs now instead of two,' the Maori snorted. 'Can't promise I'll be quick, but that ain't exactly news.'

Jenna turned back to Kunley. 'Do you have a back door?'

'Of course,' the logicator replied, looking dubious, 'but he really shouldn't be—'

'A.'s lived through worse than a broken ankle before,' Jenna assured him, casting around quickly to check that they'd left nothing important around. She picked up the two satchels of rescued belongings and slung them across her shoulders, one resting on each hip so she was as well-balanced as possible.

'Yeah, I'm hard as, me,' Apirana chuckled, although there wasn't a great deal of humour in it. He levered himself back up onto his crutches and nodded to her. 'You wanna make a move?'

'Sooner seems better than later,' Jenna agreed. She pulled up a map of Uragan City on her wrist console, grateful for her own foresight in taking it off the Spine as soon as they'd arrived and before it had been blocked off.

'This is surely foolishness,' Kunley said, worry now clearly audible in his voice. 'You don't even know what these rebels want!'

'An' by the time we do it'll be too late, if what they want is us,' Apirana pointed out.

'Besides, if the police aren't around to shoot people on the streets then there's no reason we can't try to find our crew,' Jenna added. She fixed the logicator with a level look. 'Thanks for fixing Apirana's ankle, but it's best that we go now. For you as well as us.'

'Yeah, that way you can say we're not here and you ain't lyin',' Apirana said. He took a couple of crutch-assisted steps towards the door, then stopped and looked around at Jenna with an embarrassed expression. 'Uh . . . you got my other boot anywhere? I might need it sometime.'

Jenna couldn't help but laugh, and patted her left satchel. 'Don't worry, big guy, I've got your boot.'

'Well, they're good boots,' Apirana muttered, although Jenna had no idea why he felt the need to justify himself any further.

'This way, then,' Kunley said, apparently resigned to their decision. The logicator spun on his heel and turned right out of the doorway, padding barefoot down the corridor which was walled in white, with the intricate gold filigree of the Universal Access Movement's stylised circuit design etched into the walls. Jenna knew from having made the anxious journey in watching over Apirana that each of the several other doors off it led to a surgery bay.

'Easy, bro!' Apirana called after him. He was making good speed on his crutches, but it was obviously faster than was comfortable for him and Jenna felt a surge of annoyance directed at Kunley: the man worked to fix people up, surely he should be a bit more understanding about their limitations afterwards? However, the logicator turned right again through a swing door and stopped, holding it open for them as they approached.

'Through there,' he said, pointing with his free arm towards another door, marked with what Jenna guessed was the Russian for 'Fire Exit'. 'That leads into an alley at the rear. Turn left and it will take you to the next street over.'

'Thanks, mate,' Apirana said earnestly, pausing for a moment to grab the other man's shoulder with one massive hand, his crutch trapped awkwardly under one arm. 'Best of luck to you.' Then he swung off towards the external door, leaving Jenna face-to-face with Kunley and his unreadable visor. She hesitated for a moment, and her stammer of uncertain gratitude was brought up short by the logicator raising his hand.

'Please. I can see that you do not trust the Movement, and I know that there are certain . . . *extremists* . . .

whose actions have caused us all to be painted in a bad light.' He took a deep breath, the metal plates of his chest flexing and sliding over each other. 'I just wish you to remember that although we may have less of our original bodies than you, we are no less human.'

Jenna felt her cheeks heating. Kunley only had his metal chest because he'd been shot, and it seemed cruel and unfair to mistrust someone on the basis of a life-saving operation . . . *but that could just be a story he tells. And he didn't need to join the cult afterwards.*

'Thanks for fixing A.'s leg,' she managed, then turned to hurry towards where Apirana was shuffling through the exit while trying not to knock his bad ankle on anything. She heard the other door close behind her, but didn't look around.

'You still think the Circuit Cult's so bad?' Apirana asked, shouldering the door open wider for her to step through. Sure enough, they were in a narrow alley which apparently consisted of the back doors of the various properties around them. The UAM's Uragan headquarters was no taller than anything else – every building was three storeys high and joined the roof at that point, which had apparently been denoted as the optimum height for one level of the city by some past architect – but it made up for that by being fairly wide. However, there were no stylised circuit representations on the rear walls and no shiny white lacquer. Instead, it was simply hewn with laser-edged precision from the grey Uragan rock and the door marked with a small plaque bearing Cyrillic script. On either side, and facing them, were the rears of less expansive properties: mainly retail outlets, judging by the rubbish that had accumulated in the narrow, poorly lit space.

'I just don't trust them,' Jenna replied honestly, letting the door swing shut behind her and feeling some of the nebulous tension that had been bothering her for the last few hours dissipate slightly. 'I mean, this lot seemed fine – weird, but fine – but I don't trust the *cult* itself. Do you know what I mean?'

'Uh-huh.' That was a fairly non-committal response for Apirana, and she looked up into the big Maori's face.

'What?'

'I dunno.' He made an awkward twitch of his shoulders, the closest he could come to a shrug while on crutches. 'What about if you're being unfair? I mean, I know the cult are a bit weird, but they listened when you told 'em not to put a new foot on me an' it's not like they shoved a load of metal into you, either.'

'It's . . . look, that's not the point,' Jenna replied, turning away from him. She really didn't want to get into an argument with Apirana, especially not here and now, but he appeared in her field of vision again with a swing of his body.

'I think it is,' he rumbled, his tone of voice reasonable enough but apparently either ignorant or uncaring of the fact that she didn't want to talk about this. 'If people keep not acting like you expect them to act, maybe your expectations are wrong.'

'Oh?' she snapped, whipping around to face him. 'And why do *you* care about the cult so much?'

He recoiled slightly, looking surprised at her vehemence, but then his eyes narrowed and his cheeks set in an expression of stubbornness which she recognised. 'Look, I got no thoughts much one way or the other about the circuitheads, but you obviously do. I'm just suggesting that maybe you don't need to worry so much.'

Jenna tried hard not to roll her eyes. 'So you're telling me what I should and shouldn't worry about?'

'I'm telling you,' Apirana said, and now his voice really *was* a rumble, like one of Franklin Minor's rare atmospheric storms, 'as someone who's been on the receiving end of more than his fair share of mistrust an' prejudice, I don't like seeing good deeds brushed off.' He gestured at his *moko* with one hand. 'A lot of people see these, my culture, my heritage, an' *still*, they think it makes me a savage. They expect one thing from me an' I do my best not to give it to 'em, but you know that if I *do* get in a fight it'll only be what they expect, an' if I *don't* then they'll just assume the fight'll happen somewhere else, some other time where they don't see it.'

Jenna knew that what she should do – what *they* should do – was head out of the alley and try to track down Rourke or the Captain, or preferably both. That went double for the fact that the rebels were apparently nearby looking for *something* and they had no idea exactly what it was. But she just couldn't let that lie.

'It wasn't a *good deed*, A., I paid them for it!'

'I remember – sort of – being carried off that square,' Apirana replied, 'and there ain't no way you could've hauled my carcass to wherever the hell we are now. So that was with some panicking crowd, and gunshots and gas and I don't know what else going on, and they still decided to stick around to help two off-worlders they'd never seen before because one of them had fallen like a damn fool and broke his ankle.' He shook his head. 'Five hundred stars don't cover that sort of danger.'

'Some of them *not* being assholes doesn't make their cult any less creepy!'

'But just because you've met some creepy ones don't mean that—'

'Damn it, A.!' She was shouting now, but she didn't care. Apirana had been the one person on the crew whom she had really and truly counted as a friend, and now he was being infuriating and confusing in equal measure. 'Do you think I'm just some dumb rich kid who looks down her nose at everyone?!'

His expression abruptly shifted from stubborn to aghast. 'What? No, I—'

'These . . . "*people*" abducted my friend! A girl I was studying with was grabbed on her way out of college by circuitheads and I *never saw her again*! Don't you *dare* try to tell me their fucked-up cult might not be as bad as I think it is! It's probably *worse*!' She stepped back, biting her lip to keep from saying more.

Apirana's lips narrowed and he turned his head slightly, as though eyeing the building behind him. 'Maybe we should get moving.'

Jenna nearly hit him. She'd been trying to get him to move away and stop talking but he'd provoked her into what, okay, had possibly been an unwise outburst given where they were standing . . . and now *he* wanted to say it was time to move?

'Fine.' She turned away from him and started to walk towards where the alley bent at right angles to meet the next street over. Behind her, she heard a shuffle of crutches and Apirana's one good foot.

'Jenna! Damn it, hold on!'

She was possibly moving faster than she needed to and, yes, she'd been annoyed at Kunley earlier for doing the same thing and, yes, it was possibly petty, but . . . she'd been so *worried* about him! She'd never seen Apirana look so helpless, even when she'd been watching over the camera system on Kelsier's asteroid and had seen him get shot. And then he'd woken up and . . . well, it wasn't that she was unhappy he was up and around again, far from it, but did he have to be so damned contrary?

She followed the alley to the right, avoiding a discarded packing crate and some smashed glass, and stepped cautiously out into the substantially wider street it led onto.

'Hey!'

The shout came from her right and she couldn't prevent herself from whirling around guiltily. When she did so she found herself only a few paces away from a familiar-looking, skinny pale youth wearing overalls which left the tribal tattoo on his right arm visible.

Shit.

She backed hastily down the street and across the mouth of the alley, away from the member of Moutinho's crew whom she'd last seen in Cherdak. He advanced after her, one hand outstretched and his mouth starting to form the first syllable of another word.

'*Hoi!*'

The only audible word, however, came from the throat of Apirana just before he erupted from the alley mouth about as fast as a human could reasonably move on crutches. Moutinho's crewman had just enough time to turn towards him, which in turn gave Apirana a larger target for the thunderous kick he unleashed with his good leg that caught the youth square in the chest, much like he had in Cherdak. The difference in their respective masses was so great that the youth was sent sprawling to the ground while Apirana simply killed his momentum enough to land on his foot with a satisfied grunt. He looked towards Jenna and his face twisted in alarm at the same moment as she became aware of the presence of someone behind her. She whirled and lashed out instinctively, and the heavy metal casing of the EMP generator on her right forearm collided with someone's skull.

'*Puta de merda!*'

Ricardo Moutinho staggered sideways on unsteady legs, clutching at his face. His situation didn't improve much when Apirana crutched up to him, readjusted his grip on one of his supports to hold it like a club, measured the *Jacare*'s stricken captain for a moment and then swung his improvised weapon with enough force to take Moutinho off his feet completely. Jenna took a couple of quick steps to Apirana's side and gave him a shove towards a narrow street on the other side of the main concourse on which they'd come out.

'Over there, go!'

Even when the big Maori was on crutches it was still somewhat akin to trying to push a wall, but thankfully Apirana was rather more amenable to suggestion and he hobbled off with her following after. She looked around, but apart from the two floored gunrunners everyone in sight looked like a Uragan native. That wasn't a massive comfort, however: their brief scuffle had attracted a lot of interest and Apirana on crutches was even more distinctive than usual, which was saying something.

'So where now?' Apirana huffed from ahead of her. His best pace was little more than a jog for her, but it was better than nothing. She checked her map.

'Take a right at the next street. That'll take us towards a justice station, maybe the rebels will be steering clear of that.'

'Never thought I'd see us runnin' *towards* the cops,' Apirana grunted as they passed another narrow alley to their right. 'Still, needs must, eh?'

Needs must, indeed. Jenna wondered for a moment what her parents would think if they could see her now. Apirana might have spent most of his life on the wrong side of the law, but she'd grown up being taught that the purpose of the justices was to keep people like her safe from the dangerous, the criminal and the poor (which in her father's opinion were usually one and the same), and yet since joining the *Keiko*'s crew she'd broken most laws she could think of. As a teenager she'd always maintained that her increasing interest in slicing had been due to an interest in getting a job as a security tester. However, they normally waited to be contracted before finding out how easy it was to break into an organisation's records whereas she . . . well, by that point she certainly hadn't been fooling herself anymore.

Still, even that was a long way from being part of a smuggler crew and running from revolutionaries in a Red Star mining town. But she'd needed to get off the Franklins somehow and the *Keiko* had been her only way out, so . . . *needs must.*

She placed a restraining hand on Apirana's shoulder, holding the big man back as they approached the next junction. 'Hold up a second, let me look first.'

'Not complaining,' the Maori puffed, coming to a grateful halt. Jenna slipped past him and sauntered out into the street, as casually as she could manage with her heart pounding, and cast her eyes down the street towards the *politsiya* station. She was hoping to see a quiet, law-abiding street, but her stomach sank when she saw the station's doors thrown wide and the yellow-and-black flags of the Free Systems flying from its windows with a group of armed civilians milling around in front of it.

'Shit!' she hissed, retreating back into the side street while trying to look like she'd simply realised that she'd come the wrong way.

'Problem?' Apirana muttered.

'It looks like that's their damn headquarters!' Jenna told him, trying to fight down the frustration building inside her. Why the hell was the galaxy against her today? To make matters worse, an elderly Uragan woman was already eyeing her suspiciously from across the street. She turned to Apirana. 'Back the way we came and into that alley on the left, casual as you can.'

'Next time we see the Captain, remind me to yell at him for bringing us here,' Apirana grunted, turning and hobbling in the direction she'd indicated. He cut left into the alley and she followed him in, then grabbed the back of Apirana's jumpsuit as they passed another opening to their left.

'In here!'

Apirana looked at it dubiously: it was little more than an inlet between two stone walls leading up to a small rear door and dominated by two large refuse dumpsters. 'It's a dead end.'

'We can't outrun anyone chasing us anyway,' Jenna told him as reasonably as she could, 'just get down the end and hide! And quickly,' she added, feeling a thrill of fear as voices rose into the air behind them and she recognised a couple of the Russian words. 'Someone's shouting about the "American woman". They've recognised me.'

'Ah hell,' Apirana grunted, and started edging his way down the alley as fast as he could. He nearly slipped over when one of his crutches slid sideways on a piece of discarded plastic, but caught his balance at the cost of jarring his ankle and swearing sulfurously, albeit quietly, and managed to stumble into the deep shadows behind the rearmost dumpster with no further incident. Jenna squeezed in after him and tried her best to support him as he sank down into a sitting position to get his head out of sight. She ended up next to him on the floor, back pressed against the cold metal of the dumpster and listening to the breath rasp in and out of his big chest.

'All in all,' Apirana said quietly after a few moments, 'this has not been one of my better days.'

Jenna said nothing. She wasn't sure what to say.

'Sorry for giving you a hard time about the circuit-heads,' he continued a moment later. 'Didn't mean to cause a fight. You helped me as much as they did, anyhow.'

'A.,' Jenna said carefully, after a pause, 'have I . . . done something?'

'How d'you mean?'

'You've been . . . weird. Towards me.' She fiddled with her wrist console, theoretically studying the map but in reality it was so she had an excuse to talk to Apirana without looking at him. She didn't even know why she'd started this conversation again, other than she had the worrying notion that they were going to be found by people harbouring bad intentions towards them and she wanted to get at least one thing straightened out first.

There was a pause, slightly too long. 'Have I?'

'Yes, you have.' She felt some heat creep into her voice. 'And don't play innocent either, I can tell that you know it.'

There was a huff of breath from beside her, and a faint reverberation as something gently hit the dumpster. She looked around to see Apirana's head tilted back, eyes open and staring upwards.

'Didn't mean to be.'

'For *fuck's* sake, A.!' She managed to keep her voice low with an effort. 'I don't really give a damn what you *meant* to do, but you've been making me feel worried and on edge since we set foot in this hole and I just want to know why!'

He looked sideways at her, his face tight and his expression uneasy, so far as she could make it out in the dim light thrown up by her wrist console. 'You sure this is the right time?'

'This is the *only* time,' she replied firmly. 'I'm not running around this city with you any longer until I know what's going on. I thought you were my friend.' She tried to keep the last sentence from being overwhelmed by bitterness, but only partially succeeded.

'Okay,' Apirana muttered after a second, sounding about as subdued as she'd ever heard him. 'Just remember I ain't much good with words, right?'

'That's a lie to start with,' Jenna retorted, 'you *are* good with words. You remember how you came and talked to me about you, and your family, after we'd loaded that cargo from Kelsier's ship? That was about the most open and honest anyone's ever been with me. Just because you can't spin bullshit around like the Captain doesn't mean you're not good with words, A.' She turned towards him slightly, trying to get him to understand. How was it possible for one man to sometimes be so perceptive about what she was thinking but completely oblivious at others? 'They just have to be *your* words. So tell me: what's going on?'

There was another pause.

'Guess I just noticed something that's been under my nose for a while,' Apirana rumbled eventually. 'I've seen a fair few crew come and go, an' each of us, an' pretty much everyone I've met since I were a kid for that matter, we're all one sort of bastard or another. Maybe it's what this life turns us into, maybe you've just gotta be that to stick at it for any length of time, I dunno.

'But you're different. You ain't just good at what you do, an' smart, an' pretty, you're *nice*. You're a real good person, and I'd kinda forgotten what they were like.'

Jenna almost started in surprise. That was the most compliments anyone had paid her for a long time, and Apirana had just tossed them out as though they were accepted facts.

'Don't get me wrong, the others ain't so bad,' the big Maori continued, 'but if we all got rich tomorrow an' I could settle down, I'd probably wish 'em well an' not think much more about 'em. But not you. I . . .'

He broke off for a second, his voice thickening a little, and coughed awkwardly.

'You said you thought I was your friend, an' I am, an' I always intend to be. But I want to be more than that too, if you're willing, an' I just realised that. I didn't want you to just move on an' leave one day, not without telling you how I felt, but here's me, wrong side of forty an' I've never even met someone I could say I . . . liked. Let alone figured out how to say it to 'em. So while I was trying to work out words for it all, I just tripped over myself and messed shit up.'

Jenna sat very still and very quiet while she tried to process what she'd just heard. She knew that a response was probably called for – a carefully thought-out, honest and tactful response – but she was finding it hard to formulate one because most of her brain seemed to be off flying in circles somewhere else and all that remained was one small part loudly asking, *Does this qualify as being 'gob-smacked'?*, which really wasn't helpful. She blinked a few times, in case that helped.

'I . . .'

Footsteps. Footsteps coming into the alley behind them. She bit down almost gratefully on the barely formed sentence and held her breath.

The footsteps slowed.

Stopped.

'You really shouldn't have your console lit up if you're trying to hide, you know.'

The voice was low-pitched enough to be borderline between masculine and feminine, carried the accent of North America and, perhaps most tellingly, was devoid of much in the way of humour. Jenna's momentary shock at being addressed by the unseen person evaporated into relief as she recognised the speaker and she scrambled to her feet, stepping out into what passed for the light in the alley.

A silhouette stood between them and the street beyond: shorter than Jenna, with its shape lost in a flowing coat and a wide-brimmed hat, and with a familiar-looking rifle slung casually over one shoulder. Jenna could have hugged her, only that would have been weird and she wasn't entirely certain she wouldn't find herself with a dislocated shoulder from some sort of self-defence move.

'You have no idea how glad I am to see you,' she breathed, a relieved grin spreading of its own accord across her face.

'Likewise,' Tamara Rourke nodded. 'Where's Apirana?'

'Here,' the big Maori grunted, levering himself up with some effort. Jenna instinctively moved to help him then stopped herself in sudden fear of what that might be seen to imply, and by the time she'd sorted her brain out enough to decide that no, she really *should* be helping him, he'd managed to make it up to his good foot anyway. *Jesus Christ, what the hell is wrong with me?*

'Moutinho told me you were on crutches,' Rourke said. 'What happened?'

'I— Hang on, *Moutinho*?' Apirana looked about as shocked as Jenna felt.

'Long story short, we've agreed not to be pains in each other's asses until we're off this dirtball,' Rourke said perfunctorily. 'Can you move?'

'Long as you don't go too quick,' Apirana offered.

'Good.' The hat turned back towards Jenna. 'I need you.'

Jenna tried to look attentive, eager for a distraction that might give her time to think. 'What for?'

'Another long story short,' and now there was the very faintest hint of a dry smile in Rourke's voice, 'we've just joined the revolution. And they need a slicer.'

S hit, I've been shot.

Drift experienced a moment of quiet panic, oddly isolated from what was going on around him. Even the noise of Muradov barking an order and a presumably thunderous hail of gunfire erupting from the transports and their disembarking *politsiya* seemed muffled and distant. Then his brain caught up with events and registered that although he was winded from the impact and fall and he was going to have a bastard of a bruise in a few hours, he could feel nothing to suggest that he was bleeding and all his arms and legs still seemed to work. His armavest had done its job.

The realisation that he still had all his health to lose hit at about the same time as a fresh adrenaline rush. He scrabbled into what was probably a poor approximation of the knees-and-elbows crawl he'd seen in countless war holos, but which served well enough at getting him towards the shelter of the transports without putting him in anyone's line of fire. The thicket of boots he was heading for obligingly parted to let him through and he scrambled gratefully up into the back of the transport they revealed. Two hands hauled him in and he looked up into the faces of the Chang siblings, one on each side of him. Kuai immediately went back to fiddling with his dragon pendant and Jia looked about as stressed as he'd ever seen her.

'Thanks,' he said with some feeling, thumbing the safety of his rifle on and sitting up. 'You two alright?'

Jia's face congealed into a thunderous scowl and he thought for a moment he was going to be on the receiving end of one of her vituperate bilingual rants. However, she simply turned away and did as creditable an impersonation of someone storming off as could be performed inside a somewhat cramped armoured vehicle. Drift stared, confused and not a little annoyed.

'*Me caga en la puta*, I just got *shot*!' he shouted after her, then turned to Kuai. 'What the hell's her problem?'

The little mechanic shrugged. 'She left her hat in the hotel.'

Goddamn pilot hat. Drift lowered his voice. 'We need to find some way for her to deal with things without that stupid "lucky hat" of hers.'

Kuai shrugged again, managing to make the motion accusatory with the ease of a practised passive-aggressor. 'I tried hiding it once, but you made me give it back.'

'Well, yeah, because she . . .' *threw a tantrum and I needed her to fly us somewhere*. He sighed. 'Never mind.' Sometimes being a freelance captain was a little like how he imagined parenting to be, although so far as he was aware it was generally frowned upon to fire a child.

He became aware that the sound of gunfire from outside had ceased, and a moment later the vehicle began to rapidly fill with black-armoured shapes. One of them removed his helmet as soon as the doors were shut behind them, revealing the face of Chief Muradov. He gave Drift an appraising look. 'Are you injured?'

'I'm sore, but I've had worse,' Drift informed him, then frowned as they lurched into motion again. 'What about your wounded?'

'They are in the other car,' Muradov replied, gesturing about them. 'We are trying to fit three squads plus civilians into two vehicles, so things are a little . . . cramped.'

'I'd noticed,' Drift muttered as the benches became occupied by *politsiya* backsides. On the upside, he was clapped on the shoulder in comradely fashion by the woman who ended up squeezing in on his left: clearly his efforts to stay in one piece by keeping as many armoured bodies as possible alive to help him had convinced people that he was a team player.

'You said you're pulling back to Level Four?' he asked Muradov above the noise of the engine. The security chief nodded.

'There have been no reports of rioting above Level Five. We can close off the lower half of the city until the unrest has run its course, so you should be safe.'

Drift didn't much like the idea of being sealed off from half of his crew, but did his best not to let it show on his face. 'Could you relax your restriction on crews not being allowed to stay on their ships?' he asked instead.

Muradov pursed his lips. 'I will consider it.'

'We've got nowhere else to go,' Drift pushed, 'and I'd like to be somewhere the rest of my crew can—'

'I said, I will consider it,' the security chief stated with finality, and Drift subsided. The thing was, he was fairly certain that Muradov *would* consider it, which made it more difficult to dislike him for not giving an immediate answer. Drift liked being able to dislike authority figures; it made it easier to ignore his conscience when he inevitably broke their rules.

+Kommandir!+

Muradov looked up sharply as the driver activated the intercom, and he reached over to answer it. A quick exchange in Russian followed, and Drift looked to Kuai for a translation while belatedly fumbling with his pad to activate the translation function on his comm earpiece. He didn't want to drain his pad's charge too much while on the move, but it looked like he was going to be surrounded by Russian speakers for a while yet.

'Civilians in the road,' the Chinese mechanic murmured, just loud enough for Drift to hear. 'The driver thinks they're off-worlders, judging by the clothes.'

Tamara? If anyone could track them down in a city with no comms and in the middle of a mass riot, it was his business partner. *But what if Muradov decides it's another trap?* He took a breath to protest if the security chief gave any indication of ordering the gunners to open fire, but instead the Uragan swiped at a holoscreen to bring up an image of the road in front of them. There were two people visible, one larger and one smaller, both waving their arms desperately and growing larger by the moment as the car rumbled closer.

'Captain,' Muradov said, looking over his shoulder at Drift and gesturing at the screen, 'do you know these two?'

Drift got to his feet and picked his way as quickly as he could through the forest of boots and legs to stand next to Muradov. As soon as he got there his hope of seeing Apirana and either Rourke or Jenna evaporated into bitter disappointment. For a moment he considered denying all knowledge, but he'd already decided that lying to Muradov wasn't something he wanted to try unless he absolutely had to.

'They're members of Ricardo Moutinho's crew,' he said reluctantly. 'The man's called Dugan; I don't know the woman's name.' *Although she was willing to go one-on-one with Apirana if needed, which makes her batshit crazy at the very least.*

Muradov seemed to consider that for a moment, then activated the comm again and gave the order to stop. The vehicle began to slow in response, to Drift's surprise and mounting apprehension.

'Chief,' he said in alarm, 'this could be another trap!'

'Which is why everyone will have their guns ready,' Muradov snapped. 'Captain, I appreciate you and Captain Moutinho are not on the best terms, but I have the same duty to these people as I do to you and yours.'

'And what if Moutinho was involved in the gun-running?' Drift demanded. 'You said yourself he's been here several times over the last few months.'

'Well then,' Muradov said quietly, 'I will need to be having conversations with his crew, will I not?' He turned away and began barking instructions to the *politsiya* officers, who readied their weapons. Drift watched uneasily as the hull-mounted camera tracked closer and closer to the frantically waving smugglers, then glided past them as the vehicle slowed to a halt. Someone threw open the back doors to reveal Dugan and the woman, whose expressions of relief were replaced by alarm as they realised they were facing a dozen gun barrels.

'Get in, please,' Muradov ordered from behind a small wall of *politsiya*.

'But—'

'That was *not* a request,' the security chief snapped. His officers shuffled backwards a little to make room and the two off-worlders reluctantly clambered aboard into the increasingly crowded transport. The doors were pulled shut behind them as soon as all their limbs were inside the passenger bay and Muradov signalled another officer, who hammered on the driver's door to set them in motion again. Drift picked his way back to Kuai, mainly so neither Dugan nor the woman ended up stealing his seat.

'I am Security Chief Muradov,' Muradov announced without preamble, 'and Uragan City is currently in a state of martial law. You have both been identified as crew of the *Jacare* and are being placed in protective custody until the current state of emergency is ended. Your names?'

'Dugan Karwoski,' the big man replied, still eyeing the guns nervously.

'Lena Goldberg,' the woman added. 'Identified by who, anyway?'

Muradov jerked a thumb in Drift's direction. 'By the good Captain here.'

The pair's eyes tracked to Drift, seeing him for the first time, and widened almost simultaneously. Goldberg's face hardened instantly. 'Son of a—'

'Captain Drift is also in protective custody,' Muradov said over her impending curse, 'as are the members of his crew here. Where are the rest of yours?'

'Hell if I know,' Karwoski said, not without a hint of despair. 'Captain was meeting someone, Lena and I headed out for a drink. Next thing we know there's sirens everywhere, and everyone's looking at us a bit strange, and our comms don't work anymore. Then we heard gunfire, and *then* we saw your vehicles.'

'Thought we'd flag you down and find out what was going on,' Goldberg put in, a little sullenly, 'not get taken for a ride.'

'Who was Moutinho meeting?' Muradov asked, deceptively quietly.

'Some contact about a shipping contract,' Goldberg replied, a little too quickly if Drift was any judge. 'I don't know the name.'

'Where're you taking us, anyway?' Karwoski asked, changing the subject fairly blatantly.

'The fourth level,' Muradov replied after a second or two of studying their faces. He held up one hand to silence their protests, and both were at least smart enough not to try shouting over him. 'Martial law is in effect on Level Five and the streets are not safe.

Since you have no homes to go to, you are coming with us.'

'And what about our crew?' Goldberg shouted after him as the security chief turned to pick his way back to the tactical comm unit at the other end of the vehicle. Muradov stopped and looked back over his shoulder.

'Hopefully, they are not doing anything stupid.'

He turned away again immediately and so didn't see the look that passed between the two, but Drift had been watching for it and knew guilt when he saw it. The more he thought about it, the more convinced he became that Moutinho had not only been bringing in the guns but had pinned it on the *Keiko*'s crew as a combination of petty revenge and a smokescreen. And now some sort of revolution had kicked off . . . but it had apparently taken these two unaware, and presumably Moutinho as well. Had they really not realised who they were selling to? Then again, Drift knew full well that asking too many questions could simply get potentially lucrative doors shut in your face. Sometimes you just took the job and did it.

One other thing was tugging at his mind, though. He could remember all too clearly how unhappy his crew had been on their dark run into Amsterdam when they'd found out that he *had* known who their employer was, despite his previous protestations to the contrary. That – and the subsequent revelation of his previous identity as Gabriel Drake, notorious pirate – had sparked a near-mutiny. No one liked being kept in the dark by people they felt they should be able to trust, and he'd have put money on Goldberg and Karwoski wondering, right at the moment, whether Ricardo Moutinho had been as honest with them as he could have been.

And that was something he might be able to use, should he need to.

'So when they were shouting about "the American woman" . . .' Jenna began, understanding starting to dawn.

'They were telling each other to find me,' Rourke finished with a nod. The pair of them, with Apirana hobbling behind, were making their way towards the *politsiya* building that was now apparently serving as the headquarters of Level Five's new government.

'And you've joined the revolution?' Apirana put in. 'Seems a bit reckless, I gotta say.'

Rourke turned and looked at the big man, her expression serious and her voice low. 'It wasn't my choice. I wound up in the same place as some of Moutinho's crew and Tanja, who seems to be in charge around here at the moment. Moutinho tried to land me in it as soon as he saw me, of course, so I had to throw Tanja a bone to keep myself alive.' She shrugged. 'Thanks to a bit of lucky timing that bone worked quite impressively, and now here we all are.'

'So this isn't actually some well-disguised GIA plot?' Jenna asked. She didn't genuinely think that – although the Galactic Intelligence Agency was rumoured to be very, very underhanded in its activities – but Rourke pursed her lips and seemed to be seriously considering the question.

'It seems unlikely,' the older woman said a couple of seconds later. 'I'd have expected to run up against another agitator by now, if that was the case. No, I think this is purely organic. Which is probably why they had so little idea what they were doing.'

'Come again?' Apirana asked.

'Almost invariably, any native with enough understanding of the system to bring it down has too much invested in it to want to see it fall,' Rourke replied absently, turning away from them to head towards the main doors. 'That's how the system protects itself. Even if you set out to sabotage it, by the time you're in a position to influence anything you've probably been caught up in it one way or another. Although there are always exceptions.'

The three of them attracted a fair amount of stares as they approached the headquarters. Jenna had become used to that since she'd been spending any time with Apirana, but now it wasn't just the Maori who was being studied. She got the uncomfortable feeling that she was being weighed up by many pairs of eyes, and as they reached the maglev pad that would take them to the next floor up without Apirana needing to brave the stairs, she leaned close to Rourke. 'What exactly did you tell them I was going to do?'

'You're going to slice into the Spine to find instructions on how to work the broadcast equipment on this level so the revolution can spread the good news,' Rourke told her placidly as the clear plastic doors whispered shut behind them. 'Oh, and find some way for us to contact the others.'

Jenna blinked. 'You want me to do *what*?'

Rourke turned to look at her, dark eyes cool. 'I'd have thought that would be your area of expertise.'

Jenna closed her eyes and swallowed an urge to swear violently, but when she opened them again Rourke was still studying her. 'There is a hell of a difference between slicing a . . . a starport records system, where things are changing all the time and it's probably cobbled together on out-of-date software and no one follows the security protocols because they're too busy . . . and trying to slice through a *governmental block*.'

'Well, we'd better talk fast then,' the other woman said with a grimace. A moment later the platform rose up past the level of the next floor and slowed smoothly, bringing the corridor into view.

'I'm touched by your faith in me,' Jenna muttered as the elevator's doors opened, 'but did you ever think that governmental security measures might not be vulnerable to a university graduate?'

'Not when that university graduate is you,' Rourke whispered back, a comment which Jenna found both complimentary and infuriating in roughly equal measure. She took a deep breath and tried to project an outward calm to match Rourke's. It was clear that their standing in this proto-state was somewhat dependent on the results they could deliver, and sweating profusely and stammering was unlikely to engender much confidence in her abilities.

The room Rourke led them into had clearly originally been some sort of conference or presentation room, dominated as it was by a large holotable in the middle which was currently displaying a three-dimensional map. The windows had been blacked out to maximise the efficiency of the display and the other people in the room were mainly illuminated by the light it was giving off, which gave them a slightly sinister, unnatural-looking aspect in Jenna's eyes.

'Everyone,' Rourke said in English, 'this is Jenna and Apirana, two of my crew. Jenna is our slicer.'

Four pairs of eyes turned to Jenna. She tried to meet them evenly, as though being introduced to the leaders of a Free Systems revolution was an everyday occurrence.

'This is Tanja,' Rourke continued, gesturing to a woman in some sort of uniform – probably a mining company – with short hair that was light enough to be coloured alternately red or green depending on which part of the display was most lit up at that moment. 'She's in charge.'

'To an extent,' the woman identified as Tanja replied with a slightly strained smile. Jenna's first impression was that she was at least Rourke's age – although Jenna had only ever been able to guess at that figure – but when she looked closer she realised that in actual fact the Uragan woman was probably only in her early thirties. The lines on her face belonged to someone a decade or so older, and the bags beneath her eyes told volumes about how well she'd been sleeping lately . . . which was probably not that surprising, if she'd been waiting for the right moment to start a revolution. Her eyes themselves were bright and sharp, however, and Jenna suddenly had an uncomfortable flashback to those rare moments when she'd done something as a child that had warranted her mother's full, ferocious attention.

Tanja gestured to the other people around the table, in turn. 'This is Abram, who works for the power board; Marya, who served in the army; and Inzhu, who is . . . helping me organise everything.'

Abram, whose dark hair was receding at the temples and who appeared to be compensating for this by growing a bushy beard, mainly under his chin, laughed nervously and said something in Russian. Rourke muttered a translation, just loud enough for Jenna to hear: 'I'm not sure who I work for now.'

Marya tutted at Abram's words, just audibly. She was a robustly built woman in early middle age, with short ginger hair framing a face that carried the beginnings of impressive jowls. There was a pistol holstered at her right hip, and – Jenna felt her heart speed up a little more – her left arm looked to be mechanical. Jenna fought her body's response down: it was unremarkable for an ex-soldier to need augmentation, and besides, she'd just walked in and out of the Circuit Cult's headquarters here without anyone grabbing her. Marya responded to Abram, waving her natural fingers to make a point.

'Marya says that Abram still works for the power board, but there will just be a different government in charge,' Rourke translated quietly as the conversation continued. 'Abram wants to know how he and his wife can buy food for themselves and their child when the revolution has disowned their own currency. Marya is . . .' Rourke paused for a moment in the face of a particularly aggressive rattle of Russian, '. . . being impolite.'

Inzhu, a pretty, round-faced girl with dark hair pulled into two narrow pigtails, snapped something which apparently stopped the argument in its tracks. Abram and Marya both managed to look a little shamefaced, which surprised Jenna a little given that Inzhu was almost certainly the youngest of the four Uragans. Then she took in the sheet after sheet of plaspaper covered with scrawls, diagrams and reams of Cyrillic script that obscured most of the non-holographic part of the table, and noticed how they were spreading out from where Inzhu was standing. *Ah, a logistical genius. I wonder if they'll expect* her *to solve everything, too.*

Tanja cast a grateful smile at Inzhu, favoured the other two with a brief but pointed glare, then turned back to Jenna. 'Tamara said that you can get onto the Spine.'

Jenna tried not to grimace. 'Maybe. It's going to depend what sort of connection I can get. Rourke said there's a broadcast terminal on this level?'

'Not far from here,' Tanja replied, tapping the table and causing a small section of the holo to start flashing, which wasn't massively helpful given that Jenna hadn't studied it enough to work out where she was right now.

'Okay,' she said, the faint ghost of a plan starting to form in her mind, 'that's a start. If it's a government building then I'm likely to be able to find a terminal in there with a more direct link to the Spine, so I can at least eliminate some levels of the block outright. After that . . .' She exchanged a glance with Rourke, who clearly seemed to think that she should be selling it more, but Jenna really didn't feel like promising these people anything she wasn't absolutely certain she could deliver. 'Well, I'll be working in an unfamiliar alphabet and my translation algorithm probably isn't foolproof, but—'

'Please,' Tanja said, holding up one hand with a slightly pained expression. 'I speak enough English to know I will not understand what you are about to say.'

Beside Jenna, there was a very faint noise which might just have been Tamara Rourke suppressing a snigger. Jenna allowed herself a moment to glare sideways at the shorter woman, then addressed Tanja again. 'If I'm inside the broadcast hub I can probably get you *something*, but I'm not sure how long it'll take.'

Tanja nodded. 'It will take as long as it has to.'

Great, so what you're saying is that I won't be leaving until you've got what you want?

'We have not yet tried to get inside the hub,' Tanja continued, 'since we did not want to give the government any more warning than we had to of our plans. Marya will come with you to coordinate our operation.'

Marya nodded briskly and made her way around the table. Jenna watched the other woman's eyes and saw them skitter over her dismissively to focus on Rourke, who had one thumb casually hooked under the strap of her Crusader. The ex-soldier and former GIA agent simply regarded each other for a moment, each apparently waiting for the other to make the first move or acknowledgement, and Jenna was suddenly put in mind of the antique holos her father used to watch where two nineteenth-century gunfighters would stand facing each other in a street.

'Uh, can we get moving?' Apirana asked apologetically into the suddenly tense silence, 'I could do with sitting down soon, if it's all the same to everyone.'

The big Maori's interruption seemed to break the spell. Rourke nodded an affirmative and turned to lead the way out of the room, with Marya following behind. Jenna gave Apirana a smile which she hoped conveyed her gratitude at his timely (and almost certainly deliberate) intervention between their companions' respective egos, but stopped short in the face of his pained expression. Of course, he'd been left hanging, and badly. But that was due to the circumstances – he had to understand that, surely?

'A.,' she said quietly as she slipped out of the door just ahead of his bulk, 'we'll talk, I promise. But later, when this is . . . done.' She looked up at him, hoping he'd understand. 'But we *will* talk.'

Although I have no idea what I'm going to say.

'*The problem won't be getting inside,*' Marya said in Russian, '*the problem will be preventing those already in there from disabling the equipment before we can use it.*'

Rourke pursed her lips, studying what she could see of the blocky hexagon that formed the Level Five broadcast hub. Protective shutters had come down to cover the doors and windows and it currently looked more like a fortification than a media centre. '*Do you think that's likely?*'

Marya nodded once. Rourke got the impression that it wasn't just the other woman's career in the military that had bred this curt manner; she had an air of someone who had never suffered fools gladly, yet saw them most places she looked. '*The government controls this world closely and everyone in there will be working to their agenda. They will not wish for us to be able to communicate across levels, or off-planet.*'

'*I would have expected an ex-servicewoman to . . . have a greater affiliation to the government's agenda,*' Rourke replied. She'd nearly said *be more loyal*, but decided at the last moment that it was probably not very diplomatic.

'*The government are quick enough to send people out to fight for them,*' Marya replied stiffly, '*but I have found that they are somewhat less eager to provide for those who come back injured, or for the families of those who don't come back at all. They do not respect the sacrifices others make in their name, so they no longer have my support.*'

'*And you don't think anyone in there would share your views?*' Rourke asked, although she was fairly certain she knew what answer she'd receive.

'*Not enough of them,*' Marya replied, as Rourke had predicted. The other woman didn't seem the sort of person to be easily swayed from an opinion once she'd formed it.

Rourke sighed. '*Well then, I guess we do this the hard way. There will be security personnel, I imagine?*'

'*Certainly,*' Marya confirmed.

'*And I assume they won't start disabling or destroying anything unless they think it's likely we'll get inside?*' Rourke asked. Getting into buildings surreptitiously wasn't anything new to her, and she was starting to put a loose plan together. It was a good job she'd never been claustrophobic.

'*Unlikely,*' Marya said, '*they would be responsible for such damage.*'

'*Then that gives us an opportunity,*' Rourke said decisively. '*I'm going to need a laser cutter, a maintenance vehicle capable of reaching the roof, and a shockgun with plenty of ammunition.'*

'They will see us trying to cut in through any window, even one on the top floor,' Marya warned.

Rourke managed not to roll her eyes. *'Which is why I'm not going in through the windows.'*

'You?' Even though Marya was speaking a language which was not one of Rourke's native tongues, the disdain and mistrust was audible in the Uragan woman's voice. *'Tanja asked me to coordinate this.'*

'You will be coordinating it,' Rourke assured her, *'but I'll be the one doing it. You will be standing very obviously outside the front doors trying to talk them into opening up. You don't have to do a good job of it,'* she added, perhaps a trifle nastily, *'just don't stop.'*

'I will be leading the infiltration,' Marya corrected her, turning sideways as though to try to intimidate Rourke with her greater height and bulk. *'What is your plan?'*

For answer, Rourke just pointed upwards. Overhead, running along the ceiling like a network of silvery veins, was Level Five's ventilation system. The broadcast hub was supplied by one of the main pipes, but even that was hardly huge. Rourke wasn't looking forward to it, but she'd been in such tight places before. Marya, on the other hand, with her broad shoulders and wide hips . . .

'That's ridiculous,' the Uragan said after a moment, suddenly looking less certain.

'Do you have a better idea?' Rourke asked. *'I'd advise against trying the sewers.'* Subterranean settlements tended to use pressurised suction systems

instead of gravity to move their waste, mainly because it often didn't end up going downwards anyway.

Marya was clearly reluctant to back down, but after a few moments of indecision her stubborn expression faded slightly and she nodded. '*Nothing that can be put into action quickly. Very well. We will attempt to reason with them to let us in while you get into position to act if we cannot.*'

Rourke didn't challenge the other woman's reassessment of her role from glorified distraction into main player. So long as Marya did what Rourke wanted, she wasn't much bothered how the other woman thought of it. '*Fine, just keep their attention on the front of the building.*' She nodded towards where she could see Jenna. Oddly, her and Apirana seemed to be keeping their distance from one another, and Rourke wondered what had passed between them while she'd been elsewhere. '*For everyone's sake, keep that girl out of sight. If they decide to open fire and she's hit then you can kiss goodbye to this plan.*'

'No one is indispensable,' Marya snorted.

'*That's the kind of thinking that wins fights but loses wars,*' Rourke said, removing her hat. She turned to fully face the Uragan for the first time, catching her eye and holding it. '*More importantly, that girl is part of my crew. My participation in your revolution is conditional on being reunited with all of them, not losing someone to a hothead with a gun because the person in charge couldn't keep them safe. Am I clear?*'

'*Perfectly,*' Marya replied icily.

'*Very well then.*' Rourke shrugged out of her coat somewhat reluctantly. She found it helped with people's attitudes towards her due to it partially offsetting her diminutive stature, but it would be nothing but an inconvenience where she was going. '*Let's get on with it.*'

With communication systems out it took a little time to get the necessary equipment together, but soon enough Rourke was being raised up towards the ventilation ducts on the work platform of a maintenance vehicle. They were hidden from the broadcast hub by another building to avoid their plan being immediately exposed, which meant Rourke was going to have to navigate through a couple of bends instead of getting a clear run at her target, but it was nothing she hadn't done before. The echoes of a slightly distorted voice informed her that Marya had found some sort of vocal amplification equipment from somewhere and was hailing the hub. *Good. I'd put money on her being able to talk at a wall for at least an hour.*

She activated the laser cutter and set to work slicing through the galvanised metal above her head, idly trying to remember the last time she'd had to go into a building through the ventilation system. *New Ghayathi? Recovering some sort of weapon plans, I think. I probably should have convinced Ichabod to take a peek at what they were, but I was likely happier not knowing.*

The last cut was nearly done: she braced the panel with her free hand, directing it so it fell safely into the rail-bordered work platform instead of plummeting three storeys to potentially hit someone below her. A gust of wind hit her as some of the air coursing along the pipe's length escaped, and she ducked down to check her bag while she gave the super-heated sides of the new void above her some time to cool. As well as some more general-purpose tools, she had a shockgun taken from the *politsiya* armoury and two full magazines of shockbolts, a pistol firing regular ammunition as a backup in case she needed the threat of lethal force, several restraints to keep troublemakers out of the way and, perhaps most crucially, a two-way radio scavenged from somewhere. It was short-range and prone to interference or having its signal blocked by walls, but unlike the more sophisticated comms it didn't rely on piggybacking through a planetary communication system or that of an orbiting satellite or ship. She looked over the edge of her platform and saw Jenna's red-blonde hair beneath her.

'Jenna, do you read? Over.'

A pale face turned up towards her. +*Loud and clear. Are you going in? Over.*+

'Any second.' The metal was no longer glowing but would still be hot, and she had no wish to burn her hands. 'Stay alert, I don't know how good the signal will be from in there. I'll basically be opening a window and hoping, over.'

+*Roger that, I'll be listening. Over and out.*+

Rourke clipped the radio to the belt of her bodysuit and reached up to cautiously pat at the hole she'd cut. The metal was still warm but not enough to hurt, so she pushed her bag up into the hole ahead of her, then pulled herself up after it and flicked on the flashlight strapped to her forehead.

The pipe stretched away in front of her: a narrow, more-or-less rectangular space which made her feel momentarily as though she'd been swallowed by a whale of Old Earth, had they been made of metal. It was dirty, too, where dust had built up along the welding lines despite the stiff breeze she could feel pushing on the backs of her thighs. She gave her bag an experimental push and it slid away from her for a couple of feet before its progress was arrested by one of those welding lines, which stood just proud enough of the silvery surface to snag on the irregularly shaped contents.

Rourke sighed. This minor detail of careless engineering was going to exponentially increase the effort she would need to expend to reach her destination. She nudged her bag over the obstacle and pushed it on again, then followed it using her elbows and knees. Lift, shove, crawl, repeat. Lift, shove, crawl . . .

This is ridiculous. I could have been getting paid *for this bullshit instead of just doing it because we happened to wind up on the wrong planet at the wrong time. I could have had a pension to look forward to, maybe somewhere to retire to. But no, I had to take issue with the morality of it, like I ever thought the Agency would be a bastion of ethics, then go and find a job with a stars-damned ex-pirate.* She sighed, trying to ignore the ache in her shoulders that wouldn't have been there twenty years ago. She'd been lucky, but age was starting to catch up even with her. *Maybe I* should *look into sourcing some Boost and take a few years off my joints. I'm sure it's not being vain if you're only doing it to make sure you can still crawl through air ducts.*

She reached a junction and turned left. Lift, shove, crawl, repeat. She needed to be as quiet and careful as she could, since sound would travel easily along this giant metal tube, but she didn't have limitless time. Marya's distraction would only work for so long before someone got suspicious, and Rourke didn't fancy dropping into a building where people were on the alert for intruders.

There. Ahead of her was an upwelling of light, distinct from the jerky beam of her forehead-mounted flashlight: a vent into an illuminated building, and that meant the communications hub. She advanced cautiously, listening for voices as best she could over the echoed sounds of her own breathing and shuffling, but not hearing anything. This was where she trusted to luck, because even someone as light as she couldn't crawl along a ventilation duct, while pushing a bag of equipment, without making enough noise to alert anyone standing beneath it. Hopefully the vent was only just inside the building.

Ten feet away. Now she could afford to slow down a little, and she crept the last distance as silently as possible until she was directly over the grate that blew fresh air down into the building beneath.

It looked to be a corridor, which was exactly what she'd hoped for as it would avoid the potential nuisance of being locked inside a room. No one was standing directly beneath the vent, certainly, and there were no shouts of alarm, but she wanted a little more certainty. She pulled an engineer's imager from her bag and tapped the display to turn it on, then cautiously threaded the narrow camera wire though the grate. The device was intended to allow mechanics, engineers or electricians to see into narrow, enclosed spaces and around corners, but it also served admirably as a way to reconnoitre a potentially hostile environment.

All clear in all directions. She dropped the imager back into her bag and tested the vent, which shifted agreeably. Not screwed in. Good: cutting through it would have taken more time than she'd have liked, as well as hardly being subtle. It took both hands and a braced foot for leverage, but she pulled it up and away from its fitting, slid it out of the way and followed her bag down through the gap. The corridor was some six feet wide with rooms on either side and was perhaps thirty feet from end to end, where it took sixty-degree turns inwards as it followed the building's hexagonal shape.

The appearance of a shadow on the carpet of the corner to her right was the only warning she had that someone was approaching. Short of them showing up at the very moment she'd started to lower herself down from the vent, it was about the worst possible timing. She had no cover, no plan, and no time to prepare.

What she *did* have was a shockgun, and hopefully the very faint element of surprise.

She'd yanked the weapon out of her bag, flicked the safety off and aimed it down the corridor in about the time it took for the shadow to be caught up by its owner. He turned out to be a security guard, *six feet two inches, early thirties, physically fit, slightly over 200 pounds,* with a shockstick at his belt and a commpiece in his left ear.

Rourke shot him before his eyes had finished widening at her presence. She had no way of knowing if his transmitter was already activated, and, if it was, then he'd have blurted something to whoever was listening before she could threaten him into silence. He spasmed as the shockbolt delivered its electric payload, and his collapse brought into view his colleague who'd been a step or so behind him. *Five feet nine inches, early fifties, well over 200 pounds which is mostly fat, probably at considerably higher risk of heart attack when exposed to strong electrical stimulus.*

A good thing she'd started running towards him as soon as she'd pulled the trigger on his colleague, then.

Rourke hadn't known there'd been two guards, but she'd known that if there was anyone else then she needed to narrow the angle so they couldn't put the corner of the corridor between them and her for long enough to get off a shout for help. She didn't want to shockbolt this man, but she also couldn't have him raising the alarm any more than his colleague's spasmodic grunts already might have, so she dropped the gun and put all of her momentum into a running kick to his sizeable gut. The breath huffed out of him and he doubled over, momentarily unable to speak, but his fingers clutched at the shock-stick on his belt.

He was wide and her legs comparatively short: if she got behind him then she could certainly get an arm around his neck for a blood choke, but her legs might not be able to reach around him to prevent him from shaking her off. She leapt upwards instead, wrapping her legs around his neck and right shoulder and locking her right foot into the crook of her left knee in a flying triangle choke. She took a moment to rip the commpiece out of his ear, then pulled his head down with both hands.

He realised what was going on and staggered forwards as the blood flow to his brain was restricted, perhaps intending to ram her against the wall. She leaned back instead, turning his unsteady forwards momentum into a full-blown roll which ended up with him on his back and her on top, her legs still locked in place. He tried to batter at her with his free left arm, but he was already going red in the face and his eyes were starting to glaze over, so she took the hits and gritted her teeth against the pain in her ribs.

He went limp a moment later. She kept the choke on for another second to ensure he wasn't faking, then hastily disentangled herself, as there was little point in avoiding shocking someone for fear of giving them a heart attack only to inflict brain damage with an overzealous blood choke. Both guards had restraints on their belts but she didn't risk attempting to use those, in case they were voice or thumbprint activated. She took some constrictor bands from her belt pouch instead: the autoshrinking plastic strips were designed for easily securing cables and the like, but anyone who'd spent time in any sort of situation where you needed a quick, easy and not necessarily legal way to restrain humans knew them as reliable for this alternative use, and one which was less likely to cause comment than traditional cuffs if found on you.

She did the second guard first, pulling his arms up behind him and tying his wrists in the small of his back, then doing the same to his ankles. He came around a moment later, still instinctively fighting against the choke which was the last thing his body remembered, and let out a panicked whine as he found himself trussed and face down on the carpet.

'*Quiet!*' Rourke snapped in Russian, fitting his commpiece into her ear and moving on to his partner. '*Don't make me knock you out again.*' To her surprise he fell silent.

The first guard had never lost consciousness, but the shockbolt had done its work and right now he would be feeling like a team of men had worked his body over with clubs. He put up a half-hearted attempt at resistance when she pulled his arms behind him, but despite their size discrepancy she barely had to exert herself. She quickly had him tied up as well, although she had nothing to gag either of them with and nor would she be able to move them anywhere less obvious: she might be able to incapacitate two men twice her size, but hauling them around after-wards was beyond her. They'd have to stay here in the corridor, and she just had to hope that no one happened upon them too soon.

She returned to her pack and withdrew her pistol, then slung the bag over her shoulder and walked back to the older guard. He looked up at her with a fearful expression which didn't alleviate in any way when she pointed the gun at his face.

'*Which way to the front door?*' She disabled the safety with an audible buzz. '*If I have to come back this way because you lied to me, I will not be happy.*'

'*That way!*' the man whimpered, nodding desper-ately in the other direction to where the two of them had come from. '*First stairwell on your left, it leads straight down.*'

Rourke nodded. '*Thank you.*' Another thought struck her. '*And the main broadcast suite?*'

'*First floor, centre of the building.*'

'*Thank you again.*' She activated the safety again and tucked the pistol into a belt pouch, then retrieved her shockgun from where it had been lying on the floor. '*I'll send someone to release you as soon as we have this building under control.*'

She had no way of knowing if he'd been telling the truth, of course, but having asked for the information it made sense to use it, so she made for the stairwell and found it just around the next bend in the corridor. She went through the door cautiously, shockgun poised, but no one was waiting on the other side. Her ear was empty of comm-traffic, too: how many guards were there in this building? She had no doubt that there would be surveillance cameras in the corridors and stairwells, but was anyone watching them? Or was everyone concentrating on the large, noisy distraction orchestrated by Marya?

She descended the stairs to the first floor by her usual method of sliding down the handrails, then paused. She needed to get the doors open, but she was having second thoughts about trying to do it all herself. If whoever was in charge of the controls wasn't paying attention to their surveillance feeds, then she might be able to walk up and take them by surprise, but that was a big gamble. The shockgun was a useful tool, but a glancing hit wouldn't deliver the charge and some people were simply more resilient to its effects anyway. The pistol's threat of lethal force was only effective for as long as she proved willing to utilise it, and when it came down to it she didn't particularly want to start leaving corpses in the name of someone else's cause. Besides which, she had a notion that although the revolution might turn a blind eye to Uragan casualties caused by its members, they might not be so forgiving to an off-worlder. She had to minimise their excuses for turning on her and her crew.

Sometimes, solving a problem wasn't a case of how much brute force you could bring to bear. Rather like a chokehold, knowing exactly *where* to apply the pressure was usually more valuable.

She pushed the stairwell door open and edged cautiously into the corridor on the other side of it. Directly opposite her was another door, this one with a sign over it reading 'Production Suite' in Cyrillic script.

Standing in the doorway was another security guard: a stocky, black-haired woman over whose face an expression of surprise was rapidly stealing.

Rourke fired the shockgun from the hip and the bolt struck the other woman in her belly. She gasped and started to spasm, but Rourke had no intention of waiting and swept her right leg up in a roundhouse kick. The point of her boot caught the guard behind her ear and the other woman collapsed bonelessly, muscles still twitching even in unconsciousness thanks to the shockbolt's discharge. Rourke waited a couple of seconds for the current to dispel, then quickly used two more contraction bands to secure her and pulled an access card from the guard's belt. Shockgun once more in hand, she swept the card through the reader and stepped through the door.

She was greeted with the sight of a large room full of terminals and the sound of a raging argument consisting of at least four different people. She was on a raised area that ran around the edge of the room, which was hexagonal. In the sunken hexagon in the middle, and clustered around what looked to be the equipment that was the main focus of the place, were a group of Uragans yelling at each other so continuously that she couldn't make head nor tail of what they were actually arguing about.

There were several other techs in the room, watching the show put on by their probable superiors with airs ranging from the amused to the annoyed to the down-right worried. One of the worried-looking ones, a girl with curly blonde hair and a prosthetic eye, glanced towards the new arrival. Her natural eye widened comically for a moment as she saw Rourke, and then she screamed.

The sound achieved what no amount of aggressive shouting had apparently succeeded in doing, and the argument in the middle of the room abruptly ceased as every head turned first towards the sound, and then towards the small, dark-skinned intruder clad in a bodysuit and holding a shockgun. Rourke took in their faces for a second and wondered if this was such a good idea after all, but the die was cast now. She wished that Ichabod was here with her; his natural talent for wordsmithery would have been very useful right about now.

She raised her voice enough to hopefully be heard by everyone, and hefted the shockgun just enough to let people know that they shouldn't try anything funny. '*Good evening. I represent the revolution that is currently taking place outside your building.*'

Sharp breaths, worried glances, a whimper from somewhere . . . but thoughtful, evaluating expressions on some faces. Exactly what she'd hoped for. She let her eyes travel around the room. Government employees these people might be, but they were still broadcasters. Their lives were about creating content and transmitting it to an audience. Surely, this deep on a backwater mining planet, there must be someone yearning to be noticed?

'Who *wants* to get the exclusive on the Rassvet System's most shocking political event of the century?'

THE GAME CHANGES

Drift could taste the tension in the air.

Uragan City's Level Four was obviously supposed to be functioning normally, but even an off-worlder like him could feel that wasn't the case. They'd stopped at the first big *politsiya* station they'd come to after exiting the vehicle ramps and passing through the heavily guarded checkpoints, and Alim Muradov had disappeared to presumably lead an emergency briefing. That left Drift and his motley collection of tag-alongs somewhat in limbo, and with the Chief not keeping a close eye on them, Drift had stepped outside to get a feel for the air.

There were people everywhere, many more than he supposed was normal at this hour of the early morning. These weren't the chanting mobs of the revolution further down but worried-looking clumps of citizens that formed on street corners, then drifted apart and reformed again elsewhere with different members. Drift didn't need to be fluent in Russian to understand why everyone was so concerned: as he well knew, all communication with Level Five and below had ceased.

Any city on any planet would have comms glitches at times when wires broke, or a relay faulted, or a satellite's circuitry was fried by an electromagnetic surge from a solar flare. People understood these things, but half of a city simply dropping off the communications map? Drift guessed that there'd been no official announcement about why this was, because what government would announce that half of its capital city had erupted in bloody revolution? The fear of the other half joining it would be too great.

However, as time marched on, whispers would start flying – not over the comms, which might be monitored, but out on the street with neighbours – and people would surely begin to guess that this was more than just a technical fault. The powers that be would look either incompetent or scared, or both. He didn't know how long it would be until reinforcements from other cities or from elsewhere in the system arrived, but the storm raging above would surely shut them out for at least a couple more days. If the revolution gained enough momentum, if it could bubble up beyond the lowest, poorest sectors where it had fermented . . .

His train of thought was cut off by his comm buzzing. To his surprise and great relief, he recognised it as Rourke.

'Hello?!'

+Ichabod, where the hell are you?+

'Where the hell am *I*? Where the hell are *you*?' He frowned, realising there was only one explanation for how this call was even possible. 'Have you got out of Level Five too?'

+No, of course not, we're . . . wait, are you saying you have got out?+

'Yes, I'm with the Changs and the Shirokovs on Level Four. But if you're still on Level Five . . .' He looked around at the *politsiya* station, but he knew full well there'd been no mass mobilisation of force to take the lower levels back. It was impossible, but he still had to ask the question. 'Has the government opened the comm channels again, then?'

+No, the revolution's taken control of a broadcast hub here and . . . well, someone's managed to remove the block on communications.+

Drift looked around. Here and there on the street he could see surges of activity, and groups of people clustering around someone avidly listening to a comm. Word about what had happened below was spreading already, to friends, to relatives. He could imagine the message leaking out: We're fine, there's been no catastrophe, but everything's changed . . .

His brain belatedly latched onto the momentary catch in Rourke's speech, a sign that she'd changed what she'd been about to say at the last moment, and his gut clenched in alarmed response. If Rourke was close enough to know that the revolution had taken a broadcast hub then that was either one hell of a coincidence, or . . . 'What do you mean, "someone" managed to remove the block on communications?'

+It looks like the revolution managed to find a slicer from somewhere.+

Drift closed his eyes for a moment and groaned. Of all the . . . At least Jenna was still alive, if he was interpreting Rourke's words correctly, but even that piece of happy news was scant comfort.

+*Ichabod?*+

He gritted his teeth and looked around quickly to make sure no one was close enough to overhear him. It was just as well that no one was: he might have burst if he'd had to hold the words in.

'I nearly got shot in a bar!' he hissed. 'I *did* get shot in the street, and my damn armavest is the only reason I didn't take a bullet in the spine and lose control of everything below my waist! I got taken into protective custody by Alim Muradov and then the fucking police vehicle I'm travelling in gets *blown up* by some goddamned booby trap, and I have to fight my way out! All of those things were done by the rioters, and you are fucking *helping* them?!'

+*What . . . why are you in protective custody?*+

He sighed, trying to calm himself a little. 'It seems that someone matching my description *might* have been caught up in a clash between rioters and officers of the law, and ended up helping the cops get away before they were killed. Chief Muradov decided that it was safer not to leave us to fend for ourselves on the streets.'

+*Someone matching your . . .*+ Rourke trailed off. She knew full well how long the odds were that there could be another rangy, blue-haired Mexican in Uragan City. +*Motherless son of a flyblown whore.*+

Drift blinked. 'I beg your—'

+*Not you, Ichabod. I was just . . . thinking out loud. But of all the times you could choose to help out the law, why did it have to be this one?*+

'Because Muradov's actually competent and I figured he'd get the situation under control quickly!' Drift snapped. 'What the hell are you doing throwing in with the rebels, anyway? GIA instincts too hard to break?'

+*Oh, piss off! I stumbled into a meeting between them and Moutinho, and they were going to kill me! I gave them some useful tips, then figured I could use them to help find the half of my crew who'd been out getting drunk when this all kicked off. I never thought you'd have actually defended the polit-siya instead of keeping your head down in a bar somewhere.*+

'The bar was full of choke gas because some of your new friends had just opened fire on the cops!' Drift protested angrily. A couple of faces were starting to turn towards him, and he fought to moderate the tone of his voice. Arguing over the comm wouldn't help, in any case: they needed a solution, not a quarrel. 'Look, I don't suppose there's any chance you can get out of there?'

+*Surely you've seen that we're blockaded in down here? Even if you could fast-talk us a way through the checkpoints from your side, there's no way the revolution are going to be letting us leave. We can't sneak out, either: A.'s broken his ankle, so he's on crutches.*+

Drift bit back a curse. 'Well, there's no way *we* can get to *you*, even if there weren't people who might want to shoot me on sight. Muradov seems to actually trust me now, but that will last as long as spit on an afterburner if we try to get into revolution territory.'

+*Damn it.*+ There was a brief pause. +*I suppose you should know now, and if you make any sort of joke about this then I will shoot you when I next see you . . .*+

Drift frowned. 'Go on.'

+*I've called a truce with Moutinho. We were both missing crew members and we agreed to help each other find them.*+ Her voice lowered until it was almost inaudible. +*I don't trust these Uragans. Their revolution's nothing to do with us, and I want as much help as I can gather when someone decides to play 'get the off-worlder'.*+

Drift considered this, then nodded grudgingly. He couldn't stand Moutinho, but he had at least some trust in the Brazilian's self-interest. 'I can't fault you, I just hope the bastard realises it's his best option and doesn't try sticking the knife in at some point.'

+*Well, he's unlikely to try to sell the revolution out to the law. It turns out he* was *the one running guns into here, and now everything's kicked off he's kind of tied to them.*+

Drift snorted a humourless laugh. 'So he *was* double-bluffing with that tip-off, the cheeky bastard. I figured so.' He looked back at the station again. 'There's two of his here, actually. They flagged us down to try to find out what was going on and Muradov pulled them along. They're the only two who wanted anything to do with the cops other than shoot at them, or blow them up.'

+*There's only two he's looking for, so that must be them. At least I can tell him we know where they are.*+

'Hooray,' Drift grunted, 'we can all be one big happy family. Assuming we can ever find a way to meet up.'

+*Ichabod, this revolution isn't going to stop here,*+ Rourke said, and now her voice held a tone of warning. +*They know they have to take the entire city: it's all or nothing. The longer you stay with Muradov, the more eventual danger you'll be in. Get clear of him and get to the starport. We'll find you there, if we can.*+

'He's not going to be the easiest person in the world to give the slip to,' Drift replied doubtfully, 'but I'll see what I can do.'

+*Well, he might be too busy to pay much attention to you soon.*+

'Why do you—' Drift cut himself off as there was a sudden upswing in activity from the knots of people he could see. They were no longer crowding around people on comms, now they seemed to be focused on anyone who had a pad out, clustering around and watching . . . something. 'Okay, that's strange.'

+*The broadcast's started.*+ The background noise filtering through from Rourke's end of the comm suddenly increased. +*I have to go.*+ She didn't wait for a reply: there was simply the *click* of a terminated call in his ear. Moments later, however, his comm buzzed again. This time, he was surprised to see that it was Kuai.

'Go ahead.'

+*Captain, you need to see this. We're in the canteen.*+

Drift turned and headed back for the station. The two officers stationed on the doors were eyeing the street with a mix of confusion and burgeoning uneasiness, but they knew Drift had arrived with the city's security chief so he was able to re-enter the building without any issues.

'What am I missing?' he asked the mechanic as he was buzzed through into an area which would normally be for officers only. Truth to tell, Drift wasn't sure how happy Muradov would be if he learned that Drift had been coming and going at will, but the old 'hive mentality' trick seemed to be working again: once you were inside somewhere, everyone generally assumed that you had a reason to be there and decided it was someone else's job to challenge you.

+*Uhh . . . the revolution has been holovised?*+

Kuai was tired, and irritable, and possibly a little scared. Coffee was only really helping with one of those.

The police canteen was a fairly grim and soulless affair, and reminded him why he didn't like being off-ship. The *Keiko* wasn't huge and the *Jonah* was significantly smaller, but that didn't trouble him in the slightest. He had his own space and he could put his own imprint on it: not just in his cabins on the respective vessels, but in the engine rooms where he spent so much time. Everything was in its right place, and that place was the one that *he* had designated, and there was room for his own individual touches to make it all feel homely. He felt like an outsider here. Besides, you only had to walk into this canteen and look around to realise that no one lived here and no one loved it.

Jia was sitting on his right, either arguing or flirting with one of the officers they'd ridden in with, or possibly both. The Captain had once suggested that Jia constantly picking fault with him was simply her way of showing affection, but Kuai knew better. It was actually her way of showing that she was an obnoxious little brat, to the point of always trying to ensure that any men in the vicinity were concentrating on her, not him. Still, she was an obnoxious little brat whom he'd promised their parents he'd look after, and he kept his promises. Even when they took him to the far side of the galaxy and deep into the crust of a backwater mining planet where someone had apparently stirred up a revolution.

Kuai had grown up in downtown Chengdu on Old Earth, in the middle of a conurbation stretching for tens of miles all the way to the foothills of the Hengduan Mountains, and the grip of the Red Star Confederate's government there was an invisible omnipresence in the same vein as gravity. The notion of any meaningful action being taken against the state was laughable: you would get the occasional political rally or outspoken commentator, but even they were looking to change things in line with the existing order. The notion of simply saying 'we don't want this anymore' and dumping the entire system was a fanciful dream, and a dream that most people wouldn't want. The uncertainty, the insecurity, the very real possibility that the government would just march in and take everything back anyway . . . how did that appeal? Jia had been the one to rail against the rules, the regulations, and even the confining walls of their parents' apartment. Kuai would have been happy to stay on the planet that had birthed humanity and get a job in a repair shop, or similar.

But, as always, his sister had gone and got in trouble, and in trying to protect her he'd ended up well outside his comfort zone. Sometimes he was grateful to the Captain and Rourke for bailing Jia out when she'd got herself arrested, sometimes he was still mad that they'd persuaded her to jump that same bail and fly them around the Milky Way from then on. He supposed he was just lucky they'd needed a mechanic at the same time, as otherwise he'd have had to face his parents and admit that he'd let his little sister down.

There was a holoscreen making up one wall of the canteen, displaying whatever inane chatter served as entertainment for Uragan. He already knew it would either be fanciful escapism or one of the peculiarly dour Russian soap operas his mother was inexplicably fond of: 'workers or wizards', his father had dubbed it once. Kuai understood enough about how society worked to know that this sort of place, with its grim drudgery and lack of prospects, wouldn't be one where the government would want people to get ideas above their station. Of course, they seemed to be capable of getting those on their own anyway . . .

He became aware of a change in the atmosphere of the room, and that the heads of the few officers who'd been relieved of duties for long enough to grab a snack were all turning to face the holoscreen. Someone turned the volume up a moment later, and the voice of a dark-haired woman was suddenly to the fore.

'. . . you can see behind me, the revolutionaries are in effective control of Levels Five and below of Uragan City.' She was facing into the camera and speaking into a branded microphone, neither of which were necessary for reporting but which even now were still used to communicate the urgency and immediacy of A Person At The Location. 'This of course gives them control of the main mine face and the raw materials it produces, which they have stated belong to every Uragan citizen equally and will no longer be sold off with the profits going to the gov . . . the Red Star government.'

Officers were looking at each other in confusion. Voices were raised, first in protest and then, as men and women in uniforms and visors just like their own appeared in shot, walking under a Free Systems banner behind the reporter, in anger.

'. . . of the police force resisted, but many have embraced the revolution's aims and have declared themselves ready to serve this new state. As you can see behind me, the—'

Kuai grimaced and, in what he suspected was a probably futile attempt to glean good fortune, touched the dragon pendant his mother had given him. He'd been hoping this whole mess could be sorted out and put down with the minimum of fuss and trouble, but that suddenly looked a whole lot less likely. It wasn't even that he had any form of loyalty to Red Star rule, he just hated it when things were unpredictable, and there was little that was more unpredictable than an enclosed city in the grip of a determined and apparently expanding revolution. He fell back on one of his old adages: if things looked bad, make it someone else's problem. He activated his comm and entered the Captain's callcode.

+Go ahead.+

'*Captain, you need to see this,*' he said. '*We're in the canteen.*'

There was a brief pause, although the faint noises of breathing and echoing footsteps from the other end of the line suggested that Drift was on the move. Then the Captain's voice came again. +What am I missing?+

Kuai debated briefly how to get over exactly what he was watching, and gave it up. English was reportedly a very versatile language in the right hands, but he still hadn't mastered it fully. '*Uhh . . . the revolution has been holovised?*'

The canteen door banged open and the Captain strode in, ignoring the glances he got from the officers who didn't know him and exchanging a couple of nods with the members of Muradov's team who looked around. Kuai had got the impression that the Captain had actually acquitted himself well in the immediate aftermath of the transport he'd been riding in being overturned by a revolutionary booby trap, and that the officers had taken something of a liking to him as a result. Even Muradov seemed to trust him now, which in Kuai's opinion just demonstrated that the man wasn't nearly as smart as he should be.

'*Well,*' the Captain said, sliding onto the bench between Kuai and Jia and looking up at the screen, '*this really is a clusterfuck of epic proportions. The revolution's gained enough of a foothold that they've co-opted the governmental broadcast units. Besides which, I've just found out that they've managed to lift the comm blockade too: Tamara called me a moment ago.'*

'*Seriously?!*' Jia put in from the Captain's other side. '*They all alright?*'

Drift grimaced. '*Depends how you look at it. It sounds like they got separated for a bit, and A.'s broken his ankle somehow, but him and Jenna are with Tamara now.*' He lowered his voice a little. '*They also seem to have called a truce with Moutinho's mob. Where are his two goons?*'

'*Over there.*' Kuai pointed to the far corner where Karwoski and Goldberg sat. He presumed that neither of them spoke good Russian as they'd not interacted with anyone or even looked at the holoscreen, but the woman was now talking urgently into her comm. Presumably Moutinho was on the other end, giving her the same information which Rourke had just passed to the Captain.

'*Keep an eye on them,*' Drift warned, speaking even more quietly so Kuai and Jia had to lean in to hear him properly. Thankfully, the officers in the room were still transfixed by the pictures on the holoscreen. '*They were the gunrunners, Tamara's confirmed that, but we've got a bit of a problem ourselves. It sounds like the revolution have found themselves a very good slicer, and she's been involved with lifting the communications blackout.*'

'*His mother's dick,*' Jia swore in Mandarin, immediately realising Drift was referring to Jenna. She switched back to English. '*So, she been coerced then?*'

'*It sounds like Tamara had to make herself useful to avoid being killed, and that meant dragging Jenna in as well. I don't think they'll just be slipping quietly away from anything any time soon, that's for sure.'*

'Plus, if Muradov finds out about Jenna then we're screwed,' Kuai grunted.

'So maybe don't go throwing their names about?' Jia hissed at him in Mandarin.

'Most of these don't speak English as well as us,' Kuai retorted, although he glanced about to see if any of the officers had looked around at the mention of their chief. It seemed not. 'They'll speak Mandarin though, you think of—'

'Shut up!' Drift snapped. Kuai sometimes thought '*Bì zuǐ*' was the only Mandarin the Captain knew. '*I'm not in the mood for you two to start squabbling. Tamara thinks we should try to get to the Jonah and wait for them there; she seemed to think that the revolution's going to push upwards and that maybe they'll be able to reach us.*'

'Wouldn't surprise me,' Kuai admitted, 'they've done alright so far.'

'Yeah, but they won't be taking the government by surprise any more,' Jia argued.

'Oh, and you're some sort of exper—' Kuai cut himself off as Drift's natural eye narrowed in his direction. He settled for downing the last of his coffee in a gulp, then grimaced as he registered how cold it was. '*Whatever. It still seems like the best chance we've got. Plus, at least we'll actually be on the shuttle in case something goes wrong.*'

'Something has gone wrong,' Drift pointed out.

'You know what I mean.' Kuai shrugged. '*The three of us: we're a pilot, a mechanic and a captain with*

*the access codes. Say the others can't get to us, or . . .
y'know . . . something goes wrong.'*

The Captain's face had become a blank mask. '*You
mean, if they get killed.*'

'*If something goes wrong,*' Kuai repeated, shifting
a little uncomfortably in the stare of that metal eye.
Damn it, why did everyone always try to make him
feel guilty for being realistic? '*I'm just saying that if
we needed to, if there was no point in staying, we
could take off and fly away. That's all.*'

The Captain held his gaze for a moment longer,
then deliberately looked away and up at the holoscreen. '*Just keep an eye on Moutinho's pair. And the
Shirokovs, for that matter.*'

'*You still thinking to give them a ride out?*' Jia
asked, astonished.

'*I'm thinking that this entire venture is neck-deep
in shit and I'll take what recompense I can,*' Drift
snapped, with enough heat to cause a couple of nearby
officers to look around momentarily at the tone of
his voice, even if they hadn't made out the words.
He waved a hand irritably. '*Never mind. I just—*'

He cut off in mid-sentence at exactly the same time
as Kuai saw something he recognised on the holoscreen. The revolution's newscast, still transmitting
in spite of what Kuai assumed must be frantic efforts
on the part of the government to shut it down, had
just shown a panning shot of the plaza outside the
guest house they'd been intending to stay at. Yellow-
and-black Free Systems banners had been draped
across building fronts and people were celebrating in
the square with apparent genuine delight, despite the
fact that Kuai was pretty sure he'd heard about people

being killed there only a few hours ago. And there, in the corner of the shot and seen only for a second in the far background, was a familiar wide-brimmed hat and flowing coat. The wearer was talking to someone else and pointing, apparently oblivious to the camera directed at them, and both the tiny hand emerging from the coat sleeve and the smudge of face visible between collar and hat were dark enough to mark them out from the vast majority of Uragans in shot. The person also appeared to have a rifle slung over one shoulder.

Kuai felt his gut clench, and glanced sideways at the Captain. '*Did you just see her?*'

Drift didn't look at him. '*No. No, I didn't. And neither did either of you.*'

'**Y**ou are certain that they cannot see what we are doing?' Tanja asked for the third time. Jenna did her best to suppress a sigh.

'No, I'm not *certain*,' she replied with studied patience, 'but we've blocked all output on the surveillance feeds that the security stations on this level had access to. I'm not saying that some big cheese up on Level One doesn't have some sort of private, hidden feed that his subordinates down here can't see, but . . .' She shrugged. 'You can't plan for everything.'

Tanja huffed. 'Well, that will have to do. And there is nothing you can do to make our comms more secure?'

Jenna winced. 'On the equipment you've got here? I've done *some* audio encryption before, but that was hard enough to set up for a one-to-one deal on systems I'm familiar with, and even then it was only to avoid casual eavesdropping. Trying to program a secure commsnet for multiple users when you'd have government-level operatives trying to decode it—'

'A "no" would have sufficed, Miss McIlroy.' Jenna's irritation must have showed on her face, because the Uragan rebel immediately held up one hand in a conciliatory gesture. 'My apologies, I intended no offence. I meant that I do not require you to explain yourself to me. You have been of great assistance to the revolution, and if you tell me you cannot do something then I will believe you.'

'Well, okay then,' Jenna nodded, somewhat mollified. 'Umm . . . good luck, I guess.'

'I fear we shall need it,' Tanja said, her expression grim as she turned to survey the scene behind her. 'This will be neither easy nor bloodless.'

They weren't far from Vehicle Gate 2, one of three main routes up into Level Four. The huge, reinforced slabs of steel had been closed off, of course, with their hydraulics locked down. On the other side there were certainly armed security personnel waiting in case of a breach. However, on *this* side was a mass of humanity all the way down the ramp back into Level Five, wearing and waving the colours of the Free Systems.

Tanja was no fool; she was well aware that taking the *politsiya* by surprise wouldn't work the same way twice. A headlong charge by lightly armed and largely unarmoured men and women into the teeth of waiting guns would be a slaughter, and not in their favour. Even if they overwhelmed the waiting troops with sheer weight of numbers, the death toll might be simply too high for people to maintain faith in the revolution.

Besides which, Tanja and her fellows didn't want to smash the systems which ran Uragan City, they simply wanted control of them. Some of the *politsiya* had already decided to join the revolution, either due to previously hidden personal political beliefs or simple awareness of which way the tide was turning. If the rest could be persuaded to follow suit with no more fatalities, so much the better. What was needed was an overwhelming demonstration of how organised and comprehensive the revolution was, and how standing in its way was simply delaying the inevitable.

For all that Rourke had maintained that this wasn't her revolution, Jenna couldn't remember a time when she'd seen the older woman more vital than when she'd been plotting out the next bit of strategy with Tanja and Inzhu. Jenna herself was starting to wilt after what must be coming up to nearly twenty-four hours awake, and she briefly wondered how she'd managed to stay up all night when she'd been doing her degree. *Half a dozen cans of Caffeine Kick and no adrenaline dump from nearly being killed, most likely.* Rourke seemed to be having no such trouble, however, and Jenna's admiration for her had gone up another notch.

Tanja looked at her chrono. 'Five a.m. Time for stage one.' She opened a channel on her comm and began speaking rapidly into it in Russian. Jenna hadn't sat in on all the planning meetings, but she knew well enough what was going to happen. Or at least, what was *supposed* to happen.

From the communications hub on Level Five, the crew who had accepted the revolution would begin transmitting another broadcast which, thanks to their location in Uragan City, could reach every other habitation on the planet. Unlike the previous pro-revolution propaganda disguised as unbiased news reporting, this was a personal message from Tanja Mironova herself. In it she named herself as the Interim Head of the People's Council of the Free State of Uragan until such time as an appropriate election could be held to make the offices permanent. She also addressed Governor Drugov directly, demanding the immediate and unconditional surrender of power to the People's Council forthwith and guaranteeing the safety of his person should he do so.

It was no coincidence that this broadcast began at exactly the same time as mining charges placed at Vehicle Gate 1 went off, breaching the defences and opening hostilities. The idea was to put immediate pressure on the governor, but not to actually force entry. The magnitude of explosion necessary to destroy enough of the gates to allow easy pedestrian and vehicular access would risk bringing the entire roof down, and the miners in the revolution knew their tools well. The explosions which had – hopefully – just gone off would have blasted holes, certainly, but left enough cover for a firefight. That was an attention-grabber, something to start panicked messages flying across the *politsiya*'s comm systems.

'Into position if you please, Miss McIlroy,' Tanja said, her tone of voice one notch down from making it a direct order. Jenna swallowed and began to thread her way through the crowd of revolutionaries, accompanied by a trio of Uragan guards in *politsiya* armour adorned with hastily created Free Systems logos.

The sheer energy of humanity around her was astounding, but she couldn't help wondering how many of these people might make a stupid decision due to sheer overtiredness. She bit back a laugh: wouldn't it have been far more convenient to wait until everyone was well rested for the revolution to begin?

She found her way to a wall terminal, not far from the main gate. This was one of the places she least wanted to be, but Rourke had made it clear that at the moment they had to play along as well as they could to ensure their own safety. Jenna couldn't quite see how standing next to what amounted to an invasion force really ensured *her* safety, but given Rourke had infiltrated the communication hub on her own she guessed she couldn't really complain.

She hooked her wrist-mounted terminal up to the one on the wall and checked her chrono. Two minutes and forty seconds gone since the broadcast began . . .

+*Everything ready?*+ Tanja's voice asked in her ear.

'Accessing now,' Jenna replied, her fingers skating over the interface. The controls on the gates were laughably simple to access if you knew what you were doing, especially if you had access to the main terminal. Normally this would be guarded by *politsiya* of course, but they were long gone. 'Okay, we're ready to roll.'

+*On my mark. And . . . mark.*+

Jenna hit the override and the hydraulics on Vehicle Gate 2 swung smoothly into action. One panel began to retreat into the ceiling while the other started to sink into the floor. Another quick instruction activated a preprogrammed spiralling access algorithm: anyone trying to close the gates from the other side would suddenly find that their command codes no longer worked.

What was more, the exact same thing was happening at the exact same time at Vehicle Gate 3, assuming the tech Jenna had recruited from the communication hub had half a clue what she was doing.

Rourke's plan had been twofold. In the first instance, the phoney assault at Gate 1 would attract attention and, just possibly, divert *politsiya* resources away from the other two gates. In the second instance, the brute-force-and-ignorance method would suggest that this was all the revolution had to work with: in the three minutes after those charges went off, the defenders would be able to wrap their heads around the notion that any incursion from below was going to begin with an almighty noise and commotion, and would by necessity be piecemeal.

Therefore, when the other two gates opened smoothly to disgorge a horde of heavy-duty haulage vehicles intent on ramming their way through any form of security cordon, the impact would not just be physical but psychological.

Jenna flattened herself against the wall as the engines coughed into life around her with basso roars. An answering shout went up from the assembled revolutionaries, who scrambled up onto their make-shift transports or crowded alongside them in the tunnel, eager to push forwards as soon as the lower plate had disappeared. It all looked horrifically confused to Jenna, and she winced as a haulage lorry jerked forwards ahead of time and nearly squashed four people between it and the truck in front. One of them shouted abuse in Portuguese at the driver's cab, and she recognised Moutinho's men. The *Jacare*'s captain saw her and flashed a leering grin, then ostentatiously checked the action of the gun he'd been given after he and his three crew had volunteered to take part in the assault. Of the other three, Skanda looked nervous, Jack looked impatient and the youth called Achilles just looked like he'd taken a battering. Which would be about right, given he'd been kicked twice by Apirana in the last twelve hours.

Her attention was dragged back to the vehicle gate as she caught a glimpse of black uniforms on the other side running around, and moments later there was the *spanging* noises of bullets ricocheting off metal. However, the front line of the revolutionaries' convoy was made up of ore trucks with huge hydraulic scoops for lifting and dumping loose rock, and gunfire spattered off them like rain off the *Jonah*'s viewports. A moment later and the gate had fully opened, and the invasion force lurched into somewhat erratically driven action.

Jenna was no student of warfare, but she was fairly sure the initial charge of the People's Council's motorised militia wouldn't go down in any history documents as an example of slick manoeuvring. It was, however, undeniably effective. The dozen or so drivers simply gunned their engines and headed as fast as they could for the greatest concentration of security personnel and vehicles, at which point the discrepancy in sheer power between a rugged urban police vehicle and an industrial digger became painfully obvious.

Politsiya transports were hoisted partially off the ground and propelled backwards at some speed, with the more unfortunate ones being toppled onto their sides or even their roofs in the process. Revolutionaries on foot flooded through the branching streets in the wake of these trailblazers, waving flags and weapons and shouting slogans as they did so. Some gas grenades were fired in an attempt to slow the charge, but the revolution had learned from earlier clashes and Marya had ordered rebreathers brought up from the mining levels, where hitting subterranean toxic gas pockets was always a risk. Jenna watched in slightly terrified awe as Level Four's official resistance to the Free State of Uragan, consisting of nearly 300 black-clad officers, crumpled in slightly under a minute.

+*Marya reports overwhelming success at Gate 3,*+ Tanja's voice crackled over her comm. +*Well done, Miss McIlroy: your programming worked like a charm.*+

She heard a faint crackle in her ear, a signal that Rourke had switched to the scrambled channel Jenna had prepared for the two of them and Apirana, without telling Tanja. +*Jenna, are you still at the gate?*+

'Still here,' she confirmed.

+*Don't go anywhere. We'll be with you shortly.*+

In fairness, there wasn't really anywhere Jenna could go, as the revolution's bodies continued to surge past. The lower levels of Uragan City were mainly the mine workers and other menial labourers, and the revolution's promises of better wages and a fair share of their planet's riches had quickly found eager listeners even among those who hadn't been party to it before it erupted. The upper levels were generally more affluent, however, and potentially much less welcoming. Inzhu had been adamant that as much visible support as possible should be shunted upwards to 'persuade' the rest of the population not to thwart the will of the people, and so the mines stood still and everyone who could be roused from their beds and given a flag or a sash was sent on their way.

Even allowing for those who couldn't or wouldn't get involved, Tanja's best guess still put that at slightly more than 50,000 people pouring through the three gates and bellowing slogans.

A jeep rolled to a halt next to her, and Jenna nearly jumped in until she realised that it was Tanja in the passenger seat and not Rourke. The Uragan leaned over towards her and raised her voice over the engine noise. 'Do you need a lift?'

'You go on ahead!' Jenna shouted back, gesturing at the terminal behind her. 'I just want to make sure that there are no problems with the security algorithm I've installed!'

Tanja frowned, but nodded. 'Fair enough. Make sure you come and find me when you have finished, though.' She tapped her comm meaningfully, then said something to the jeep's driver and the vehicle rolled onwards.

Jenna huffed out a breath and turned to fiddle with the terminal on the wall. There was absolutely nothing wrong with her programming of course, nor would she have cared even if there was given that she had no intention of returning through this gate once she'd gone past it, but she needed to be out of Tanja's way for a while. She busied herself for a minute or two doing pointless things on her wrist console until a horn sounded and she looked around to see Apirana's tattooed face peering out of the window of a bulky flatbed truck.

'All aboard who's comin' aboard!' the big Maori boomed. He looked at Jenna's three guards. 'You boys still babysittin' our girl here? We can look after her, no trouble.'

'We have orders,' one responded, his English broken but intelligible. 'Must guard McIlroy, take back to Councillor Mironova.'

Rourke's head, complete with wide-brimmed hat, rose up above the truck's cab on the driver's side. 'That's where we're going anyway, so jump on the back if you want. Jenna, there's room for you in the front if you don't mind squeezing between A. and me.'

'Sounds good,' Jenna replied, disconnecting her wrist console, 'I'm done here anyway.' She headed around to the far side of the vehicle where Rourke momentarily disembarked to allow her to scoot across the bench-like front seat, while her three guards climbed onto the flatbed at the back. She was careful not to knock Apirana's braced ankle with her feet: luckily, there was enough space for her between the big man's bulk and Rourke's diminutive figure to avoid her being uncomfortably crushed up against anyone.

'We still goin' through with this?' Apirana murmured, looking straight ahead and barely moving his lips as Rourke put the truck into gear.

'You have a better idea?' Rourke asked, pulling away carefully.

'Jus' seems a bit cold-blooded, is all.'

'You say that like it's a bad thing,' Rourke replied. Her tone wasn't defensive, but there was steel in it nonetheless. 'Look around you, A.: this hot-headed revolution would have led to a bloodbath without me. It was going to happen anyway, but I've given them ways of making it as efficient as possible. People will die, but people always die in revolutions. Hopefully, my cold-blooded input will lessen the body count.'

'That ain't what I was talking about,' Apirana rumbled, 'an' you know it.'

Rourke shrugged. 'It's true on a large scale or a small. Just trust that everything I'm doing is based on getting all three of us to where we need to be with as little risk to us as possible.'

'I ain't necessarily doubting that,' the Maori sighed, 'I just wish there was another way.'

'So do I.'

They were through Vehicle Gate 2 now and into Level Four proper. The remnants of the *politsiya* presence were scattered around, what parts of it hadn't been gathered up to be used by the revolution itself as it surged through the streets. It seemed that some of the locals had already been swept up in the tide of bodies that was pushing onwards, and here and there Jenna could see walls daubed with crude yellow-and-black symbols or presumably triumphant graffiti.

Rourke drove the truck with quiet assurance through the streets, checking the schematic Jenna had downloaded for them all as she went. She mainly stuck to the larger routes, but at one crossroads she took a right onto a smaller street, then a left into one much narrower still. This was little more than an alley; there would barely be space for another vehicle to pass them here, and the buildings on either side seemed to loom despite their relative lack of height.

A helmeted face appeared at the window, its visor raised so that the Uragan's face could be seen as he leaned forwards somewhat precariously from the flatbed behind them. 'This is not route!'

'I'm taking a shortcut,' Rourke replied, sounding slightly irritated. They rounded another corner and she braked, hissing in vexation. 'What in the . . .?'

Two shot-up vehicles blocked the road and in front of them were four figures apparently arguing with each other, figures whom Jenna recognised as Rourke rolled the truck to a halt not ten metres away.

'Moutinho!' Rourke called, half leaning out of her window. 'What the hell are you clowns playing at back here?'

Ricardo Moutinho turned around, his eyes flashing over his bristling moustache. 'Go suck an afterburner, Rourke!'

'You're blocking my road, you Brazilian piece of crap!' Rourke retorted. 'Did you wreck these things for fun, is that it?'

'You can't just blame everything on me, you know that?' Moutinho snarled. 'This wasn't *our* roadblock: a bunch of cops decided to take potshots at us from behind it. If you'd actually been getting stuck in, instead of pissing about playing big shot, you might have seen that.'

'Well, shift them!'

'To hell with you, turn around and go back!'

'I'm not going to try turning this beast around in here,' Rourke replied firmly. 'How about we give you a hand?'

'*You?*' Moutinho snorted. 'You can't choke a car and shooting it some more won't help, so how're you going to help, little woman? Plus I know your Maori's got a broken ankle.'

'We've got passengers,' Rourke said, jerking a thumb at the rear of the truck. 'Try to look like good citizens and I'll see what I can do.' She turned the other way, craning her head out of the truck's window, and started speaking in Russian. After a few exchanges, in which Jenna thought her guards sounded a little tetchy, they clumped down from the flatbed and headed for the roadblock where Moutinho and his crew waited. Rourke slipped out of the cab and followed them, fiddling with her left sleeve as she did so.

'I still don't like this,' Apirana muttered from beside her. Jenna, fighting down the acid churning in her stomach, had to agree.

It took much sweating and grunting, except for Achilles and Rourke who climbed into the wrecks and did their best to steer them, but finally the two vehicles were pushed aside and staggered along the alley's edges so their truck could slalom between them. That done, the three Uragans dusted themselves down and turned to head back to their ride.

Rourke's garrotting wire flashed out of her sleeve as she looped it over the head of the leftmost one and jerked backwards. The man's hands flew up to his neck but the narrow polymer cord was already digging too tightly into his flesh for his fingers to get any purchase.

Skanda dropped to his knees behind the second and slammed his arm up between the man's legs. As their victim doubled over, Jack slid his heavy knife from his belt and dragged it across the guard's throat to spatter the ground with his blood.

The guard on the right had removed his helmet during his exertions. Achilles snatched it from his hand and, as the man opened his mouth to protest, Moutinho simply placed the barrel of the gun the revolution had provided him with to the back of the guard's head and pulled the trigger. The bullet exploded from the front of the Uragan's skull, carrying bits of brain and face with it.

'Damn it, Moutinho,' Rourke snarled, wrestling her choking, purple-faced victim onto all fours, 'you got his uniform dirty! That one's yours!'

After staking an unassailable claim on the hearts and minds of the proles in the lower levels, the revolution had paused briefly at the threshold between Levels Four and Five to gather its strength and transmit propaganda to the rest of Uragan City. After watching the 'news' broadcast, Drift had taken this as a cue to grab some sleep, which he'd done in the corner of the *politsiya* canteen with the ease of a long-time smuggler, on the basis that as soon as anything kicked off again someone would wake him up.

It had kicked off three hours ago, and the revolution had promptly swept through Level Four and its carefully organised government military resistance. Level Three's populace had seen the real-time broadcasts of this on their holoscreens and, presumably wishing to keep their homes in good order, had turned out onto the streets to declare for the Free State before Muradov had even had time to try to organise a new

line of defence. It was now 8 a.m. local time, and
Drift was back in Chief Muradov's transport riding
through Level Two. The security chief's normal expression of stern professionalism had been replaced with
the haggard grimness of a man aware that, short of
a miracle, he was fighting a war that was already lost.

'Chief, I'm not trying to be difficult here,' Drift
offered as Muradov studied the tactical holo as
though there was some solution to be seen in it if he
simply looked hard enough, 'but perhaps you should
just give up?'

'The revolution is unlikely to be kindly disposed
towards you, Captain,' Muradov replied without looking up. 'I would have thought you would be more
interested in keeping your skin intact than suggesting
I should surrender.'

'Oh, I'm attached to it, don't get me wrong,' Drift
replied seriously, 'but you don't get as old as I am
doing what I do unless you can see which jobs are
a losing proposition. The one you're looking at right
now is a loss all ends up, through no fault of your
own, and you deserve to be told so. You've treated
me and mine well, and fairly. You gave us protection
when maybe that would have been the last thing on
the minds of most—'

'And you repaid me by keeping my team and me
alive long enough for us to get out of that wreck,'
Muradov cut in, sparing Drift a glance and a faint,
bitter smile, 'so perhaps my judgement is not so bad
as you think.'

'I'm just saying, I'm sure that this Mironova's going
to recognise your qualities,' Drift persisted. 'You've
done your job as well as you can, as well as anyone

could, but perhaps it's just time to let the inevitable happen, you know? Maybe take up your job again under this Free State.'

'Captain, I appreciate what you are saying,' Muradov said, pinching the bridge of his nose, 'but let me make a few things clear to you. Firstly, although I have come to realise that you are not perhaps the scoundrel I initially thought . . .'

Drift put his best poker face into place and kept it there.

'. . . there is still a great difference between the somewhat, shall we say, "fluid" nature of your commerce and the responsibilities of my role.' He looked up, his dark eyes tired but focused. 'I took a solemn oath upon the commencement of my duty as Uragan City's security chief, and I will not willingly see that oath broken.

'Secondly, I strongly suspect that "heads must roll" under any new state. There must be certain changes made, lest the revolution be seen as a sham. They have already declared that the governor will be replaced, as of course they would. I can see no reason why they would let me, the man who embodies the will of the governor and, by extension, the Red Star government, keep my job. In the frenzy of revolutionary fervour, it would be a miracle should I even make it to trial on some trumped-up charge. More likely, I would be lynched by a mob before that pretence of justice occurred.

'Thirdly, the Red Star government *will* retake this city, or even this planet, no matter whether or not it is lost to the revolution. It may not be easy or quick, but it will be done. The minerals harvested here are too valuable for it to be allowed to secede. On the day when Red Star forces retake Uragan City, if I am found to be in any situation other than already dead or languishing in a prison cell, then I shall surely be tried and executed as a traitor to the state; and rightly so.

'Finally, if this is some effort on your part to convince me to let you try your luck and attempt to get back to your shuttle, I should inform you that the spaceport has already declared for the revolution.'

'What?!' Drift slumped back in his seat, suddenly feeling a lot more tired than he had been. '*Jesús, Maria, Madre de Dios!*' His admittedly somewhat loose plan, once it became clear that the revolution was going to win out, had been to ride with Muradov as close to the surface as he could and then make for the spaceport to wait for Rourke and the others when they got there. If the spaceport was already in the hands of the Free State, however . . . *but perhaps that means Rourke's already there.* He tapped his comm, but found it dead.

'Civilian communications have been disabled over all levels now, of course,' Muradov said in response to his questioning look. 'It is the only advantage we have been able to maintain.'

'Didn't the rebels manage to get them working again before?' Drift asked, trying to keep the hopefulness out of his voice.

'When we had only disabled it on certain levels, yes,' Muradov nodded. 'We have now shut down the entire network. I do not know how long it will be until they can gain control of it since they already have a foothold on Level One, but until then I am afraid you will not be able to make contact with the rest of your crew.' He frowned. 'Did you ever manage to, by the way?'

'Uh, yes,' Drift replied, 'but when we were on Level Four they were still on Level Five and unable to reach us.'

'A shame,' Muradov said, and Drift got the impression the man might actually mean it. He watched as the security chief spoke into the comm that connected him to the driver, and the vehicle turned in response. Drift didn't usually care much for lawmen, but Muradov was smart, capable and honourable, and clearly cared for the city and the citizens he was responsible for. However, it seemed that wasn't going to be enough to carry the day. It was a shame, in a way: had the man been more brutal or totalitarian he might have stopped this rebellion earlier, and if he'd turned a blind eye to some of his government's more stringent regulations then this level of unrest might never have brewed in the first place. Instead he'd followed orders and procedure, and now the poor decisions of others would see him lose his job and quite possibly his life.

All of which was a damn shame, of course, but it also meant that Ichabod Drift might lose *his* life. And despite having lived on what might be considered borrowed time for well over a decade, ever since he'd tricked the Federation of African States into thinking he'd asphyxiated aboard the *Thirty-Six Degrees*, he wasn't ready to lie down and die yet. He was out of his element down here in this enclosed, Russian-speaking city, but the closer they got to the storm-lashed surface and the sky, the more comfortable he was.

In fact, he was starting to have an idea.

He checked his pad, but he was still locked out from the Spine. It looked like he'd have to do this the long way, then.

'Chief,' he said quietly, getting up and moving to Muradov's side, 'let's say that this has tipped too far and you can't pull it back. I'd imagine that your responsibility would then be to safeguard the governor, right?'

'Indeed,' Muradov confirmed, looking sideways at him, 'although I must confess, if all else is lost then that will not be an easy task. There are few places to hide in this city, and the surface offers no shelter. However, Governor Drugov has demanded my presence and I must attend him to advise him of his options, limited though they are.'

'So what if you got him off-world?' Drift asked. 'If I know anything about planetary governors – which okay, I don't really, but still – I'd have thought he has his own shuttle, right? And his own launch pad?'

Muradov's face took on a long-suffering expression. 'Yes, Captain, but you may remember that there is a large storm overhead at the moment, through which it is impossible to fly. Were it not there, I believe you would have taken off shortly after leaving my custody . . .'

'"Impossible" is just a word, Chief,' Drift said, feeling a faint smile tug at the corners of his mouth. 'Can you bring up details of the storm, please?' He met the Uragan's steady gaze. 'Humour me?'

Muradov still looked sceptical, but finally shrugged. 'As you wish.'

He fiddled with the controls and the tactical holo showing the levels of Uragan City abruptly gave way to a three-dimensional map of the surface, complete with the swirling monstrosity of the storm above it as mapped by the city's atmospheric instruments. Drift took it in quickly, noting the pattern of the clouds and the more vivid colours which denoted greater wind speeds, then smiled more broadly.

'And the governor's private launch pad is . . .?'

'Here.' Muradov tapped something and an otherwise unremarkable part of the ground began to flash.

Drift chewed the inside of his cheek for a moment, studying the display to make sure he'd got this right and wasn't about to look like a complete idiot. 'Okay, so this here is the eye of the storm, correct? And it's due to begin passing over the governor's residence soon.'

'Captain, a Uragan storm is not like some hurricane on Old Earth,' Muradov explained shortly. 'It is many times stronger, and even in the eye, wind speeds are still far too dangerous for flight. Besides which, the eye is narrow: any miscalculation of timing would result in the shuttle being caught in the back edge of the eyewall, where the winds are strongest once more.'

'If the choice is between possibly getting into orbit on a shuttle or almost certainly getting killed by the rebellion, which do you think the governor will take?' Drift asked mildly.

'I think the governor will be reliant on his personal pilot,' Muradov snapped, 'who is unlikely to be feeling suicidal given that he can probably win favour with the revolution simply by refusing to do his job!'

Drift smirked, and jerked a thumb over his shoulder in the general direction of where Jia sat. 'Then it's a good thing we've got one with us, isn't it?'

Muradov's face stilled suddenly. Drift knew that expression: it was that of a man who'd just heard some unexpectedly good news and was wondering if he could trust it.

'Ah shit, this don't sound good,' Jia remarked from behind him. 'What you getting me into now?'

'Chief, I've got my pilot and mechanic with me,' Drift persisted, ignoring Jia's complaints. 'I'd stake my life that we can get you and your governor onto whatever ship he has waiting for him in orbit and back to New Samara, if that's what you want.'

'You didn't hear me when I told you about the storm, did you?' Muradov sighed.

'I did,' Drift countered, 'and I'm telling you that if anyone in this galaxy can get through those conditions, it's Jia. We've had to do some, ah, *unconventional* flying at times—'

'You mean smuggling,' Muradov cut in.

'Unconventional flying,' Drift repeated firmly. 'But fine, if that's an assumption you want to make, let's run with it. Who would you rather trust in a situation like this? Some jumped-up flight-school graduate in a uniform, whose most important job has been making sure that the governor's coffee doesn't spill during a landing? Or a smuggler pilot who's flown through storms and pitch-blackness, outmanoeuvred security craft, and has put down in places with no landing pad or guidance beacons? Jia's part insane and part genius, and I'm never quite sure exactly where the sliders lie on that scale, but she's still the best damn pilot I've ever met. I'm not saying it won't be a bit hair-raising, but we'll get out.'

Muradov pursed his lips. 'Even on a craft she has never flown before?'

'Hey!' Jia shouted up. 'What kind of fuckin' amateur do you take me for? It got thrusters? It got controls? It got structural integrity? Then I can fuckin' fly it!'

'And the rest of your crew?' Muradov asked Drift, frowning. 'We would not be able to wait for them to somehow make contact with you. You would be abandoning them.'

Drift had thought of that, and the prospect of leaving Rourke, Jenna and Apirana stranded on Uragan wasn't one he relished. All the same . . . 'A great man once said, "You have to be realistic about these things." Our shuttle's still in the spaceport, and our ship's still in orbit. My business partner is fluent in Russian and I don't believe they've given anyone any reason to wish them harm, so hopefully they can find their way off here. Right now, I'm more concerned with what will happen if the revolution catches up with *us*.'

'You make a convincing argument, Captain,' Muradov acknowledged. He cocked an eyebrow at a heated exchange in Mandarin coming from the Chang siblings. 'I do, however, have one question.'

'Which is?'

'What in the Prophet's name is a "pilot hat"?'

DECEPTION

As it turned out, Ricardo Moutinho didn't have to wear the hastily cleaned body armour of the man he'd shot because he was rather taller than the guard who'd been wearing it. Skanda would have been the right height, although perhaps a bit on the fat side, but he was no more likely to pass for a native Uragan than Rourke was, and was in any case unwilling to remove his turban. Achilles ended up drawing the short straw, although he hardly looked like an imposing presence. Still, Rourke supposed that since the armour had probably been 'reassigned' from its original *politsiya* owners anyway, no one would really be too surprised that there was an obvious gap between the youth's ribcage and the armavest he was wearing.

'You two, keep your visors down,' she'd ordered Jack and Moutinho, who'd managed to fit themselves into the remaining two uniforms. 'Neither of you will pass muster if anyone sees your faces. Keep your gloves on, too, and your chins tucked.'

'In future, how about we avoid planets made up exclusively of fucking white people?' Jack had drawled to his captain.

'Shut up and try to look pale,' had been Moutinho's sole response.

The three *Jacare* crewmen had taken up station on the back of the truck again, this time with Jenna sitting in their middle. Meanwhile, Skanda sat in the cab between Apirana and Rourke as they'd played a cautious game of cat and mouse up through Uragan City, following the revolution's advance while trying to stay clear of anyone who might recognise her or Jenna as people who were meant to be reporting to Tanja Mironova or her council. All of them studiously ignored any attempts from the revolution at contacting them on the comms, but this was surprisingly piecemeal.

They'd reached Level Two when the two-way radio she'd picked up for infiltrating the communications hub crackled and disgorged Jenna's voice.

+*They've knocked out the comms and the Spine again, over.*+

Rourke frowned and picked her handset up to reply. 'Do you think they've done that centrally from Level One this time? Over.'

+*I reckon. So until the revolution takes control of that, they're running in the dark again. Over.*+

Rourke pulled the truck around a bend. 'What was the state of play, last you heard? How far had the revolution reached? Over.'

+*Uh, Captain Moutinho was listening in on the comms, over.*+

Rourke sighed. 'Put him on, over.'

The radio crackled again, and Moutinho's voice replaced Jenna's. +*What do you want to know, O Tactical Genius? Over.*+

Rourke gritted her teeth. 'Have they taken the spaceport? Over.'

+*I heard someone babbling about some fighting up there before the comms got cut, but I couldn't tell you what the outcome was; I think they were still at it. You thinking we should make a break for it? Over.*+

'Have you heard anything from your two?' Rourke asked. 'Have they managed to get away from Muradov yet? Over.'

+*Um segundo.*+ There was a brief pause. +*Jack says that the last time he spoke to Dugan they were still with the cops. Your mechanic had passed on a message from Drift on the down-low about him trying to talk everyone's way clear once they were on Level One, then making for the spaceport. Course, Dugan couldn't really say much since he wasn't sure how much the cops around him could understand, I guess. Over.*+

Rourke shared a glance with Apirana and saw her own grim thoughts reflected in the big man's face. She couldn't see a likely way out for their colleagues. 'I think we chance it. We head for the spaceport, try to bluff our way onto the ships and take it from there. Over.'

+*You do realise that once we're on board we're sitting ducks with nowhere to go, right? Unless you want to try flying into the teeth of the mother of all storms, I mean. Over.*+

'We'll be in a better position to act than we are now,' Rourke argued. 'If our crews make it to us then at least we're all in the right place and we can take off as soon as there's a break in the weather. Hell, there are bound to be other ways out to the surface in a mining city, some sort of fume vents or something: all they'd have to do is get some breathing apparatus and survive long enough for us to reach them. Over.'

+*And if they don't make it at all? Over.*+

'Well, better some of us make it off than none of us, I guess.' She did her best to look apologetic in Apirana's direction, but the Maori's face was hard to read. 'Over.'

+*You're a stone-cold bitch, Tamara. It's why I liked you; I always said you were wasted on that soft-hearted Mexican bastard. Okay, you get us there, we'll get us in, over.*+

Rourke suppressed a humourless snort. Moutinho had no idea that the 'soft-hearted Mexican bastard' he'd just ridiculed had been the most notorious pirate in the galaxy and had once left his entire crew to suffocate in order to save his own skin. Perhaps that was why the Brazilian had always underestimated Drift. 'Just don't kill anyone unless you have to, over.'

+*You're never satisfied, that's your problem. Over.*+

Rourke grinned. 'We established long ago that I'd never be satisfied by you. Out.' Apirana gave a bark of laughter on the far side of the cab. It was a welcome sound: the big man had seemed uncommonly dejected since she'd met up with him and Jenna again, and Rourke didn't put that entirely down to the pain of his broken ankle. Beside her,

Skanda turned slightly to eye her curiously, and she sighed. 'Don't say anything.'

'I wasn't—'

'I could hear you *thinking* it.'

With the individual parts of the revolution no longer able to communicate with each other or, crucially, with Tanja, Rourke felt able to take a chance. She navigated through the streets of Level Two and pulled the truck up next to a crowd of revolutionaries who were surrounding the pedestrian elevators, then jumped out and beckoned Jenna over. 'You can get these working, right?'

'The elevators?' Jenna frowned down from the flatbed, absent-mindedly flicking a strand of red-blonde hair back from her face. 'If it's a software lockdown then sure, assuming there's still power running to the systems. If they've cut that, or if there's some physical lock on it, I've got nothing.'

'Fingers crossed, then,' Rourke muttered, helping the young slicer down. She beckoned to the three *Jacare* crewmen in their pillaged uniforms. 'Come on, gentlemen, time to look like you belong.'

'*Just don't get us all killed while you play secret agent,*' Moutinho grunted to her in good, if accented, Russian: presumably he was just showing off, as none of the revolutionaries were in earshot yet. Rourke bit back the temptation to tell him that actually she *had* been a 'secret agent' for years, but Moutinho didn't notice her annoyance as he hopped down after Jenna and turned back to the other two. 'Don't bother trying to look all military and precise, boys. Us revolution types probably took these uniforms off dead men, after all.'

'"Probably",' Jack snorted, following his captain's lead. Rourke had to concede that, admittedly more by coincidence than design, the trio managed to give off an air of casual thuggery that fitted their roles as quasi-official revolutionary enforcers. She looked in the truck's door and jerked her head at Skanda. 'Come on, this is your stop.'

'Are you sure this is going to work?' the *Jacare*'s lone undisguised crewman asked nervously, shuffling along the seat to get out.

'No,' Rourke admitted, standing to let him squeeze through the door, 'but it's our best shot at getting back to the shuttles. A., you holding up okay?'

'I'll live,' the big man replied shortly. He hopped out of the cab and steadied himself on his crutches, then nudged the door shut behind him with a bump of his elbow. 'Let's get this over with.'

Rourke looked between him and Jenna, standing on opposite sides of the truck and making no move to approach each other, and stifled a sigh. Digging into the interpersonal relationships of her crew would have to wait, and preferably until she could hand it over to Drift. Right now she needed to concentrate on the job in hand.

'Fall in, everyone,' she ordered. They'd already been seen, and a couple of Uragans in Free Systems colours were approaching with a mix of curiosity and caution. Everything depended on Rourke being able to take the initiative, so she stepped forwards and held her hand up in greeting.

'*Good morning!*' she hailed them all in Russian, then turned her full attention to the woman who'd been two steps ahead of her compatriot. '*My name is Tamara, I've been assisting Councillor Mironova. Who is in charge here, please?'*

The man, a bulky, dark-haired specimen, looked doubtfully sideways at his blonde companion, but she showed no such uncertainty as she responded. *'I am. My name is Olga Timofyeva. This is Yuri.'*

'A pleasure to meet you,' Rourke nodded briskly. She gestured to the elevator banks behind the two Uragans. *'I take it the transport links are currently inoperable?'*

'The displays are active but they're not responding to commands,' Olga replied. *'We have a couple of maintenance crew here, but all they can tell us is that the elevators must have been locked down on Level One.'*

Rourke breathed an inward sigh of relief. *'We have someone who may be able to assist.'* She turned and beckoned Jenna forwards. The young slicer threaded her way between her supposed bodyguards and smiled nervously; either excellent acting skills or, more likely, genuine discomfort. *'This is Jenna: she has been assisting in technical matters.'* She turned to Jenna and switched back to English. 'Do you need to access the wall terminal?'

'That's the best way in, yeah,' Jenna nodded.

'She'll need to connect to the control panel,' Rourke told the two Uragans. *'I take it you're hoping to get up to Level One?'*

'Those were our last instructions before the comms died,' Yuri put in before Olga could reply. Rourke got the impression that he wasn't too happy with Timofyeva putting herself forward as the person in charge. He gestured at the crowd of variably armed

rebels behind him. '*Once we're up there, we're meant to secure the transport links on that level, the trams and suchlike.*'

'*Excellent,*' Rourke nodded, '*we'll come with you. Jenna, if you would?*' She coughed in momentary embarrassment when she realised she'd continued speaking in Russian, but Jenna just smiled, so presumably she'd activated a translation program via her comm and wrist console.

'Gotcha.' Jenna squinted at the mass of humanity in front of her. 'Er . . . do you know where the panel is?'

It ended up being easiest for them to move as a group with Rourke providing the translations where necessary, although she didn't even bother attempting to parse Jenna's techno-speak into Russian when the slicer was mumbling to herself at the control board. Within a couple of minutes green lights started blinking up to replace red ones, and a ragged cheer went up from the rebels as the elevator doors started sliding smoothly open. Yuri and Olga stepped away to begin organising their followers, and Rourke felt her stomach unclench a little.

'Nicely done,' she muttered. 'Remind me to talk to Ichabod about getting you a pay rise when we're off here.'

'It wasn't that hard,' Jenna muttered, her cheeks flushing, 'all these utility systems use the same basic programming which means they have the same security protocols, so once you've figured out how to unlock one thing—'

'Lesson one, kiddo,' Moutinho's voice drawled out of his helmet, cutting her off, 'never turn down an offer of a pay rise.'

'You keep quiet!' Rourke hissed, looking around. Thankfully no one seemed to have noticed that the Uragan enforcer had just spoken English with a Brazilian twang.

'*What's the matter, Tamara?*' Moutinho continued, in Russian this time. '*You don't want me talking to your wide-eyed little lamb? Scared I'll lure her away from you?*'

'*You're welcome to have her laugh in your face if you try,*' Rourke retorted, '*just wait until you're not going to blow our cover when you do.*' She motioned towards the elevators. '*Let's get out of here.*'

The pedestrian elevators were a trio of large, maglev metal boxes which could comfortably take thirty people at a time. The rebels had initially tried packing more in, until Rourke had a quick conversation with Olga about the potential impact of rapid-firing weapons and grenades into an enclosed space. Even so, roughly 200 revolutionaries were able to be shuttled up to Level One in relative short order, and it was only a matter of minutes before Rourke's group were able to follow with the last few Uragans. Olga had gone up with the first party, leaving Yuri to bring up the rear along with a dozen or so companions.

'*Very impressive work, Miss,*' the big Uragan said politely to Jenna as they boarded.

'Thank you,' Jenna beamed. 'I'm happy to help.'

'*I'm surprised to find off-worlders so invested in our cause, though,*' Yuri continued conversationally to Rourke. There was a faint jerk beneath their feet as the elevator swept into upwards motion.

'*Jenna is a slicer,*' Rourke shrugged. '*If you show her a system, she wants to take it apart and play with it just to see if she can. She doesn't much mind who it belongs to.'*

Yuri made a noncommittal sound in his throat. *'And you?'*

'I made a deal with Councillor Mironova,' Rourke replied truthfully. *'I agreed to help her if she helped me.'*

The elevator *pinged* and the doors slid open to reveal Level One's tram depot, a tributary of sidings branching off the main track with the snub-nosed, silvery lines of carriages parked in them at this early hour. The elevator's occupants began to disembark, several of the Uragans running off to join their fellows who were already overrunning the depot. However, Yuri and three others didn't follow.

Rourke heard the buzz of an arming weapon half a second before she felt the cold pressure of a barrel at the base of her neck. *Stupid girl. You let yourself get tired and careless.* She held up her hands and turned around slowly, being careful to make nothing that could be interpreted as a move to unsling the Crusader from her right shoulder. Yuri's companions had also raised their weapons, and they were all covering her: too many to try to take down, even at this close and confused range. With Apirana out of commission and Moutinho's loyalty somewhat suspect at the best of times . . .

'Councillor Mironova sent a message out just before we lost the comms,' Yuri said with a sneer, *'identifying you as a deserter. Olga didn't hear it, which is why she believed your lies and why I am going to get the credit for bringing you in.'* He paused for a second, then looked past her at Moutinho and his goons in their Free Systems-daubed gear. *'You*

three! Didn't you hear me? She's a deserter! Arrest her, then get the slicer back to the councillor!'

'*Yes, sir!*' Moutinho's voice said briskly, his Uragan accent almost perfect. Behind her, Rourke heard three more guns buzz into readiness.

A FIGHTING RETREAT

They were on Level One and heading for the governor's residence. The first sign Drift had that something was wrong – well, more wrong than he'd become accustomed to – was when an unfamiliar female voice crackled over the transport's speaker. He'd turned translations off to save battery life on his comm and pad, but his Russian was good enough to recognise a call for all units to respond, and his grasp of body language was easily sufficient to notice Muradov stiffening in surprise.

The security chief grabbed the handset and snapped something in return. '*Who is this?*' Well, that was easy enough to understand. Everyone else in the vehicle was looking round, clearly wondering who had just broadcast on the *politsiya*'s open channel. Unfortunately Drift's language skills weren't up to translating the response, but judging by the thunderous expression that slid across Muradov's features, it wasn't a good one. He looked over at the Changs in search of assistance, and Kuai took a few steps across the bay to slide into the seat next to him.

'She says she's a councillor,' the little mechanic murmured. 'Sounds like she's the head of this revolution.'

'Shit,' Drift muttered. 'So they've taken the security headquarters, then.'

Muradov snarled something uncomplimentary into his handset, but the reply was calm and measured, almost imperious. Drift had never seen this woman, but he had a sudden mental image of a barely controlled smirk on her face while she broadcast across Uragan City to any *politsiya* who were still listening.

'She says Muradov has to turn himself in, or he'll be considered a traitor,' Kuai whispered before Drift's brain was even halfway through trying to decipher what had just been said. 'All security forces are called upon to arrest him in the name of the new state.' He listened for a moment more. 'Anyone who fails to do so will also be a traitor.'

'Oh, wonderful.' Drift felt his stomach tighten as he glanced as surreptitiously as he could around the vehicle. There were half a dozen *politsiya* officers in here with them, as well as Goldberg and Karwoski. Ahead of them was another transport vehicle with ten more officers plus a driver and both Shirokovs, and a third brought up the rear behind them; all that was left loyal of Muradov's security forces. *So how many of them are still willing to fight for a lost cause?*

Not enough, if he was any judge. Not if they had families to think about.

He got up, pretending it was just to stretch his back – which wasn't far from the truth, as Red Star security vehicles were not the most comfortable in which to spend an extended period of time – and took a few steps towards the two *Jacare* crew, who were sitting opposite Jia near the rear. Goldberg glared at him as he came level with them, but he ignored her hostility and bent over with one hand braced on the rack above her head. This made it look like he was continuing his stretching, but it also brought his head down between theirs.

'Any minute now, someone's probably going to try to arrest the Chief,' he muttered. 'Our only way off this rock is on the governor's shuttle with him, so we throw down on his side, okay?'

'Are you crazy?' Goldberg hissed.

'Possibly,' Drift conceded, 'but unless one of you has a brilliant plan for how to get out of this . . .?'

'Last I heard from the boss, they hadn't made it to the spaceport yet,' Karwoski muttered grudgingly. 'Lena, I reckon we gotta take this.'

'And leave them down here?!'

'We can wait for 'em in orbit, or they can wait for us,' Karwoski shrugged uncomfortably. 'You've got the access codes for the *Jacare*, yeah?'

Goldberg didn't answer, but a certain resignation flavoured her glare. Drift decided that was probably the best he was going to get so he straightened back up again and turned around, just in time to see the big officer with the moustache stand with an expression of grave reluctance on his face.

'*Komandir?*'

Muradov's stare could have cut through hull metal, but the big man ignored it except to go slightly redder in the face. 'Komandir, ya—'

Another officer, a woman with her red hair in twin plaits, got to her feet and interposed herself between the big man and Muradov and started shouting. A second later the entire interior of the vehicle had devolved into chaos, with every member of the politsiya on their feet, raising their voice and gesticulating.

In such a highly charged environment it was of course only a matter of time until someone put their hand on a weapon. In this case it was the big man with the moustache, who held his left hand out in what looked to be a simultaneously warning and accusing manner towards the red-haired officer in front of him while his right crept apparently automatically to the pistol holstered at his side. It seemed, however, that he hadn't banked on the strength of feeling of a muscular young woman with a blonde buzz cut, who took exception to this and stepped up to slug him neatly across the jaw.

The big man skewed sideways and went down, which was the cue for the other three officers to go for their own guns, or at least try to: Drift saw Karwoski explode up from his seat and tackle one of them around the waist, while Goldberg moved to grab the officer's gun hand and wrest the weapon from him.

For his part, Drift jumped on the back of the nearest man and pinned his gun arm to his side using his legs, then snaked an arm under the Uragan's chin and squeezed for all he was worth. He caught a brief

glimpse of Kuai cowering with his arms raised protect-
ively around his head – hardly surprising, given that
the little mechanic had taken a bullet in a scuffle a
few weeks before – before Drift's adversary reversed
sharply into the wall in an attempt to batter him off.
There was a flash of pain as the back of his skull
collided with the storage rack, but he gritted his teeth
and held on.

The man tried again, a shuffle-forwards-and-back
motion without the momentum of the original attempt,
but Drift ducked his head and the metal just scraped
unpleasantly up the back of his skull instead of hitting
him squarely. Then he felt the Uragan's legs start to
go as the lack of blood to the brain began to tell, and
braced himself for the man to keel backwards onto
him.

There was an unpleasant metallic crunching sound,
the entire vehicle rocked and Drift found himself
accelerating forward towards the floor. The unfortunate with whom he was grappling hit face first, which
proved to be enough to send him completely limp,
while Drift's left shoulder and hip took the brunt of
his fall and both promptly began screaming at him.
He let go of the Uragan and staggered up to his feet,
looking around in confusion. 'What the—'

The noise and impact came again, throwing everyone
about for a second time, and Drift realised what it
was. They were being rammed.

Muradov grabbed his comm handset and spat
something in Russian, but Drift was already moving
past the security chief and hauling open the door that
led to the cab. The driver was so busy wrenching at
the controls that she didn't even look around at the

interruption, and Drift got a momentary impression of wide streets lined with affluent-looking houses and gardens – with artificial sunlight and real plants! – before he refocused on the intimidating bulk of another Red Star riot vehicle swerving at them from the right. Clearly one of their escort vehicles, or at least the driver of it, had decided to try to curry favour with the new regime.

'Brace!' he yelled into the passenger bay, grabbing the door frame for support half a second before they got hit again. The jolt was bad enough to send a new stab of pain through his shoulder, but not enough to send him to the floor. He pulled the pistol he'd appropriated from its holster and aimed it reflexively at the other vehicle's driver, visible through the two cabs' respective viewports, but remembered at the last moment that the glass on both trucks would be bullet-proof and he was more likely to endanger himself or his own driver with a ricochet. However, the other man saw the weapon and seemed to have a similar memory lapse: he swerved away instinctively, allowing Drift's vehicle to recover the centre of the road just before it would have been forced into a very solid-looking boundary wall.

The escort vehicle ahead seemed to have worked out what was going on, and its driver decided to intervene by slamming on the brakes and turning so it started to skid sideways down the street. Drift thought for a moment that they were joining the attack, but then saw that it had been angled to cut off the aggressor to their right. Muradov's driver veered across the street in a sideswipe of her own, forcing the other vehicle into a collision course, then pulled away at the last moment to skim past the now-stationary third truck with an elated whoop. Her counterpart wasn't able to evade in time and careered headlong into the sudden obstacle with a rending crunch that made Drift wince even though he'd only heard the impact.

'What in the Prophet's name was that?!' Muradov barked, appearing at Drift's shoulder.

'Your car in front just took out the one ramming us,' Drift replied breathlessly. 'I'd say they're all feeling quite bad about now.' *Including the Shirokovs, I expect.* He wondered for a moment about trying to persuade Muradov to go back for the Uragan couple, but sometimes you just had to accept that a promise would be broken. *And at least this way I'm not smuggling Orlov's mole off-world.* He brought his thoughts back to the situation at hand and tried to peer past the security chief. 'I take it everything's under control in there now?'

'Your help was appreciated,' Muradov muttered. Drift got the impression the Uragan was ashamed that some of his officers had turned against him, and felt a momentary pang of sympathy for the man. It had to be hard when your world got turned upside down overnight.

Muradov leaned a little closer and lowered his voice. 'I would not have expected such a reaction from Captain Moutinho's crew. Was that your doing?'

'I told them our only way off is with you,' Drift replied quietly, 'and to be ready to step in when things went south.' He saw the surprise in Muradov's eyes, and shrugged. 'I did say I've made a career out of surviving things going spectacularly wrong.'

'You did. I still think that it sounds . . . inefficient,' the Uragan said after a moment, and it took Drift a second to notice the ghost of a smile tugging at the corner of the other man's mouth.

He snorted. 'How far is it now?'

'Five blocks,' Muradov replied, looking at the scrolling schematic by the side of the driver.

Drift nodded, then lowered his voice again as a thought struck him. 'Your people know this isn't going to magically solve everything, right?'

Muradov frowned. 'Excuse me?'

'"Get to the governor's place" is a fine aim, but what will they do when they realise the plan is to just take off and leave?' Drift asked quietly. 'Do they have families?' He paused, suddenly aware of the can of worms he'd potentially opened. 'Wait . . . do *you* have a family?'

'Not since my mother died,' Muradov replied, with unexpected openness. 'You may be correct, however . . . I had not thought of the impact on the others, or their reactions.' He grimaced. 'Clearly, I am not so expert as you at creating plans on the fly.'

'Pray you never have to be,' Drift muttered, thinking furiously. He glanced into the passenger bay again in case inspiration struck, and found it sitting back-to-back in handcuffs and covered by the two female officers. 'Okay, we play it simple. *Those* four were the ones who sided with you, but you betrayed them and left them behind. Then the two ladies here and the driver, who all wanted to join the revolution, got the drop on them when they were arguing among themselves afterwards.' He paused for a second, then added. 'And I was holding the driver at gunpoint.

Just in case anyone who saw her is still in a fit state to speak.'

'Both sides would have similar stories, with nothing to prove it one way or the other,' Muradov mused, 'so they could hopefully stay here without consequence. That may be the best outcome we can hope for.' He looked sideways at Drift, as though weighing him up. 'You are alarmingly good at this.'

Drift shrugged again. 'It's a talent with its uses.'

'All legitimate, I am sure,' Muradov said dryly, then moved to the side of his two loyal officers and began speaking to them urgently in Russian. Drift caught the eye of first Kuai and then Goldberg, and gave them both a thumbs up. Kuai just looked at him wearily, while Goldberg replied with a different single raised digit of her own.

Well, there was just no pleasing some folk.

'**T**amara,' Moutinho said in a voice thick with tension, 'duck.'

Rourke registered that the second word was in English and, while expressions of confusion were still spreading over the faces of Yuri and his men, threw herself to the ground.

'*Traitor!*' Moutinho yelled, this time in Russian, and three guns roared into life. There was a brief fusillade of shots accompanied by some screams, then someone landed on her. She bucked and kicked them off instinctively, coming up to her feet with the Crusader in her hands, and found herself staring down at Yuri. The Uragan had a weeping red wound in the centre of his chest, and she realised with some distaste that his blood had smeared down her left arm when he'd fallen on top of her. He focused on her face and opened his mouth as if to speak, but Rourke had no time for him: she kicked away the

pistol that was still loosely grasped in his right hand,
then turned to survey the rest of the scene.

The rest of Yuri's immediate companions had apparently been caught unaware by Moutinho's sucker
punch and were, if not dead or mortally wounded,
certainly out of the fight. The brief but violent commotion had understandably attracted attention and faces
were turned towards them, with a couple of revolutionaries jogging back in their direction. Most of this
group didn't have firearms, but even so . . .

'Tamara!'

She turned again and saw Moutinho, Jack and
Achilles fleeing towards a tram, one of them propelling
Jenna by her shoulder and another holding her head
down. They looked for all the world like bodyguards
getting someone away from a conflict zone, but despite
that, the Free Systems colours on their armour and
Moutinho's shouted assertion that Yuri had been a
traitor, Rourke didn't think it would fool the other
revolutionaries for long. Apirana was hobbling after
them as fast as he could, but the big man had never
been the fleetest of foot even when both his feet were
in working order, and he was already being left behind.
And Skanda . . .

The last member of Moutinho's crew, unprotected
by the body armour his colleagues had been wearing,
had apparently taken at least one bullet in the exchange
and was on his back. She bent over him for a second,
taking in the placement of the wound. *High on the
right side of the chest, probably puncturing a lung.
Not necessarily fatal if treated quickly.* She looked
around quickly at the other revolutionaries and took
in their positions, then back down at Skanda.

'Get up,' she told him bluntly, 'or you'll die.'

'Don't leave me!' he wheezed, clutching at the hem of her coat. She snatched it out of his grip.

'Sorry,' she said flatly, 'you're not my crew.' She took off after the others, Crusader clutched in one hand and the other trying to hold steady the bag of belongings Jenna had rescued from their rooms, leaving the *Jacare*'s crewman on the ground behind her but unable to shake an uncomfortable sense of guilt. Skanda had persuaded Ruslan to open the door and let her in off the street into the salon, away from the bullets flying outside. He hadn't necessarily saved her life, but . . .

Stupid. He's Moutinho's crewman and Moutinho's responsibility, and Moutinho's left him behind. Skanda wouldn't stop to pick me up if I was wounded.

Only a few seconds had passed since the confrontation that had ended Yuri's dreams of becoming a hero of the Free State, but now some of the other rebels had decided that something was wrong. Gunfire began to ring out around the tram depot again, echoing off buildings and with the occasional *spanging* sound as a bullet ricocheted. Rourke kept her head down and ran, with the lumbering shape of Apirana growing larger in front of her moment by moment.

'Gas!' Moutinho yelled, and two of them slowed for a second to pull grenades from their belts and hurl them to either side. Greenish-white plumes of gas erupted as they bounced across the ground, partially obscuring the trio and Jenna from the sight of the revolutionaries.

It also sent wisps trailing across the narrow route onto the platforms that Rourke and Apirana were aiming for.

'Hold your breath!' she yelled as she came alongside the big Maori. She waited until the last moment before grabbing the collar of her coat and pulling as much as she could across her eyes and face, then held it in place as long as she dared before removing it again. A retching sound behind her arrested her flight and she looked around to see Apirana spluttering on his crutches, eyes streaming. Clearly, the big man's exertions hadn't lent themselves well to being able to hold his breath, no matter the potential consequences.

'Go!' Apirana rasped, his watering eyes focusing briefly on her. Rourke hesitated for a moment, but the Maori was still coming gamely on. She trusted him not to be a needless martyr, and she knew better than to think she could physically help him in any way.

Besides, someone needs to make sure Moutinho doesn't leave us both behind.

Jenna and her 'bodyguards' had reached one of the trams, and the shortest one – Jack, Rourke guessed – wrenched one of its sliding doors open for them to pile inside. Rourke put on a final burst of speed and caught up with them, staggering through the doorway before they closed it again and just before her lungs gave out. *You're getting too old for this, girl.*

'Jack, get us out of here!' Moutinho roared, sending his crewman towards the driver's cab with a shove and ducking away from the windows.

'We wait . . . for Apirana!' Rourke wheezed as adamantly as she could while leaning on a standpole. She was mildly annoyed to see that Moutinho didn't appear to be out of breath, but then he hadn't been running as fast as her.

'The hell we do,' Moutinho rasped. 'Jack, get us moving!' His helmet turned towards Rourke, and although she couldn't see his face behind the riot mask, she knew he was waiting for her to try to stop the First Nations man. Once she did so, he'd have a clear shot at her . . .

Jenna abruptly swivelled and brought her knee up into Achilles' crotch, then snatched the gun from the youth's suddenly slack grip as he keeled forwards. She armed it with a buzz and aimed it down the tram car at Jack.

'We wait,' the slicer said coldly. She spoiled the effect a little by puffing to blow strands of hair from her face, but Rourke had to concede that it had been very smoothly done. Moutinho was still in his crouch under a window, and his reflexive jerk of movement to intervene had been arrested by a twitch of the Crusader's barrel.

'Y'know what? Fine,' Jack said loudly. He still held a gun too, but it had been pointed at the floor and he clearly wasn't interested in trying to win a shoot-out with someone who had him in her sights. 'We'll wait. I kinda like the big guy, anyway.'

Rourke risked glancing away from Moutinho, and was relieved to see Apirana's labouring form approaching the door. There were still occasional shots flying, but the curtain of gas back towards the elevators was now doing a fine job of obscuring them from view, and even Big A. wasn't large enough to be hit by every bullet that came his way.

The Maori stumbled inside, rivulets of sweat pouring down his face and his top soaked dark with it. He landed on a seat, more by luck than judgement, and let out a groan of combined pain and relief which was loud enough to be heard even over the noise of the door sliding shut as Moutinho reached up and slapped the closer.

'Go!' the Brazilian roared at Jack.

'Go!' Jenna echoed, putting her gun up and rushing over to check on Apirana. 'A., are you okay?'

'Think I need to lose some weight,' Apirana muttered breathlessly, huge chest heaving. '*Kai a te ahi!*' He looked up at her, his manner oddly tentative to Rourke's eyes. 'You?'

Jenna leaned down and gave him a hug with the arm that wasn't holding a gun, which seemed to startle the big man. 'I'm fine,' she said reassuringly, 'I'm just glad you are too.'

'That's all very touching,' Moutinho rasped, getting to his feet and pulling his helmet off, as a jerk of the carriages signified that Jack had got the tram into motion, 'but you ever point a gun at one of my crew again and you'll be a long way from fine.'

Jenna whirled on him, her eyes flashing dangerously. 'And if you *ever* try to drag me away from my crewmates again, you'll be the one I'm pointing it at.'

Rourke watched Moutinho's scowl deepen and tensed, waiting for the *Jacare*'s captain to do something that would spark a real confrontation. Then Moutinho glanced at her, and at Apirana's forbidding expression, and snorted a humourless laugh. He turned away and clapped Rourke on the shoulder as he passed her. 'Kids, eh?'

'*You still want to steal her onto your crew?*' Rourke asked him in Russian.

'Go die in a fire, Tamara,' he retorted without turning, then reached down to haul Achilles to his feet. 'Stand up, you little prick.'

'She hit me in the—'

'Everyone saw. No one cares. Get up.'

Rourke took a couple of steps over to where Jenna was standing and glaring at the back of Moutinho's head. 'Nicely done with Achilles.'

'Thanks,' Jenna muttered. 'I know you told me once that every guy's on alert for a nutshot because it's so obvious, but he had a helmet and an armavest on, so I thought—'

'No, you did good,' Rourke assured her. She leaned a little closer and lowered her voice. 'I'd advise against staring down Moutinho again, though. It's good to show him you're no pushover, but he's smart, vicious and vindictive, and proud to boot.'

'You don't seem to mind antagonising him,' Jenna replied. Rourke smiled slightly.

'He already hates me. Plus he knows I can kick his ass.'

The tram made a low shrieking sound as it rounded a bend on the tracks a little too fast, and Rourke had to grab a strap dangling from the ceiling for just such a purpose in order to avoid stumbling sideways. Moments later the tannoy crackled into life, feeding Jack's voice back to them.

+Everyone might want to duck about now.+

Rourke glanced ahead and saw the *Jacare* crewman hunkering to the floor behind the driver's control panel. A moment later a window shattered as a bullet passed through it, and there was a ringing sound as another was turned aside by the tram's metal skin.

They were approaching a street crossing on the way out of the depot and a couple of rebels who'd got ahead of them had apparently decided to try to stop the tram, or at least kill the occupants.

'Down!' she yelled, pulling Jenna down with her and rolling away from the glass doors as another window shattered, this one closer to them. Apirana hit the floor with a grunt of pain a moment later, but got tangled up with his crutches and couldn't seem to get any purchase to get into cover. Rourke fought with the instinct to help him, unwilling to leave him there but knowing that she wouldn't be able to drag his bulk across the floor . . .

A gun barked several times, a few yards away. She looked around to see Moutinho standing and firing through the window in front of him, then drop back down again into a sitting position with a satisfied smirk on his face. The shots from outside stopped, and as their carriage passed the crossing, Rourke saw a man and a woman on their backs and clearly in the early process of bleeding out.

'You're welcome,' he grinned when he saw her looking in his direction. Rourke sighed and cautiously got back to her feet, although now they were away from the depot there appeared to be no further immediate threats.

'Where are we actually going?' she asked, helping Jenna up.

'If Jack's got any sense, which he does, we'll be heading for the spaceport,' Moutinho replied, checking the magazine on his weapon and grimacing at what he found. 'There's a terminal right inside it.'

'How will he make sure we get there?' Jenna asked dubiously. 'Aren't there preprogrammed routes, or something?'

'Nah, the drivers know their routes and select the lines they need to go on,' Moutinho said, pulling a fresh clip from his belt. 'There's controls in the cab to choose from the different line polarities when it reaches a junction.'

Rourke studied him, grudging admiration warring with distrust. 'You studied this . . . in case you ever needed to steal a *tram*?'

'Don't sound so ridiculous now we're on one, does it?' Moutinho snorted, reloading his gun and getting to his feet. 'C'mon Tamara, you know as well as I do that it's best to research all possible ways of getting out of somewhere quickly, just in case the shit hits the fan. We'd come here a few times and took the tram more than once: all we had to do was stand behind the driver and watch what they did. Besides, Jack can drive or fly pretty much anything if he puts his mind to it.'

Rourke nodded slowly. It was easy to forget, sometimes, that Ricardo Moutinho was an intelligent and resourceful man whose crew would have been hired for specific reasons. 'So, we get to the spaceport in a tram with bullet holes in it, then what?'

'I'm thinking we see how many people are between us and the ships and how gullible they look, then bluff or shoot our way past them depending on that,' Moutinho replied, scratching his stubbled cheek. He shot Jenna a brief, disapproving glare. 'That's if your girl there wants to give Achilles his gun back.'

'Can he use it?' Rourke asked dubiously, eyeing the skinny, pale youth standing further down the tram and looking glumly out at their surroundings.

'Hell, what do you think he's on the crew for, his looks?' Moutinho guffawed. 'Kid's worse than an asthmatic grandma in a fist fight, but he's the best damn shot this side of Alpha Centauri.'

'Do you even know which side of Alpha Centauri we are?' Rourke demanded.

'Eh, like it matters,' Moutinho shrugged. 'I reckon it's still true.'

Rourke exchanged glances with Jenna, who looked a little uneasy but passed the weapon over. Both of them knew that Jenna's place on the *Keiko*'s crew was definitely not due to her proficiency with firearms, and if a fight was going to break out then it made sense for someone to be armed who would make a difference in their favour. All the same, since the earlier confrontation Rourke felt more than a little uneasy being the only member of her crew who was armed. She frowned as a thought struck her.

'Hey, Ricardo. Who's your slicer?'

'Skanda was filling in, but he wasn't exactly an expert,' the *Jacare*'s captain replied. 'What, you think I was keeping blondie there safe just because she's pretty? I knew we might need her to get us out of that concrete coffin they've got our shuttles in.'

Rourke nodded, partially reassured. At least she probably didn't have to worry about the Brazilian allowing Achilles to get any form of revenge on Jenna. Whether he'd show any restraint when it came to her or Apirana, however . . .

She pinched the bridge of her nose as her vision blurred slightly. *Damn it. I went without sleep for three days once, minus twenty minutes here and there, and now I can't stay awake for more than twenty-four hours? I really am getting old.*

'You okay?' Apirana rumbled. The big man had dragged himself back onto a seat, but he looked spent. He could still probably grab Achilles and punch his face in, but the image of Jack casually cutting a Uragan guard's throat with his heavy knife wouldn't leave her mind when she looked at the Maori. *I could take one of them, if it came to it. A. would be dead in the water. Jenna's not a fighter. We're basically alive on Moutinho's sufferance right now: that, and he's still wary of me. If he sees me flagging . . .*

'I'm fine,' she told the big Maori, but right then she wished she had Drift's talent for lies.

Kuai had to admit, he was impressed.

Their small party – him, his sister, the Captain, Karwoski and Goldberg, and Chief Muradov – had been buzzed in through the thick security gates of the governor's residence, which Muradov was even now shutting securely behind them. On the other side, the transport they'd been riding in was rumbling off somewhere else with the loyal security officers in it apparently now pretending that they were traitors. On *this* side, however . . .

'Hey, you remember that summer when Mum and Dad took us to Hangzhou?' Jia muttered, staring around them.

'I was just thinking that,' Kuai admitted. The air in here didn't have the dry, recycled tang it had held in the rest of Uragan City, or for that matter that he'd got used to from years of travelling on the *Keiko*. It was not only several degrees warmer, but humid, and held the scent of green plants. Which wasn't that surprising given that they were surrounded by the things.

The grounds of the governor's residence were huge, at least by the standard of a subterranean dwelling. Ahead of them, a wide gravelled path snaked between banks of verdant green grass, which were sprinkled here and there with what appeared to be naturally occurring wildflowers. Thick, dark green bushes with purple blossoms skulked up against the boundary wall on their right, while tucked away in the corner on the far left was a white wooden box which, Kuai realised in mild alarm, must be a beehive. Overhead in the roof were a series of lamps imitating the wavelength emitted by the sun, and providing not just light but also heat, if he was any judge.

'Those are palm trees,' Jia said, pointing. 'He has palm trees. In his garden.'

'And a stream,' Kuai replied, his eyes focusing on the thread of glittering water just visible where the landscaped terrain dipped down and the gravel path gave way to a dark-stained wooden footbridge. He frowned. It obviously couldn't be natural on this world, so presumably it was some sort of giant water feature, pumped away at one end and sent back to the start . . .

'*Restrained*,' the Captain commented to Muradov in English, the lenses on his mechanical eye widening slightly as he focused on their lush surroundings.

'*We have fled for our lives up and across a rioting city to our only hope of escape, and now we are here you want to offer sarcastic critique on the living arrangements of the man who holds the keys to it?*

He runs the entire planet, I would have thought that entitles him to something larger than an apartment,' Muradov said in apparent disbelief. He waved a hand dismissively and set off up the path with the gravel crunching beneath his feet, heading towards the white building which took up the entirety of the far end of the garden. *'Whatever. Follow me.'*

'Sure thing, Chief,' Drift replied easily. Goldberg and Karwoski were already crunching up the path as well, so Jia and Kuai fell in behind them. Jia was frowning, an oddly dejected look on her face even for someone who'd lost her damnable hat.

'What's the matter?' Kuai asked, making the effort to be a good brother despite expecting a belligerent or mocking response. To his surprise, Jia sighed and gestured vaguely around them.

'Just reminds me, is all. We haven't sent any money back home for a long time.'

Kuai shifted his shoulder uneasily. 'Well—'

'And don't say it's because we haven't had none, because we have. We were both gambling on New Samara, you know we were.'

'You more than me,' Kuai replied reflexively, although it was true.

'Like that's the point.'

'I'm just saying—'

'What fucking words are you saying?!' Jia exploded, rounding on him with hands waving. 'If you'd come to me and said, "Hey, we should send some of this money back to our parents so they can move out of that shithole in Chengdu and get a nice place on the coast," you think I'd have said, "No"?' She turned away and continued trudging up the path, hands now sunk deep into the pockets of her flight suit. 'We both fucked up, and that's the end of it.'

'Okay, fine,' Kuai replied, glancing ahead of them. The Captain hadn't turned, perhaps being so used to Jia's shouting that he tuned it out, but Muradov had looked over his shoulder curiously. 'You're right. Okay? You're right. We both should have thought about it. When we get off here and get back to New Samara, we'll send . . . what, most of our share from the account? We'll send that back to them.'

'*If* we get back to New Samara,' Jia grumbled. 'We fucked this job up royally, you think the Captain's gonna take us back to where . . .' She trailed off suddenly with a glance ahead at Muradov, then lowered her voice. 'To where Orlov can get his hands on us?'

'What, the revolution is *our* fault?' Kuai protested in a whisper. 'Even if we'd got the data back to *him*, it'd still be useless. Nothing's getting shipped out of here any time soon, so he'd have paid us for no reason.'

'Oh yeah, I forgot,' Jia snorted, 'those crime lords are always so reasonable and logical, aren't they?'

'Whiner.'

'Old head.'

'Little rabbit kitten.'

'White-eyed.' They were on the bridge, and Jia looked over the railing into the sparkling water. 'There's *fish* in this!'

The front door of the mansion opened, and a tall, slim figure clad in a dark suit with the Russian-style breastplate piece emerged. 'Alim?'

'Sir!' Muradov called, raising a hand in greeting and increasing his pace. The rest of them followed suit, and their party broke into a mild trot as they came out of the wooded valley-in-miniature and followed the path up over the lawn in front of the governor's mansion.

'Alim, who are all these people?' Governor Drugov asked in Russian as they reached him, in a tone just short of demand. 'Where are your officers?' He had fine features and a nose a shade too sharp for Kuai's taste, with a closely trimmed dark beard showing the same flecks of silver that decorated his temples, and his forehead was creased with frown lines that were currently getting heavy usage.

'Sir, I regret to inform you that the vast majority of my officers are either captured, dead or have betrayed the Uragan government,' Muradov replied, a little stiffly.

Drugov blinked, apparently unable to process this information. '*What?* I'd heard that things were bad, even before the comms went down, but . . .'

'Sir, we were able to deal with even major crimes, and we could handle riots and protests,' the security chief said heavily, 'but this . . . Less than one per cent of the population was on my staff. We simply couldn't suppress an uprising of this magnitude, especially when the rebels had an unforeseeable ability to access the security and communications systems.'

'You should have come here sooner,' Drugov replied. His eyes narrowed. 'But you haven't answered my question, Alim: who are these people, and why do some of them have guns?'

'Sir,' Muradov said, straightening a little, 'this is Captain Ichabod Drift, of the *Keiko*. He's a freelance trader who happened to be planetside when things began. He and the two crew with him intervened in a planned ambush on one of my squads and were able to assist in dispersing the rioters before any more casualties were sustained. He's armed because I trust him to be so, and he's kept me alive already over the last twelve hours.' Muradov paused for a second, and coughed into his hand. 'He, ah, also doesn't speak much Russian.'

'And he's with you because . . .?'

'Sir, with the martial-law curfew in effect and him with no refuge, I couldn't leave him to be potentially shot by my officers,' Muradov explained, 'or to fall victim to a revenge attack by the revolutionaries.'

'I see,' Drugov said, although the tone of his voice and his expression suggested to Kuai that this might not be completely truthful. 'And the others?'

'The two North Americans are Lena Goldberg and Dugan Karwoski, members of a different ship's crew,' Muradov explained. 'I took them into protective custody to prevent them from being hurt in the riots, when they'd been separated from their colleagues.

'The Chinese siblings are Jia and Kuai Chang, Captain Drift's pilot and mechanic, respectively. I thought that Jia, in particular, might be able to assist us.'

'You did?' Drugov appeared completely nonplussed. 'In what manner?'

Muradov frowned in apparent confusion. 'Sir, the revolution is seeking complete control of Uragan City, and probably hoping to spark similar uprisings in our other settlements. As planetary governor, they will be seeking to either arrest or simply execute you. They breached the security gates between city levels using mining charges in some cases, or simply overriding our security protocols in others. When they get here, and they'll get here soon, we won't be able to keep them out.' He paused for a moment, but Drugov still seemed not to comprehend. Muradov spoke again, with just the faintest hint of trying to explain something to an unexpectedly obtuse child. 'Sir, Miss Chang is by all accounts a pilot of unusual skill. The eye of the storm should be more or less above us at this moment. I believe she may be able to pilot your shuttle into orbit, where we can dock with your vessel and make our way to New—'

'Alim,' Drugov said sharply, holding up one hand to cut the security chief off in mid-sentence. 'Come with me, please.' He turned and led the way into his mansion without looking back. Muradov frowned in apparent surprise, then started after him.

'*Everything going okay?*' Kuai heard Drift ask quietly in English at the security chief's shoulder as their party moved somewhat uncertainly forwards.

'*Wonderfully, why do you ask?*'

'*Was that sarcasm, Chief?*'

'*Captain, if you would keep your mouth shut for a few minutes you may just succeed in not making things any more problematic.*'

Kuai suppressed a snigger. He'd grown so used to the Captain being the smart-mouthed one in any given company that he found the professional, sober-countenanced Muradov verbally cutting him dead rather amusing. He looked around at Jia to see if she'd heard, but his sister was more concerned with their surroundings now they'd moved into the house.

'Check it,' Jia said in awe, drawing the last word out and turning slowly on the spot. The entrance hall, which was apparently climate-controlled to several degrees cooler than the sub-tropical environment in the garden, was a high-ceilinged atrium. The walls were lined with carved panels of a reddish wood, tall potted ferns stood in the corners and there was holographic artwork on the wall that looked expensive even to Kuai's untrained eye. All in all, it was the sort of environment the *Keiko*'s crew never really experienced unless they'd just broken into it.

'Yeah, just keep an eye on the Captain to make sure he doesn't try to pocket anything,' Kuai muttered, giving his sister a nudge to keep her moving in the direction of travel. The house seemed disturbingly empty to him: this was not a building that would be kept in such neat and tidy order by a man who ran a planet from it. There should be servants, surely? Doormen, security, an aide, a cleaner, *someone*. However, it appeared that none of them had showed up for work today.

He couldn't really blame them.

They climbed a stairway wide enough for ten people to walk abreast, passed through a hallway and came out into what looked like a waiting area, judging by the luxuriously upholstered seats positioned around the edge. Kuai looked instinctively around for the security attendant such a room surely needed, but once more there was no one else to be seen. There were simply the seats, a holoscreen that was forbiddingly blank – he could understand why the governor might not want current affairs playing, given that the revolution had presumably now taken over all broadcasts – and a set of large, dark wooden double doors on the far side.

'Tell the others to wait here,' Drugov instructed Muradov, who turned to rest of them.

'*Everyone please take a seat,*' the security chief said in English, '*the governor wishes to speak to me alone for now.*'

'*We're not going anywhere,*' Drift said with a shrug, slumping into a chair. Kuai looked at him in surprise – he'd have expected the Captain to want to be at the heart of any discussions – but Drift simply nodded at one of the other seats. Kuai sat down and the rest of their motley group followed suit, with varying degrees of ease: Jia threw one leg over the arm of her seat, while Goldberg sat perched on the edge of hers as though she expected it to swallow her.

No sooner had the double doors *clicked* shut behind the two Uragan officials than Drift sprang up from his chair and beckoned Kuai over to it. '*Keyhole,*' the Captain muttered, pointing.

Kuai nodded and squatted down, putting his ear to the small hole in the wood. Archaic designs like this were all well and good, and might look rich and imposing and cultured and whatever else, but when it came to security they rather depended on having an actual person on hand to make sure that nobody was listening in . . .

'Alim,' Drugov's voice came to him, muffled but audible, 'why have you brought this group of probable criminals here?' The governor's voice was stern, sharper even than it had been outside.

'Sir,' Muradov replied, sounding uncertain of himself, 'as I said, the pilot Jia Chang should be able to—'

'I don't need a pilot!' There was a bang as something hard and heavy was slammed or thrown down onto another hard surface: probably a desk. It appeared that Drugov was a man who expressed displeasure physically. 'What idiocy is this? Yes, the eye of the storm is above us now, but look out there, Alim! Look at it! Does that look to you like something any person could fly through?!'

He's got windows looking out over the surface? Kuai frowned. *I knew we were on the top level, but I didn't realise we'd come that high. No wonder he's so grumpy, with that sort of view every day.*

'With respect, sir,' Muradov replied, 'I'm fairly certain that the pilot for a freelance trader—'

'I'd bet money that the man's a damn smuggler, Alim, and you should know that too!'

'So what if he is?' the security chief snapped, then seemed to recover himself a little. 'Sir, I know the circumstances and the company are far from ideal, but I know first-hand how tight shipping controls are on many planets, not just ours, and I also know that smugglers get around those controls! It follows that a smuggling pilot needs to be a damned good pilot, sir, able to get through conditions most people would consider impassable!'

'I am *not* leaving Uragan!' Drugov bit out. Kuai could hear footsteps on a hard floor: presumably the man was pacing. 'I don't care if that bitch—'

Kuai clenched his fist. No one talked about his sister that way! Well, except him.

'—is the best damned pilot in the galaxy, it's irrelevant! Do you know what would happen if I left here and went to New Samara, or wherever you're suggesting? I'd be arrested, for starters. Dereliction of duty! Cowardice! Collaborating with rebels!'

'Sir,' Muradov began again, then changed his mind. 'Abram. No one could blame you for leaving a planet when the capital had been taken! We don't know if the other cities will be any safer, and in any case it would make most sense for you to go to the system governor and make your report in per—'

'*Don't* tell me my job, Security Chief!' Drugov thundered. Kuai could picture his face, eyes wide and spittle flying: he had features that seemed designed to be angry. 'The capital has not been taken yet, despite the apparent inability or unwillingness of your officers to perform their roles. We still have the fail-safe.'

There was a momentary pause, which Kuai could not imagine boded well. Nothing which followed the word *fail-safe* being used ever boded well, come to that.

'You're joking.' Muradov's voice was flat, but Kuai was sure he wasn't imagining the edge of desperation to it.

'Do I *look* like I'm joking?'

No, Kuai thought, *I bet you don't*.

'Sir,' Muradov replied, his tone clipped, 'that would involve the deaths of hundreds of thousands of people. Possibly most of our population! It was supposed to be a last resort against, against *foreign invasion*, not—'

'Not what? An "uprising of this magnitude"?' Drugov's tone dripped with scorn. 'Your officers are dead or have turned against the state, Alim. The vast majority of our population has aligned with this rebellion, or they wouldn't have been able to succeed. Invaders don't have to be speaking English or Swahili for them to be our enemies, the enemies of *our government,* the authority that appointed you and I to our jobs in the first place!'

'I swore an oath to *protect* these people, not—'

'You swore an oath to protect *Red Star citizens*!' Drugov roared. 'They're not our citizens any longer, they've rebelled! The military's on its way in any case and there's a cleanse order in place. This entire damn city's going to be exterminated and repopulated, so what does it matter whether they're killed by a bullet or by breathing in the atmosphere?'

'Don't talk to me about bullets as though you know what it's like to fire a gun!' Muradov shouted, his sudden anger catching Kuai by surprise even through the keyhole. He jerked away and found Drift looking down at him, the Captain's one natural eye registering considerable concern, with the others clustered behind him.

'*There's an awful lot of raised voices in there,*' Drift said, '*do we have a problem?*'

'*I think Drugov killing everyone in the city is a problem,*' Kuai replied, standing up. He could still hear Muradov shouting, but now he wasn't next to the keyhole it was too muffled for him to make out the words. '*Something about a "fail-safe" and people breathing in atmosphere.*'

'*Me caga en la puta!*' Drift exclaimed, a piece of Spanish profanity that Kuai had never bothered to try to translate beyond excrement being involved somewhere. '*Must be something to do with the ventilation system*,' the Captain continued, glancing uneasily and presumably unconsciously up at the ceiling.

'Yeah,' Kuai nodded, '*sounds like it was built in during construction. I guess that's an easy way to gas everyone if you need to – bring in all the shit from outside, let it do the work.*'

Drift grimaced. '*Tamara and the others are still out there. To hell with this genocidal chingadera.*' He pulled the pistol he'd appropriated from his belt and backed up a couple of steps, eyes on the door. The others retreated from him in alarm, a sentiment Kuai abruptly shared given that he knew at least one person on the other side of the door was also armed.

'*I, uh, don't think it's locked,*' he offered.

Drift actually glared at him, and Kuai got the feeling that the Captain resented being told that piece of information. '*Fine, we'll do it your way.*'

He stepped up to the door, turned the handle smartly and opened it a crack. Then, with a swift grin at Kuai, he took a step back and kicked it wide open with a loud bang, entering with gun raised. Kuai ducked aside, unwilling to be in the line of fire when either of the Uragans started shooting, and noticed that the rest of their party had followed suit.

'*Gentlemen,*' he heard Drift say, '*we need a new plan of action. One which doesn't involve murdering an entire fucking city.*'

It was strange to be riding through a city in turmoil. Level One of Uragan City was still going through the process of the revolution taking hold, but there was an air of inevitability about the whole thing given the rest of the city had succumbed. Jenna watched it all from the windows of their stolen tram with everything taking on a slightly dreamlike, disconnected air. She was hellishly tired, and the aftermath of the adrenaline invoked by the shoot-out in the tram depot and her subsequent confrontation with the *Jacare* crew wasn't helping. She sat in her seat, leaning back on the headrest behind her, and watched people waving yellow-and-black banners breaking into what looked like some sort of public building while, two streets over, neighbours gathered in worried-looking groups on the sidewalks and glanced around nervously. Another couple of streets on and two *politsiya*, or at least people wearing those uniforms, had joined with half a dozen youths in Free Systems colours to apparently apprehend some looters.

They went over a road crossing – Jack was ignoring all traffic signals and just sounding the tram's horn to tell everyone else to get out of the way – and through some railings she caught sight of a play-park with its rubberised safety surface, fake plastic trees, slides and swings and a small electronic bumper buggy pool. A boy and a girl, perhaps eight years old, were spinning round and round on a roundabout. They'd presumably snuck out of their homes while their parents' attention was elsewhere. Assuming their parents were still alive.

Very few people were taking much notice of the tram, which was the odd thing. Everyone was too preoccupied with whatever people felt when their entire way of life was turned upside down and the structures were ripped apart. Trams were a part of the normal background scenery of Level One, she supposed: this, at least, appeared to be something working as usual, even if it was slightly battle-scarred. No one was waiting at the stops to get on, in any case. It was only when Jack ignored the rules of the road that anyone really paid attention, and even then not for long.

'We're coming up on the spaceport now,' said Rourke, who had appeared in the seat beside her with her usual unnerving silence. 'I think we're going to have to take Moutinho's lead on this, so be ready to do whatever you need to do.'

Jenna glanced sideways at her and was suddenly struck by how old the other woman looked. Well, it wasn't that she looked actually *old* as such, but the lines on her face and the faint bags under her eyes had stripped some of the usual ageless nature from her features. 'You look like I feel,' she said, not unkindly.

'Well, keep it to yourself,' Rourke snapped. Jenna recoiled a little, stung by the retort, and Rourke's expression softened slightly. Only slightly: this was Tamara Rourke, after all.

'Nothing personal, Jenna,' she muttered, 'but I don't want *them* thinking that we're weak or tired.' There was no need to specify who *them* was: the slight tilt of Rourke's hat at the black-armoured shapes further down the tram had been all the explanation necessary. The tram was a continuous unit with flexible membranes at the joins between the carriages, so there was little practical division between one carriage and the next. However, Moutinho and Achilles had left the length of one between themselves and the *Keiko*'s crew, which Jenna didn't object to in the slightest.

'They'll be tired too, right?' Jenna asked quietly.

'Perhaps,' Rourke conceded, 'but they weren't up all night planning insurgencies with Uragans or slicing into communications systems. Or recovering from ankle surgery,' she added with a glance at Apirana, whose chin was now touching his chest and whose eyes were shut.

'What are we going to do when we get to the *Jonah*?' Jenna asked, trying to steer the conversation onto a slightly more positive subject.

'That might depend on what we've had to do to get there,' Rourke grimaced, 'but I'm still holding out that Ichabod and the Changs can get away from that security chief. If there's anyone who can talk his way out of a situation like that, it's Ichabod. Although I must admit, they'll still have to get to us.'

Further down the tram, Moutinho got to his feet and picked up his rifle. 'Look alive over there,' the Brazilian called, 'we're coming in!'

Rourke adjusted her hat and took a grip on her Crusader. 'Just don't get us all killed!'

'You'd best keep up then!' Moutinho replied with a laugh that Jenna didn't like the sound of at all, before pulling the *politsiya* riot helmet back over his face. Beside him, the dark visor of Achilles' mask seemed to be staring at her in a manner she found quite unnerving.

'A.?' Rourke said, looking over at the big man.

'M'awake,' Apirana muttered, 'just restin' my eyes.'

'Well, up and at 'em,' Rourke told him as the tram began to slow, 'it looks like we're here.'

Jenna sucked in her breath as she saw what awaited them. The station was inside the spaceport's boundaries and had several different maglev lines leading in and out of it, to take passengers to the various areas of Level One. There were a few visible bullet holes in the walls, and one platform was blackened in places with dark blooms of damage as though from fire.

'Molotov cocktails,' Rourke grimaced, 'or something similar.'

The rail itself appeared undamaged, and they glided into a station which proved to be oddly deserted. Only the digital displays presumably showing scheduled arrivals and departures gave any indication that this place would normally be bustling with people.

'So far so good,' Moutinho commented as Jack brought them to a halt. His helmet turned towards them. 'I'm thinking we're escorting some off-worlders to their ship.'

'Prisoners or guests?' Rourke asked warily.

'Prisoners would work best,' Moutinho shrugged, 'or at least, the sort of foreigner scum we want out of our new Free State. You know, place 'em in the ship, keep 'em under arrest there until the storm lifts when they get sent on their way. That sort of thing.'

Rourke snorted. 'That would involve me handing over my gun, wouldn't it.' It was a statement, not a question.

'Got some restraints on our belts, too,' Moutinho said agreeably, 'might as well make it look convincing.'

Rourke shook her head. 'Not happening.'

Moutinho barked a short, humourless laugh. 'What, you don't trust me? I want to get back to my ship too, y'know?'

'No, Ricardo, I *don't* trust you,' Rourke said flatly. 'I'm not giving over my gun, and there's certainly no way you're putting any of us in cuffs.'

'You're making this harder than it has to be.'

'My heart bleeds for you,' Rourke retorted. 'You can be escorting us, but we're not prisoners.'

'That might prove problematic if anyone else picked up that transmission from your friend the councillor,' Moutinho pointed out as Jack appeared at his shoulder, having left the driver's cab. 'Someone sees you already in custody, they might not make an issue of it. Someone sees you wandering around free with a gun in your hands . . .'

'We'll improvise,' Rourke shrugged.

'You mean we'll shoot people.'

'Probably, yes,' Rourke sighed.

Jenna couldn't see Moutinho's face, but there was less irritation in his voice than she'd have expected. 'Okay, we play it your way. Lead on.'

'You're the escort,' Rourke pointed out, nudging the door control with her elbow and sending them sliding sideways, 'after you.'

'*Puta que pariu!*' Moutinho muttered, but he jerked his head and his two crewmen followed him out of the carriage, forming up into a wide triangle on the platform. Jenna stuck close to Rourke's side as they also exited the tram, with the dual *clack-scuff* of Apirana's crutch-assisted locomotion bringing up the rear. The air around them was bitter with the after-taste of burned chemicals: presumably whatever had been used on the next platform over.

'I'm still not getting anything on the comms,' Rourke said as they walked towards the gently hissing escalators which led up to the many spaceport berths. 'Have you heard anything from your people?'

'Nothing yet,' Moutinho replied, turning towards her, 'the systems must still be down. But we got a new problem.'

'What?' Rourke brought the Crusader up slightly, her hat turning from side to side as she scanned for threats.

'Well, right now Achilles is holding a gun on the Maori,' Moutinho said almost apologetically as his own barrel shifted slightly to cover Rourke, 'and unless you hand that rifle over nice and slow, he'll pull the trigger.'

Rourke froze, but Jenna couldn't stop herself from turning her head as her guts turned to ice water. Sure enough, the lanky shape of the *Jacare*'s apparent marksman had his gun unwaveringly aimed at Apirana, close enough for the threat to be imminent but far enough away that even a swing from one of the big man's crutches wouldn't reach him.

'You are bottom-feeding scum, Ricardo,' Rourke bit out.

'Playing nursemaid to your crew's already cost me one of mine,' Moutinho bit out, his voice suddenly hard. 'Sure, Skanda could piss me off at times, but that doesn't mean I was happy he got shot because you thought you were cleverer than you are. And just because I know when to cut my losses and leave the dying doesn't mean I don't have loyalty. So hand the fucking gun over and behave, and we'll take you to your ship. Try to fuck with me, and we'll leave all three of you bleeding here and go to our shuttle without having to explain why we're with your worthless asses.'

'Bro, you might wanna move that pea-shooter,' Apirana rumbled, turning to face Achilles.

'I don't think so,' the youth replied, his voice level.

'See, that's where you're wrong,' Apirana said firmly, 'cos right now I'm tired, and I'm angry, and my foot's hurtin' me and I probably ain't thinkin' too rationally, but if you don't point that someplace else then as the gods are my witnesses I will shove my hand so far up your *nono* I'll be able to use you as a *fucking hand puppet*!'

Achilles took half a step back instinctively in the face of the big man's sudden bellow, but kept his gun steady.

'Okay!' Jenna shouted. 'Everyone calm down!'

All faces turned to her.

'Hear that, big man?' Moutinho said, although his gun covering Rourke didn't waver. 'Your slicer's got the right idea.'

Oh, I do.

'Ricardo *fucking* Moutinho,' Jenna spat at him, pulling back the right sleeve of her jumpsuit to reveal the heavy metal bracelet encasing most of her forearm, 'do you know what this is?'

The *politsiya* helmet tilted slightly. 'Should I?'

'Probably not, because you don't have a master's degree in electronic engineering and circuit systems from one of the best damn universities in the galaxy,' Jenna told him coldly. '*This* is a person-portable electromagnetic pulse generator: an EMP, as you might know it. And while you were all concentrating on Rourke and Apirana, I've been entering the detonation sequence so that all that's required now is for me to press one more button.' She rested her left forefinger lightly on a red button near the centre of it.

'Jenna . . .' Rourke said, a tone of alarm audible in her voice, even through the pounding of Jenna's heartbeat in her own ears.

'Sounds impressive,' Moutinho conceded, 'but I ain't a robot, and neither are my boys. So why should I care if that thing goes off?'

'Because I reckon I'm close enough to knock out the main systems governing this spaceport,' Jenna said, keeping her hand steady with an effort of will. She did *not* want her finger to slip. 'I don't trust for one second that you'll actually take us to our ship if Rourke hands over her gun: I think that's just a ruse so you can kill us all anyway with no risk. So you tell Achilles to put his gun away, and you stop pointing that at Rourke, and tell Jack to stop trying to creep up behind me—'

Rourke gave a very slight nod.

'—or I make sure that you're not getting off this planet without someone rewiring and rebooting the entire *fucking* system. Are we clear?'

There was a pause. Jenna resisted the temptation to look over her shoulder, but did turn her head ever so slightly sideways to try to keep Jack's dark shape in her peripheral vision. 'I said, are we clear?'

Rourke shifted position. It was meant to look like nothing more than uncomfortable shuffling, but Jenna had taken enough lessons with the former GIA agent to recognise the signs. Getting her feet slightly more side-on, changing the angle of her arms slightly . . . She wouldn't be able to bring her rifle around to shoot at Moutinho without him reacting first, but from that position she'd be able to strike him with a reverse elbow and maybe disorientate him for long enough to get into a firing position.

'Achilles?' Moutinho said. Jenna readied herself to press the button. Damn it if she *wouldn't* trap them here . . .

'Boss?'

'If the Maori tries to grab you, you can shoot him. Otherwise, put the gun down.'

'But—'

'*Do it.*' Moutinho cautiously shifted his own aim by a few degrees, taking Rourke out of his line of fire. 'That girl is too smart for our own good. We do this their way.'

Very slowly, Achilles lowered the barrel of his gun until it was pointing at the platform just in front of Apirana's feet. The big man nodded, very slightly.

'Good call, bro.'

'Let's get moving,' Jenna said, trying to prevent herself from collapsing in the wake of the sudden exhaustion that washed over her and left her feeling decidedly wobbly. 'I'm not taking my finger off this button until we get to where we're going, and the longer that takes the more likely it is that I fuck up and trap us *all* here.'

'Fine,' Moutinho replied, his voice now clipped and brisk. Once again, the Brazilian seemed to have shunted his feelings away and was all business. 'Big man, you're on point with me. We go at your best pace.'

'You got it,' Apirana rumbled, turning his back on Achilles and moving across the platform with surprising rapidity. Jenna saw the new sweat staining his top and wondered how long he could keep it up. *He has to. And he will, I'm sure he will.*

Moutinho fell in beside the big Maori, gun held crossways and helmet turning from side to side, for all the world as though he genuinely was a body-guard. Jenna followed the pair of them with an uneasy glance at Jack and the heavy knife in his belt, and wondered how close she'd come to having him open her throat with it from behind. The *Jacare*'s pilot struck her as the one she'd trust most out of the trio, but she had little doubt that he'd kill her if he needed to.

'Thank you,' Rourke muttered, falling in alongside her. The older woman's expression was grim. 'I got sloppy. Could have screwed it up for all of us.'

'No one can stay one jump ahead of everyone all the time,' Jenna whispered encouragingly. 'You've been carrying the ball for the last twelve hours straight. You drop it, I pick it up.'

'Is that thing actually armed?' Rourke asked, nodding at her forearm.

'Sure is.'

'Well . . . try not to trip over or anything, I guess.'

They rode up the escalators in uncomfortable silence, with Jack and Achilles behind them. Jenna hadn't liked the idea of having their backs exposed, despite her threat, and Rourke apparently shared that view as she rode it backwards to keep their 'escort' in view. Jenna nudged her at the top to warn her and the older woman took a calm step backwards onto stationary ground without missing a beat.

'Okay, I'm starting to get a bad feeling about this,' Moutinho said, looking around. They were in the long concourse that ran down to the customs and immigration suites, and short of some graffiti on one wall which Jenna didn't recall from before, they were entirely alone. 'Where the hell *is* everyone?'

'I don't want to come across as reckless,' Rourke replied dryly, 'but does it matter? We need to go that way anyway.' She gestured with the Crusader's barrel in the direction of the docking bays. 'I don't see how anyone could know we're coming, even if we're worth the trouble of setting a trap. Let's just push on before someone *does* show up.'

'Eh, I guess it's not like we have a choice,' Moutinho rasped. 'Fine. Stay close and watch your backs.'

Jenna managed to suppress a laugh. *Way ahead of you there, at least if your boys are standing behind me . . .*

No one else came up the escalators from the other tram platforms, but Jenna doubted that anyone else had stolen a tram and ridden it to the spaceport. When the *Keiko*'s crew had come this way before, the hallway had been busy: not necessarily rammed tight with people, but enough that you couldn't walk in a straight line from where you were to where you wanted to go. Now it was empty, save for the holographic displays on the walls, which were still (probably) welcoming people to Uragan City and reminding them of local laws and the like, and the vending machines selling their ubiquitous products. Governmental boundaries might restrict the movements of currencies, people and even ideas, but Star Cola got *everywhere*.

'What do you think happened to the security?' Rourke asked Moutinho as they advanced cautiously towards where the corridor ended and opened onto the immigration gates, another long hall which ran at right angles. 'There was enough of them.' Jenna had noticed that when talking about their surroundings or methods, Rourke appeared to value the Brazilian's input. It was only when any conversation shifted to themselves or their crews that they clashed.

'Less than you might think,' Moutinho replied, 'which is just as well, given how often we had to bribe the greedy little bastards.'

'I had wondered how you'd smuggled the guns in,' Rourke commented, her tone neutral. 'Not many places for a surreptitious landing on this rock.'

'Nah, just good old-fashioned palm-greasing,' Moutinho laughed. 'You know how it is: there's always someone coming up to retirement and doesn't give a shit anymore, or who likes the cards more than the cards like him. The trick's working out who it is and what their price is.'

They were starting to cluster close to the near wall, eager to stay out of sight of the immigration hall for as long as possible. Apirana was hanging back now and Rourke ghosted forwards until she was at the corner, then removed her hat and cautiously peered around it. Jenna stared at the back of her head, waiting for a shout, a gunshot . . .

Rourke resettled the hat on her head and stepped out. 'Clear.'

'You certain 'bout that?' Jack spoke up from the rear.

'I'm standing out here, aren't I?' Rourke demanded, turning back to him. She turned away sharply and disappeared out of view, but not before Jenna had caught the beginnings of a yawn on the other woman's face. She nearly glanced at the *Jacare* crew to see if they'd noticed, before remembering that she wouldn't be able to tell behind their helmets anyway. *Plus, Rourke's not the one they need to be wary of now, it's me.*

No pressure.

They followed her out into a long hangar of white surfaces, blinking digital signs, blocky seats with uncomfortable-looking upholstery, and turnstiles with accompanying security cubicles. And no people, any-where, although the smashed glass here and there and occasional bullet hole gave at least a partial explanation for that.

'Yeah, I'm not seeing them being ones to stand against the revolution,' Moutinho admitted, his helmet apparently taking in yet another yellow-and-black smear of paint down one wall. 'Too much effort for too little reward.'

'So where's everyone else?' Jack asked. 'Why aren't they all trying to get out of here?'

'Because everyone knows there's still a storm going on up there,' Rourke pointed out, lifting one finger towards the ceiling. 'Also, all the off-worlder accommodation's several levels down, remember? Odds are most people couldn't even get here, and wouldn't want to try until things have settled down one way or the other.' She looked at Moutinho as though weighing something up. 'This might be easier than I thought. If no one even knows we're here we could just sit tight on the ships until the storm blows over. Once the comms system comes back online we can contact the others, find out where they are and build a plan from there.'

'Yeah, maybe,' the *Jacare*'s captain replied. 'Let's just make sure we haven't got any nasty surprises waiting for us first.'

The turnstiles were the only real obstacle they encountered. The rest of them could vault over (or crawl underneath with one finger hovering near her EMP generator, in Jenna's case), but Apirana found it more of a struggle. After that it was simply a case of getting on the moving walkway and waiting until they reached the airlock into Grazhdansky Dok 2.

Which was locked.

'*Puta merda!*' Moutinho swore, jabbing at the release button. 'Look at the readout! Goddamn air's fine inside, so why won't it open?'

'Move over,' Jenna told him, then abruptly remembered exactly why she'd been holding one finger in place over her right forearm for the last few minutes. 'Damn.'

'Pity's sake girl, you ain't causing us any trouble now,' Jack protested, 'we've got no excuses to make for you, no stories to come up with about you, we just want to get in there like you do.' The pilot slung his rifle across his back and folded his arms. 'See?'

Jenna looked at Rourke, who shrugged, then at Moutinho and Achilles. Both of them reluctantly shouldered their weapons.

'Isn't that more polite?' Jenna murmured, and switched the position of her hands so she could access her wrist console. She fired up the translation protocol and squinted at the screen as the Cyrillic script was rendered into the Latin alphabet. 'Yeah, here we go. It's on a standard emergency lockdown. Shouldn't take a moment to . . .'

The airlock began to grind open, showing the dimly lit hanger beyond.

'. . . override,' she finished happily.

'I'll give you this, kid,' Moutinho said, pulling the helmet from his head and looking at her with eyes which she was sure contained grudging respect, 'you're good at what you do. And you're no coward, either.'

'Ricardo,' Rourke said warningly.

'What?' Moutinho protested, his face all innocence. He looked back at Jenna. 'You fall out with these clowns for any reason and you need a job, you come looking for me, you hear? I know we might seem a bit rough—'

Apirana let out a snort.

'—but we're just direct,' Moutinho finished, giving the Maori a glare. 'With someone like you on board to ease things along, maybe we wouldn't need to be.

Reckon you could help a lot with ghosting in and out of places. Maybe keep a few more people alive.' He winked at Rourke as he replaced his helmet, and now his eyes held nothing but ugly humour. 'Until the next time, Tamara. Come on boys, let's see if the baby gator's array can boost our comms any.'

The trio of *Jacare* crewmen sauntered through the airlock and away across the hangar bay floor towards the sleek, predatory lines of their shuttle, apparently unconcerned about any risk from behind them. Rourke followed them through, eyeing their backs warily, then turned back to Jenna and Apirana. 'Let's get onto the *Jonah*.'

'Sounds good t'me,' Apirana grunted, putting his crutches to work once more and heading off towards the squat shape of their trusty shuttle. Jenna came last, closing the airlock behind them and finally deactivating her EMP. The walk to the *Jonah*'s ramp seemed to her to take longer than it should, and her shoulders were itching the whole way. She didn't trust Moutinho or his men not to take a potshot out of spite, despite the fact that Rourke kept checking on them, but finally the three of them stood beneath the *Jonah*'s blocky nose. She activated the shuttle's systems from her wrist console and called the entrance ramp down, sending warm, welcoming light spilling over them in contrast to the shadows of the bay.

'Tell you this, I ain't never gonna call this girl a rat trap again,' Apirana commented, although he eyed the ramp's incline dubiously. 'Ah man, this is gonna hurt.'

'You'll be fine,' Jenna said encouragingly, putting one hand on his shoulder. 'Come on, let's go.'

As it was, after the first couple of steps Apirana threw his crutches into the shuttle and simply went up the ramp in a sort of three-legged crawl, his injured foot held up out of the way. Jenna followed, trying not to laugh at him no matter how odd he looked, while Rourke brought up the rear. Once at the top she called the ramp up again and collected Apirana's crutches for him, then breathed a final sigh of relief.

Then she became aware of Rourke sliding down the wall.

'Whoa!' Panic gripped her and she reached out to catch the older woman, abruptly becoming aware of exactly how light she was. 'Tamara?!'

'I'll be fine,' Rourke muttered, setting her gun down on the deck with a *clank*. 'I'm just so damn tired . . . I'm getting too old to stay up all night organising revolutions.'

Jenna tried to laugh, although in truth she was more shaken up than she wanted to show. Rourke was made of steel: always had been, always would be, so far as Jenna had been concerned. She might look tired, might talk about dropping the ball, but there was no way that she could *actually* burn out, right?

'Let's get you two to your cabins,' she suggested, looking between them, 'you can both get some—'

There was a deep thud on the sort of scale of a leviathan clearing its throat, and the *Jonah* actually seemed to shake a little.

'—rest,' Jenna finished uncertainly. How loud did something have to be for them to be able to hear it inside an airtight spacecraft, for crying out loud?

'Bridge,' Rourke gasped, trying to lever herself to her feet. 'Go, I'll catch up!'

Jenna got to her feet and ran, clattering up the steel steps at the side of the cargo bay and hammering at the release on the airlock at the top until it opened. She flew down the short corridor that led to the bridge, slapped the release for its door and was through before it was halfway open, just in time to feel another thud which seemed to reverberate through her bones. The cockpit's viewports gave her a little over a 180 degree arc of vision, and she craned around to see what was going on. The hangar bay seemed lighter than it had before . . .

Her mouth fell open in genuine shock as she saw the *Pouco Jacare* hovering on thrusters, its nose angled upwards roughly forty-five degrees to the horizontal. Above the far side of the hanger was a hole, an actual *hole* in the doors that sealed the hangar bay off from the world above and the storm raging there. Through that hole was pouring light and, more ominously, sand and rocks.

She snatched up the comm and fired it up to broadcast on an open channel. '*Jonah* to *Pouco Jacare*, *Jonah* to *Pouco Jacare* . . .' She paused for a moment, trying to summon the right words. 'What the *fuck* are you doing, you demented idiots?!'

+*Jenna, that you?*+ Ricardo Moutinho's voice crackled jovially over the comm. +*See, we've logged into the automatic weather sensors they have here and taken a reading on the storm up there. It's not so bad at the moment, the gusts are only a few hundred miles per hour – nothing Jack can't handle, if he's careful. So we're going to get some altitude and start broadcasting using this girl's comms system, and try to reach our people that way, since the*

Uragan comm systems are still offline and I don't intend to wait for hours until they come back on again. Over!+

Something streaked from under the nose of the *Pouco Jacare* and detonated a split second later on the hangar bay roof with another titanic impact and a corresponding widening of the hole, causing Jenna to flinch in terror. Bits of debris tumbled down, clattering off the luckless shuttle which was berthed on the far side, and the flow of sand and rocks from above increased.

'You'll bring the damn roof down!' Jenna almost screamed at him, blinking away the white after-images of the explosion.

+*Well, yeah. That's sort of the idea, over.*+

'Do you have any idea the size of rocks which these storms can shift?!' Jenna yelled. 'If one of those gets in we'll be crushed!'

+We *won't be, we'll be in the air. You're welcome to follow us. If you can.*+

Another missile erupted from the *Pouco Jacare*'s concealed and highly illegal guns, and in the wake of this explosion the remaining part of the huge door covering that half of the bay fell in with a rending crash. Jenna covered her face reflexively and uselessly, but it was at least on the far side of the hangar: the shuttle directly beneath the falling door seemed to crumple under the immense weight of metal, although she couldn't see exactly what had happened, but nothing struck the *Jonah*.

+Pouco Jacare *out.*+

The *Corvid*-class shuttle, held in place by Jack's expert piloting, fired its thrusters and roared up through the hole it had created into the maelstrom beyond, leaving nothing behind except more temporary damage to Jenna's retinas. She wiped at her eyes desperately to try to clear them, then jerked aside with a yelp of alarm as a rock the side of her head clattered off the *Jonah*'s nose, narrowly missing the viewshield. She was fairly sure it could have taken an impact of that sort anyway . . . but as she looked at the volume of sand, dust and rocks already pouring into the hangar, she had a nasty feeling that larger ones were on their way.

'What the . . .?'

Rourke had appeared behind her. The older woman's expression was surprisingly blank, although in that moment Jenna wasn't sure if it was because Rourke had recovered her usual composure or was simply too tired to react.

'I . . .' Jenna waved a hand helplessly at the scene in front of them.

'Too much to hope for that he would leave without a parting shot,' Rourke muttered. 'What a wonderful choice he's given us: stay to be buried or crushed, or follow him into the storm and die out there by being blown into a ridge.'

'What do we do?' Jenna asked desperately, looking at her.

Rourke just gazed out at the storm with tired eyes, and said nothing.

Muradov had reached for the gun at his belt the moment Drift stepped through the door, but froze as Drift covered him with his pistol. 'Captain . . .'

'Chief,' Drift replied cautiously. 'I'm really sorry to do this, but there are still three members of my crew out in your city and I can't be having them suffering breathing difficulties.' His attention was very nearly arrested by the huge window directly behind the desk where Governor Drugov was standing: it appeared to look out over what might have been a canyon on Uragan's surface, although it was hard to see anything much given the thick yellowish clouds of gas and detritus whipping past. On the other side of the office was another window, this one looking out over the lush garden they'd come in through. He pulled his gaze away with an effort and refocused on Muradov, whose face twisted in frustrated consternation.

'You idiot, Drift! I was arguing *against* him!'

Drift frowned. 'Kuai?'

'Yeah?' the mechanic's voice came from somewhere outside the doorway.

'Is that right?'

'Why d'you think they were shouting? 'Course he was arguing, I told you *Drugov* wanted to gas everyone.'

'Well, shit. Sorry, Chief.' Drift shifted his aim to cover the governor instead, whose beetling brows lowered still further at this impudence.

'Alim!'

Muradov brought his gun up to point directly at Drift's temple. 'Captain, please lower your weapon.'

It wasn't like Drift wanted to be shot in the head. For a moment he considered backing down and just letting the two officials have it out between themselves, but when he'd intervened Drugov had simply needed to say Muradov's name and the Chief had immediately moved to obey. Drift didn't think that boded well for the people inside Uragan City. Rourke, Jenna and Apirana were his top priority, of course, but they weren't the only ones out there. He couldn't help but think back to the *Thirty-Six Degrees*, crippled and hiding in the ice belt around Ngwena Prime, where a dozen men and women had died as he'd overridden the airlocks to vent their precious atmosphere into the void. They'd been bad people, to be sure, people who'd sought profit through theft and violence, but they'd been at least nominally *his* people. And if he wouldn't be the one to kill these people in Uragan City, well, perhaps the fact that there were two million of them was enough to make him stand firm to ensure they didn't suffer a similar fate.

Someone had once said that for evil to prevail, all that needed to happen was for good men to do nothing. Drift didn't consider himself a good man, but perhaps he had his moments.

'Chief,' he said, trying to sound as calm and reasonable as he could with a gun aimed at his head by someone he was pretty certain was a former Red Star Army veteran, 'I think I'm on your side here.'

'You are pointing a weapon at my planetary governor,' Muradov snapped, 'that does not fit my criteria for "my side".'

'I thought he wanted to kill everyone in this city?' Drift demanded, not looking away from the bearded Drugov and wondering how much of the conversation the governor could understand. He'd have expected a planetary official to have a good grasp of all the major governmental languages, but he hadn't heard Drugov speak anything except Russian so far. 'Do you think that makes him qualified to *be* a governor?'

'Captain, how are you expecting to solve this by threatening him with a gun?!' Muradov demanded, sounding truly exasperated.

'Simple,' Drift replied flatly, 'if I see him doing anything that looks suspicious, I'm going to shoot him.'

That got a reaction: Drugov couldn't hide the widening of his eyes and the colour starting to drain from his face. Drift severely doubted the other man had ever been in a life-threatening position before, and possibly hadn't really believed until this moment that Drift would actually do anything. *Well, I hope you believe me now.*

'Captain—'

'Damn it, Chief, you know I'm right!' Drift snapped, trying to ignore the black hole that was all his peripheral vision could see of the barrel of Muradov's gun. 'You were arguing with him too.'

'I was hoping that reason could prevail, I never intended to *threaten him with a lethal weapon!*' Muradov snarled.

'Well that's what he's doing to two million people, right now!' Drift shouted back. 'I saw you when you realised that troops were being called in, Chief. You didn't *want* war on Level Five, even after rebels bombed your transport and tried to kill you and your squad. You didn't want *anyone* to die!'

'Of course not, but—'

'That's what *he* wants!' Drift continued furiously. 'He'll kill them all! Hell, he'll probably kill us, too: are you really prepared to risk that this mansion's airtight and its oxygen supply won't get compromised?'

'As to that,' Drugov spoke up in English, cautiously raising one finger, 'there are twenty full environment suits and additional rebreather masks in that cupboard.' He pressed something on his desk and a partition in the wall to the side of his desk suddenly slid aside, revealing what looked like nothing more than a wardrobe for a chemical spill clean-up team. 'Despite this disrespectful behaviour, you and your people may use them if necessary.'

'Word of warning, amigo,' Drift said, 'the next time your finger touches anything on your desk, I pull this trigger.'

'So what would you have me do, *Captain*?' Drugov demanded angrily, his placatory facade vanishing. 'Sit and wait until the rebels break down my doors and kill us all?'

'Sooner that than kill an entire city,' Drift told him, 'but no. I was thinking we all get into your shuttle and my pilot gets us off this planet.'

'That is not going to happen,' Drugov bit out, resting his knuckles on the desk in a vaguely simian gesture which Drift supposed was intended to make him look intimidating.

'So how about if I shoot you and then we take it anyway?'

'Only I have the access and ignition codes,' the governor sneered.

And Jenna's not here. If she was, I might be inclined to chance it. 'I don't buy your act,' Drift told him bluntly. 'Once the rebels start coming through your garden gates, I reckon you'll reconsider.'

'I do not intend to wait that long,' Drugov replied, then switched his attention to Muradov. '*Alim, ubei etogo cheloveka!*'

Drift's Russian was good enough to recognise an order to kill him, despite what Drugov might have thought. There was a fleeting moment of terrible indecision when he wondered whether to pull the trigger, spatter Drugov's brains over the wall and have done with, and then . . .

'*Alim!*'

Drift risked a glance sideways to see Alim Muradov still staring down the barrel of his gun at him, and with an expression of agonised conflict on his face. He breathed again. 'Chief, I—'

He'd noticed Drugov shifting his weight very slightly, but didn't realise the significance until something hit him in each thigh and every nerve in his body overloaded. He was dimly aware of landing half on his back and half on his left arm with his body attempting to draw in on itself like a crushed spider, while the shockbolts spat out of Drugov's desk by the foot-activated floor trigger did their work on him.

Drugov flipped up a section of the desk and lowered his hand, palm downwards, towards the green light grid of a palm reader. It had to be the security protocol for activating Uragan City's 'fail-safe'.

The shockbolts had exhausted their charge in a second, but the after-effects left Drift's muscles still unwilling to obey his commands. He tried to raise his gun, but his arm just spasmed.

There was a gunshot.

Drugov's face had time to register the faintest flicker of shock before he crumpled like a puppet with its strings severed, a bloody hole blown through his forehead. Turning his suddenly aching neck with an effort, Drift looked up and saw Alim Muradov. The security chief also had shockbolts attached to him at thigh level, but it seemed that his *politsiya*-issue gear had protected him. He was lowering his gun, which was pointed at where Drugov had been standing, and he looked suddenly haunted.

Drift opened his mouth before deciding for once that it might be better to say nothing. Instead he rolled onto his right and craned his head around to look back at the door into Drugov's office, which was conspicuously absent of anyone else.

'Kuai! Jia!'

His voice came out as little more than a pained wheeze, but after a second or so both Chang siblings stuck their heads around the door, one from each side in an unconscious stereo movement which made him chuckle despite himself.

'You alright, Captain?' Jia asked uncertainly, her eyes narrowing as her gaze moved to Muradov.

'I'm fine, I've just been shockbolted,' Drift said through gritted teeth. 'Help me up, would you? Don't worry about the Chief,' he added, 'he's just saved everyone's life but had to kill a friend to do it.'

'I thought he was my friend,' Muradov agreed, his voice sounding slightly vacant as Jia and Kuai cautiously entered the room. 'But perhaps I never knew him.'

'Careful, careful!' Drift gasped as the Changs grabbed an arm each and hauled upwards. He staggered, his legs still uncertain beneath him, and Kuai had to catch him with a grunt.

'You're getting fat,' the mechanic told him.

'You should work out more,' Drift retorted, holstering his pistol. *Fat? Not a spare ounce on me.* He tested his legs again and found them to be more capable of taking his weight, so he disentangled his arm from over Kuai's shoulders. 'Chief? First of all, thank you for doing what I would have done, had I not been incapacitated.'

'You realise, of course, that I have effectively signed our death warrants?' Muradov replied gloomily. 'He was not lying about being the only person with the access codes to his shuttle.'

There was a deep *crump* from the direction of the garden, echoed a moment later by a wailing klaxon as the mansion's alarm system started sounding. Drift didn't need to look to guess what had just happened: someone had attached a mining charge to the main gates and blown them in.

'Drums,' he muttered, feeling his guts stir uneasily, 'drums in the deep.'

Muradov had crossed to the window overlooking the garden, his melancholy air abruptly gone. It seemed that the security chief – or former security chief, as he surely had to be thought of now he'd killed the planetary governor – wasn't the sort to let introspection get in the way of practicality. He looked around as Drift spoke, an odd expression on his face. 'They are coming.'

Despite himself, despite the gravity of their situation, Drift laughed. *At last, someone who appreciates the classics!* 'Chief, are there any other ways out of here? Any panic room?'

'None we can use,' Muradov replied briskly, checking his weapon, 'everything was coded to the governor's fingerprints.' He stopped, then looked up at Drift as the same thought occurred to both of them.

'Well, we still have his hands,' Drift pointed out, brain racing. 'If we can use him to open the panic room, but leave him outside it with a gun in his hand and make it look like suicide then maybe they won't realise we're—'

'New plan!' Lena Goldberg shouted as her and Dugan Karwoski burst into the office and made a beeline for the environment suits. 'Grab a mask and get the fuck out of here!'

'What?' Drift watched in bewilderment as the two *Jacare* crew grabbed rebreather and goggle combinations and pulled them on. 'Where are you going?'

'Out there!' Lena replied, her voice slightly muffled as she pointed at the window looking out over Uragan's surface.

'Out *there*?' Drift echoed incredulously, turning on his heel to look at the foot-thick window of perspex, reinforced to survive the battering of Uragan's incredible storms. 'How the hell are you going to get it ope—'

He stopped. Descending into view was a dark shape, swaying unsteadily in the wind but still undoubtedly under human control, with floodlights cutting through the thick atmosphere to stretch new, wavering shadows out across the floor of Drugov's office. He recognised the sleek, angular form as a *Corvid*-class shuttle. The *Pouco Jacare*.

And, as Goldberg and Karwoski fled the office again, Drift realised that there was only one way for Ricardo Moutinho to get rid of that window.

'Move! Move!' he yelled desperately, shoving the Changs towards the office door. He dashed for the closet and grabbed more rebreathers, then followed his crew with Alim Muradov close behind him. The Uragan slammed the door shut after them and snatched one of the masks from Drift's hands with almost unseemly haste.

'Put these on!' Drift ordered, pressing masks on Jia and Kuai, then pulling one over his own head. 'Get away from the door! Get behind the wall!' He grabbed Goldberg by the shoulder. 'Why the hell didn't you mention this before?!'

'They only just came into comm-range,' she spat, knocking his hand away, 'and you were—'

This explosion was much, much louder than the one that had signified the arrival of the rebels, and it shook the building itself. The wooden office door was nearly knocked off its hinges by debris flung outwards from the force of it, and Drift was still trying to shake off the roaring in his ears when Goldberg and Karwoski barged past him and back into the office. He suddenly became aware that the roaring wasn't an after-effect of the *Pouco Jacare*'s guns. It was wind noise.

They had armed rebels coming for them in one direction, possibly already inside the mansion, and an escape route in the other. There was only one sensible course of action, although given it involved charging into the teeth of a toxic hurricane, the word 'sensible' was probably relative.

'Come on!' he yelled, waving his small party onwards and following Moutinho's crew into the office. The room was already filled with a swirling, ice-cold mess of pus-coloured gas and dust as Uragan's frigid atmosphere billowed in through the ragged scar created by the *Pouco Jacare*'s armament. Virtually all of the window was gone, save for a few chunks of thick perspex along each side, and some of the wall was missing at the top as well. The shuttle itself hung immediately outside like a monstrous predatory bird, its ramp down and giving the impression of a distended jaw. Drift found himself grudgingly admiring the skill of Moutinho's pilot at holding the craft more or less steady in the cruel crosswind, which was pushing hard against him even in his current position of relative shelter.

Goldberg was already on the ramp, crawling up it to present as small a profile as possible to the vicious gusts. Karwoski followed, leaping the small gap between the window and the ramp and almost being carried away even in that short distance. He landed on the ramp with a clatter though, and began scrambling up it after his crewmate. At the top, silhouetted against the internal lighting, was someone wearing *politsiya* riot gear including a full-face helmet with gas mask. From the height and general build, Drift guessed it was Moutinho himself, an impression which was heightened when it pointed a gun at him. His comm beeped, alerting him to a broadcast on an open channel powered by the shuttle's transmitters, and he answered it with a grim sense of foreboding.

+Olá, *Ichabod!*+ the Brazilian's voice crackled cheerily into his ear. +*Thanks for keeping my crew safe.*+

'Tamara told me you'd struck a truce,' Drift replied through gritted teeth, aware of the others at his shoulders. Possible salvation lay in front of them . . . but so did a gun. 'Where is she?'

+*Sitting safe and sound in your shuttle where I left her, I expect,*+ Moutinho said, +*and no doubt waiting for you to get back there with that pilot of yours. You'd better hurry though: we made a bit of a mess on our way out.*+ He hit a button next to him as Karwoski scrabbled up past him into the hold proper, and the ramp began to rise. +*Best of luck.*+

'Damn you, Moutinho!' Drift snarled. 'We could have left your crew high and dry!' Which was true enough, so long as the 'we' included Muradov, whose decision it had been.

+*Which is why I'm not telling Jack to blow you to pieces with another missile,*+ Moutinho pointed out. +Adeus, *Ichabod*.+ The transmission ceased as the ramp whined shut, and the *Pouco Jacare* banked away into the swirling clouds with a roar of manoeuvring thrusters audible even over the screaming wind.

'So that's it then,' Jia said from beside Drift's right elbow, her voice barely audible through the muffling effect of the rebreather and over the wind. 'We're fucked.'

'Not yet,' Drift growled, more out of stubbornness than anything else.

'We're about to get shot, man!' Jia protested, gesturing back towards the office door. 'They're gonna be here any second!'

'They cannot breathe in this!' Muradov cut in, tapping his rebreather. 'We shut the door, we get something to barricade it, and we dare them to come in and get us!'

'What, and freeze to death instead?' Jia demanded, throwing her arms up. 'That's just a different flavour of fucked!'

'Are your crew always this upbeat?' Muradov asked Drift. The Uragan had his gun in his hand again, and seemed to be thoroughly himself once more.

'They're an absolute riot,' Drift replied, slapping the shorter man on the shoulder. 'No pun intended.' He looked around at the Changs. 'Jia, grab some of the big chairs from out there, I don't think this desk is moving anywhere. Chief, take another look out of the garden window and see if they've actually got through the gate yet, or just damaged it. Kuai—'

The little mechanic was pointing past him, out into the storm. Drift whirled, expecting to see the shape of the *Pouco Jacare* dropping back down and a crackle in his ear as a preface to Moutinho saying he'd changed his mind and was going to blow them up anyway. Sure enough, there were running lights approaching unsteadily through the storm, and he opened his mouth to shout for everyone to run for it.

But the lights were configured slightly differently. In fact, they almost looked like . . .

+*Captain, are you there?*+ It was Jenna's voice in his ear, coming in on the *Jonah*'s private frequency that his comm was programmed to automatically accept.

'Yes!' he shouted, fighting the urge to jump up and down and wave his arms, joy warring with relief in his chest. 'Yes, damn it, I am!'

+*Jia?*+

+*You bet your ass!*+ Jia's voice crackled over the comm now she was included in the broadcast network, echoing the more muffled words he heard coming from behind her mask.

+*Then get ready to get aboard ay-sap,*+ Jenna said, her voice somewhat grim, +*because A. and Tamara are having a hell of a job flying this thing.*+

+*Gotcha!*+ Jia replied, pushing Drift aside as the *Jonah*'s bulky shape materialised out of the maelstrom. Sure enough, where the *Pouco Jacare* had been shaky but clearly controlled, Drift's shuttle seemed barely able to keep upright, let alone on course. He watched with his heart in his mouth as it veered drunkenly, overcompensating sluggishly to gusts with too-enthusiastic blasts from the thrusters, but a crack of light appeared at the front and kept widening as the ramp began to lower.

+*Hold her steady!*+ Jia yelled, setting herself for a running jump.

+*Trying!*+ was the curt response, a taut voice which Drift took a second to recognise as Tamara Rourke's, so great was the stress in it.

+*Well, try harder!*+

The ramp was nearly down now, with Jenna visible at the top and holding onto the control panel for support as the floor repeatedly tilted under her. Jia clearly didn't trust in her crewmates' abilities to keep it in the right place for long because she made a leap as the *Jonah* lurched forwards, launching herself into mid-air.

Just as the wind gusted viciously again.

The shuttle rocked to one side a little, but Jia's slight frame had nothing like the *Jonah*'s bulk and her headlong leap was abruptly turned into a sideways trajectory. Drift reached out reflexively and uselessly as his pilot windmilled her arms and legs desperately, seeking some purchase on the air and failing to find it.

She did, however, just manage to snag the hydraulic support on the far side of the *Jonah*'s ramp with one hand.

+*Fuck! Fuckfuckfuckfuckfuckfuckfuckfuckfuckfu—*+

Jia latched on with her other hand almost immediately but the *Jonah* wasn't holding steady in a wind still gusting strongly enough to blow her sideways, and she seemed unable to haul herself to safety. Drift backed up a couple of steps and prepared to jump, trying to swallow the bile churning in his throat as the ramp swayed in front of him and doing his best to block thoughts of the potential fall from his mind.

He was taken by surprise, therefore, when a shape in *politsiya* blacks sped past him and vaulted athletically across the gap between window and ramp, landing with a sure-footed and metallic thud. Alim Muradov crouched low on the ramp and splayed himself to minimise his own risk of being blown off, then reached out to grab Jia's wrist and hauled the pilot to him with a strength that belied his modest build.

+*Captain, is he with us?*+ Jenna asked, sounding a little confused.

'He is now,' Drift confirmed. He turned to face the office door and raised his gun, just in case there were any particularly enthusiastic rebels closing on them: he didn't fancy taking another bullet in the back, armavest or no. 'Off you go, Kuai.'

Kuai muttered something in Mandarin which Drift didn't quite catch, but didn't delay in making his leap. Muradov, now upright and holding onto one of the hydraulic stanchions with his right hand, caught the little mechanic and steadied him before sending him up the ramp after Jia.

+*Get up to the cockpit,*+ Jenna told the younger Chang as she reached her, then pulled something down which had been wedged into place next to the control panel. +*Here: you'll need this.*+

Jia snatched it from her eagerly. Drift realised what it was as she pulled it down over her head, and laughed. 'You saved the goddamn pilot hat?'

+*We grabbed a couple of bags from the hotel,*+ Jenna's voice replied. +*Hadn't had a chance to look in them until just now.*+

'Captain!' Muradov shouted from the ramp, barely audible through his rebreather mask and the howl of the gale. 'Are you coming?'

Drift smiled despite himself. Finally, after everything going wrong, they were—

A *politsiya*-issue gas mask appeared in the office doorway above a rifle's barrel. He squeezed his trigger instinctively and the mask's wearer ducked back into cover as Drift's bullet chewed into the door. 'Ah, shit.'

He turned and ran, making the leap as Muradov began to retreat towards the cargo bay. There was a heart-stopping moment as a dim, yellow gulf opened beneath Drift's feet and the wind tried to throw him sideways, but he landed on the ramp. It was hard on his knees and cold on his hands as he sprawled forwards, but it was reassuringly solid beneath him. At least, for the moment: he holstered his pistol and started scrambling up the ramp before either the weather or pilot error tilted it. 'We're all on, go!'

+*Gotcha, Cap,*+ Jia's voice replied. +*Come on, get out the way . . . no, the* other *way, I need that chair!*+

There was a faint lurch and then the *Jonah* started to swing up and away from Governor Drugov's ruined office, far more smoothly than it had been moving before. As the shuttle turned, Drift caught a quick glimpse of the blasted window, set in the top of a sheer canyon wall that formed what must have been one edge of Uragan City. Above it was a windswept, dusty plain that presumably led back towards the spaceport, although the thick, stormy atmosphere limited his visibility too much to make anything out. Then the ramp hissed shut, bringing him and Muradov fully up into the *Jonah*'s hold.

+*Repressurising with oxygen,*+ Jenna said as she operated the controls, her voice reaching his ears through the remnants of Uragan's atmosphere as a weird, muffled counterpoint to her words coming through his comm. Drift could hear the whine of the fans even above the *Jonah*'s engines, towards which Kuai had already disappeared, and the yellowish haze that had drifted in was starting to thin. The slicer seemed . . . different, somehow. More confident, perhaps.

'Why didn't you contact us earlier?' he asked. 'We were about out of hope down there.'

+*Moutinho thought we were grounded and trapped,*+ Jenna replied, +*we didn't know if he'd turn around and blow us out of the sky if he realised we were following him, so we kept quiet. He'd already said they were going to try to contact their crew, so we figured that you might be in the same place and just tailed him, hoping they were too busy flying to notice us.*+ She shrugged. +*I guess it either worked, or they didn't care after all.*+

'Well, good thinking,' Drift laughed. 'For a moment I thought you'd done it to be all dramatic.'

Jenna mock-saluted. +*No, sir! Just trying not to die.*+

Drift snorted, and removed his rebreather as the light on the cargo bay control panel flashed green to indicate that the atmosphere was now safe to breathe.

'Far too much of my life so far seems to have consisted of "trying not to die".'

'You've spent most of it flying around hard vacuum inside a tin can,' Jenna commented dryly, following suit, 'it shouldn't really come as much of a surprise.' She lowered her voice and nodded towards Muradov. 'Who's that?'

'That's Alim Muradov,' Drift replied, 'former security chief of Uragan City.'

'Oh. Um . . .' Jenna's eyes widened. 'Why's he here?'

'It's sort of a long story,' Drift said wearily. 'Can you just check in on the cockpit, please? I need to have a conversation here.'

'The good sort or the bad sort?' Jenna asked, running a hand through her hair and achieving precisely nothing.

Drift grimaced. 'I'll let you know when I find out.' He left her side and walked over to where Alim Muradov was sitting against the wall. The Uragan had apparently noticed them taking their masks off and had followed suit. The face thus exposed was wearing a dolorous expression once more.

'So,' Drift began, sitting down next to him, 'you're ex-military, right?'

Muradov looked sideways at him. 'It is that obvious?'

'Maybe,' Drift shrugged, 'but I saw you take command in a stressful combat situation, and I also saw you shoot. Given Uragan doesn't allow guns for civilians, you either spent a hell of a lot of time on the security force's range or you did it for a living for a while.'

'Red Star Army. Four tours of duty. Twelve years.' Muradov's voice was mechanical, as though reciting by rote.

Drift nodded. 'Why'd you join?'

'Why are you interested, Captain?' Muradov sighed.

'You're on my ship, and you're armed,' Drift pointed out. 'Humour me.'

'Very well.' Muradov fiddled with the mask he'd just removed, holding it in his hands as though looking at someone's face. 'My father was a miner, as most are on Uragan. He died at the mine face when I was five. From that moment I saw mining not as the proud, working tradition of our planet but as a hazard. When the opportunity came to sign up for the defence force at sixteen, I did so immediately.'

'And you were good enough to get bumped to the military,' Drift nodded.

'As you say,' Muradov confirmed. 'I showed a natural eye for tactics, for understanding combat. I began active service at eighteen. I won regimental marksmanship awards. I became my squad's official sharpshooter. And after five years, I was officially reassigned to a sniper unit.'

Drift whistled, appreciatively.

'It was merely a combination of a steady hand, good eyesight and great patience,' Muradov shrugged. 'There are other professions for which those attributes would be suited, and I grew tired of killing. At first I had told myself I was protecting my planet, but I saw that I was not, for no enemy came near Uragan and I was stationed far from here. Then I told myself that I was protecting my government's people, but I saw that I was not, for often we were sent to combat zones on contested worlds, or even worlds already claimed by others. Then I told myself I was at least earning money to aid my mother, who had fallen ill shortly after my father's death and had never been able to work properly again. My childhood was hard, even by Uragan's standards, but she deprived herself further to ease the impact on me. I swore that I would find a well-paid job to ensure she did not want again and that, at least, I managed.

'Then she died when I was twenty-nine, and I found that I had no further reasons to kill people for money. I comfort myself somewhat with the knowledge that someone would have been sent to do what I did anyway, and the fact that I did it efficiently meant that my comrades suffered less in combat.'

'So you came back to Uragan and joined the security force again?' Drift surmised.

'Indeed,' Muradov nodded. 'I was honoured in a small way by the military upon my departure, for the services I had performed. I was initially assigned to train our forces in weaponry, but I was not content merely to create inferior copies of myself. I wished to do something more, to make a difference, and I turned my energies to it. I was promoted upwards and sideways, learning more about the civilian side of the job as I went – crime detection, investigative procedures and such. I left my instructional role and eventually became security chief, perhaps partially aided by Abram Drugov's desire to have a *military hero* in charge.' The final words were flavoured with bitterness.

'And now?' Drift deliberately kept his tone neutral.

'Now . . . I do not know,' Muradov conceded. 'I have failed. I did not see the threat to my city, or I misjudged its scale. A revolution was plotted under my nose, and I heard nothing but whispers until it was too late. My response was inadequate, and my officers either died or were forced to change sides in fear of their lives . . . or I had simply recruited the wrong people in the first place, people without the necessary loyalty to my government. And now I have killed the man I should have protected above all others, because it seems I also lacked that loyalty when my government ordered the death of two million of their own people.'

'It doesn't sound like that was a government that deserved much loyalty,' Drift offered.

'Do not try to convince me that the United States of North America rules its worlds with smiles and honey cakes,' Muradov snorted.

'I know full well that they don't,' Drift replied easily. 'The way I see it, all governments are just a different flavour of bastard.' *I know for sure that the Europans aren't saints, given what they employed me for.* 'That's why I have nothing to do with them, if I can help it.'

'That does not sound like such a bad idea,' Muradov admitted wearily, leaning his head back against the cargo bay wall and closing his eyes.

Careful, Ichabod. 'How do you fancy giving it a try?'

Muradov's eyes opened again and he turned his face towards Drift, his expression guarded. 'I beg your pardon?'

Drift took the plunge. 'I have a vacancy on my crew. Have had for a couple of months now, ever since a guy named Micah bought the wrong end of a stardisc when we got mixed up in something rather unpleasant. It's left us a bit light, especially in the fighting department. My business partner Tamara has all sorts of useful skills, and you can imagine that Apirana's no slouch in a fist fight, but sometimes you need someone with a different mindset. Someone who sees things *strategically*.'

'Let me get this clear,' Muradov said slowly. 'You are offering me . . . a *job*?'

'Yes,' Drift replied simply. 'You're smart, adaptable, calm under pressure and one of the best shots I've seen. You've got a strategic brain and, most importantly, you don't *want* to fight but you will when you have to. None of us here *want* to fight. But sometimes we have to, to protect what's ours.'

'So tell me, Captain,' Muradov said, 'what is it that you *really* do?'

Drift became aware again that the Uragan had a gun at his side, but he'd come this far and honesty was the only real policy. 'Whatever we need to, in order to get by. Within reason, I mean. We work transport jobs. Not all of them are legal, I'll be straight with you, but we never traffic people other than consenting passengers. Goods, yes.'

'Guns?' Muradov asked, and Drift had a sudden mental image of ice cracking under his feet.

'We have done,' he admitted, 'but I swear to you, not on your world.'

'Oddly, I find myself believing you, Captain,' Muradov said after a moment. 'Continue.'

That would have been the sticking point, I'm sure of it. 'Sometimes we've done bounty-hunter work,' Drift continued, his confidence in his pitch growing. 'I like to keep within the law when I can: not because of any moral conviction, really, it's just easier. But sometimes a legal job is hard to find, and sometimes something's falling apart in the engine room and the only way you can make enough to get a replacement in time is to take a black-market job that pays well.'

'Anything else?' Muradov asked quietly.

Okay, there was one more potential sticking point. 'You'd find this out anyway, so I may as well tell you now,' Drift said seriously. 'Years ago, and I mean over a decade ago, I was a pirate. Quite a notorious pirate. Well, I guess I was technically a privateer: I was hired by the Europan government to hit specific shipping targets when they couldn't risk the political fallout of sending their military after them.'

'You mean you were hired by a government to kill people?'

'Mainly just to take their stuff.'

'Then you were better than me,' Muradov grunted.

Drift tried not to look too guilty. The story about killing his own crew could wait until they had a little more time.

Muradov sighed, apparently not noticing Drift's moment of awkwardness. 'I have always prided myself on being a pragmatic man. I have no loyalty towards governments not my own, so I do not object to breaking their laws. I now have no loyalty to my own government either, as I have seen first-hand what they will do to protect their material wealth. I will be labelled a traitor by New Samara should they learn that I killed Abram Drugov, and I have already been labelled a traitor by the revolutionaries on Uragan. I am a man without a home.' He looked Drift square in the face, his dark gaze direct and open.

'I have no reason to refuse your offer, Captain, so long as you understand that I will not kill save in defence of my own life, or one of your . . . of *our* crew.'

Drift grinned, relief washing over him as he extended his hand. 'Then welcome aboard, Chief. I'll take you to meet the others; a more informal introduction than at your old headquarters.'

'Very well.' Muradov levered himself to his feet. 'I am a man who needs purpose in his life, I confess. Having some responsibility for a ship, a crew, even if I am not in command . . . that would suffice, I think.'

'Glad to hear it,' Drift said, following suit and leading the way towards the steps which led up towards the canteen.

'Just one question,' Muradov said from behind him.

'Yes?'

'If you were not gunrunning . . . what were you *actually* doing on Uragan? I never did believe your story that you were looking for honest shipping work, and I still do not believe it now.'

Drift chewed the inside of his mouth for a second while he considered his answer. He turned back to Muradov and clasped his hands in front of him.

'Let me begin my answer with a question. I imagine you do not consider yourself to be among the favourites of Sergei Orlov?'

Muradov's face darkened. 'The New Samaran mobster? I should think not: he might have half this system's government in his pocket, but he never had me.'

'Well then,' Drift said brightly, already planning where they could run to that was a long, long way from any potential retribution, 'at least one thing will remain a constant between your old life and your new one! And, uh, here's why . . .'

A TALK

Jenna was tired. So very, very tired. They'd survived the storm's buffeting and were burning through the upper layers of the atmosphere, heading towards where they'd left the *Keiko* in high orbit. It seemed that Alim Muradov was part of the crew now: she wasn't sure how she felt about that, but since he'd apparently killed Uragan's governor she supposed he at least wasn't likely to try to arrest them, which was where her concerns ended. She didn't really care about anything right now, in all honesty, other than the fact that she really wanted to go to bed. However, she still had one thing left to do before she could sleep.

She stopped outside a cabin and raised her fist, then paused. The last time she'd been on this shuttle, she'd have hammered on the door without thought. Things had been different then. Uragan had changed so much in her life.

But she couldn't go to bed until she'd done this, so she pounded on the door three times, ignoring the dull pain that striking the metal always caused in her hand. There was a buzzer next to the door, but she'd never used it before and she wasn't going to start now.

'*Haere mai!*'

No going back. She jabbed the release, which was indeed unlocked, and waited for the door to hiss aside before stepping into Apirana Wahawaha's cabin.

The big man had the second-largest cabin after the Captain's, in deference to his sheer size. Even so, it seemed small with him in it, lying on the bed and making it look like something designed for the proportions of a young teenager. He'd made it homely, though. One wall was taken up with a huge holoframe that altered images from day to day, all of them apparently of New Zealand. Today's was one of her favourites: the majestic, snow-capped peak called Taranaki.

'Hey,' the Maori rumbled, his tone and face neutral. A pad was resting on the bed beside him, but judging by its dark screen he hadn't actually been using it for a while.

'Hey,' Jenna replied. The door closed behind her, and then there was just the two of them in this suddenly enclosing space. She gestured to his ankle, propped up on a pillow. 'How is it?'

'Not so bad,' Apirana replied, 'managed to find some more painkillers. At least I'm not gonna need to do much movin' for a while, except over into the *Keiko*. Might not even bother, to be honest.'

'Right.' Jenna simply wasn't awake enough for further small talk, so she screwed up her courage and went for it. 'Look, A., I'm nearly asleep so I apologise if this comes out wrong, but I said we'd talk later, and now it's later. So we're going to talk.'

Apirana blinked. 'We are?'

'Yes, because I said we would talk later, and I keep my word.'

'Okay.' He sounded a little uncertain, and possibly slightly alarmed. Jenna was suddenly struck by major doubts as to whether this had been a good idea, but she was damned if she was going to back out now.

'I have had two boyfriends in my life. One was called Kris, when I was thirteen, and we watched two holos together which he paid for, and then he kissed my best friend Emma and I swore I would hate them both for ever, because I think that's what you do when you're thirteen.'

To his credit, Apirana didn't laugh. He just nodded soberly. 'Right.'

'Then I had another boyfriend called Paulo, when I was . . . sixteen, going on seventeen. We were together for about two years, and we did . . . you know, boyfriend and girlfriend stuff. The stuff you do.' She stumbled to a halt. When Apirana had been seventeen he'd already been in a street gang for two years after fleeing his family home when he'd nearly beaten his own father to death. Swimming pool parties when Jane Hudson's parents had been away, sneaking out after dark to watch stars under Franklin Minor's benevolent skies instead of doing homework, staying up late trying to scratch-build your own terminal out of scavenged parts just to see if you could . . . these were not things she suspected he could easily relate to.

'That ended when he moved away to go to college. We didn't try to make it work, because I was enrolling on one of the most demanding courses the university had and I didn't think I'd have time for a relationship. And I didn't. And then . . . well, a couple of years after that everything happened with the Circuit Cult and I just . . . ran away.'

'Uh-huh.'

'So the relationships I've had,' she said carefully, 'have been with people my own age, and . . . from the same background as me. At least from the same *planet*.'

She saw his neutral mask start to crack and fall away.

'So I want you to understand,' she plunged on, 'that when you said what you did on Uragan, it took me by surprise. I never expected that from you, just because you are so, *so* different to anyone else I've had a relationship with or have ever considered the *possibility* of having a relationship with. And that's not a bad thing,' she added, 'but it's a true thing.

'And so I couldn't wrap my head around that straight away, which meant I clammed up and said nothing, and then Rourke arrived, and then because I hadn't said anything so far it got harder and harder to start the conversation. And I'm really sorry for that, because you are my friend and you were honest with me.'

'Nah, I get it,' Apirana said. His voice was somewhat thick and choked, and he seemed to be fascinated by his feet.

'I haven't got there yet, silly,' Jenna said gently. She sat down on the edge of his bed and he looked up in surprise. A couple of days ago she'd have done that without thought: now it felt like a big step. 'It took you saying it to make me realise it, A. I never thought of this ship as anything other than a way out of something I needed to escape, and I never thought I'd want to stay, but after everything that happened down there I've realised that I feel like I belong here. And the biggest part of that is you.'

The big man's eyebrows climbed so far she thought they'd shoot off his face. 'Oh. Uh . . .'

'I've done a whole load of things I'd never expected that I'd do, and never wanted to have to do,' she admitted, feeling her stomach twist slightly. 'I know you talk about being a thug, but it wasn't so long ago I was opening a blast door so a revolution could get through to attack a planetary security force. I guess I've realised that you pick the people who matter to you and do what you need to do for them. So I hope you can accept that about me. Sometimes I struggle with it.'

'That's been a whole lotta my life,' Apirana rumbled softly, 'I just picked the wrong people for a while.' He looked at her searchingly. 'So are you saying . . .?'

'I'm saying that we're two adults and I don't think we need to label anything,' Jenna told him, smiling slightly. 'But . . . yeah. I knew I liked you and I trusted you, more so than pretty much anyone else I've met, but I guess you just have that expectation of what something's going to be like for you? And then you might need to readjust your thinking when something totally different comes along. So I have, and . . . you and me. I'd like to see where that goes. If that's okay with you.'

A huge, genuine and possibly ever-so-slightly goofy grin spread across the big Maori's face. 'Hell *yeah*, that's okay with me.'

Jenna exhaled as tension left her body, and suddenly found that words didn't work any longer. 'I, look, I'm really tired and I'm going to bed, but I wanted to speak to you first, because . . . because. So, we've spoken, and I'm glad of that, and I reckon we both need sleep and then we talk again, tomorrow?'

'I'd like that,' Apirana nodded. His eyes were still a little wide, but not from the furious anger she'd witnessed on occasion. He looked more like someone had dumped a pail of ice water over his head, but he was oddly happy about it. 'Um. Goodnight, then.'

'Goodnight.' She smiled nervously and got up, waved and felt immediately stupid for doing so, then pressed the release button on the door behind her and stepped out into the corridor. As soon as the door hissed shut again she collapsed against the wall. 'Holy shit. That should not have been that hard.'

'What shouldn't?'

Jenna had never truly appreciated the term 'jumped out of her skin' until now, as she whirled around in a roiling mixture of terror, anger and sleep deprivation. Tamara Rourke stepped out of the slight recess of her own cabin's doorway, her expression bland.

'You . . .' Jenna fought down a sudden impulse to lunge for the older woman. Only the sure and certain knowledge that it would lead to at least moderate injury stopped her, but she still marched up to Rourke and leaned down into her face. 'Were you spying on me?!'

To her astonishment, Rourke leaned back slightly. 'Yes.'

'Well, I—' Jenna paused as her brain caught up with her ears. 'Hang on, what do you mean, *yes*?'

'You and Apirana have been acting weirdly since I met up with you again on Uragan,' Rourke said simply. 'It's not like you, either of you: you're easily the closest two on this ship, and I include myself and Ichabod in that.'

'And what business is that of yours?' Jenna demanded.

'First of all, this ship and this crew survives on us all pulling together,' Rourke said. She still looked tired, but she'd collapsed into her cabin immediately after Jia had taken over the *Jonah*'s controls and she'd shown a remarkable ability to at least partially recharge her figurative batteries on minimal sleep. 'We can just about deal with the Changs' squabbling, but if you and A. fell out properly then that's the sort of dynamic that could tear us apart.' She shrugged. 'Secondly, I used to be a damn spy. Information was my life. I'm nosy by nature.'

'All you need to know,' Jenna told her haughtily, 'is that we have *not* fallen out, and if I catch you spying on me again then you and I *will* fall out. And you won't enjoy that, even if you *can* kill me with one hand!'

For a moment she thought she'd pushed too far, as the realisation dawned through her anger that Tamara Rourke had been nearing the end of her tether through stress only an hour or so ago. Being shouted at, being *threatened* by the *Jonah*'s youngest crew member might just be the straw to break this particularly stoic camel's back.

Then Rourke nodded, perhaps a little sadly. 'I under-stand. And I apologise. It wasn't my place.' She smiled, ever so slightly, but there was melancholy there. 'Ever since Old Earth . . . well, I didn't want any other surprises coming out of this crew. I don't think anyone's hiding the sort of skeletons that Ichabod was, but all the same . . . but I guess I just have to trust people, or I'll become the sort of problem I'm trying to avoid.'

She stepped back into her cabin doorway and activated her own door release. 'Goodnight, Jenna. I'm sorry, again.'

'Goodnight, Tamara.' Jenna waited until the door slid shut behind the former GIA agent, then turned and made her way towards her own cabin before she could bump into anyone else and start another fight. Tomorrow was a new day, if such a thing really existed up here away from all units of time other than the purely arbitrary, and it would contain new things. Exciting things. Possibly slightly scary things.

And the *Jonah* climbed on, far enough up now that terms like up and down were starting to become simply a case of where you were standing, towards the *Keiko*.

Towards home.

ACKNOWLEDGEMENTS

I will, once more, start my acknowledgements with an apology.

When I was creating the universe of the *Keiko* and its crew, I wanted to keep much of the cultural individuality that marks the world today. Although it can be a source of conflict, I also feel that humanity's diversity is one of our most interesting attributes. However, as someone who has never lived (indeed, has rarely even travelled) outside of the UK, my personal experience of other cultures is somewhat limited. In *Dark Sky* I have once more used Apirana Wahawaha the Maori, possibly the crew member with a culture most starkly different to my own, and I apologise to the Maori people individually or collectively for any inaccuracies in his portrayal that may cause offence. However, this time I've also set the novel on planets with strong Russian influences, and I hope just as fervently that no readers feel that my depiction is unfair (I make no apologies for individual characters – there are bad apples everywhere, after all).

With that out of the way (again), thanks go first to my agent Rob Dinsdale, whose assistance got me to the stage of, for the first time, writing a novel where I knew *before I started it* that I'd get paid for it. That was a hell of a feeling, let me tell you. I am indebted to both him and my editor Michael Rowley for their insight, suggestions, and willingness to put up with my default initial position of WHAT DO YOU MEAN I SHOULD CHANGE THAT, IT'S FINE AS IT IS AND HERE'S WHY.

Speaking of Michael, I should also mention and thank the entire team at Del Rey UK including Emily, Tess and Clarissa, who've not just made sure that all the things that need to happen for a novel to work actually happened, but also that it's been suitably and enthusiastically waved at people to persuade them to buy and/or review it (or 'publicity and marketing', as I believe it's called). Also, the cover art. I *love Dark Sky*'s cover art, even more than I liked *Dark Run*'s.

Special thanks go to Liudmila for ensuring that the Russian in this book is as close to authentic as you can get with the Latin alphabet. Any errors in the text are most definitely mine, not hers.

Thank you to everyone who's read anything I've written so far and has said anything nice about it . . . and even the people who've been critical, because I want to get better at this writing thing, and I'm unlikely to do that if I'm in an echo chamber of unconditional praise.

And finally, and most importantly, thank you to my wife Janine for being supportive of my wish to make stuff up and have other people read it, and the corresponding demands on my time. And also being interested to read what I'm writing without going, "Haven't you finished it yet?" or other such unhelpful comments. In this, as in so many other things, you are the best person I could share my life with.

DEL REY UK

The home for the best and latest science fiction and fantasy books.

Visit our website for exclusive content, competitions, author blogs, news from Del Rey HQ at Penguin Random House, musings on SFF and much much more!

Ⓡ Follow Del Rey on Twitter @delreyuk for weekly giveaways

Ⓡ Visit www.delreyuk.com

Ⓡ Sign up to the newsletter

Join the conversation on: